TOUCHED BY THE MORNINGSTAR

COMPLETE VOLUME ONE

RISE OF THE FALLEN

LISSA KASEY

Touched by the Morningstar

1st Edition

Copyright © 2022 Lissa Kasey

All rights reserved

Cover Art by Atra Luna Cover & Logo Art

Edited by C. Duke

Published by Crafty Fox Limited

http://www.lissakasey.com

Please Be Advised

This is a work of fiction. Names, characters, businesses, places, events and incidents are either the products of the author's imagination or used in a fictitious manner. Any resemblance to actual persons, living or dead, or actual events is purely coincidental.

Warning

This book is licensed to the original purchaser only. Duplication or distribution via any means is illegal and a violation of International Copyright Law, subject to criminal prosecution and upon conviction, fines, and/or imprisonment. This eBook cannot be legally loaned or given to others. No part of this book can be shared or reproduced without the express permission of the Author.

TRIGGER WARNING

Listed below are the trigger warnings for this book. If any of these things bother you, please proceed with caution:

- NSFW Why Choose Series
- Monster Romance depicting scenes not possible in regular human life
- Mental illnesses including Anxiety, Depression, PTSD
- Toxic families, culture, and religion
- Violence and gore
- Talk of disasters and the end of the world
- An Agnostic view of Christianity

Night with the Morningstar
A YURI AND STAR SHORT

Alone for centuries, Star wants to watch the world burn, but he never expected to encounter Yuri and find love amidst the darkness.

Will Star find a way to keep Yuri in his arms after the world ends?

A Kiss to End the World

Humans mastered a special kind of chaos. Thousands of other worlds, years, and species, and none quite made the mark humans did. From the rewriting of already mistranslated texts into religions to justify murder and rape for physical wealth, to war, to the death of their planet. The dragons, with their love for shiny things, had nothing on humans' greed.

Who hadn't seen the end coming?

Star wandered the spaces between, little more than a ghost, watching the worlds change, observing mortals live and die, wars and kingdoms rise and fall. Many ages seeming like the end, but only now as the planet itself began to collapse, stripped of the rare resources that kept the magic from running wild and all of existence from caving in on itself, did Star agree that the time of humans was ending. Would they survive this final destruction? He struggled to care anymore, though it had once been his job and passion, to help them thrive.

His fault, perhaps? Had he broken his love's creation? Or had this always been the intention?

Star wandered the streets of Chicago. He'd memorized a thousand giant cities, explored them all as little more than a shadow, but returned to this one time and again. Why?

He paused outside a nondescript bar. Nothing outside special at all, inside the food was passable, the liquor only mid-shelf, but something kept pulling him back.

Star waited until someone else entered and slid inside behind them, conserving his muted energy, the chains heavy on his limbs and throat as a constant reminder. His heart thumped, cracking the ice around it as he caught a familiar shape behind the bar. The man was young and barely old enough to drink. Mortal laws were strange and inconsistent, but he provided others with alcohol and a smile. Star had savored that smile a handful of times to memorize the nuances of politeness and rare glimpses of welcoming.

The man's chocolate brown hair shimmered with a thousand natural highlights in every shade of color, a spectrum of life and light growing from his head no human would see, but he had pulled his hair up high on his head into a bun, only a few stray strands escaping to touch his face, a sign the night was bustling despite the unravelling world outside the bar's doors. The touch of a well-maintained beard hid the sharp jawline Star longed to touch, but it was his eyes, a blue swirling with a universe of colors that kept bringing him back.

Yuri.

Yuri never remembered Star. Twice Star had dared to speak to him. Drawing enough power to manifest even for a few minutes made Star weak, sometimes sending him into a coma-like slumber for weeks. But as with most humans, Yuri dismissed their encounters as dreams and allowed them to fade. Star returned a dozen times to stare at the man's beauty with longing, not understanding the draw exactly. He'd met a thousand humans with bright auras wrapped in rainbow colors to remind him of his lost love. Humans couldn't perceive the variation, the spectrum of light and dark too muted for them and their eyesight too weak to decipher, but Star wanted to explore and memorize every trace of color change in Yuri.

Star paused near the door, watching. His heart thawing by simply being in the room with the man. He waited until Yuri moved down the length of the bar to serve another customer before slipping into an empty seat at the counter.

Tonight would be the end of civilization. The veil would tear another Fracture in time and space, dropping everything into madness. It was a familiar enough feeling to give Star a sense of peace. Each time it happened, he hoped it was the last, longed for his end, and prayed to find the love stolen from him several millennia ago. He longed to bask in the warmth of his lover again. If it meant the end of humanity, so be it.

His only regret was Yuri.

Star wrapped waves of power around himself, manifesting in the human world as he rarely did. The coming rift gave him added strength. Not enough to break the chains, but perhaps sufficient to stare into Yuri's beauty, listen to his sweet words, and maybe share a touch or two?

But touching Yuri would cause more trouble than any human deserved. It would put a target on Yuri's back, awakening any latent abilities the man might have, and open him up to a world of nightmares as the shadows always sought to devour anything Star adored, a curse of his brethren's jealousy. The rainbow blend of colors painting Yuri's aura meant the man could see through the veil, and might even have the power to untangle the end of days, but who wanted to know all about the end? Who would want the pain, terror, and grief of knowing and being powerless to change it? Fate was a cruel and unrelenting bitch.

Star flinched and stared down at his hands. They blinked from human fingers to the clawed monstrosity of his curse as he tried to regain control of his anger. He clenched his hands into fists, crossing his arms over his chest to hide them.

Yuri appeared in front of him, making Star suck in a deep breath of joy and grief all at once. The desire to touch the man, memorize his sighs, and examine the mix of colors woven through his aura made Star tremble. Yuri gave him a sweet smile, genuine and charming, and absently asked for Star's ID. This modern world, so strange with its rules. He manifested an ID and shared pleasant words with Yuri about drinks. The background noise of the television news broadcasting disasters as the world fell apart sank into Star's subconscious like a ticking time bomb.

So little time left. To say he didn't long for the implosion of humanity would have been a lie. His brethren fought with him forever, claiming humanity was a blight to be extinguished, their dreams finally coming to fruition.

Star disagreed because his lover had created them. The imperfections of humanity adding an unusual ability for thought and creativity that no other creature seemed to have. Millions of species and worlds, yet none as filled with inner magic, beauty, and monstrosities as humans. Did he care anymore?

As he watched Yuri move, he thought, for this one, *yes*.

Humans entered the bar and approached with scathing words. The shadows always drew the dark ones to Star. Yuri tried to dissuade them, his concern over Star endearing. Star could have struck them dead with a thought, but not in front of Yuri. He didn't want the man to fear him. When a human touched Yuri, it was a step too far. It was all Star could do to control his rage. He reacted without thinking, grabbing the human's wrist, his touch sliding a wave of darkness through the human like slime devouring his soul. Even if Star did nothing, the man wouldn't live through the night.

Star decided none of them would. The weakening veil meant he felt strong, his ability to manipulate this world tangible. He could tear them to shreds, work out his aggression, and since the world was about to end, it wouldn't matter. He could return to the bar, and his gentle flirting with Yuri, and wait until it all caved down around them.

He spared a brief look at Yuri, sighing internally with a thousand ideas of how he'd like the man beneath him, and teach him to sing of pleasure, show him what love could be through physical touch. Could he erase the sadness that stained Yuri's heart? It had been growing long before they met. Star's sadness echoed Yuri's, as though they were bound without Star ever daring to touch him, but standing in his presence made his heart beat, and the frozen emotions inside him begin to crack free of their prison.

Desire, the first to leech through, anger quickly following with jealousy and need hot on the trail. A combination of emotions often woven together and long cast into the frozen abyss, he marveled at their awakening. Yuri's doing?

Star followed the humans outside, cracked his knuckles and let his hands turn to claws, not caring if they all died. He could play a little. How long had it been since he'd had a real fight? Not that humans were strong enough to fight him, anyway. But they came at him and he enjoyed the stretch of muscles long stiffened from his chains, dodging their attacks, delivering a light hit here or there to draw it out, not unlike a cat playing with a mouse.

They would never have landed a hit if the door behind Star hadn't opened and he sensed it was Yuri coming out of the bar. One of the human's smashed Star in the face, splitting Star's lip on fangs rising from his loss of control. The rush of pain awakened a thousand nerves and needles of sensation Star forgot existed in his human form. He needed to end this before Yuri got involved and worried the man's heart would turn away from him if Star actually killed them. He sped through an attack to knock them all unconscious. The curse of his touch spread over them and the shadows pooled in the alleyway, anticipating a feast as the last man went down and stayed there.

"Holy fuck," Yuri said. "You okay?" Yuri reached for Star, his gaze going to the trickle of blood on Star's lip. Star stepped away, composing himself to hide fang and claw. Since Yuri didn't flinch away, Star's hold on his beast must have been firm.

"Fine. I apologize for the trouble," Star said, his heart hammering not from the fight, but speaking to Yuri, being seen even if it wasn't his true form. Star licked away the blood from the side of his lip. It would heal, but the way Yuri's gaze followed Star's tongue lit a fire in Star.

The end of civilization, he reminded himself. If Yuri survived the coming catastrophe, he wouldn't want to be cursed with Star's touch.

"Not your fault these assholes pulled shit," Yuri said. "Come back in, and I'll refill your glass."

An invitation that felt a thousand times deeper than the words. Yuri's gaze, filled with heat, melted another layer of ice encasing Star's heart. It was all he could do not to reach out and shove the man against the wall to show him pleasure as the world erupted around them. Star hugged himself to keep from touching and glanced back at the fallen humans as the shadows ate. He needed to get Yuri back inside.

"They look fine. I'll lock this side door when we head back in and let everyone know to let them wander off on their own."

Star nodded and stepped past him into the bar, hoping Yuri would follow. Thankfully, he did, making his way back behind the bar and filling a fresh glass for Star. The money Star had left him was on the counter, untouched as he knew it would be. Another couldn't take a gift he gave. But Yuri slid the cash back across the bar.

"Why?" Star wondered.

"Seems shitty to make you pay when some assholes tried to pull shit," Yuri said.

"You are too kind for this world." Star slid the money back. "Take it, and I will keep drinking, refuse, and I shall go." The value of money in this world was survival, but only for a few hours more. He could give Yuri peace of mind, if nothing else.

Yuri took the money and refilled Star's glass, though his gaze never strayed long from Star. It made Star burn with anticipation. Did Star have any scions left in the mortal world strong enough to protect Yuri from what was to come? And what would be the point? If humanity died, that meant Yuri, too.

Star swallowed the alcohol and buried his rage in focusing on the TV and the rising wave of disasters. A server came and went, calling Yuri by name. She was pretty and young, but Yuri paid no attention to her in the way men usually noticed women, rather he acted brotherly, protective, watching all the employees as though he were some giant to stave off all evil.

"Yuri?" Star asked, hoping for more conversation. It was a dance they'd played. Star pretended they had never met. Yuri never remembered him anyway.

"Yeah. My mom saw it in an anime and liked it. What can I call you?" Yuri asked.

A thousand names, stories, and tainted histories marked him, but after first finding him months prior when Yuri had remarked on the brightness of the stars that night, Star had decided for Yuri, he would be "Star."

Yuri grinned. "Yeah? It suits you."

Why did it feel like lying? Translations aside, Star could be anyone he wished. The world was coming to an end. Only for Yuri, he wanted more.

"I mean, you sort of shine like a star, right? That action in the alley was crazy, but you're the guy everyone notices?"

He shouldn't have noticed any of it. Had Star manifested too much strength, or was it the weakening of the veil that showed Yuri more than he should see?

"Sorry. Bad way of saying 'You're pretty', I guess? Handsome, whatever. Sorry."

Star's heart warmed. His mortal visage, while not his true form which had been cursed by his brethren thousands of years ago, was as close to what he looked like when his love had created him as possible in the modern human world. It had been ages since anyone found him attractive. The monster near the surface made everyone run. Any who couldn't see it still sensed the demon within.

"You think I'm pretty? A lovely gentleman like you?"

"Uh, yeah? Is that okay? I'm not lovely. Or a gentleman, really. Just Yuri."

Star studied Yuri. Wanting everything and fearing the worst. He could coax Yuri to follow him into the dark across the veil, delivering himself to Star, but he imagined Yuri's light fading quickly when locked in the dark. The shadows found the taste of human flesh alluring, which meant he'd be fighting to keep them off the man and draining his strength. One slip up and they'd take Yuri from him in the most gruesome way.

"Sorry. I'm not trying to come on to you. I know that's rude. You're here to drink. I try not to be one of those guys. I just..."

"I'm not offended," Star said. "Surprised."

"Why? You're gorgeous. You probably have people throwing themselves at you all the time."

"And you? Do you have people throwing themselves at you, sweet Yuri?"

"People flirt sometimes." Yuri shrugged. "I think they are drunk."

"You are lovely," Star said. "Doesn't take drowning in cups to see that."

Yuri's face turned a delightful pink, and the rippling rainbow of color in his aura shimmered. Joy, pride, hope, adoration. It was a bright well of emotion Star hadn't seen in a long time. "Thank you."

Star felt the gears shift as the veil tore. Out of time. The ground shook and chaos fluttered around them.

"What the fuck?" Yuri asked. "Everyone, stay calm!" Yuri turned on the light on his flashlight on his phone, his gaze pausing on Star for a moment as though he saw something. Star locked down on his power although waves of energy rippled through the very fabric of reality.

The end of the world. This one, at least. Star ducked his head.

"You okay?" Yuri asked.

Star moved away as Yuri tried to touch him again. "The end is never pleasant," he said. Yuri followed everyone to the door, holding it open, waiting for everyone to pass, even Star, who could have vanished rather than facing the shifting skies and booming fires. Star slid out into the night, careful to keep his distance from Yuri while wanting to grab onto the man and escape with him while he could.

Buildings crashed and imploded, the ground shook, lights flickered and died, leaving fire and screams billowing into the darkness. Death rising beneath the fires and rubble. The end was always a nightmare, fast in some ways and painfully slow in others.

Yuri trembled; his hand pressed to his chest as everyone bolted off in other directions. Star eyed the growing movement of shadows congregating. Even without his touch, they would find Yuri's light a feast.

"You okay?" Yuri asked, working hard to breathe, though Star could hear his racing heart. "Can I walk you home or anything?"

"You are anxious about me," Star said. "Are you well?"

"I think the world is ending," Yuri said. He took a few steps and stumbled. "Fuck, sorry. Panic attack." Yuri half fell to a spot of risen pavement, trying to catch his breath and slow his racing heart. Fear, a bittersweet emotion, wafting from him. Star glared at the shadows, who slinked away, not willing to face his rage. He crouched close to Yuri, not touching him, though he badly wanted to hold Yuri and chase away the fear.

"It's okay," Yuri said. He counted for a few seconds, lips moving and only sometimes speaking the numbers. "This will pass in a minute. You can touch me if you want."

"No one wants my touch," Star said. A gift of nightmares from the most hated being in all the worlds—mostly propaganda—but Star had done plenty.

"That's stupid. I would love your touch," Yuri confessed. "End of the world, right? Fuck it. What's the worst you could do? Beat me up like you did those guys in the alley?" Yuri asked.

He sounded earnest, and Star couldn't help but smile. Self-destructive, perhaps? It reminded Star of the seraphim in a lot of ways. But that was what Yuri was, wasn't he? A flawed creation mirroring the seraphim? Something meant to grow, learn, and create rather than birthed into light, perfection, and stagnation.

Yuri reached for him. Star could have stopped him, should have. There were a few seconds of Yuri's hand lingering near Star's jaw before Yuri's touch, warm and bright, slid over Star's skin and drew him forward to press their lips together. It was all Star could do not to crush the man into the pavement and make his body sing right there with the world collapsing around them.

There was an innocence in Yuri, not necessarily from his lack of experience, which Star knew from his hesitation, but a rising sense of wonder, like touching could be good and he wanted so much more. Star slid his tongue between Yuri's lips, basking in the man's heat and pulsing waves of life, his heart hammering in his chest with both anticipation and fear. The shadows moved around them, inching closer, waiting to take Yuri, but Star surrounded them with a shield as he sank into Yuri's kiss. How many times had he longed for this? Watched the man from a distance, intrigued and yearning, not understanding why exactly? Was it worth it?

Star's touch slid through the man, his curse slipping right off Yuri, though the waves of rainbow color brightened. An awakening of his abilities. How much would he see, Star wondered as he pulled back to stare at Yuri? That brightness of his aura blazing hot enough to burn. Star sucked in a breath, unwilling to let go, the ice melting inside as he ached with a need he hadn't encountered in thousands of years. He worried Yuri would see him in his cursed form and run, and for a few seconds, as Yuri's gaze focused on the fracture of worlds in the distance, and then on Star's face, Star thought he saw everything.

"You're so beautiful," Yuri said. His eyes glistened with colors, any last resistance holding back his abilities falling away. If he saw the monster within Star, it didn't frighten him as he didn't pull away.

"Oh, Yuri," Star said. "I would never wish my curse on you."

"Curse?" Yuri asked. He gripped Star's shirt, clinging to him, gaze focused on Star's face, eyes half-lidded with longing. "We're going to die, right? End of the world and all that? I want..." He leaned in for another kiss.

Star devoured his lips, diving deep, despite his fangs pushing through, and Yuri didn't seem to notice other than to press his hard cock against Star's thigh, arms wrapping around Star's waist. It was everything Star wanted and feared. The world falling apart around them, and Star could hold on to energy for a while, maybe even create memories to last them all of eternity?

Star sighed. "You're so pure, you should not be mine. I should not have touched you, spoiled you..." He tried to pull away, but Yuri clung to him.

"Please," Yuri begged. "It's the end of the world. Can't I be me for five minutes?"

"And who are you, Yuri? Who do you want to be?" Star asked. It was a larger question Star asked himself, trying to understand why he wanted Yuri so badly. Millions of humans crossed his path, and Star had lovers from every world to pass his days even in the icy prison of hell, but Yuri had somehow reached through time and space and tethered Star with need.

"Yours?" Yuri asked breathlessly. "Please? Is it okay? To not feel like I'm evil for the last minutes of the end of the world?"

"Evil?" Star asked as he cupped Yuri's face. "Why would anyone think you're evil?"

"Because I want this. If this is the end, I want to feel everything. I want to feel adored, loved for a few minutes, even if it's nothing but a lie. I'm so tired of being alone."

But Star was a lie, everything about him. Would Yuri run if he really knew? Star kissed him again. "Then let that be my gift to you. In exchange for the ill that will come from my curse, let me show you how beautiful feeling can be."

He created a doorway and manifested a private space for the two of them. A bedroom, like a modern magazine picture with a soft bed and all the things he could ever imagine providing comfort for Yuri. It wouldn't last, even if he locked Yuri away to protect him. Eventually the chains would drain Star's power and Yuri would fall prey to the shadows and curse Star's existence.

Star slid his hands over Yuri's face, his power glowing beneath his skin. Did he see? Was the horror of Star's form unveiling itself before him? Star had to know. "I give you one last chance to run," Star said.

Yuri looked confused. "Why would I run?"

But Star unwrapped the glamour holding back his true form and the curse of his brethren. Their jealousy meant to unravel his beauty because the creator had loved him beyond all others. His hands were no longer human, but tipped with claws, and the size of Yuri's head. Yuri felt small and delicate in Star's embrace, a familiar sensation that made Star's gut flip over with a rise of memories. He studied Yuri's expression for signs of fear, but found only wonder.

"Don't you see how monstrous I am?"

"You're beautiful," Yuri whispered. "Am I dreaming?" He reached up to put his hand over Star's, blinking at the size difference, and the shadow-laced skin. Shadows had thousands of years to stain Star with their darkness, devouring the last touches of light within his soul. They fed on him endlessly, but he couldn't die. What must he look like to Yuri? Grotesque most likely. His transformation into a beast meant to give rise to fear in humans. Star tried to pull away, hoping to deliver Yuri home and give him a chance to survive the worst few hours of the collapse of the human world.

"Please," Yuri asked, not letting go.

"Can't you see what I am? Who I am?"

Yuri stared up at him with wonder. "Mine?"

That word cracked more ice encasing Star's soul, and he couldn't help but press his lips to Yuri's. The need to claim him leaving Star aching. Thousands of lovers, and he wanted no one as bad as Yuri. Still, he hesitated, his heart awakening as though it had been gripped in stone and the rock walls shattered by Yuri's light.

"If you become mine, I will never let you go," Star said, holding Yuri's face between his hands to force the man to meet his gaze. "My affection is not for the weak."

Yuri turned them, and pushed Star back onto the bed, sliding his hips over Star's lap, hard cock pressing to Star's stomach with need. He held Star's face between his hands, foreheads resting together, Yuri's breathing labored, heart racing, but not in fear. "If this is a dream, I never want it to end," Yuri said.

He crushed his lips to Star's, trying to mimic all Star did, learning and seeking all at once. Star breathed him in, hand cupping the back of Yuri's neck with delicate claws and drinking in his warmth. He sank into Yuri's touch, basking in the heat of him and that glowing light long stolen. Star traced Yuri's body, hesitating to remove the barrier of clothing between them for fear he'd go mad with lust and frighten the man away.

Star dragged waves of power back around him to suppress his size, making him appear mostly human again, and Yuri made a small sound of protest.

"You don't have to..." Yuri said, his gaze focused on Star's face. "I find you beautiful both ways."

"You tempt me terribly," Star confessed. "So innocent and fragile. I don't want to hurt you, but my need is great." He slipped his hand down between them to cup Yuri's hard cock through his pants. The man thrust his hips into Star's touch, desperate for pleasure. "I promised you pleasure for the night, a memory to last until the end of your days."

"Yes," Yuri hissed, clinging to Star. "I don't know what to do, just that I want..." He didn't even know how to express what he wanted, but that was okay, Star knew.

Star leaned in and kissed Yuri again, slowly working Yuri's cock through his pants and exploring Yuri's mouth with his tongue, memorizing it all. "There is so much to show you," Star said. He tugged Yuri's hair from its bun, letting the messy curls fall free. Star badly wanted Yuri naked beneath him, sinking into him, and screaming in pleasure. He shoved up Yuri's shirt, and the man chucked it off to the side, clinging to Star's touch as Star traced his fingers over Yuri's bare chest and the bright colors of ink etched deep. Did Yuri know some of that art was soul deep, as though the stories had become living magic beneath his skin? Star longed to examine and memorize it all.

He pushed them both off the end of the bed, forcing Yuri to his feet to unbutton his pants and shove them down, casting aside the shoes, underthings and any fabric barrier Yuri kept between them.

"You too," Yuri begged, "please."

Star leaned in to kiss him, his hand wrapping around Yuri's length and gently squeezing. The man was beautiful in every way. Flawless, and still so delicately human that Star felt as though it was madness to touch him at all.

"Please," Yuri begged again. He wove one hand through Star's hair and the other beneath Star's jacket, seeking flesh.

Star nipped Yuri's lower lip. "Up on the bed. Get comfortable against the headboard." He stepped away, not waiting for Yuri to comply, as he stripped off his jacket and unbuttoned his shirt. He could have magicked his clothes away. His presence in the modern world was mostly a projection of his soul anyway, but he wanted Yuri's eyes on him. He wanted to watch the lust in Yuri's gaze build as he revealed himself. Part pride, and a lot of desire, but Star knew the heat of those emotions and had almost forgotten how delicious that fire could be.

Yuri stumbled, half falling backward on the bed and crawling backward until he rested against the headboard, his gaze not leaving Star for a second. His breath hitched as Star slid off the shirt, baring his shoulders, chest, and stomach. Star kicked off the shoes, unbuttoned the pants and let them fall open, revealing no underwear beneath, only the hot spread of flesh with Star's need thrusting between. Yuri gasped, his gaze focused on Star's groin as Star shoved the cloth down and stepped free.

The half-lidded desire in Yuri's gaze ignited an inferno of craving in Star's gut, a longing to devour him, the light, the heat, and his body all at once. Star let out a long and controlled breath, steadying himself. Yuri was human, breakable. He would have to be careful, but he also imagined his massive cock, rippling with shadows beneath his skin, splitting Yuri wide and filling the man as he writhed and begged for more.

"Please," Yuri said as though he somehow could see inside Star's head and all the things Star wanted to show him.

Star climbed up onto the bed and crawled toward Yuri, all of him on display. He slid over Yuri, capturing the man's lips and palming his cock all at once. Yuri thrust into Star's grip, but Star was only beginning. He nipped Yuri's lower lip, chin and down his torso, Yuri's chest heaving for air as Star sank lower to lick the tip of Yuri's shaft.

"Star," Yuri cried as Star lapped at the sensitive head and finally took him into his mouth, sucking and swallowing Yuri down until Star was nose to pelvic bone. Yuri came apart beneath him, his hips bucking wildly, and Star knew the man wouldn't last long, but they would have plenty of other rounds. He swallowed deep, his throat working the head of Yuri's cock while Yuri muttered incoherent things and came. He shot down Star's throat, the spend filled with light, joy, and life.

Star swallowed and sighed sweetly, his gaze on Yuri's face filled with wonder. Yuri gripped the bedding as though fearing he'd fall into a void if he let go completely. Star lapped at Yuri's dick. It remained hard, needing, begging for more, part of Star's magic, but a lot of it was Yuri's desire, still endless pools of need reflected in his eyes.

Star climbed over Yuri's lap, his body aching for more, to fill or be filled. The light inside him from Yuri's spend beginning to thaw parts of him he long thought dead. Yuri wrapped his arms around Star, pulling him closer, breathing into his touch, and accepting a kiss flavored with Yuri's come.

"Round one," Star said into Yuri's lips.

Yuri's eyes widened, his desire naked and laid bare in his gaze. "Yes," Yuri said, his hands careful, but opening and closing as if he wanted to touch but was afraid. "You have wings," Yuri whispered, one hand on Star's hip, the other in his hair.

"I do," Star agreed, surprised Yuri could see or sense them at all.

"This must be a dream," Yuri said, sounding sad.

"Is it not a good one?" Star slid his hips over Yuri's, gliding their cocks together in a playful thrust.

"Yes," Yuri agreed.

"Then why not make it memorable?" Star manifested a container of lube, setting the slick down to open it and coat his hand, then wrapped both of their cocks in his fist. "Dance with me, love," Star teased as he moved his hips. Yuri held on tight, adding his own rhythm. It wasn't graceful, but the zing of their cocks together sweet and stirring. Star released his hold on them to push Yuri down onto the pillows and lean over him, legs spread, thoughts focused on what was to come. He wanted Yuri inside him, more than just the waves of light and spend, but his body buried deep.

Yuri gasped at the sight between their bodies, Star's cock hard and weeping, while Star guided Yuri to his entrance, teasing them both as he skimmed Yuri's cock around his rim before finally holding him and pressing down to ease Yuri inside. Yuri trembled as Star's ass swallowed his cock to the root. Star waited, reveling in the heat, stretch and desire joining them. He leaned forward to capture Yuri's lips again. Yuri thrust his tongue into Star's mouth and Star moved his hips, holding Yuri in place and fucking himself on the pretty man with abandon. The sound of their bodies working together was slick and decadent. Yuri fed at Star's lips, the sounds falling from them incoherent but filled with desire.

Star took Yuri's hand in his and wrapped it around Star's

cock, his hand covering Yuri's, guiding him. "Sweet Yuri," Star whispered into Yuri's mouth, their bodies linked and pleasure building wave upon wave until Star saw flashes of light. He came hard, painting Yuri in ribbons of come, Star's ass clamping hard on Yuri's cock, milking him as Yuri cried and loosed himself inside Star in a fiery rush of light.

"Fuck," Yuri cried, unable to stop moving his hips as he slammed into Star, riding the wave of pleasure as it rose and fell a half dozen times. Star's hold on his magic waned. He shuddered, the chains suddenly heavy, but his body also returning to the natural form, huge, and dark. His thighs were massive as he adjusted his weight to not crush Yuri, but without the glamour and suppression, the sensation of Yuri inside him was ten thousand times better.

Star eased his grasp, careful of his claws, half expecting Yuri to run away, but the man gripped Star's cock, his hand barely wrapping around the enormous girth of the shaft and pumping, desperate for more. Star clenched his ass, squeezing Yuri tight inside and slowing their pace. He painted swirls in the come on Yuri's chest with a careful fingertip, bringing the digit to Yuri's lips to lap it clean.

Yuri let out a frustrated sound, his body demanding the mad rush for more pleasure. He touched Star's face, fingers sliding up Star's cheek and to his forehead and the horns that were part of his curse. One more piece of him revealed that didn't send Yuri running.

"Can I?" Yuri asked, his gaze focused upward. "Will it hurt?"

Star gasped as Yuri caressed one of his horns carefully, as though it could break with the slightest touch. "Grip my horn and I shall fuck you, love. My body buried within your heat."

"Really?" Yuri asked in wonder. He looked between the

massive size of Star's cock in his true form and the horn beneath his fingers. "Can we?"

Star groaned. Could Yuri take him like this? Most humans couldn't, in fact most species couldn't, even those crafted for sex. But Star longed to try, and could imagine how beautiful Yuri would look, split wide on his pulsing length, writhing and begging as Star claimed him. He took a handful of Yuri's hair, forcing the man to meet his eyes. "You will tell me if I hurt you and we will stop."

Yuri bit his lip.

"That is not a request, love. I want to be inside you. You promise to tell me if I hurt you or we stop here."

"Promise," Yuri agreed.

"You've never even taken another before," Star said.

"But I want you."

Star growled and lifted Yuri, flipping him over. "Let me see how loose I can work you, and how many times I can make you come, love. Once your muscles feel like jelly, I will ram my cock deep, caressing your insides until you pass out from the pleasure." He shoved a pillow under Yuri's hips, tilting the man's gorgeous ass upward. Star spread Yuri's thighs, pressing his legs open to stare at the sweet depths of his ass. Yuri made a needy noise as Star traced a careful finger over Yuri's rim. Star couldn't suppress his claws, his need overwhelming him, but it meant he'd have to use other ways of loosening Yuri and preparing him to be filled.

Yuri turned his head on the pillow to stare back, gaze half-lidded and filled with need, almost drunk with it. Star brought his lips to Yuri's cheeks, kissing one and then the other, nipping lightly, not enough to break skin, but the light beneath the surface glowed brighter with every touch. Not unlike the archangels of old and the way their skin would reflect the light of creation.

"You are a puzzle, Yuri," Star said, leaning in to take Yuri's balls in his mouth, sucking on them, rolling them around with his tongue. A thousand nuances of sound fell from Yuri's lips, nothing Star could define as spoken language, but they were sign enough that Yuri was enjoying what Star did. The man was fearless, lying there beneath Star's unsuppressed form. Star knew he looked like the mortal depiction of a demon, his curse meant to strip him of his beauty and render him unlovable, but Yuri didn't run. He struggled to keep his body still beneath Star's touch, begging for more. Star slipped between Yuri's cheeks and traced his tongue along Yuri's taint, tickling the rim in a circle, sliding back down, his tongue larger, wider, and more pointed in this form. Yuri sank into Star's touch, gripping the bed, but gaze never leaving Star for a second.

Star expected Yuri to recoil from the tongue, more serpent-like in this form than human, but he shivered, ass clenching and gaping as if begging to be filled. Star flicked his tongue around the rim, pulling more sounds of pleasure from Yuri. He pressed the tip inside, waiting and watching for any sign of tension or discomfort in Yuri. He wrapped a careful hand around Yuri's dripping cock and stroked him slowly, easing Star's passage inward while the man's body dueled with itself over pleasure.

"Yes," Yuri trembled, hips trying to shove backward for more, then ground his hips into Star's fist, adding friction to his hard cock.

Star gripped Yuri's waist, holding him in place, and shoved his tongue deep. There were advantages to this form that the human form could never replicate. The length and size of his tongue part of it, but also the ability to control. The tip teased Yuri's prostate, pressing in as Star dug his face between Yuri's cheek to get himself as deep as possible. It wouldn't be as deep or wide as Star's cock would spread him, but the heat and teasing was enough to send Yuri over the edge again.

Yuri screamed and came hard, body clamping down on Star's tongue, but Star continued to work him, his cock throbbing to be inside and feel that gripping heat. Star expected Yuri to black out from the waves of pleasure as his skin glowed with added light, illuminating the tattoos painted into his flesh as though he were a stained-glass window. But Yuri gasped and shivered, begging for more.

Star eased his tongue out, Yuri's hole clenching, trying to keep Star inside.

"Please," Yuri begged, hips moving as he ground himself against the bedding and into Star's hand. His gaze found Star's cock, and he licked his lips, ass gripping hard as if he could already feel it inside of him.

"You must be one of my get," Star said quietly as he slid up behind Yuri and teased Yuri's hole with the tip of his cock. "To be so wanton." He added more slick until he dripped with it, and pressed into Yuri, expecting resistance, or complete denial of entry. But Yuri swallowed the head of his cock with a pop of the outer muscle easing and the shaft gliding in like Yuri's body needed to devour it. It was insane, the sheer size spreading Yuri wide, and the man took it, his expression filled with wonder and pleasure, unlike any human Star ever encountered.

"What are you?" Star whispered, seating himself deep inside the man, the heat and grip nearly his undoing.

"Yours," Yuri whispered earnestly.

That rang true more than anything else in all of time. Star lifted Yuri, dragging him back into his lap and grinding himself hard. He could feel the beat of Yuri's heart through his cock, the pulsing of his blood, the heat of his body gripping and begging. Star held the man against him, feeling massive in this form beside Yuri's sweetness, and stared down Yuri's fine body to the lovely cock jutting from Yuri with desperate need.

Star thought for a few seconds it was sad they were alone, as he could imagine watching a handful of lovers bring Yuri pleasure while Star made the rules. Someone would drink down Yuri's cock, another would lick at where their bodies joined, still another would worship Yuri's nipples, and perhaps Star would find another fine cock to nestle between Yuri's lips, bringing noises of delight to his throat each time a cock sank deep. Star could imagine Yuri fucked in a thousand ways, all of them beautiful, not unlike worship in the old days when the creators surrounded themselves in love and life before the wars began.

"Mine," Star agreed as he pressed his fangs into the flesh of Yuri's shoulder. He cupped Yuri's cock with a careful hand. "I want you to feel me forever," Star said. "To remember how deep I'm buried, and how much you stretch to accommodate me."

"Yes," Yuri begged, lost in pleasure even as Star's fangs drew blood. Star lapped at the puncture. The two small marks felt as enormous to his soul as his cock buried in Yuri's ass. It was like the ambrosia of stories, sweet, divine, and addicting. Was it the centuries without light that made Star mad with need for all of Yuri?

"I'm going to fuck you until you cry," Star promised. "And you never forget my touch."

"Yes, please," Yuri begged. He turned his head to catch Star's lips and slid a teasing touch of fingertips over Star's horn. "Let me be yours."

Star captured Yuri's mouth with his, sliding his tongue inside as his body worked in and out, slowly at first, but building to a grind that would send them into a hundred climaxes as long as Star could keep pulling power from the Fracture. It didn't matter that the room wavered from time to time, or the weight of Star's chains creaked as he moved. All that mattered was how hot, tight, and needing Yuri was beneath him. If he could brand Yuri's body as his forever, let the world know, he would.

Star caught movement out of the corner of his eye and turned, thinking the shadows had already found them, but was surprised to find a large mirror on the nearby wall, reflecting everything they did. He hadn't remembered manifesting that with part of the room and glared at his massive form, the swirling shadows living beneath his skin and the mutations cursing his beauty, stilling as nothing looked like the creature he remembered other than the eyes, a reflection of his long-lost love.

They were watching, weren't they? Were they waiting for Yuri to reject him? Wanting to watch Star wake with Yuri's corpse clinging to his cock or alive with a murderous intent and words of rage on his lips? What nightmare or curse did they have planned for him now? Weren't eons in the dark enough torture? Existence after the death of his beloved? Could he not find a few moments of peace and pleasure in the arms of a pretty man?

Star snarled at the reflection, wanting to break the mirror and shatter the beast he was. He didn't deserve Yuri's beauty, even while the man begged him for more.

Yuri reached up, fingers sliding over Star's cheek, their gaze meeting in the reflection briefly. There was no fear in his eyes, only desire. Yuri pressed himself up to meet Star's lips, an awkward sideways kiss, but accepting and filled with adoration. Didn't he see the monster Star was?

"You're so beautiful," Yuri said into Star's lips.

Star growled and pressed Yuri into the bed, slamming into him, and Yuri taking it with a grateful grunt and shoving himself back into Star. His vocabulary completely lost beneath the pounding to moans, grunts, and gasps for air as Star's cursed form held him down and showed him heaven all at once.

They could watch, Star decided at that moment. Let them see Yuri's beauty and never touch it. He belonged to Star now, and Star would savor every sound, sensation, and sight until they dragged him back into the dark, locked in nightmares until all worlds finally ended. He traced his fingers in circles over Yuri's tattooed skin, memorizing it.

Yuri cried and came again, his body gripping Star tight, and Star sank his teeth into the joint of Yuri's shoulder, a claim that would heal, but be an invisible mark. None to touch him, harm him, or take him as long as Star's strength lasted.

The power would fade. Star could feel the spinning of the Fracture slowing and he'd have to retreat, eventually. The chains would drag him into the darkness, possibly even locking him in a coma-like dream state as he was using more power than he ever had to be in this moment with Yuri.

Star would have Yuri over and over until then, burning himself deep into the man's memory, even if he muted the monster side of himself, leaving Yuri only with the memories of his human self. Would Yuri hate himself later if he knew he submitted to the thing Star was? Star didn't want to know, instead lazing in the divine touch of him and grafting memories of them as if they were equals together with Star little more than the pretty man Yuri met at the bar the night the world fell apart. Their lovemaking inspired, but not monstrous, even while Star wanted to never forget a single moment.

The end of the world had few perks, but Star thought being nestled in Yuri was probably the best he could ever imagine. If he could curl up and rest within Yuri's skin until the end of time, that would be okay, and a fine way for the king of demons to finally die.

"Sweet love," Star whispered as he worked Yuri up again, determined to breathe him back to arousal until they were both too tired to move. "Let me live in your dreams as you will live in mine."

TOUCHED BY A STAR

Yuri met the man of his dreams the night the world ended.

When Star vanished back into the shadows leaving Yuri to find a way to survive, Yuri returned home, hoping to hide from the Fracture of worlds and the monsters that spewed from the rift. Time passed and Yuri's memory of that night faded into dreams, until their camp was raided by vampire warriors from another world.

Taken by the warriors and delivered to the feet of their leader, Yuri finds himself facing a Master of magic, power, and desire.

Will Yuri find his way back to Star or lose his heart along the way?

THE NIGHT THE WORLD ENDED

H e kicked their asses like some super-powered being in a video game.

Yuri stood in the doorway, open-mouthed, shocked. The small, pretty man, with a teal streak through his dark hair, moved like water, beating the shit out of the four guys who'd lured him outside.

The group of drunk frat boys had started this mess, bothering pretty boy at the counter of the bar where Yuri worked the closing shift as a bartender to pay for chef school. When the pretty boy sat at the counter, Yuri had instantly asked for his ID, though he didn't really think the man was underage. Yes, he looked young, but something in Yuri's gut said he was older than he looked. World-weary eyes, perhaps? He flashed a sardonic smile and pulled out a wallet to flash an ID for another state, but the date put him closer to thirty than twenty.

Yuri threw him a nod, not more than glancing at the card. "What'll you have?"

Tuesdays were never busy nights, usually the same crowd in those who wanted to drown in the alcohol. Yuri expected, from the fit of his clothes, and the high end look of him, that he'd order something fluffy or fruity, but he said, "Vodka. Top shelf. No ice."

"I don't have Grey Goose," Yuri said, knowing a lot of the younger crowd wanted names rather than the best. "But I've got Van Gogh or Tito's."

"Van Gogh Oranje?" he asked.

A drinker then. Yuri nodded and set a tumbler before him, a fresh bottle of Van Gogh at the ready. The man waved a hand at the glass and Yuri poured. More than a shot, this type was best on the rocks, mixed in a drink, or smoothly sipped. He wasn't the chatty type either, focusing instead on the overhead TV playing the news on mute with subtitles talking about the latest disasters.

The world was plunged into a nightmare with a growing ripple of natural disasters. Everything from tornados, hurricanes and floods to earthquakes and volcanic eruptions. The past year had been chaos, and seemed to get worse, every day something else on the news, another natural disaster, thousands dead, or feared dead, and there seemed to be no end in sight.

Chicago, the city in which Yuri worked and went to school, a supernatural level of wind storms brought a new meaning to the windy city. On the outskirts of the city, he hadn't noticed a difference, but the wind had brought down a handful of the downtown towers, crashing in chunks over the city. The rumbling made everything rock and roll, and the plume of debris and dust had choked the city for days, leaving the sky a strange orange haze.

"Never seen before," "record-breaking," and "biblical level" were words often on the news. The world was coming apart at the seams, and Yuri tended bar and attended school to feed the grind of the capitalist machine. He thought often it was better than the cult life he'd escaped, but also wondered what the point to any of it was. Surviving disaster after disaster alone, working for pennies, barely surviving. Why?

With the world dying and him stuck working like a zombie, his depression and loneliness grew. What was the point?

The pretty boy at the counter gave him something to look at. He tended a handful of others before returning to the pretty boy and motioning to his glass.

"Please," the young man agreed, and Yuri refilled.

"You want to order any food?" Yuri asked.

"Are you cooking tonight?" The man threw back, a touch of an accent in his tone.

Yuri smiled. He did from time to time, testing his culinary skills when the bar was slow to offer delights that the type who frequented this space rarely got to try. "Too busy for me to play chef tonight," Yuri said. Had the man been in before? He thought he'd remember that, since the pretty boy was the type to make anyone look, even if they weren't into guys like Yuri was. There was something about him, an edge of charisma or an aura of something that dazzled. The hair was an unusual distraction, the color blending as if it were natural rather than some rebellion of brightness among the inky darkness that fell around his high cheekbones in waves.

He was lean, barely six feet, not lanky, but narrow. Face prettier than most men, lips full, eyes with a slight uptilt, but marginally wider with a button nose that made him look almost fae-like, or as if he'd stepped off some movie set.

Yuri had never met a celebrity in real life, but he suspected the pretty man was something like that. "You've tried my cooking? I would have thought I'd remember seeing you in here before," Yuri said.

The man smiled, a light reaching his eyes as he brought the glass to his lips again, sipping his vodka. "That's kind of you."

Did people not notice him? Were they blind?

"I'll cook for you anytime you'd like, as long as it's not a night that I'm the only tender on duty. Let me know if you need another drink or food, or anything," Yuri said. He could imagine wrapping his arms around the pretty man and holding him for a time. "It's a crazy world out there, and we could all use a few minutes, right?"

"Indeed," the man agreed. He held the glass in steady long fingers, the length of them disappearing beneath long sleeves of a fitted navy sweater, and ink colored each digit.

"You're a tattoo fan?" Yuri asked. "I have a few myself."

The man glanced at his hand and nodded, pulling back the sleeve to show more color. It looked like snakes, or a multiple headed serpent, like something out of a fantasy novel, the colors shifting with iridescent purple, teal, and aqua which Yuri hadn't known was possible in ink.

"Cool," Yuri said. "My art is a bit fantasy inspired, dreams." He kept his art hidden by clothing; the fear ingrained in his youth rising at the mere thought.

"Perhaps sometime we can share stories," the man said as he continued to sip his vodka. "When you have more time."

Yuri nodded, smiling. Another patron waved to him. He headed their way to refill a glass and attended a handful of other customers.

The group of frat boys arrived a few minutes later and Yuri knew they'd be trouble right off, but their normal bouncer had lost a family member to the downtown collapse and had quit, so that meant Yuri against more brawn than brains, and he wasn't the biggest guy in the room, more average—average height, average weight, average everything. It made blending in a crowd easy, but turning away bullies a touch harder, and after midnight a group like that wasn't looking for quiet drinks. They wanted a fight.

They seemed to zero in on pretty boy as a target, commenting on everything from his hair to the fit of his clothes, which were more European trending than American, fitted to him, not off the rack.

The man, despite all the surrounding noise, didn't acknowledge them at all.

"Enough," Yuri snapped. "Find another bar. Taps are closed for you."

"We're paying customers. You can't shut us down," one of them said.

"Since I'm in charge of the bar, I can," Yuri said. "You want trouble? Take it outside. Plenty of bullshit to find out there. Careful a building doesn't fall on you."

One of them reached across the bar and grabbed Yuri by the collar. "How about we take you outside? Show you the way back to your country?"

Yuri narrowed his gaze, knowing they were zeroing in on the slant of his eyes and cut of his cheekbones that made him obviously mixed race. "American born and raised, asshole. Now get the fuck out."

The man balled up his fist, and Yuri braced for a hit, thankful he could divert their attention from the pretty man, even if that meant he'd go home bruised, but the hit never came. Pretty man put his hand on the jock's wrist and twisted, breaking his hold on Yuri. He shoved the man away from the bar and toward the far door.

"Let's," he said, giving the brute a toothy smile. He motioned for the door that led to the side, out to the alley and the trash.

"That's not a good idea," Yuri said to the pretty man. But the man threw a few big bills down on the counter to cover his booze and disappeared beyond the side door. The jocks laughed. The one who had grabbed Yuri gave him a shove before they followed the pretty boy out.

Should he call the cops? There hadn't been a unit available since the towers came down. Lots of search and recovery, digging through rubble to find thousands of bodies. The military had shown up to help with the aftermath, although something new and awful was happening every day somewhere in the world and plenty of it right here in the US of A.

Yuri glanced around the bar. But it was him, two servers, and the cook, who was a man in his sixties. The servers were slips of girls who did well at running the room, delivering food and drinks. No one else seemed to need much in that moment, so Yuri darted to the door, expecting to wade in and get his ass kicked too, but found the pretty boy moving like only people in movies ever did.

It was a sort of dance of martial arts and magic, height for a jump that didn't seem physically possible, speed, precision, and the strength to smash a jock halfway down the alleyway with a single kick. Was Yuri being punked? Was his whole life a movie set somehow?

In seconds the group of jocks were on the ground groaning, all unable to get up, but no one looked injured enough to actually need medical care, which was good because Yuri didn't know of any EMTs or hospital space available. They were breathing, that much he could tell.

"Holy fuck," Yuri said as the pretty man stepped away from the group. His expression changed to one of sadness and worry for a few seconds before a mask of blank indifference went up. "You okay?" Yuri asked him, reaching for a drop of blood that trickled from the edge of the man's lip. Had one of them got a good hit in?

The pretty man stepped out of reach; his smile strained. "Fine. I apologize for the trouble." He dabbed away the blood, his tongue darting out to lick the drop away. Yuri felt something in his stomach tighten with need. A rising desire he couldn't recall ever feeling before. To take care of him? Or something more? Like that drop of blood should have been his to claim. He swallowed hard at the crazy thought. Must be the insanity of the world finally getting to him.

"Not your fault these assholes pulled shit," Yuri said. "Come back in, and I'll refill your glass."

The man hesitated, a half-lidded gaze landing on Yuri that made Yuri's cock harden, his jeans tightening, the zipper biting into him. Bedroom eyes? Was that what all the books meant? A gaze of longing, interest? Was he misreading? Or imagining things?

He'd learned in his cult days how to lock those feelings down and stepped back to open the door. He held it and motioned for the man to head back in and waved at the frat boys. "They look fine. I'll lock this side door when we head back in and let everyone know to let them wander off on their own."

The man tilted his head, studying Yuri, but then nodded, carefully stepping by to enter the bar without touching Yuri at all. Was it strange that Yuri burned for a touch? He followed the man inside and went back to the counter, finding a fresh glass and filling it, taking the money the man had left and sliding it back across to him.

"Why?" the man asked.

"Seems shitty to make you pay when some assholes tried to pull shit," Yuri said. It meant he'd go home without tips tonight to cover the cost of the drink, but that was okay. With the world ending, money seemed to matter very little. Maybe tomorrow would end with a meteor falling on his little studio and blasting him to bits. Fast seemed better than this brutally slow demise the planet was taking.

"You are too kind for this world," the man said, sliding the money back. "Take it, and I will keep drinking, refuse, and I shall go."

Well, that was an ultimatum if Yuri ever heard one. It didn't normally matter if someone came or went. Yuri got good at ignoring everyone at the bar. People flirted with him, all genders and races, but he'd never taken that path. His youth of cult brainwashing, hard to overcome. But his heart flipped over at the thought of the man walking away.

Yuri took the money, counting out bills that were higher than his rent and a lot more than the entire bottle of booze. He frowned. The pretty man smiled. Yuri refilled his glass.

The man's gaze went back to the TV and endless news of disasters. One server passed Yuri. "Thanks, Yuri," she said. "Those guys are always handsy when they're in."

Yuri had done nothing, but she didn't acknowledge the man at the bar as she passed to grab up a tray from the kitchen delivery counter.

"Yuri?" the man said, his accented voice seeming to dance on the name.

"Yeah," Yuri agreed. "My mom saw it in an anime and liked it." She'd been barely fourteen when forced to have him. He shoved those thoughts away, going back to focusing on the bar, cleaning the counters, and filling any dwindling glasses. His depression was drowning on the best of days. He worked to keep it from overwhelming him, distraction his vice.

"What can I call you?" Yuri asked after a few minutes of

background noise. The bar was too quiet, the madness of the end of the world on the news playing, but everyone else still, watching in horror.

The man turned his gaze back to Yuri's. "Star."

Yuri grinned. "Yeah?"

The man, Star, shrugged.

"It suits you," Yuri said.

Star frowned, a few expressions crossing his face, and Yuri felt bad. Maybe he hated his name?

"I mean, you sort of shine like a star, right?" Yuri tried. "That action in the alley was crazy, but you're the guy everyone notices?"

None of that seemed to help Star's troubled expression.

"Sorry," Yuri finally said. "Bad way of saying 'You're pretty', I guess?" Fuck. He shouldn't have said that either. Men didn't like to be called pretty, right? Toxic world they were in and all that. "Handsome, whatever. Sorry."

"You think I'm pretty? A lovely gentleman like you?" Star asked. Yuri tried to place his accent. A touch of British, perhaps? European at the least. Yuri leaned in a little, hoping to hear more.

"Uh, yeah? Is that okay? I'm not lovely. Or a gentleman, really. Just Yuri."

Star's gaze returned to that half-lidded thing he'd done in the alley that made Yuri's gut clench with longing. A need to touch. He touched no one. Had learned in his cult days that touch was bad. Well, he knew that was wrong, part of his brainwashing, but he was still working to decode all that crap. He'd been out two years.

Star studied him, and Yuri tried to shove his anxiety down.

"Sorry. I'm not trying to come on to you," Yuri said quickly. "I know that's rude. You're here to drink. I try not to be one of those guys. I just..." He didn't know how to explain his war of emotions. Attraction and desire he'd never felt before, rising in conflict to his childhood trauma.

"I'm not offended," Star said. "Surprised."

Yuri squinted at him, confused. "Why? You're gorgeous. You probably have people throwing themselves at you all the time?"

Star seemed to consider his words, sipping the vodka in quiet reflection for a minute or two. "And you? Do you have people throwing themselves at you, sweet Yuri?"

"People flirt sometimes." Yuri shrugged. "I think they are drunk." He wasn't pretty like Star. Not overly tall at five nine, his long brown hair touched with red, giving it a slight mahogany sheen, but he kept it pulled up in the ever-scorned 'man bun' when he worked. He'd grown it out the second he escaped the cult. The severe military style cut had always irritated him, but the newfound curls that barely brushed his shoulders when loose reminded him he was free. He never thought his face was much to look at, a mix of his Texas father, with pale blue eyes, and the sculpted cheekbones and skin tone of his Asian mother. His body was lean and muscled from the years of hard labor, but not what graced movie screens or magazine covers. He wore a medium in everything, felt average in most everything. And in the big city of Chicago, even his mixed genes weren't all that unusual.

"You are lovely," Star said. "Doesn't take drowning in cups to see that."

Yuri flushed, his face feeling on fire. "Thank you."

A shuddering thud shook the entire building. Like an earthquake, the ground wobbled and rolled, a roaring rumble of grinding stone shattered the quiet. Yuri threw his hands over his ears trying to ease the assault of the sound, metal on glass scraping, the noise near deafening.

Everyone froze, some screamed, terror on faces as the ground continued to move and the sound slowly faded. The lights flickered; the TV turned to static. Had something else fallen much closer this time?

"What the fuck?" Yuri asked when the sound and movement ended. The lights flickered again and died completely, leaving them in complete darkness. The servers shrieked, and Yuri heard movement, but didn't know where to go.

"Everyone, stay calm!" Yuri called. He dug in his pocket for his phone and turned on the flashlight, which was blinding, but the actual phone itself said no service. He tried to illuminate the space to see the movement. The door opened, people rushing out. Something outside glowed in the distance. Fire?

Yuri's stomach flipped over in fear. The flashlight touched on Star's face, still having remained at the bar. The light cast shadows over him, and he blinked, looking a little ghastly, the planes of his face seemingly stretched with shadows in the low light.

"You okay?" Yuri asked again, reaching for him.

Star rose from his seat and slid easily out of range. "The end is never pleasant," he said.

Yuri rounded the bar and headed for the door, holding it open to direct everyone out. Even the cook passed him by as all the power had died, leaving them in darkness. He held the door and Star was the last to leave, Yuri behind him. The image in the distance was one of wonder. A giant arch pierced the landscape, eclipsing everything. The city beyond, which had once been central Chicago, completely gone, vanished beneath the rainbow light of the arch and the dancing shadows beneath.

Things poured from the base of the arch, like legions of

spiders or something, tiny but fast racing movement in the distance. Yuri's heart flipped over in fear. What was it? All of it? Had something fallen from the sky? Had there been a satellite as big as the city? Perhaps an alien attack?

There were screams and shrieks around them. People running in every direction. Fires burned from partially collapsed buildings, smoke stinging the air. The surrounding landscape, any building over three stories, had fallen from the movement. Rubble filling the streets, bodies too, lying unmoving. Some appeared untouched by anything, others crushed in falling debris. Yuri trembled. It looked like a war-zone, the stuff from movies or those novels he'd always been told were evil growing up.

The employees and the patrons of the bar vanished into the night, leaving Yuri standing there gaping at everything, his chest tightening in pain. Star lingered a few feet away, his gaze cast at the arch, expression filled with sadness.

"You okay?" Yuri asked again, looking him over for sign of injury. "Can I walk you home or anything?" Did either of them have a home to return to? He looked toward the distance and thought it was going to be a long walk to find out if he still had a studio apartment. His car had vanished beneath a wall of rubble.

"You are anxious about me," Star said. "Are you well?"

"I think the world is ending," Yuri said, pain tightening his chest, the sign of a panic attack, first since leaving the cult. He put a hand to his chest and tried to breathe. "Fuck, sorry. Panic attack."

He struggled to sit, finding a clear spot in the road to tuck his head between his knees. End of the world and some big bad he was, panicking and almost passing out. Star crouched nearby, hand hovering inches from him as if to help, but hesitant.

"It's okay," Yuri said, wheezing as he tried to count his breaths, forcing his mind to focus even while his lizard brain told him to run. Running wouldn't save him, nothing would anymore. The world was ending. "This will pass in a minute. You can touch me if you want." He wanted Star's touch, even while chaos reigned around them.

"No one wants my touch," Star said.

"That's stupid," Yuri grumbled, sucking in gulps of air. Yuri had spent most of his life avoiding touch. Now, if it was the last thing he ever experienced, he longed to be touched, especially by this pretty man who set his soul on fire with his presence. "I would love your touch," he confessed, not caring about the consequences because it was the end of the world. "End of the world, right? Fuck it. What's the worst you could do? Beat me up like you did those guys in the alley?" Yuri asked.

Star smiled and leaned in close enough that Yuri could smell him over the scent of ash and fire coating everything. It was a warm smell, not unlike the fire, but a touch of sugar too, sweetness, toasted, like marshmallows. Yuri reached out to touch Star's face, wondering at the strange play of shadows across his features. Did Yuri look as ghastly to Star in this rippling light of fire? Not that it mattered, because when Yuri's fingers touched Star's cheeks, the pretty man re-solidified before him. The shadows vanished and the light beneath his skin drew Yuri close. He was so incredibly beautiful it brought a clarity and focus to Yuri's mind, helping him breathe, and fading the panic. Star hesitated to close the distance, expression guarded, but Yuri tugged him down, and pressed his lips to Star's, wanting one taste if this was the end, the feel of another's lips on his, one brief encounter with a star...

Yuri didn't know how to kiss. He never had before, only seen it in movies after he'd escaped into the real world. He didn't know how to start it or if Star even wanted it, but the man took control, wrapping his hand around Yuri's neck and pulling them close. Star's lips danced over Yuri's, his tongue gently prodding for entrance, and Yuri let him in. Star tasted of toasted marshmallows and heat, with a metallic bite almost like blood. Yuri didn't pull away, instead sank into Star's touch, wanting things he'd never allowed himself to long for in his entire life.

The end of the world made it all okay, right? Star wasn't pulling away, beating him or berating him for daring to touch. It was okay to want, right?

Yuri sucked in a deep breath as Star pulled back, tugging Yuri to his feet. They were almost the same height, and the dancing of the fire and distant rainbows made Star's eyes go from pale blue to rippling oil-spill black. Fascinating. Wondrous.

"You're so beautiful," Yuri said.

"Oh, Yuri," Star said, his voice soft and pained. "I would never wish my curse on you."

"Curse?" Yuri asked absently, lost in the beauty of Star's face. He trembled, pulling Star closer. Wanting everything and not understanding what he wanted. Touch? Sex? Love? Need? Long denied the chance to explore any of that. He didn't know where to start. "We're going to die, right? End of the world and all that? I want..." He leaned in for another kiss.

Star let him, guiding, coaxing, and teaching, his hips pressing to Yuri's and building a need like Yuri had never let himself indulge before. He knew men liked other men, had swallowed the desire himself a million times, but this was so much better. Not evil or painful, as the cult had made him fear. His body sang at the touch of Star's erection grinding into his.

Star sighed. "You're so pure, you should not be mine. I should not have touched you, spoiled you..." He tried to pull away, but Yuri clung to him.

"Please," Yuri begged. He didn't know what he wanted. Not really. And yet his mind, filled with a thousand thoughts they had taught him, were wicked. "It's the end of the world. Can't I be me for five minutes?" Without all the sadness, pain, and guilt.

"And who are you, Yuri? Who do you want to be?" Star asked.

"Yours?" Yuri said dumbly. Even if it was only five minutes. He wanted that touch. "Please? Is it okay? To not feel like I'm evil for the last minutes of the end of the world?"

"Evil?" Star asked, his hands cupping Yuri's face. "Why would anyone think you're evil?"

"Because I want this." Yuri gripped Star tight. "If this is the end, I want to feel everything. I want to feel adored, loved for a few minutes, even if it's nothing but a lie." Tears blurred his vision, the loneliness and fear of rejection rising. "I'm so tired of being alone."

Star gave him a sad smile but kissed him again. "Then let that be my gift to you. In exchange for the ill that will come from my curse, let me show you how beautiful *feeling* can be."

CAPTURED OR SAVED?

TEN YEARS LATER

Yuri dreamed of Star's touch every day, long after the night had passed. Star had guided him to a building, somehow still standing, and a place within, with a giant bed, soft sheets, and an insane amount of pleasure. Star had gifted him memories that Yuri hoped would last until the end of his days. The hours spent, skin to skin, Yuri soaking up the feel of warmth and affection, studying Star's body, lean and lithe, memorizing his tattoos, and the taste of his skin beneath Yuri's kiss. They didn't speak more than moans of pleasure or begging for more in Yuri's case. The night burned into his skin indulgence to override the terror of the world coming apart.

Yuri had thought he'd die quickly in the end, but persevered.

Time faded the memories and his hope of ever seeing Star, or experiencing that incredible desire again, died. Yuri had woken alone in his small studio, somehow still standing, while the world around him fell into chaos.

Monsters poured from beneath the arch. Dark shadows became creatures from a thousand worlds. A devouring presence of *other* that descended on humanity, crushing everything that ever was. He'd found his way back south, searching for safety, and winding up in the Texas cult of his youth because it was familiar and had walls to keep out the rising terrors of a new world. He'd barely made it back, hiding a thousand times, watching countless others die beneath fang, claw, and horror. Screams forever burned in his mind. Ten years had changed none of it, nor given any sign that there was hope for humanity. Would today be the day his life finally ended? He hoped he'd die with the memory of Star's touch burned into his skin, but time stripped that memory bare. Was it real? Had it really happened? Or had it been a dream conjured by the explosion of everything he ever knew? Yuri wondered if dying would answer that question.

"Death to the monsters!" The Leader screamed seconds before a giant bat-like monster bit his head off. The gush of blood wasn't the same as in the movies that Yuri could recall. Less outward gushing, but it had been years since he'd seen a movie. Maybe he misremembered.

Death was all too common these days in innumerable forms. Rarely was death peaceful or even gentle.

The whining metal screech of the last barrier gate wailed as they ripped it open. Border walls tumbling inward, some landing on the few surviving fighters. Hordes of demons, followed by vampire warriors, rushed through the breaches, the last of the resistance falling beneath to brutal death.

Yuri's stomach cramped with fear. He ran back inside and closed the door to the kitchen, barring it to the outside. Not that he thought it would slow them down. If today was his day to die, nothing would keep them out. He tightened his mask around his face, hoping to keep from being noticed. The air quality had plummeted over the years, making it hard to breathe. Though many were used to the suffocating lack of oxygen, Yuri used his mask as a shield as much as a tool.

Something had changed the night he'd touched Star, not only inside his soul, but to him. Too many people noticed him, staring at him in a way he had never experienced before, with lust and longing. He kept himself at a distance, masking the lower half of his face as an added barrier. It didn't always work, but the few who would force the matter were busy dying outside. He could only hope that whatever monster came through the door next wouldn't fall beneath whatever spell he'd been cursed.

Yuri sat down at the table. The last of the living children, women, and servants deemed too important or weak to fight scattered around him. If his mother, the cook prior to him, hadn't died from tainted water two years ago, he'd have been out there dying under the onslaught of the monsters as well. If he had lived this long at all.

Water boiled behind them on the wood stove. The remaining food, as scarce as it was, was being sorted between the survivors. A final meal, Yuri supposed. He had passed on his share since he wasn't hungry. Not really. Hunger pains merged with all his other physical pain, and oncoming death made it all pointless. He couldn't remember the last time he'd eaten or even bring himself to care.

The loneliness had been gnawing away at his soul for a decade, leaving him feeling like little more than a shade of a person. Dying was only the next logical step. He hoped he'd fall asleep one night and not wake the next. Only finality hadn't blessed him with an end.

The sound of screams vanished. Nails on the roof and walls

flickered away, and time passed achingly slow. Maybe the wards on the doors and windows helped. The Leader had broken down and hired a *witch* to save them. Trading some of the last of their MREs for the spells to protect the buildings. Not that protection did them much good if they couldn't step outside, breathe the air, or died from starvation and lack of water.

Eric paced and snapped at anyone who got close to him. "My father sacrificed himself for all you ungrateful pieces of shit," he chanted.

Yuri's father too, technically. Never acknowledged as thus, but the Leader had over a dozen children. Some still in diapers. A way to repopulate humanity, the man had claimed. Yuri doubted the man had intended *his* creation that way. Not thirty years prior and born to an Asian American child who served as an assistant cook to the household in what used to be called Texas.

Eric was almost forty himself. His mother dead and gone before Yuri's birth. Blond and blue-eyed, Eric looked more ragged by the day. He refused the masks, claiming his body would fight off whatever toxins filled the air. But his faith didn't stop his wheezing when he moved. He was the sort of blond American Christian Jesus appearance they proclaimed proved God sent them.

Eric should have been outside fighting. His job had been as a guard, and not as important as he would have claimed, else the Leader might have let him reproduce. But the Leader denied Eric his pick among the women, and the last few of the Leader's favored command had just died in that last assault.

Yuri didn't think any of the crying or whimpering in the room came from lost fathers. More likely fear about coming death or enslavement. Family meant little when death's fangs were coming for you.

"You don't have more food?" Eric demanded. "It may take them days to leave."

"There's water," Yuri offered.

"You let them eat what's left? How stupid are you?"

There hadn't been enough left of grain or even dried meat to fill the belly of even one of them. The scraps they all got were little more than watery gruel. What was the point of drawing it out? The hunger cramping, starvation, or a fast death beneath monster teeth? Yuri thought he might prefer the latter, though wasn't too weak to admit that terrified him. Years of them preaching about a great beyond burned into his mind like a poisoned nail in his soul.

His last night working that bar seemed another lifetime, perhaps a memory that wasn't really his. Did that mean Star had been a dream? It was the only memory that kept him moving these days, an irrational hope he would someday see Star again. Or taste a moment of that affection.

Star was probably dead. Like everyone else Yuri had ever known. Like Yuri wished he was. He planted himself facing the door. He hadn't really wanted to watch death coming at him but didn't want to play the coward either. Death came for them all, eventually. He'd watched thousands of people die in the past decade. He prayed his death was quick and would send him to his reward for being obedient. After all, why live through this mess, surviving the worst of the end of the world, only to be delivered to more torture and pain? The Leader promised God cast disbelievers to the lake of fire to live eternity in agony, but weren't they already in endless suffering and pain? Would he be able to tell the difference? Could there be some place worse? Maybe they were all already dead, and this was the hell of damnation.

He wanted an end. A void would be fine. No gardens or lakes of fire necessary.

The far door opened, locks popping and snapping as the mechanism broke under brute strength, shattering the wards as if they were nothing, though Yuri had felt something from them to believe they were real. The door swung wide, slamming into the wall behind it and rattling the space hard enough to shake ceiling dust down on them.

Eric raised his gun. The echo of bullets erupted in the small space, followed by screams, women, children, and even Eric, who shouted like he was some sort of monster himself. The bullets stopped in midair, never meeting their target. They paused, frozen, then clattered uselessly to the ground. The magic was thick enough to make Yuri's teeth ache, a vibration, but started at his core instead of externally.

What stood in the doorway didn't look like a monster, though he towered over everyone in the room. Easily six and a half feet, and muscled like a giant, his face mostly covered with a helmet reminiscent of the many stories Yuri read as a child, with narrow vertical slits of the eyes and a large piece over his nose. But the fangs were hard to miss as the creature snarled at them all.

Vampire.

Not the creature of storybooks or even movies, but warrior giants with bloodlust beyond comprehension. He swept out a meaty paw and knocked the gun from Eric's grasp and the man himself halfway across the room. Eric hit the wall with a thud and slid to the ground like a broken doll.

Silence fell over the room instantly. Yuri's hearing already muted from the sound of the bullets. A hollow whipping wind noise resonating through his head. He wondered if Eric was dead. The man lay battered and unconscious, his face to the floor, but his chest rose and fell with stuttering breaths.

No one else attempted to attack the warrior who stomped inside, followed by several others as large and intimidating as he was. Yuri felt the intensity of their gaze sweeping the room, searching for threats. The children and the rest of the survivors huddled together, silent as the grave. His hearing returned with the sound of bubbling water behind them as the only noise for the stretch of several minutes.

It was a little anti-climactic. All the stories they'd heard the past decade, made Yuri expect them to come in and start devouring the children whole, crushing skulls beneath their giant boots and raping the women on barbed penises. Yet the warriors stood there, assessing the space, more like people than the animals everyone said they were.

Outside, the sky was a deep navy blue, filled with stars and half darkened rainbows of clouds near the circular ring of the Fracture in the distance. Yuri could see it framed in the doorway behind the group. He'd thought it beautiful at first until he'd seen what had come from beyond it.

Another creature stepped through the open doorway, this one willowy and unsoiled by blood and dirt. Though Yuri knew by the robes and the shimmer of the cloth draped over them, they were cloaked in magic. Perhaps to look more human? They weren't as tall or broad as the warriors, appearing more an aristocrat, without the metal armor, fine robes inlaid with glittering thread instead, dark silver hair long, but pulled back in elaborate braids, and expression stern. Female, perhaps? They had women among their warriors?

Beautiful, yet severe? Almost like a fae of legend, with pointed ears and cheekbones so sharp they could cut glass. Her eyes were narrow, but quick to peruse the space. A pretty man stood behind her, his hair blond, long, pulled back in a braid, but his face glowed with an edge of something that almost made Yuri leap from his seat, a familiar draw of something ethereal. A bright luminescence that Yuri craved. The man stepped to the side, ignoring them all. He wore armor, but not like that of the warriors, more elite like the woman's, with designs swirled into the layer of mail.

The warriors let them in, deferring to them. Were they generals of some sort? The woman crossed the space in quick strides, looking over the group, Eric, who was still prone, her gaze assessing everyone, and finally falling to Yuri. He met her gaze unflinchingly, expecting her to order an attack, but steadying himself for whatever came. She seemed surprised that he focused on her. A small smile tugged the corner of her lips, as though amused by something.

"You speak American?" She asked in an accented tone, taking his attention from the pretty blond man.

English, Yuri thought, though the language hadn't been called that in almost a decade.

"Yes," Yuri answered softly, and a few other languages, though he was admittedly out of practice. He kept his hands on the table in plain sight and tried not to breathe too hard. Yuri was not in any way a warrior. He had never fired a gun, though he could butcher a cow or a fish easily enough. Not that they'd had either in a long time. He'd been a pastry chef in training, not a cook. The rest of his education had come out of necessity. Not much need for cakes and sweets in a world where food was scarce.

"I'm looking for the central power source of this compound," the woman said.

"We use mostly wood now," Yuri said, pointing to the

wood-burning stoves behind them. They had solar, but it didn't work in the perpetual night that had fallen since the Fracture. The sun vanished, not buried by clouds or even the long-expected climate change, but completely gone. Though Yuri didn't know if there were scientists left to research where it had gone. Ripped through the veil into another world, maybe? The plants and trees died, leaving nothing but barren stalks for them to harvest and burn. That too, ran low, the trek to retrieve wood becoming too dangerous without a legion of guards.

The woman nodded. "Yes. We've detected more. Is there an interior room?"

Yuri didn't have access to it. If there was anything of value left, it had been in the gun stores. He didn't know what the vampires might want from the space, but he nodded. "I don't have a key or a code to get in, but I can show it to you." Yuri glanced at Eric, who might have known how to get in, but he didn't appear conscious.

"Up then," the female commanded. "Show me." Her gaze narrowed. "Try anything, and I'll leave you choking on your insides."

That sounded unpleasant, and not the quick death he'd been hoping for.

Yuri rose slowly from the chair, showing he was unarmed, too thin, and in little more than rags, he had nothing to fight with and nothing to gain other than a quick death. He headed to the back of the kitchen, to a wall of shelves, mostly empty, and worked to push them aside. He didn't get them to move much more than an inch or two. They were too heavy, built from solid timbers. Wood they probably could have burned last winter to save lives when the cold had really dropped subzero for three months. He wasn't strong enough.

The woman brushed him aside and shoved the shelves with

one hand, sending them across the room as though they were little more than paper flowers. The door to the safe room, outlined in black, bore several locks, including a digital type that Yuri wasn't certain worked at all anymore due to lack of power.

The locks snapped, and the door wailed as the woman yanked it open. What point were locks if brute strength could break them apart as easily as pulling weeds? The door gaped into a dark space, windowless and sprawling, but heaped with boxes.

The female grabbed Yuri by the neck and shoved him into the room, her other hand outstretched. A ball of glowing light formed there, illuminating the space. Yuri stumbled, the grip on his neck tight, biting, with nails digging in, but the strength of the fae creature's grasp kept him upright. Stacked boxes filled the space, some appearing to be ammo, others perhaps fabrics. Yuri wasn't certain. And he didn't know what the vampires wanted. What sort of human creation would matter to beings of magic?

"You're old enough to be familiar with computers? Electronic devices?" The woman holding him asked.

"Yes," Yuri replied. It had been ages since any of them worked.

"They should be in here," the creature stated. She dropped Yuri, who fell, unable to keep his feet. He landed hard, blinking at the dusty ground and the slew of boxes. "Empty boxes until you find them."

Yuri fumbled to his feet, looking around for what might be electronic storage. Everything looked like weapons caches. But the Leader had been a doomsday prepper before the Fracture. Already a fanatic when the worlds converged, his transition to fascist leader had been flawless.

Yuri opened a few, finding them empty.

"Most of these look like weapons boxes," Yuri said. "Empty." He pointed to the old electrical boxes on the wall, which used to house the solar and electric supplies, but had long been useless. "That used to be our power source. Grids haven't worked for a decade."

The giant warriors filed into the room, squeezing through the tiny entry and adding more light with glowing orbs. They began opening boxes, moving things, speaking in another language that sounded both guttural and lyrical all at once. One of them opened the power box and began pulling things out of it.

Yuri spied a box near the corner. A plastic thing he thought he recalled from years ago. He pointed to the box. "That one, I think? Computer stuff, phones, tablets, electronic things. It's been a long time since they worked."

The fae woman crossed the room and kicked the box first before bending to open it. Inside was a mess of dusty electronics. Computers and phones of all types. She exclaimed in joy and dragged the box out, uttering something Yuri didn't understand to the nearest warrior, who picked up the box as though it weren't big as a garbage dumpster and filled with metal and aluminum, and carried it off.

The warriors were digging with fervor now, as though trying to find more electronics. The fae looking woman returned to Yuri, grabbing him by the throat. Maybe he'd still die today.

"I don't know if there is more," Yuri said through the squeeze. He knew the woman could probably pop his head off with a flick of her wrist. Were all fae so terrifyingly strong? Was she really fae? And working for the vampires? How was that possible?

"Such beautiful eyes," she remarked. "Swirling with supernatural energy."

He flinched, worried someone would hear.

"What do you hide beneath the mask?" she asked.

"The ability to breathe," he said. His lungs didn't sound like they had rocks in them like everyone else's did.

She stared at him like she didn't believe him, then brushed aside the damaged shoulder sleeve of Yuri's shirt, revealing emaciated muscles and tattoos long since forgotten. From the age of eighteen to shortly before the Fracture, Yuri had been obsessed with skin art. Adding colors and designs he could find only in the big city and far from this cult-like life he'd thought he'd escaped. Images from dreams, and concepts pulled from an imagination as vivid as a memory. The art inspired him when his days got hard. That was before the Fracture had taken away his hope of freedom. The Leader had only let him stay because of his mother, and a vow from Yuri that the art meant nothing and he would keep it hidden. The entire cult had considered him tainted and bound for hell. A sign of demons in him, the Leader had said.

"Few like you remain," the fae said.

Tattooed? Demon-cursed? What did she mean?

The woman traced a design in another language. A poem about magic a friend had written for him, as they had shared a love of stories. It seemed another lifetime ago.

"You speak other human languages?" The fae inquired.

"Spanish, some Chinese. Learned a bit of Russian too, but I'm out of practice. Leader wanted nothing other than American spoken here," Yuri replied.

The fae nodded as if she'd heard it many times before. "What about books? My Master is quite fond of your human blatherings," she said.

Yuri's gaze flicked toward the door and the others beyond. "They burned books after the Fracture." All except the Bible, which the leader had insisted they read every day.

"All the books?" The creature asked quietly, dragging Yuri close. The woman's gaze was a glowing roll of opalescent white swirls, beautiful and terrifying all at once. Yuri felt a little lightheaded staring into those eyes.

"Leader had a Bible," he mumbled, his tongue feeling heavy.

"And?" the creature insisted.

Yuri trembled. A sense of compulsion, that was all he could describe it as, a mental demand to speak the truth. "I have a few hidden. Buried in the dirt beneath my sleeping mat." Saying those words hurt. He hated the idea of losing them and watching them burned in front of him. Some were little more than novels he'd enjoyed as a kid. Two were medical guides, a handful of others, cookbooks he'd brought home for his mother on college break that Christmas before the Fracture. And one journal with sketches he'd drawn over the decade. In the middle, hidden between the pages, was a drawing of Star he'd worked on for months. He had once thought of having the picture tattooed into his flesh if the world ever returned. Now he used it from time to time to freshen his memory of that single night of joy he'd found.

"Take me to where you sleep," the creature demanded, dragging Yuri to the door.

"They will burn them," Yuri whispered, feeling tears sting his eyes. They'd have burned him at the stake if they knew he had them. What if he lost that last piece of his happiness? Would there be any reason at all to live?

"There is no *them* to burn anything, only us," the creature stated as she dragged him into the kitchen and beyond to the long bunkhouse where most of them slept. "Which of this hovel was yours?"

None of it, Yuri thought. He'd spent most of his nights out back, curled up beneath the tree near his mother's grave. A pig pen it had once been. They hadn't had swine in years. He preferred distance to the chance that someone would try to force themselves on him in his sleep.

"Outside," Yuri said. Would the monsters swarm them? The vampires used the demonic sort of things as soldiers. Like the doors of hell itself opened and let them all out. Leader had often said the Fracture was the door to hell opening. Stuck within the confines of the compound for a decade, Yuri couldn't really disagree.

The woman opened the back door from the kitchen and dragged Yuri out, dropping him to the ground as soon as they were in the cool air. Everything was quiet. If the demons were still around, they'd finished their feeding and vanished back outside the gates of the compound.

The blond man followed them at a distance, the vampires keeping close to him. But he didn't look worried or alarmed. His gaze focused intently on Yuri, too. Did he know Star? Why did he glow bright enough to make Yuri want to touch him?

"The books?" the fae demanded. The compulsion clawed at Yuri's brain, a demand to move, as if Yuri would still have to crawl his way across the distance even if he was dying, intestines trailing behind him. He slunk to his feet, moving slowly and swaying to keep upright as he made his way toward the back of the property.

A high wall built from lumber and broken-down farm equipment acted as a barrier there and surrounded the graveyard as the sort of dystopian nightmare it was. The warrior vampires were pulling apart the wall, digging into the old machines, seeming to search for something. Perhaps the computerized parts that had long since stopped working? Though Yuri didn't know what good a computer was in a world of shifting magic.

The fae woman followed him through the mud and into the tiny hut that had once been a home for the dirtiest of creatures. Little more than boards and a mat, Yuri had often thought he'd eventually fall asleep there and never wake up. A fitting place to pass, curled up with a few of the crosses jutting from the ground several feet away, on top of the last remnants of his normal life. His mother's grave was unmarked despite her giving in to the Leader's demand of Christian fealty. But Yuri knew the outline of her grave at a glance, a smattering of stones placed on top to keep her in his memory.

Yuri crawled into his small space and peeled back the mat. He dug; the ground soft but not wet. A few inches down was the oilcloth covered box. A plastic remnant of the world before, slow to decompose, and strong enough to keep out the worst of the elements. He pulled the box from the ground, feeling as though this was his heart and soul, maybe even the last of his humanity, wrapped up and hidden away.

"Please don't burn them," Yuri begged.

The creature snatched it from him, opened it, and then carefully examined each book. She lingered a few seconds over the medical guides and cookbooks but seemed most fascinated by the stack of novels beneath. She mumbled a few words in that language Yuri didn't understand. The journal she flipped through, not pausing to more than glance at it, for which Yuri was grateful. There were sketches of sex acts in there. Bits pulled from his memory of the night with Star that kept him sane. No faces, mostly a study of positions and his memory craving a few moments of happiness long lost to time.

She stuffed everything back inside and closed the box, then dragged both Yuri and the box out of the little shelter. The woman lifted the box and shoved it into Yuri's arms. "Consider this part of your value, human. You will take this to the Master. He will see if he has a use for you and your secrets."

That didn't sound pleasant.

"Can you kill me quickly?" Yuri asked quietly. He didn't remember the books being that heavy, but he also couldn't remember the last time he ate more than a spoonful of watery weeds.

"You wish to die?"

"I would rather death be fast than slow," Yuri said.

"That will be for the Master to decide," the woman said. She led Yuri around the house and to a convoy gathered outside the main entry. The remains of the fighters were strewn across the yard in a bloody mess. Parts a red wash of discarded meat and metallic browning blood. The survivors sobbed and clung to each other as they all stood in a row in front of the warriors waiting to be loaded into transport carriages. The horses pulling those carriages glowed with black shadowy manes and red eyes. Otherworldly and a little terrifying. Some children whispered questions, "are we going to hell?" and "why are their horses demons?"

The fae turned to speak to the blond man, who kept his distance from all of them, distaste clear on his face. Yuri clung to his box, blinking at the sight of what little remained of humanity, less than two dozen ragged and starving humans. He'd worked hard to not grow close to any of them. Even the ones related to him by blood. They had all treated him as if he were shit clinging to their shoe, taunting him, and ignoring him. They never came when he needed help anyway. Survival had a way of stripping everyone of allies.

CAPTURED OR SAVED?

Yuri didn't look at any of the weeping children they dragged away, or the women who pleaded for mercy, though no one touched them. The vampires examined the handful of men who remained, laborers like himself, or Eric who had stood to inherit the wealth of the Leader's purpose. Back, teeth, skin looked over as though they were cows to market. But that's what they were to vampires, weren't they? Cattle? Food for blood suckers and demons.

He couldn't help any of them. He couldn't help himself. Yuri swayed when a warrior reached him.

The fae-looking woman called out something, and the warrior paused before dragging Yuri forward to a smaller carriage and shoving him roughly to the floor inside. Shortly after, they dropped Eric beside him, little more than a sack of potatoes.

Yuri clung to his box of books, sliding it away from Eric, who would as soon shit on it than open a book to read it. The door to the carriage closed, leaving them in the closed space, the windows barred as though it were a cage. Yuri curled himself into the corner, tucking his knees into his chest and breathing back the onslaught of emotions too wild to sort out. He didn't know when he passed out. Only that he lost consciousness before the carriage moved.

A Floating Castle

Yuri woke to a kick in his side. A sharp pain that caught him in the rib, but it took him a few minutes to blink through the exhaustion and pain. Eric was snarling at him. They were alone, and the carriage moved fast, the world outside speeding by.

"What the fuck?" Eric demanded.

Yuri could have asked the same himself. Eric was not as thin or unwell as any of the rest, a perk of being the Leader's chosen progeny. Whatever that bullshit meant. The Leader, Eric, and the other generals had always gotten the best of everything, food, clothing, and the women. At least Yuri hadn't had to suffer that indignity. The one general who had cast his gaze Yuri's way had found himself gutted by the Leader for being tempted by Satan. Was Yuri Satan? Or simply the lust for male-on-male flesh? Yuri hadn't ever been much interested in any flesh, other than Star, his one adventure into the ultimate sin. Years of beatings beneath the Leader's disapproving gaze had forced him to avoid humans leaving his desires in his unspoken dreams.

"Did you give us over to the monsters?"

Right, because Yuri had some sort of supernatural power to stop them? He said nothing but turned his gaze toward the bars and the night sky outside.

Eric kicked him again.

Yuri grunted, but curled himself up tighter around the box, keeping it behind him, and hopefully out of notice. If the books had value, letting Eric ruin them would not help Yuri at all.

"Fucking useless freak," Eric snarled at him. But he seemed to grow bored with the attack and eventually curled up in the opposite corner.

Yuri's stomach made a noise, but he could hardly keep his eyes open. When the carriage jerked to a stop, he jolted awake and stared at the far door and the dark luminescence beyond. A shape almost like a castle, or a giant mansion, lingered beyond the faint light from the bars. The door opened and one of the vampire warriors leaned in, reaching for Eric.

Eric fought, biting, swiping, and trying to kick, but it was like a toddler fighting uselessly. The warrior smacked him, knocking the man cold and dragging him out of the carriage. The head trauma would cause brain damage soon. Would anyone notice in a jerk like Eric? The vampires probably wouldn't care if they were planning to feed on him.

Yuri carefully picked up the box and crawled toward the door.

The fae-looking woman appeared, waving at Yuri to get out, not offering a hand at all, but that luminescent gaze sharp. The blond man was far ahead of them, already on his way inside. Yuri slipped out of the carriage and onto a path leading to a giant gate and a floating house beyond. Not a castle exactly, as it looked more mansion-like, sprawling wings branching outward, but it had a few turrets far up into the sky. It appeared to be a mishmash of buildings, sort of medieval in the middle, the towers looking ancient, and the wings more modern, strange and fascinating all at once.

The path snaking off through the gate narrowed and didn't have edges, a sheer drop into nothing but darkness projecting from below. The mansion looked like a reflection on water, hovering, but maybe not? Yuri wondered if he'd taken a hit to the head he had forgotten, which might have messed up his vision.

Had they passed through the rift? Yuri had never seen such a thing before. Yet as he glanced to the side, he could make out the stretch of a city. The horizon was oddly familiar, though it had been years since he'd seen it.

Dallas?

Half of it, at least. One of the towering, gear-looking spires that arched through the sky had pierced the middle of the city, destroying everything nearby. Roaming black shadows filled the space. The remains of the city, broken and battered, perhaps not surviving the apocalypse despite some structures still standing. There were no lights from within the city, only the remains of skyscrapers and buildings that might have once been malls, apartments, and office buildings.

And this house, or floating castle as it might have been, perched on a hillside overlooking the mess. A cliffside that hadn't existed as far as Yuri's memory could recall. This area had been flat, stretching out for miles in all directions with sprawling suburban life. All of that was gone now. Broken and ripped from reality by the Fracture of worlds, and swirling with magic energy.

The Leader had called it demonic, though never once

mentioned that magic looked more like dancing rainbows of semi-iridescent color than shadows. Yuri had never gotten close enough to the Fractures to examine them before. He could see the teeth of the gears, as if they were part of an ancient clock, with light illuminating the arch, rainbows refracting all around, beautiful and terrifying. Did demons come from all that light?

The fae shoved Yuri toward the path. The vampire warriors were already on their way in, hauling Eric with them. Yuri followed at a subdued pace, keeping his distance, but acutely aware of the fae at his back and how easily that creature had taken his mind. Did their control mean that humans went mindlessly to their slaughter? Yuri wondered if the stories were elaborated, but mind control had been underestimated in his opinion. Did that mean the rest was real? He prayed not. Not that he'd ever been a praying man. But the last thing he wanted was to be some vampire's dinner. It sounded like an anticlimactic way to end after surviving ten years into the destruction of the world.

He clung to the center of the path as it twisted and turned in sharp corners, trying not to sway or wander too close to the edge and the drop into darkness. He had never thought himself afraid of heights until he stared down into that abyss and thought falling forever would really be terrible. But he had to work to keep pace with the others, as the path was long and his legs were much shorter compared to the massive warriors.

The door to the palace stretched wide open. Large enough to fit a cruise ship at full sail. The inside entry was cavernous and yet filled with stairs leading in a hundred directions. It seemed confusing and thrilling all at once. A memory of a dream or something from a storybook, perhaps.

Was Yuri awake?

At the end of the entry stood a smallish man, with cropped short, pale brown hair and a scowl. "They stink," he remarked to the fae-looking woman.

"All humans stink," the fae woman replied. "It's their mortality staining their blood with the slow ticking away of their life." She jutted a finger at Yuri. "This one is poorly fed, but the cache of books is his, and he is marked by the seraphim."

What? Did the woman mean Yuri's tattoos? Seraphim was a word for angels or something, wasn't it? He did not have any angels tattooed on him. Nothing religious at all. Most of his art was watercolor bits from his favorite novels and occasional dreams. His imagination giving life to other worlds full of magic, he had thought fascinating until one had landed on his head.

"The other was the son of the resistance leader. The Master will wish him questioned," the fae woman continued.

The smaller man sighed heavily, as though put upon by having to deal with them. "I'll have to get them cleaned. The Master won't want them stinking up the house." He approached Yuri, gaze sharp, and Yuri realized as the man got closer that he seemed to be human. He didn't have fangs, or pointed ears, or even the swirling eyes.

The warriors said something in their guttural language and headed off down another hall toting Eric. "We'll take care of this one," the fae woman said. "I will leave the touched one to you."

The smaller man didn't question them. His focus was solely on Yuri. "You speak, human?" The man demanded.

"Yes," Yuri agreed, his grip tightening on the books.

"Come with me. You'll bathe before you meet the Master."

He glared at Yuri; gaze unflinching as it rolled over Yuri's emaciated form. "Perhaps eat something. Will do the Master no good if you die of starvation the moment you meet him."

The prospect of food made something in Yuri's stomach twist. A tease? Or hope? He sucked in a hard breath and followed the man out a side door and through several long hallways. All the spaces arched upward as though it were the home of giants. The vampire warriors had been big, many reaching close to seven feet, but not that large. Perhaps their Master was something even more colossal? Yuri tried not to linger on that thought.

The man led him to a large room filled with steaming pools of water built into the ground. It reminded him vaguely of an old Roman style bath he'd read about in history books. There were a handful of lingering people in the bath. Some with their feet in the water, and most dressed in very little, their hair up, long in all cases of male and female. But they all rose and left the room in silence without the man saying a word or acknowledging them.

The man stopped at the edge of one pool and pointed to the bench. "Set your box down. Strip and bathe. I assume you know how to wash and haven't forgotten that very basic function?" His expression said he actually thought Yuri had forgotten.

"Yes," Yuri said. "I know how. We didn't have enough clean water to—"

The man cut him off with the wave of his hand. "There is soap there." He pointed to a tray of round cakes near the edge of the pool. "I will bring clothes. Leave those infested rags there." He motioned to a spot several feet from the water.

Yuri hesitated to remove his mask, not only because he

worried about the toxic air, but because it had become a barrier between him and the world, a shield. "Is it safe?"

The man's gaze narrowed on the mask. "Magic purifies the air within the castle."

Yuri slowly tugged off the mask. The man barely looked at him. Perhaps the strange attraction that surrounded him for years had faded? Or maybe it only worked on humans.

"Do you have lice? Never mind. You probably do." He let out a long put-upon sigh. "Strip already. I'll have to find someone who can cleanse the filth from you. Touched..."

"I don't know what that means," Yuri said.

"Means you're useful, boy. We shall see how useful soon enough. Now strip!"

Yuri set the box down, surprised, as the man turned his back and left the room. Yuri stripped out of his clothes. Not that they could really be called that. Held together with a thousand broken stitches, and so threadbare they'd barely kept the chill from his skin on even the hottest days. He dropped them into a pile on the mat and carefully climbed into the pool of water. It was deliciously warm. Almost painfully hot.

He might have felt shame for the roll of dirt that slunk off of him in the water, but he'd been far too long without a true bath. They boiled what little water remained to keep it drinkable. This water scorched his skin, decadently warm, a few degrees shy of pain, and for a moment he didn't mind if he became soup.

He sucked in a deep breath as he sank down until his chin touched the top of the water. Could he sit here forever? The aches and never-ending chill that had ingrained itself in his bones seemed to be leeched away by the soothing heat. He couldn't smell anything in the water. No chemicals, and that strange luminescent light of magic didn't dance around the room. The pools of water appeared to just be water. No drain or on and off switch that he could find. More like a hot spring?

He should probably wash before the man came back, but he sat on the edge of a stone seat beneath the water for a while, half dozing from the soothing heat. How long since he'd been warm like this? Years at least.

Yuri wasn't certain what had changed. He heard nothing, movement or otherwise. But he felt something, almost like the magic of the Fracture? Sometimes the gear-like swirls would move and shift, making everything ripple for a while like an earthquake. He'd spent those days bedridden, sick, and still longing to see the movement.

When he opened his eyes and looked up, there was a man, maybe a man, slowly headed his way. He was very androgynous. He didn't shimmer with magic but looked ethereal. Beautiful, with hair white as snow, braided into one of those multi-strand elaborate styles that Yuri could only recall from books or movies. He was small. Smaller than Yuri, with a delicate build, and lean musculature. Maybe five and a half feet or so? His face was bare and young, pretty more than handsome. The man was dressed in a sleeveless top that hugged his chest, and soft pants that seemed to float around his legs. Almost a Middle Eastern style?

Was there still a Middle East, or had that vanished in the Fracture? His brain was too tired and scattered to form actual words out loud.

Yuri blinked at the man, curious, but not threatened. The presence of the man actually projected peace, or at least a sense of calm.

"Can you see me?" The man asked softly in a voice that was light and melodic. He carefully approached the edge of the pool and knelt down near the water's edge.

"Am I not supposed to see you?" Yuri wondered.

The man smiled radiantly, blinding Yuri for a moment with its brightness. "Sono will gloat. She loves being right. Not all touched can see or feel much."

Who was Sono? The fae woman?

"Can I help you bathe? You look tired," the man said.

Yuri stared at him, uncertain what to make of the man.

"You can call me Theo," the man said. "What is your name?"

"Yuri."

Theo clapped his hands together lightly. "Wonderful. Can I help you, Yuri? Wash your hair? Help you dress? You must be exhausted."

"Why would you want to help?" Yuri sighed, not that he had the energy to protest or really do much at all. "Fine."

He thought Theo would strip, but he jumped into the water and grabbed a cake of soap before making his way over. "Relax," Theo assured him. "Let me help. Then we will see about getting you some food and maybe some rest. After the Master has spoken to you."

Yuri tensed at the mention of the Master again. "Is he a vampire? The Master?" Was Theo some kind of demon? Weren't demons supposed to be monsters? Terrifying and ugly?

Theo set about rubbing the soap gently on Yuri's skin in slow circles. It was strange how intimate it felt, and yet lulling, as the touch made Yuri's eyelids heavy.

"Yes, I suppose. That is a term you can understand easily enough."

Yuri didn't know what that meant. "You don't call them vampires? Those who drink blood?"

"In your language, it is a close enough translation," Theo admitted.

"Will I be his food?" Yuri wondered as Theo cupped the water to wet Yuri's hair and rubbed soap into it. Yuri tried to focus on the long end of the braid floating between them. The color of Theo's hair refracted those rainbow iridescent colors in the water. Magic? Yuri couldn't see magic cloaked around Theo. And why cloak only his hair? Was there magic in the water?

"Perhaps. You are lovely and the Master adores the beautiful," Theo said. He paused as Yuri tensed. "It is nothing to fear. There are very few touched as you are."

Touched. That word again. Crazy? Maybe there was a language barrier. Yuri could hear the edge of an accent in Theo's voice, but not identify where it might be from. He spoke perfectly clear English, yet Yuri knew sometimes meanings got lost in translation.

Theo massaged Yuri's scalp, working in the soap, and carefully helping Yuri lean back to rinse the suds away. Yuri was so tired. The anxiety from the attack, the vampires taking him away, and even this short time inside some kind of magic mansion made his head swirl. He didn't realize he'd laid his head on Theo's shoulder and fallen asleep until the human-looking man shook him awake. He held a stack of clothing and didn't more than glance at Yuri, expression annoyed.

Theo was gone.

Yuri blinked. Had it been a dream? But his skin felt clean and soft, hair no longer a matted mess when he reached up to touch it. The mass of brown curls was still damp where it tumbled over his shoulders, but drying on top. His minimal facial hair was gone. It was a strange sensation being barefaced. He was nude, but that wasn't why he felt naked. Yuri sucked in a deep breath, fearing the sting of his lungs without the mask, but the air was clean and lightly scented with lavender. Face and tattoos on display gave him an obscene sensation of vulnerability, like everyone would see the demons inside of him, and instantly think he was evil.

"Let's get you dressed. Once you have met the Master, you can eat," the man said.

Yuri carefully climbed from the pool to stand on a towel laid out at the edge. The man handed him another towel, which was soft against his skin. The air chilled him as he dried off, the warmth of the water vanishing fast. But the clothes the man gave him weren't much different from the ones Theo had been wearing. Soft and somewhat loose pants, a fitted sleeveless top, and he also had a sort of robe that covered his arms but didn't tie. It reached his ankles, and when he wrapped it around himself, he found it warm.

He slipped a pair of sandals onto his feet. They fit well and didn't slide or cause him to stumble as he walked. Yuri followed the man out of the baths and through a dozen other halls. He was more than a little winded by the time they finally stopped before a set of enormous doors. The castle was as massive on the inside as it appeared to be from the outside.

The man glanced back his way, pausing and sucking in a deep breath. He frowned, staring at Yuri as if it were the first time he had actually looked at him. His jaw tightened, then he pointed to a circle drawn elegantly into the floor like some elaborate decoration. Swirls of metallic rings, intertwined, cogs of gears or almost like the spires of the Fracture. "Kneel in that circle. The Master prefers his food submissive." The man set the box of books outside the circle and stepped away.

Food. Submissive. Kneel.

Yuri bristled. Old dregs of pride rising when he'd thought it had been long dead. He'd always been told to obey. Only the demons rebelled, fought, and defied what they were. Demons. Or humans with demons inside them. They had thrown some from the camp. Never seen again. Others died slowly on the walls outside. A few lingered in his memory, their screams making his heart race. Yuri hid beneath his mask and away from the group to keep from being the next to suffer that slow end. He didn't want to be cast out to die, fast or slow. Was it foolish to still cling to life?

He made his way to the circle, stepping into the center and slowly sinking to his knees. The stone beneath him, cool to the touch, smooth and defined with fascinating lines. The swirls messed with his head, similar to the gaze of the fae-looking woman, Sono, Theo had called her. If any of this was real, was the circle magic?

"Back straight, chest forward, hands in your lap. Do not meet his gaze unless he commands you too," the man instructed. "His tastes are not as dark as his brother's, nor his anger as fast, but you'd be wise to gain his favor quickly."

Yuri sucked in a breath, centered his weight back on his ankles, knees flat, and straightened his back. Forehead to the floor had been the Leader's command for submission. This pose was strange. Not as vulnerable? Not as submissive?

The man touched Yuri's shoulders, pushing them back until he felt his spine aligned and straight. His touch lingered a few moments as Yuri sank further into his hips, finding a bit of comfort in the strength of his core. The man hesitated to let go but took a few steps backward.

Yuri rested his hands in his lap. The easiest place for them. He stared at his fingers, trying to resist the urge to look up. Especially when the sound of a door opening, a scrape along the stone, made him want to see.

He glared at his hands, head slightly bowed, hoping it would be enough. Would feeding a vampire hurt? Before today, Yuri had thought it meant death. But the others here wouldn't have cleaned him and treated him relatively kindly only to kill him, would they? Theo had seemed kind. But again, Yuri wasn't certain that hadn't been a dream.

THE MASTER

An echo ricocheted across the stone from hard-soled shoes in resounding footsteps that drew closer. Yuri clenched his hands into fists, his shoulders tightening in fear. It was all he could do to not look up. Was death coming at him again? Or something more terrifying?

A million images of gargantuan demons crossed his mind. Thoughts put in his head from years of fear-mongering. Though he'd seen his fair share of demons, strange bug-like creatures sometimes, mutated animals in others. What would a master of demons look like? A king of vampires? Would he be a giant with terrifying fangs, massive wings, and razor blades for hands?

The echoing footsteps stopped. At the edge of the circle and Yuri's vision, boots, the tops of which were stuffed into dark trousers, lingered. He feared looking up, having been told not to, and worried at his lower lip with his teeth. The boots didn't look massive, or like they hid some monster's feet.

It hurt to breathe, as if his heart worked too hard. And maybe it was. He had been too long without proper food and was now over-stressed, fearing everything and nothing defined. Some people died of fear and anxiety. Yuri had known a few lost that way. They dropped over, heart stopping, eyes staring out in terror, forever locked that way in death.

"He smells of the resistance," a deep, sensual voice came from above. The voice sank into Yuri's bones, a thick baritone that stirred something inside of him he hadn't known was there. A need buried within him arose, to be touched, caressed, or even sink into the sound of the voice filled with praise.

His English accented, but clear, a subtle edge that showed it wasn't his first language. The hint of it was familiar, as though Yuri had heard it before. He strained to listen, aching to hear more. Anything. Even if it were insults about how he smelled.

"I had him bathed. The rest will fade in time once he's fed and acclimated to living in more than a hovel."

A heavy sigh. "You may go, Regis," the male said.

Footsteps retreated from behind Yuri. After a few moments, he could sense they were alone. His gut cramped with worry, but that voice continued as though it were a caress, soothing and demanding all at once.

"Speak your name," the deep voice demanded.

Yuri said softly, "Yuri Wen."

"You worked for the resistance leader?"

"I was his cook after my mother passed." Would they expect Yuri to cook for the vampires? What did that even mean? Would he be cooking people? Blood? He couldn't help the tremble that started in his legs and worked its way up to his clenched fists. Part terror, part exhaustion. A panic attack was coming. He hadn't had one since that night he had submitted completely to Star.

"Relax," the deep voice soothed. A semi-growl that should have been terrifying, but it rolled over him like a freight train of ease. The panic attack evaporated. Yuri's tremor vanished, and he unclenched his hands. "Shoulders back, spine straight, good boy."

That voice...

Yuri blinked at his hands and the floor in front of him. He wanted to melt like jelly. Not compulsion at all, but as though all his inhibitions had dissipated, the caution dissolving with the fear, leaving peace and a desire to hear more.

"You should know the Leader was my biological father," Yuri whispered. "He didn't want me. Never claimed me, but if you seek to destroy all that was him and his line, I am part of that."

Tainted by insanity. Would he someday turn mad? Perhaps he was already mad, and that was why he'd seen things like shadows, demons, and dancing rainbows of magic. Maybe that was why his night with Star had changed him and everyone wanted him now, even hidden away behind the mask, avoiding all of humanity. He saw the way others looked at him. Only fear of the Leader had kept them away.

"He killed many of your kind," the deep voice said.

Yuri didn't disagree, even if the Leader hadn't looked like the monsters that broke through the gates of the compound and ate people. But if there was a heaven, and it was filled with men like the Leader, Yuri would rather go to hell. He knew not all monsters had fangs; many wore human faces.

"You won't defend him?" The Master inquired, because only the Master could be this incredible swell of power. No rainbows of magic here, rather an edge of red and orange dancing waves on the fringes of his vision like magic fire, but plenty of that overwhelming sense of *too much, too much, too much*, that had kept Yuri behind the gates of the compound for a decade. He knew when the demons were close. Their energy burned in his skin, and this was a thousand times that. Not painful, simply too much. He had never shared what he felt for fear it would get him murdered for being a witch.

"No," Yuri said, unwilling to offer a long list of the Leader's horrors. They'd all experienced nightmares none of them wanted to remember.

The Master walked around the circle, shoes clacking on the stone, echoing like they were in some giant mausoleum. He said nothing for a few minutes, but Yuri found the silence didn't breed anxiety; rather, it helped him relax. Maybe he wouldn't die a horrible death beneath vampire fangs today.

"Theodorus helped you bathe," the Master finally said, changing the subject.

"Yes. He was kind," Yuri offered. Beautiful, unearthly so, a dream? Or more.

"The seraphim often are. At least to the rare few who see them. Sono tells me you have books."

Theo was a seraph? Yuri had so many questions. "Yes, Master." He didn't move more than to open his hand in the box's direction. It sat outside the circle in front of him. "Sono was the fae woman?" Yuri clarified.

"Impressive that you not only see her but know what she is. Yes." The Master completed his walk around the circle and knelt to open the box. Yuri fought not to look. He could only see a little through the fall of his lashes and the down tilt of his head. The man had to be tall, probably over six feet, hair long, dark, and loose with a slight curl. Yuri couldn't make out much more than a tailored cut to his clothes, not a suit exactly, but somewhat formal, and broad shoulders. He didn't present as a monster or a demon, not even like the massive vampire warriors Yuri had seen. Strange. Was he a different sort of vampire? Or could the warrior vampires transform into the giants?

The books came out of the box one by one; the Master examining each. Yuri wished they hadn't been smudged with dirt, with bent spines, and torn covers. He'd tried to treat them well over the years, but sometimes he had to hide them in a hurry.

"Treasures of your world," the Master remarked. The last he paged through was the journal, glimpsing only a few pages, pausing a moment over a picture. Heat filled his cheeks, worrying the Master stared at the porn he had drawn. Yuri wanted to protest but couldn't find the will. After a moment the Master returned all the books to the box, stacking them carefully and closing it, then standing again.

"Your warriors were looking for computers," Yuri said. "I'm not sure how my old books are treasures." They had been to him, but what worth could they have to creatures who lived in magic mansions and had angels for servants?

"Not computers, but the precious metals inside of them. Necessary to repairing the *Fractures*," the Master said, "as you call them."

"You're trying to repair the Fractures?"

"I think we all want our worlds back the way they were. Humans were very efficient at destroying this one. I hope their destruction does not create a ripple effect through all the worlds."

"I'm sorry," Yuri said.

"Hmm," the Master said. He walked around the circle again. Slow. The sound of his shoes comforting in their rhythm. "Sono said you asked to die quickly."

Yuri tensed again.

"Do you wish to die?" The Master asked. "I have no use for mortals with a death wish. You all die too easily as it is."

"Do you plan to hurt me?" Yuri asked. He was so tired of

being hungry, beaten, cold, and not quite dead. "I'd rather be dead than in constant pain."

"That depends on your submission."

Yuri had a bit of a rebellious streak. It was why he still had the books. Why he'd tried to get away from the compound to go to school. He had hoped he'd build a life solid enough to spirit his mother away. Even if they were living in the dregs of a city somewhere. The Fracture had destroyed all of that. Ten years of obedience had ended with all of this. Would they reward him with a slow, painful death? He never really meant to disobey; but it happened sometimes. Maybe that's why he'd always been told he was evil.

"I would be lying if I promised to always obey," Yuri said quietly. "I kept the books, and didn't pray, even killed a man once." His throat tightened at the last confession. "One of the Leader's generals was trying to rape a girl. Not a woman." Not that rape is ever okay, no matter what the Leader said. Yuri's stomach hurt with too many memories of that. "She was eight..." He hated the memory and the long list of horrors that he'd grown numb to over the years. Yuri had smashed the man's skull with a rock. Had never known he could do something like that until that day. The girl had looked at him with terrified eyes. But Yuri had dragged the corpse off into the space beyond the wall where the demons would eat it. If the Leader ever found out, they'd have slaughtered Yuri. The girl too. Years ago, and that general was rumored to have run off. Yuri still tensed every time they mentioned the general's name. Murder was bad, but it happened. Was there a balance somehow? Killing to save a life? Maybe he was evil.

"I've lain with another man, found pleasure in his touch." Yuri admitted, laying it out all there In case the Master wanted to kill him for those acts as well. "The Leader said I am evil, but I'm not evil."

The Master had stopped walking, which made Yuri's heart rate rise again. "Not evil?"

How often had Yuri been called evil? Why? Because of his tattoos? His appearance and the way it seemed to draw others to him? His lack of compliance? Would that matter to a vampire? "The Leader called all of us evil. Commanded us to repent."

"And you didn't?" The Master asked.

"No." Yuri had spent years on his knees, but he'd stopped praying long ago. Instead of words to some god he didn't believe in, he dreamed, and let himself fall into those waking bits of fantastical thought as though it were meditation, a raft of serenity in his life of chaos.

Memories of Star. Dreams of a life they might have had if the world hadn't ended. He always shoved away the thought that they might never have found even a single night together if the world hadn't ended. And Star had been gone the morning he woke, meaning he had no intent to stay. But it was all self-delusion Yuri never shared with anyone. A fantasy to warm him when he wished the world would end already and take him with it.

"Your Leader was good?"

"He claimed he was. Chosen by God."

"Which god? There are many."

That made Yuri pause. He had never really thought much about some invisible being he couldn't see or would ever experience, but the Master made it sound like they were real. "Is there not one true God?"

The Master scoffed. "Of many worlds? Sounds like a lot of work."

"But there are angels?"

"Beings of another world."

"Aren't they good?"

"Are they? Did your own scriptures not speak of angels fallen to humanity? And angels killing people for not obeying? Slaughtering entire cities, or generations of newborns, or cursing humanity with plagues and disasters?"

Yuri thought about the stories and realized that angels really hadn't been all that good in the stories. Then there was the Lucifer thing. All the times he'd zoned out listening to the rereading of the Bible and he couldn't recall the story of Lucifer actually falling being in there, or much about the angels being good at all. They didn't sound all that divine. More dangerous. Theo hadn't seemed dangerous, by design, or some sort of act?

"Many worlds think of their creators as gods, though they aren't all powerful beings. Creators, like parents, birth a being, a world, a species, whatever, but do you think they have complete control over it? How much control did your parents have over you? Do you believe all gods or creators are good? Was your world so black and white?" The Master asked. "The *touched* aren't usually so naïve."

"I'm sorry. I still don't know what that means. Is it because I can see the seraphim? Touched?" He had hoped for a few seconds that seeing the angels meant he was good, but maybe the Leader had been right about all that, and he was evil.

"It means you can see beyond the worlds, even when there are no Fractures. A rare human is born that can see the seraphim. How much you experience from beyond the veils of a thousand worlds is yet to be seen. It is a useful skill."

Being useful couldn't be bad, right? Unless that meant he was helping hunt humans for the Master and his people to eat.

That couldn't be good. "A thousand worlds?" Were there so many? He was stunned by the possibility.

"The Fractures have converged many together. A mix of thousands if not millions of creatures wandering from world to world. It never occurred to you they might be from some place other than Earth?"

"Demons..."

"We've seen no actual signs of a breach to the demonic realms."

But Yuri had seen them. Weren't the demons working for the vampires? What about the nightmares Yuri often had? The monstrous shadows with razor-sharp teeth seeking to devour the world? Only in his head?

The Master was silent for a few minutes, then said, "You've seen demons?"

"The monsters who work for you?" Yuri had to admit that the creatures who ran with the vampires often appeared like mutated animals rather than the devouring shadows of his nightmares. What would true demons look like? "They eat people..."

The Master scoffed. "Hardly demons. Other beings. Mortals have no place to judge. Demons are things that would strike a mortal dead with its very presence." The Master sighed. "They are also impossible to control. Their only desire is to feed and destroy. If your camp had encountered an actual demon, there would have been none of you left."

"Wasn't Lucifer the king of demons? The Leader told us stories..." Yuri wondered where that story came from. Not his few hidden books. Maybe something he'd read long ago. The Leader had always said the demon armies of Lucifer would someday come for them.

"Lucifer was a warrior among seraphim. He sacrificed

himself to close a Fracture long ago, single-handedly defeating legions of demons, sealing them and himself, off in their realm to save all the worlds from absolute destruction. Yet your texts vilify his sacrifice. A *Fallen*, they called him, giving up light and beauty to save all existence. Seems if they had a god, the seraphim, that god would be the real monster for casting out a savior, don't you think?"

Yuri considered that for a minute but didn't reply. It was monstrous to consider. But part of that was the idea that Lucifer had been an actual being? Person? Seraph? It seemed silly to think after all he'd experienced in the past decade, that things like fallen angels couldn't exist. He was kneeling before a vampire. Something he would never have thought real for most of his life. Though he'd suspected things when he was young and felt more than he realized most others did.

He thought hard about his dreams, as terrifying as they were. They happened when the gears of the Fractures moved. Worsening for a time, then fading. Was that part of him being *touched*, or whatever that meant? He worried that sharing his dreams would get him cast out into the darkness again. Evil, always evil.

"Lucifer isn't evil?" Did that mean Yuri wasn't inherently evil, either?

"That word again. Do you know what it means?"

"No." Yuri answered honestly. He'd been taught a thousand meanings, none of the things they had blamed him for were things he had control over, but somehow granted him the label of evil. Except maybe his rebellion. But sometimes that too, just happened. "Sometimes I don't obey, is that it?"

The Master gave a small laugh. "At least you're honest. Disobedience isn't inherently evil. Evil is knowing the right and wrong thing to do, but doing the wrong thing, anyway. Sometimes it is based on circumstance. Humanity often has trouble with this differentiation. Would you murder a child to take their food if you had plenty of your own?"

"No," Yuri said.

"If someone else tried to murder the child to take their food, when they had plenty of their own, and the only way to stop them was to kill them, what would you do?"

"Kill them," Yuri said without hesitation.

"Good. You're not completely lost in mortal existentialism then. With some retraining, hopefully you'll have a better view of all existence."

"What if I disobey?" Yuri wondered.

"Depends on the reason," the Master said. "I am not inflexible, but I am strict."

"I promise to try my best," Yuri said. It was a half-hearted promise, as he didn't know what he was promising. "To submit," he added. Submission was something familiar, much like obeying. The Leader demanded it often. It ended beatings sooner, allowed him to eat, and he rarely had to lie as long as he bowed in submission and kept silent.

"Human promises mean little," the Master said. Yuri couldn't tell if that statement was derogatory or annoyed. Were monsters obedient? And the seraphim, did they always do as they were told? It would make for sad stories if they did.

"I don't know what else to offer." Yuri had nothing left, if he had ever had anything at all.

"An exchange then. Mortals like bargains. You all bargain with the fae often enough, to your detriment," the Master said. "I offer to provide you with a place to live, food, and a relatively comfortable life."

"For?" Yuri asked. Blood?

"I have a vast library of rescued texts. Far too many for even a hundred avid readers to peruse. But I'm looking for information. Help me find it. Lend a hand in repairing our worlds."

Yuri blinked. The Master wanted him to read? "You won't be feeding on me?"

"All humans are food, but you've hardly anything left of you. Seems pointless when it's your mind I need. Humans do not think the same way as us." The Master sounded amused.

"The books I have are fiction. I'm not sure what you're hoping to find." Did that mean if he couldn't find what the Master needed, would they kill him? It was way too much energy to debate all the terrible things that could go wrong.

"The Fractures were foretold," the Master said. He walked again. Twice around. Soothing, that sound, a rhythm Yuri's heartbeat could fall in line with. "A convergence of worlds. Many like yourself; touched with a sight to see beyond the veils. Laced into fiction, sold as fairytales. My kind cannot see into those depths, no matter how we try. Perhaps it is only a mortal calling? Though from time to time a seraph arises who can see between."

That was a lot to unpack, and Yuri wasn't well enough to catch it all. Stories had predicted the Fracture? "You think there is a way to repair it in the stories?"

"It's a lead. One of many. The original creator has long been lost to all worlds, leaving us to flounder at the meanings for their design. Were we intended to mingle and something stopped it? Is this chaos planned at all, or a mess of broken worlds? Is there a way to fix any of it? The questions are endless."

"And you want me to help?" By reading. It sounded like a dream. Except possibly feeding the vampires part.

"Yes."

"I will try," Yuri offered. He didn't know if he could actually tell the difference between a story and something that merged with a fix for the worlds being broken.

"Like the obedience thing? *Try?*"

Was he angry? "I'm sorry," Yuri said.

"Human nature is contrary."

How many times had they beaten Yuri when he didn't obey? Threatened with death or more beatings? Why did he still sometimes disobey? Because. No other actual answer, just because.

"I always try. I don't always succeed. Do vampires succeed at everything they do?"

"A fine question indeed," the Master said. "A contract then. It will bind you to the end of your days. Long or short as they might be. Should you try to renege or run away, the contract will kill you. Are you prepared for that?"

"And if you don't provide *a relatively comfortable life* for me? Will that kill you?" Yuri wondered. Magic was a fascinating thing.

"It would break our contract at the least. Perhaps give you the strength to kill me. Many have tried." And failed obviously.

There were a thousand more questions Yuri knew he should ask. But what other option was there? Refuse and be killed, or thrown out back to the Wilds as fodder for demons? Or a chance to spend his days reading and searching for a cure for the worlds? It sounded grand. Too good to be true.

"I don't really have a choice, do I?" Yuri whispered.

"You always have a choice."

"If I say no?"

"You'll join your brother. Questioned and disposed of. He will probably go to auction if he survives the questioning. Someone will enjoy breaking him. I have better things to do with my time. We keep the mortals out of power. They've already proven corrupt, so he won't be allowed to rise again. Humans are superb at destroying everything. Parasites in the view of a lot of other species. We keep them contained, monitored, and powerless. In your case, being touched is an advantage. There are collectors of the *touched* among other races. You'd likely find yourself a favored pet."

"A pet?"

"They completely depend on their masters. They will strip you of any lingering free will until you lie at their feet in complete submission. The training is often brutal and thorough. Not all collectors are kind. You would be leashed and contained at all times. Monitored, perhaps spoiled if you had the right owner, but as a pet, they would reward any disobedience with severe punishment."

"I would have more freedom here?" Yuri asked.

"Until you prove you deserve otherwise," the Master agreed. "I don't keep pets. They are too much work. And breaking the *touched* destroys their usefulness."

Yuri sighed. "Fine. What do I have to do? For the contract?"

"Submit," the Master said.

Yuri narrowed his eyes and had to fight not to look up and deliver a glare at the man. He *was* submitting. Wasn't that why he was kneeling in this strange pose? Though he had to admit at least his knees and back weren't hurting like they often did when they forced him to bow.

The Master set a cup at the edge of the circle in front of Yuri. Gold and decorated with glittering and elaborate gems, the cup could have fit well in the hand of some king or queen.

"Take the cup and drink," the Master said. "By your will, the contract will be sealed."

Yuri reached for the cup and stared down into the dark

recesses of it. The liquid inside was shallow, but dark and thick. Not wine. He swallowed hard as he stared at it, recognizing the viscosity of it.

"Blood? Will this turn me into a vampire?" His stomach churned at the thought of drinking it. It wouldn't be the first time. He had only had animal blood before. In the early days before all the livestock were gone and the group was suffering from serious iron deficiencies. It seemed so long ago, one of many plagues forcing them to do terrible things. If it turned him into a vampire, he'd certainly be evil, wouldn't he? Death or turning evil, was there another choice? All he had ever wanted was a quick death or to be left alone.

"One must be born a vampire to become one. Another twisted myth of those who have glimpsed between the worlds. It is my blood. My part of our contract. Magic to bind us both."

"I won't become a vampire?" Yuri confirmed. "I will still be me? *Touched* or whatever it is you find useful?"

"Yes," the Master agreed.

BONDED TO A VAMPIRE

Yuri licked his lips, gripping the cup with both hands. "Where do vampires come from?" He wondered, staring into the blood that didn't look different from the gallons of mortal blood he'd seen in his life, no flecks of magic or glowing color, just a thick red liquid.

"A curious mind."

He felt his face heat, reminded that once again he was asking questions. Everyone always told him to stop asking questions and behave. He'd really sucked at that. "Sorry."

"It isn't an uncommon trait of the *touched* to seek answers. My kind are remnants of Lucifer. Those he birthed to quell the demon surge. He was our creator, but never our god, as he hated that type of worship. We were always his children, adored by him, even when he led us to slaughter. Do you wish to learn more?"

"Yes," Yuri thought, staring into the cup like it held a million answers. "But I feel this is all a dream. Do I have to do anything else?"

"Drink and seal the contract."

At least it didn't smell like blood. Yuri brought the cup to his lips and tipped it back. He let the liquid fill his mouth and tried to swallow it like a shot. Fast. Down without the flavor really touching his tongue. He breathed out, set the cup back down, and felt a little disappointed. He'd expected it to do something. Taste awful. Anything. It tasted thick, but not like the pig's blood he'd had a few times in the past.

There was no copper bite of pennies or romantic flare of honey and juniper like in the stories. Yuri sat there for a minute, feeling triumphant. That he'd passed some sort of trial with no real hardship. That was when his stomach flipped over and he gagged, doubling over.

Would the contract be void if he threw up the blood?

Fire erupted in his gut. Heartburn times a thousand. Acid carving a path through him. Yuri curled around himself; eyes squeezed shut. The swirling magic compulsion he'd felt from the fae mage Sono was nothing compared to this. Yuri's insides were trying to climb their way out of him. His veins raged with fire, every joint and cell, even his teeth and hair screamed with pain.

He could feel the bond. Every part of him tied up and delivered in rolling waves of magic. The surrounding circle glowed with power bright enough to blind, and his skin burned as lines seemed to be etched within it. Had they fooled him? This was not a relatively comfortable life reading books. This was excruciating pain.

He couldn't breathe. His lungs tightened, jaw stuck shut. Not even a scream could escape. He prayed to black out, hoping a single breath of unconsciousness would ease the suffering for even a minute.

And then, like a candle flame, the pain vanished, and he sucked in a breath so deep he choked. Curled over on his side, he saw stars and swirls fading around him, the ring's magic dwindling. He couldn't help but look up as he lay utterly exhausted, staring outward. The man beyond the circle, the Master, not a monster at all. Didn't even appear to be vampire, not like the armored warriors Yuri was used to.

He had fine cheekbones, a narrow jaw, decorated in a well-trimmed beard, and lush lips. That drawing glow of internal light, familiar now, echoed a need in Yuri, reminding him of Star and the blond man. Did that brightness mean vampire? Maybe a different type of vampire? It made more sense when Yuri recalled the way Star fought, how he moved like magic, strength beyond any mortal man. He hadn't been a mortal man, had he, but one of these otherworldly creatures?

The Master's eyes were a luminescent, almost burgundy brown, like a superb whiskey Yuri would want to drink long and deep. His long hair cascaded over his shoulders, reaching at least the middle of his back. And he was tall. Probably well over six feet, shoulders wide, waist narrow.

The suit wasn't anything Yuri was familiar with, but it fit him well, topped with a sort of fitted trench coat that reached his ankles. No fangs that Yuri could see, but his mouth was closed, those lush lips set in a neutral line.

He was beautiful. Like the actors Yuri could remember from old. Not pretty like Theo had been with his ethereal and androgynous beauty, but a handsome of Middle Eastern European type that had populated media before the Fracture.

The Master, a king of this world, of vampires, of angels? Yuri had endless questions.

He let out a long sigh, feeling his energy fading. "That hurt," he said. He could lie there admiring the beauty of the Master and expire, and that would be okay, he thought briefly as the pain vanished. He felt boneless, exhausted, but unhurt. "You could have warned me."

The Master's lips curled upward, a slight smile. "I find if I warn of the pain, temporary as it might be, the contract is refused. A waste, really. It is why I didn't give permission to have you fed first. No point in you eating if you'll throw it up."

"Do we have to do that again?" Yuri asked. Memories of pain faded fast enough, even if the message attached didn't evaporate with it. But he also didn't look forward to experiencing it again.

"The bond, no. Can you stand? I will show you to your room."

He was going to get his own room? Yuri breathed another minute or two, trying to decide if he had the strength to actually move. He lifted a hand and found new lines around his wrist, running up his arms, not through his previous tattoos, but appearing much like them. Black lines of characters appearing like links as much as possibly words in another language. The bond? Magic chains?

He didn't feel enslaved, though he wasn't dumb enough to think it was otherwise. Bound to a vampire until death. That sounded a lot like being enslaved. "You won't make me eat bugs or anything, will you?" Yuri should have thought to ask that before.

"No. Though I'm told they are full of nutritional value for humans."

Yuri wondered if he was joking, but couldn't tell by the expression on the Master's face. Right, he wasn't supposed to look at him. Yuri sat up, testing his body for pain. He didn't hurt, though he was weak as his muscles ached from being overworked. He carefully pushed himself to his feet, trying to test his steadiness.

"Do all vampires look like you? I thought the warriors were all vampires?" Yuri asked, wondering about the glow and that binding draw that made Yuri want to touch him. None of the many vampire giants Yuri had seen, ever had that glow.

"Not all vampires are the same. Only humans use that term for our species."

Species. Yuri thought about that for another minute. "I can walk," Yuri finally said. "Slowly." He stared at the Master's legs rather than tempting fate by staring at his face again. Yuri was at least a foot shorter, which meant the Master was over six foot nine. "Your legs are much longer than mine."

"An astute observation. Follow me."

Yuri expected the last two words to wrap another bond of compulsion around him and make him move, but they didn't. The Master turned toward the massive door and it opened on its own. A scraping of stone on stone, the doors towering over both of them. Yuri followed, stepping free from the circle and bending to pick up his box. The cup was gone, though he didn't recall the Master picking it up. He didn't know if the Master had it when he arrived or how and when he'd added blood to it. Maybe it was magic?

The area beyond the door stretched before them as more of an upscale manor, not as large or as grand as the chaos of winding staircases in the previous areas Yuri had passed through. The Master headed for the stairs, which branched in the middle, a long path heading upward, one to the left and one to the right. At the top center before the stairs split was an old painting which Yuri had seen in books.

"Vlad Tepes?" Yuri inquired. "Dracula? Was he real? I mean, I know the vague history..."

"It's an unflattering painting. I kept the painting because it reminds me of how the Fractures skew reality. Humans are peculiar in what they remember. More vulnerable to losing fact in distorted belief. He is real."

Is. Not was. "He's still alive?" The Master couldn't be Dracula, right? Yuri's heart sped up with fear. There was no resemblance in the picture.

"He is. You'll meet him eventually, I suppose." The Master turned to the left and guided them upward. "My brother doesn't visit as much as he used to. His time during the last Fracture left a foul taste in his mouth, and unfortunate stories dictated as history. He has a lot of pets, though they don't last long."

"You're the brother of Dracula?" Wait, the worlds had been Fractured before?

"One of many, I assure you. Though most are long gone now. Lost in the last Fracture. It is only Vlad and I who remain in our direct line. He is no longer on this side of the veil and has no interest in restoring the convergence." The stairs turned near the top, opening into a long hallway. The ceilings were maybe twelve or fifteen feet rather than the cavernous spaces Yuri had already seen. This section of the castle or mansion or whatever it was, felt more homey or alive than the odd spaces of the rest so far.

"Vlad Tepes. Vlad the Impaler. Had one brother according to human history," Yuri whispered, trying to remember his world history classes in college. He knew a real person inspired the fiction. A monster in actual flesh, but truly a vampire?

"He hates that name, but it fits. Still uses that method to get people to leave him alone. I admit it works well. A garden of corpses on stakes jutting outside of one's home is likely to deter most visitors." The Master led Yuri down the hall and around a bend to a double door. Before he could reach for it, the door opened and Theo stood in the entry, smiling at them.

He bowed slightly. "Master."

"Yuri will need some rest," the Master told him. "We'll be moving soon. I have much to finish up before we do."

"Are you, Radu?" Yuri wondered. History or myth? Radu the beautiful, that fit well enough. The man was devastatingly handsome. Yuri could see the allure of such a handsome man. And so different from Theo, who really looked like an angel now that Yuri examined him again. Would Theo have wings? Did the Master have fangs? Yuri's mind spun with questions.

"I'm Master to you," he said. "You've not earned the right to call me anything else. Help solve the riddle of the Fracture, and perhaps that will change." He waved his hand at the door and Theo, who stood in the entry. "Theodorus will get you settled. You'll find the seraphim more accommodating than most of the others in this household. Humans are disliked because of their constant ripping of the veil."

With that, he turned and walked away, back down the hall. Yuri stared until he was gone, drawn to follow, even if he'd been told otherwise. He took a step away from the door and his legs gave out.

Theo caught him. "Master says to rest."

The temporary bit of strength that had allowed Yuri to follow and walk up the stairs had vanished beneath the heavy weight of exhaustion. He blinked, his gaze darkening around the edges. "Guess drinking his blood doesn't make me invincible."

Theo's smile was bright. "Not until after you've had some rest. Let's get you to bed. The bond is always draining."

"Are you really an angel?" Yuri asked as he closed his eyes and lost touch with all but gentle darkness.

THE MASTER AND HIS MOVING CASTLE

Yuri finds himself on his knees before a prince of legends.

Captured and delivered by a magical carriage drawn by demon horses to the steps of a floating castle, surrounded by vampires and seraphim, Yuri wonders if he's stepped into a dream or a nightmare.

The Master offers Yuri the chance to bask in the depths of a hidden library, seeking out answers to the world's end, avoiding the shadows stalking the halls and twisting the worlds, at only the cost of a blood bond.

Will the bond keep Yuri from finding Star, or awaken a deeper need inside?

BLOOD AND DREAMS

He dreamed of the bar, the surrounding streets untouched by the madness that had taken the world apart, but empty. Everything cast in a motionless spell like a video game stuck loading, NCPs off-screen unable to complete their loop.

Yuri wandered the streets, memories stirring as he passed a dozen places that had given him a sense of freedom before the end. His escape from the cult, short-lived, but he had found excitement beyond the walls.

The tattoo parlor, the tiny studio apartment three floors up that was barely enough to move around, the bar and the kitchen that had become his second home, and the bus stop to culinary school. All bits of his past, he thought long lost and faded with time.

He reached for the door of the bar, expecting it to be locked, but it opened, and the scent of smoke and booze flooded his senses. It was suffocating for a half second as he stepped inside, chatter coming from the TV and a handful of occupied tables. No one had faces, just blurred blank spaces as he gazed around.

The shape at the bar made his breath catch.

Yuri trembled, taking a few steps forward, fearing the man would vanish, but the outline stayed the same. The lithe form, with inky black hair and teal streak down one side, leaned forward in his seat, glass gripped in his grasp. Hunched in on himself as though trying to be small and go unnoticed.

"Star?" Yuri whispered, his heart flipping over with joy and fear. Fear that it was all a dream. He couldn't recall a time it had been so vivid, though he'd often dreamt of being in Star's bed, his body singing beneath Star's skilled touch.

The man turned, a slight tilt of his head at first, then set the glass down to slide off the stool, his cool blue gaze like ice filled with refracting rainbows. So real Yuri felt frozen in place, terrified of breaking the dream.

"Yuri," Star whispered. "I didn't think you survived."

"Is this real?" Yuri blinked, everything still frozen around them. Only he and Star moved and breathed.

Star held out his hand. The ink serpents colored over his fingers, clear and familiar. Yuri reached for him. His body yearning to be touched. Star's warm hand slid into his, drawing him close. Star touched his face with his other hand, studying him.

"My sweet Yuri, what have you been through?" He studied Yuri's face, fingers dancing over Yuri's cheek, and Yuri realized he was crying, tears leaking from his eyes to coat Star's fingers. It was part joy and part pain. Yuri clung to him, trembling and praying it wasn't a dream. But the black etched bond coated Yuri's hand as he held Star's. What was real?

"The end of the world."

"It happens," Star agreed. He leaned in to press his forehead to Yuri's, delivering a soft kiss to flutter over Yuri's lips.

"You left me," Yuri accused, recalling too vividly the heartbreak of waking the next morning alone in his studio, wondering if it had all been a dream, but finding the world beyond in chaos.

"I didn't mean to. My strength in your world is limited." Star cupped Yuri's face. "Time passes differently from world to world."

"A decade," Yuri said bitterly. "I thought you were a dream." He'd been the only happy memory Yuri clung to, but pain and loneliness touched even that.

"So much time?" Star asked. "I apologize. Does it help that I have missed the touch and taste of your sweetness? You are like the sun to me, distant and untouchable. Bright enough to burn, but I long for your caress. Dream of your kiss. You remind me of a long-lost love, giving me hope and pain all at once." He brushed his lips over Yuri's. "Perhaps when I return, you can bake that delightful lemon strawberry cake of yours? We can paint ourselves in frosting and find pleasure over and over until the last of this madness ends and the worlds are finally reborn."

Yuri recalled the memory, how he'd spent weeks perfecting the recipe, and brought the results to work because why would he, one man, need so much cake? Everyone had enjoyed it, but he couldn't recall seeing Star that day. He would have remembered, wouldn't he?

"You promised you'd cook for me anything I wished," Star continued.

"I didn't know you were there."

"Your eyes were not fully open yet. The veil untorn. Not until the night I gave you pleasure."

Yuri sighed as his body reacted to the word, as if experiencing it all again.

"Even now, I'm not free. The chains they used to ensnare me only stretch so far. But eventually..." He shrugged. "The end always comes."

Was the end of the world Yuri's fault because he wanted to be touched? But that had all started before, even prior to Star taking a seat at Yuri's bar. Maybe it was Star's curse that made him *touched*. Was that what he'd meant when he said no one wanted his touch?

"I saw things before I met you..." Only brief glimpses. The sign he had been *touched*, even before Star? The veil hadn't been torn. Not until the Fracture dropped on their heads.

"*Touched*," Star nodded. "You would never have seen me at all if you couldn't peer through the veil." Star studied him, his fingers tracing Yuri's face with reverence. "So beautiful, filled with light, though I'm saddened to find your hope buried. You've been bound by the Onari." Star lifted Yuri's arm and traced the lines. Yuri shivered with need.

"I don't know what that means." The bonds from Radu?

"Can you find safety among them? They are a powerful people, both ruthless and brutal, but not unkind, mostly. They can be protective of those they find of value. And you are very valuable, Yuri. Wait for me?"

Yuri blinked. Star would find him? It had been a decade. He tried to pull away, hating this dream and the false hope it gave him in that moment, but Star held tight.

"Yuri."

"Don't lie to me. Everyone lies to me. Uses me," Yuri whispered. "I've been alone for so long. Betrayed a thousand times." His hope buried. That was the truth. Yuri felt as though he had long ago hidden away the kernel of hope of ever seeing Star again, or ever experiencing love or joy again. The world ended, and it seemed unfair that he survived only to suffer. Hope wasn't dead, but only because he'd hidden it deep, and allowed it freedom only when he dreamed.

Star curled himself around Yuri. "I can make no promises until I'm free. But," he held his palm up between them and slashed the middle of it with a sudden sharp fingernail, drawing blood, "let this be my vow to find you. That you are mine." Yuri stared at it, confused, but Star brought his palm to Yuri's lips. "Drink."

"Are you a vampire, too?" Yuri wondered. He licked a bit of the blood tentatively, finding, like the Master's, it had no real taste, but beneath it, was the familiar flavor of toasted marshmallows burned into Yuri's memory from that night, long ago. Yuri sucked at the wound, lapping up the blood if only for a taste of Star's skin again. He sighed as warmth filled him to chase away the chill that had etched into his bones from starvation. He relaxed into Star's embrace, finding peace and sudden deep sleep drawing him down. He fought it for a few seconds, not wanting to lose a moment in Star's embrace, but the pull was too strong, and he dropped into a deep well of warm, rocking, sleep.

THE MASTER AND THE PRINCE

The floor to the main part of the mansion had begun its slight uptilt again. Radu glared at it as though his ire would change it. But he knew what it meant. Regis awaited him in the main hall.

"The other one?" Radu inquired.

"Cleaned and being questioned by Sono," Regis replied.

"No sign of him being touched?" Radu wondered as he made his way toward the back dregs of the castle. "Yuri said they shared a father. Perhaps the gift came from his mother."

"Nothing so far," Regis said. "He's like most of the resistance leaders, dumb and belligerent. More willing to let their entire species die than submit to simple facts and the rule of others."

An unfortunate trait that was stubbornly human. "Send word. We'll be moving soon. Get everyone inside."

Regis sighed heavily. "I'll be grateful to leave the stench behind, but the shifting is never pleasant. Perhaps we'll land on the other side of the veil this time?"

It was rare but could happen from time to time. Radu shrugged. He had stopped trying to predict where the castle would land each time it moved after the first year and a half. Now he focused on trying to stop it from moving, and seeking why it paused each time, and what would make it move again.

"At least it means we have found what we needed here," Regis offered.

"Anything substantial in the supplies?" Radu asked. He would need to go through the reports.

"Other than the touched boy, not really. Equipment, bits of metals, a handful of books and notes. Two dozen survivors from three camps, most barely living. It will take time to nurse them back to health and make them useful. That's all."

They had been here only a few weeks. Cleared out most of the resistance hovels, sending the remaining survivors to areas rebuilt and more sustainable to life. Radu found removing those in power allowed the others to rebuild and find a future. Perhaps the point of this stop was to retrieve Yuri. Time would tell.

"The survivors have been relocated?" Radu confirmed.

"On their way to the train as we speak. We have notified everyone. The caravan guarded. The others will have to rejoin us after the move." Regis warily eyed a wall that twisted unnaturally.

Radu paused at the top of a stairway leading into darkness. "Get everything locked down. It seems we won't have long before the shift."

Regis bowed and bounded off. Radu made his way down a labyrinth of corridors and stairs. A nightmare of space that would frustrate anyone not familiar with the palace's quirks. Even he grew irritated after the eighth trip down but steadied himself as finally the door to the crypt opened before him.

Sono's magic pulsed from within.

Radu entered to find the other human on the floor, in a circle not all that unlike the binding circle Yuri had been in, on his knees, bleeding but still protesting. Yuri was lovely in a way Radu had never thought of humans before. He didn't keep pets because he found humans too fragile, and their humanity couldn't compare to the ethereal beauty of the Onari or even the seraphim. But Radu had to admit that Yuri had been exquisite there, with his back straight and painted skin, even as underfed as he had been, the sharp cut of his cheeks and beautiful eyes, beguiling. The submissive pose stirring something Radu hadn't felt in a long time.

Interest?

More than the power of the *touched*. Radu had never found humans all that appealing. Though Vlad hadn't either until he'd met Celeste. Perhaps Yuri was like Lucian, mixed blood? Radu sighed and tried to clear his mind to deal with matters at hand.

Hopefully, the bond and rest would heal Yuri and clarify his sight. The other mortal and Yuri looked nothing alike, and Radu could not sense any magic in the man. If he was at all *touched* like Yuri, he'd buried it deep.

"Any information?" Radu inquired as he stepped up beside Sono.

"Two other resistance locations, neither close," Sono offered. She glared at the prone man. "Their own people were barely alive. I doubt the other locations are much better. United for survival seems very difficult for mortals, at least on this side of the world."

It was a sad fact that they were reaching the end of humanity. The previous convergence hadn't lasted this long. Nor had they had the extreme loss of human life. Radu wondered if the worlds would collapse on themselves without the continued presence of humans. Perhaps they'd be unable to close the gaping holes between the spaces. Fae like Sono had been locked out of their world for centuries. Left with the small bits of magic they could find between the veils of the remaining worlds. What if the death of humans locked out all the worlds, leaving them only the dying remains of the mortal realm? That sounded like a nightmare.

"We will move soon," Radu offered, annoyed. "Can we send raiding parties to the other two locations? Meet up with them at Heartbridge or Castelle?"

"Already done," Sono said. "The walkway outside was twisted, dangling over the void."

Radu sighed.

"The boy is *touched*?" Sono confirmed.

"You know he is. Saw right through you, didn't he?" Radu said. "Theodorus has already accepted him. If the others do... perhaps we will have another tool to solve this puzzle."

"Or a pretty toy. The others didn't even notice me," Sono said, not at all upset about that. She had no love for humans. "Humans are so blind to what is right in front of them. Perhaps the boy is what we were meant to find here." She stared down at the resistance's remains. "This one is as useless as the rest."

"What has Yuri told you?" The man on the floor demanded. He would not have understood them since Radu and Sono were speaking the language of the Onari, or vampires, as the mortals call them. "He's useless, you know. Nothing more than a cook. A bastard born to that immigrant woman. He's touched by the devil. We had many attacks on the camp over the years with monsters coming to retrieve him. My father hid him, kept him alive, only to use him as a buffer between the monsters and us."

"Is that so?" Radu asked in English. Fascinating. Yuri had mentioned none of that. "Monsters came for him?"

"None would ever hurt him. Even if they caught him outside the walls, somehow, he'd always end up coming back unharmed. He's unnatural. He makes men want him. Even the beasts," the man said indignantly. "Take him, if that's your desire. Let me and my people go."

Radu had never heard of a mortal touched in a way that even the scattered masses of beasts roaming between the worlds would leave him unharmed. He cast his gaze to Sono to see if she was taking note, and she nodded. "Release you and your people? To what end? Your people were almost dead."

"Better dead than slaves to the monsters."

Radu crossed his arms over his chest. "Your people are already on their way to a settlement where they will be fed and clothed. Call it slavery if you wish, but they will have an easier life than the hovel here. You may not, depending on who buys you at auction."

"You can't sell me. My God will save me from demons like you! I was Chosen."

"Hmm. Your god? Which god is that? And why is he silent? Doesn't seem powerful to me, leaving you all to die." Radu flicked out a spell, silencing the man, and binding him. "Deliver him to auction. If someone wishes to break him or eat him, I don't care. Though warn he has a sibling who is *touched*. The ability might be latent."

"Consider it done," Sono vowed. "I will also send word to the transport and see if I can corroborate his story about the *touched* male."

Radu nodded, then turned and made his way toward the barracks. He would have to listen to reports from his generals and review the supplies they'd found. Precious metals, books,

115

and now Yuri. One of those things was the reason for them landing on this torn up landscape. The books hadn't looked like anything Radu didn't already have in the vault of his library. Metals, those were slowing the churning of the gears that tore the worlds up, but the amounts were so small, he wasn't certain it was helping anymore. If Yuri had some sort of ability to calm the many beasts of the jumbled worlds, that might be something more than sight through the veil. But what? Radu had encountered nothing like that in his many centuries of life.

He ran into Lucian on his way up and frowned. "Nephew?"

"We're moving soon?" Lucian inquired.

"Yes." Not that any of them could change that fact or slow it.

"And the one *touched* by the seraphim?"

"What of him?"

Lucian was almost a head shorter than Radu, though one of the most skilled fighters of the entire population of remaining Onari. He was half Onari and half human. Vlad had insisted his son train to overcome the weaknesses of humanity. However, patience wasn't one of Lucian's virtues, nor a love of any human, even touched ones. Bitterness ingrained by his father's loss of his love made Lucian cold and ruthless. Was he feeling a draw to the mortal, too?

"I wondered what might happen with him?"

"He is upstairs in their wing, recovering. Like most of the remains of humanity, he was dying. He accepted my bond. The last pockets of rebellion are unlikely to have much time left." Their raiding parties had already discovered a dozen camps, much like Yuri's, that had all been long dead. Nothing but rotting corpses and the scavengers of a thousand worlds gnawing on their bones. Radu gave Lucian an assessing glare. "You despise humans. Have you forgotten?"

"He's lovely," Lucian admitted gruffly.

"Was he not wearing a mask the whole time you saw him?" Radu had reviewed Sono's observation of the mortal before finding his way to the binding chamber. He'd been unprepared for the delicate beauty of Yuri's face, the chiseled lines of his cheekbones, thick and lush lips, and bright eyes. The human would have created a war at auction, everyone fighting for a taste of that beauty on his knees. Even Radu wasn't immune. Lucian cared for humans even less than Radu did.

"Did you want him, nephew?"

"His eyes are drawing."

"Only his eyes?" Radu asked, tone teasing. "Or the thought of him on his knees at your feet."

"He'd have made a beautiful pet," Lucian whispered, not meeting Radu's gaze.

"The *touched* rarely make good pets unless they are broken. Would you have liked to break him, nephew?"

Lucian swallowed hard, his back straight as though preparing for battle. "One of the seraphim said something..."

"About?" Radu inquired. He hadn't spoken to Theodorus for more than a few seconds.

"One of them mentioned that his power glows to them. Like godfire. Like the archangels of old. I thought they might misremember as it's been so long..."

That was another interesting discovery. First, the beasts wouldn't attack him and now the seraphim found him blinding. More than a little *touched* then. Or that close to the grave. "Time will tell. He is resting." Radu studied his nephew, who fidgeted, looking more than a little uncomfortable. "Lucian?"

"Octavia said he reminds her of my mother," Lucian finally said. "She glimpsed him in the bath."

"Celeste was exceptional as *touched* went," Radu said as he made his way past his nephew and up the stairs.

"She helped fix the last convergence," Lucian said softly as he followed Radu up. What he didn't add was that they had lost Celeste when the last Fracture had sealed, banished back into the mortal realm, which had sent Lucian's father into madness only tempered now by his isolation.

"I recommend you don't fall in love with the mortal then," Radu stated. His gut tightened over the idea of Yuri being lost. He had only known the man for minutes and already felt a bond that had nothing to do with the magic in his blood. Had this been what Vlad had encountered with Celeste?

"As if that would ever happen. But perhaps he is the key to finally going home?" Lucian followed.

"You can go stay with your father," Radu offered. "There is no reason you have to remain here since you hate it so much."

"Do you think I could keep my sanity?" It wasn't even a teasing question but inquired with genuine honesty. Without something to ground him, it was unlikely Lucian would survive under the dark cloud of his father's depression. A projection of madness blanketed Vlad's space, magic shifted and distorted by centuries of pain. Radu had sometimes wondered if this new Fracture was part of that growing spread.

"I suggest you find something that catches your interest," Radu said.

"Like the human?"

Radu stared at Lucian. His nephew was beautiful, more pretty than handsome with his gold spun hair and defined features. More of his mother in his appearance than his father.

But Lucian wasn't known for seduction, despite having centuries of life and encounters of all species. His patience limited, attitude aloof, and a pretty face didn't solve all of that. "Could you pretend long enough to convince a human to share your bed?"

Lucian stiffened. "I've bedded plenty of humans."

"A night perhaps. But more? Without using magic to bespell them? Yuri is bound to me until death, short as that may be for humans. If you used him for a night, rape his mind to use his body, would he wish to continue seeing you?"

"You shouldn't allow them so much free will. He's a servant to the court. A slave."

Technically yes. "And how earnestly do slaves serve? Especially mortal slaves?" Radu turned away from his nephew. "Sometimes I think there is too much of your father in you, and not enough of your mother."

"She's been gone a long time."

"Does that mean you have lost the humanity she gifted you?"

"It's a weakness."

"And yet still survives."

"I'm uncertain that is a good thing."

"Without it, we would have no chance of repairing the worlds."

"I don't know if I agree with you."

Radu shrugged. They had enough recorded history to indicate that humanity was exactly what was needed to repair rifts. Even if they hadn't figured out how yet. "Your belief is unnecessary."

He made his way past his nephew, and toward the war room set up for his generals. He'd never been the warlord his brother had been, but he wasn't actually planning the genocide of humanity. Simply a purge of the pockets of the dying, placing the survivors in cities, and trying to find a way home. Radu hoped Yuri had some answers, as he wasn't certain how much time remained before giant chunks of this world broke apart and closed off.

Angels of Creation

Yuri woke to a grinding squeal of metal that pierced his senses, and the world ripping apart around him. He sat up to clap his hands over his ears to stop the noise, though it didn't help at all. The shrieking came from something hard to identify, magic, or life perhaps, but inside his head. He felt the vibration in his gut and wanted to scream. He floundered in disorientation and didn't know where he was, only that he was in a soft bed in a room that looked like it belonged in a fairytale rather than the survival camp.

Theo appeared beside the bed and crawled up next to Yuri. Not a dream then? Where was Star? Had that been a dream?

"What's happening?" he asked.

"We're moving," Theo said. He wrapped Yuri in a firm hug. "It will only last a few minutes."

"Why does it feel like something is tearing?" Time? His sanity? Yuri couldn't explain the sensation, only that it was intense and painful.

"Each time we move, something of the landscape gets stuck,

and yanked away, becoming part of the castle. It is the Fracture. Each move is worse than the last as we get bigger."

"What?" That didn't sound possible.

"You saw the outside, right? It's a mash of lots of things?"

Was that how it got all messed up? "This is a crazy dream if it's a dream."

Theo hugged him harder. "You want me to be a dream?" His tone filled with sadness.

"You'd be the nicest part of this dream." Yuri thought for a minute. "Okay, this dream wouldn't be so bad. I got a bath, and a pretty room. But am bound to a vampire who lives in a moving castle?"

Another jerking tear rumbled through his bones, painful and jarring enough that he saw stars. He couldn't help but tremble and suck in gulps of air. He only vaguely felt Theo's hands stroking his face and back, trying to comfort him.

"It's not usually this bad for humans. Your kind isn't all that sensitive to the subtle magics between the worlds," Theo said. "Breathe, focus on me. It will pass." Theo spooned around him, wrapping him in a warm embrace and covering them with blankets. "Once it passes, we will get you some food."

Yuri didn't think he could eat. Was it the castle moving that made him feel so nauseous? He couldn't stop trembling like he was freezing, but he didn't really feel cold, disoriented maybe, like chaos swirled around them and threatened to suck him away into madness at any second? He struggled to turn into Theo's embrace, facing the seraphim and curling into his shoulder. "This is almost as bad as the bond," Yuri muttered.

"Yeah?" Theo asked. "I've heard accepting the bond is bad. This is similar?"

"Aren't you bonded to the Master?"

"No. The seraphim serve freely."

Right, Theo was seraphim. Angels. "Do you have wings?" Yuri asked, to keep his mind off the rolling edge of chaos tugging on him. He could feel everything moving, the walls, the bed, all seeming to lurch and spin around him. Theo was smaller and more delicate in appearance than he ever expected angels to be. He thought them fierce warriors with giant muscles, or maybe even the many bits of art that featured them more like flying babies. Theo was neither of those, but breathlessly beautiful and ethereal.

"I do. Once we stop moving, I'll show you."

"I bet they are beautiful," Yuri whispered.

Theo hummed. "You have lovely color painted on your skin. Some archangels glowed with light like paintings, but never had it drawn on their skin." He ran his fingertips over the tops of Yuri's shoulder and arm. It was grounding, and strangely arousing. Yuri was grateful for the chaos in that moment, as he was certain it was the only thing keeping him from embarrassing himself at such a minor touch. "Am I hurting you?"

"No. I'm not used to being touched," Yuri said out loud what he'd been thinking. And he missed Star's touch and wondered how something from a dream could feel so real.

"Do you want me to stop?"

"No." Yuri sank into the sensation. "It's strange. A memory of a memory? No one at the camp really touched." Especially not him. There had been sex around him, used for reproduction mostly. He'd been mixed race and nothing more than the cook's son. Worthless. But somehow a temptation for a handful of those who had approached him over the years. One man was rewarded with death, the rest were female and traded out to other camps to keep his evil from spreading, anything else forced and kept buried deep in the back of his mind. "They thought me evil, but let me live," he said after another few minutes passed. "I had to keep the mask on because others were drawn to me, but the Leader ordered everyone to stay away."

"Why would they think you were evil? Weren't they all people like you? Humans?"

He'd never been one of them. The drive for survival could make a person do a lot of things. Hurting others for the sake of feeling powerful had never appealed to him.

"I don't know. The Leader claimed I tempted people. I don't know with what. I learned to avoid everyone, and I never told them I could feel the monsters coming," Yuri admitted. He didn't know if Theo would share what he heard, or if being an angel meant he was really something good, like a guardian. Even if he was good, Yuri thought, Theo's loyalty may be to Radu, the Master, rather than a barely living mortal creature like himself. Yuri bit his lip and tried to remind himself not to speak. It had saved him from harm in the past.

"How did you feel them?" Theo inquired. "The monsters? Did you dream of them?"

"No dreams. It always started with anxiety in my stomach. Like a vibration." Doom coming. Different from the Master. Darker. Heavy. Like its power was too much. Something in the movement of the Fracture called to Yuri, almost tangible, like he could reach out and hold a link to them, but he kept those words silent. Too many years of learning to hide in plain sight. It kept him alive. Could he trust Theo? He hoped so but would tread carefully until he was certain.

"Outside, I saw the Fracture close for the first time, and there were rainbows. Seems odd to have demons and monsters coming from rainbows." Yuri recalled the shadows beyond. Maybe those had been the monsters trudging through the veils between worlds. "Angels are real?" He let out a long breath. "I guess if demons are…"

"I don't think demons have broken through the Fracture from the hell dimensions. The Master would have told us about such a breach. If the Fractures between worlds remain long enough, it will happen. Neither the seraphim nor the demons were ever human, though sometimes we walked among the mortals. Very few are on this side. Our world has been cut off for centuries." Theo sighed and sounded sad when he said, "Since the last Fracture."

"You haven't seen the rest of your people for centuries?"

"Only those already walking the mortal realm have remained, and humanity has destroyed many of our kind. Without the archangels and direction of the higher ranked seraphim, we have little to do here." He waved his hand at the room surrounding them. "It is why we serve the Master. Many of us were guardians who have long since lost our wards, or even messengers, without words or tales to deliver."

"Is that why I can see you? Because you're a guardian and I am *touched*?" Yuri wondered. He sank into Theo's embrace. With the world spinning in his gut, he closed his eyes to narrow his focus to the warm touch. If he squinted, he could almost see the outline of wings. Were they white? Yuri imagined they were soft as down feathers and warm as a thick blanket. It gave him something to ground him as the inside of his mind swirled with rolling waves of power.

"Perhaps. Those who could see us rarely had guardians when the worlds were as they should be. Maybe because they could perceive the other terrors of the worlds, they didn't need us to guide them?" Theo stroked Yuri's back in a soothing caress. "My wards were often children. I would follow them, protect them, and try to guide them until they had a secure place in life. Sometimes it was only a handful of years. Others until they had children of their own." He breathed a heavy sigh. "Sometimes I failed."

"I'm sorry," Yuri said.

"Nothing for you to be sorry about. It was a long time ago."

"You miss your people? Your world?" How insane to think of completely different worlds and how magical they must be. "What was a world of angels like?"

"Not all that unlike the human world. Angels enjoyed the creative beauty of humans, with art and some structures similar. Trees and forests, oceans, rivers, and lakes. Our kind are not as inventive as mortals. Most of the longer-lived beings lack the creativity of the short-lived. Mortals burn bright, even if only for a short time."

"A world without all the war, maybe?" Yuri wondered. Humans were good at war, death, and killing. Destruction of environments for profit and personal gain.

"There were angels who learned that from humans as well. Jealousy and arrogance turned some against our kind and fueled a war. It is where the Fallen came from. Though I have not seen one since the last Fracture. Stories exaggerate the truth, but it was jealousy that ripped the seraphim from grace."

"Fallen angels, like Lucifer?"

"Indeed. Though that was not really his name, mortal translations and mistranslations change a lot of history. But there was a first supreme archangel cast out because of jealousy and rage. First Fracture of worlds, which is incorrectly recorded by a handful of human texts. The war of the heaven realms expanded to the mortal ones very quickly."

"The Master said Lucifer created the vampires to fight the demons."

"He did. But he had already long since left the heavenly

realms to walk the mortal plane. The creator of humanity had crafted a fascinating thing. Most angels were angry, but Lucifer adored humans, found them fascinating. Even though they were primitive, he gave them knowledge, and with that wisdom came both beauty and horror. Some say it cursed us all because it awakened mortals from simplicity to greed, but the Master thinks mortals always had free will, which is why they are both short-lived and bright with creativity, even if sometimes that innovation is negative."

"Lucifer wasn't angry at the creator for giving life to humans?" Yuri recalled the story he'd heard a hundred times in his life, though couldn't remember it actually being in the Bible as it had been read to them.

"It's a rare few who rise in power to become a creator," Theo said. "Lucifer loved them more than anything and wanted humanity to succeed in honor of his love of the creator. Not everyone agreed. Many thought the humans should obey and be subjected to the rule of the seraphim since their creator was one of ours. The creator and Lucifer disagreed."

"The creator was a seraph? I thought the creator made the angels?"

Theo smiled at Yuri and traced Yuri's lips with his fingertips. "Crafted in their image, much like us. Seraphim are born of light. The creator was one of the first and brightest of our kind. They used their divine brilliance to create an entire world, not unlike all the stories written in mortal books. Rather than words on a page, they gave life to angels first, thought they were too perfect and beautiful, and used the power they had remaining to create humanity. Rather than creating humans with perfection and beauty, humans were given the ability for imagination and creation. A mix of light and dark to gather for inspiration."

"That makes sense," Yuri said.

"But giving that much of themselves, creators often burn themselves out. Lucifer loved the creator and vowed to protect their creation, which caused a rift among the supreme archangels. The archangels demanded the first angel return. He refused. The archangels began a war, vowing to destroy humanity to force him to return, which caused the first Fracture. Demons rose from rifts between the worlds, devouring everything and everyone. The war turned from angel against angel to one of survival. Lucifer crafted beings from mixed worlds, designing them powerful and beautiful to fight the demons and mix with the mortals. But only an archangel could seal the gates of hell that had opened. Lucifer sacrificed himself to save all the worlds, locking himself inside in the darkness, stripped of all light and beauty. The supreme archangels of the time called it his punishment for wandering among the mortals and betraying his true love. Though some believe it was the creator who betrayed him first, others suspect it was the archangels who began the war that are to blame. I'm not old enough to know. The archangels fashioned guardians from their excess power and many other types of seraphim after the worlds split the first time, halting creation."

"No more new worlds were built after the first Fracture?" Yuri asked.

"It is forbidden. The archangels policed those who rose to creator status, allowing only smaller creations until none had enough power to design a new world. The idea is too many worlds cause more Fractures."

"How many Fractures have there been before?"

"Dozens, perhaps? Lucifer's was the first I know of. Though I don't think it was his fault at all. Was finding beauty among mortals so bad? I had many orders that took me to the mortal realms and I found it fascinating and filled with wonder. Does that mean I should have Fallen like the first? My wings are still white." He sighed and shrugged. "Each Fracture tears the veils between worlds. They come and go with time. Getting worse, creating more Fractures, perhaps? More mingling worlds? Unfair to blame all the stuff that happened on an archangel locked away in a hell dimension."

But they had been closed? Stopped? Something? Left as only minor mentions in stories, it made sense why searching texts would lead to ideas about fixing them again. "And worlds are closed off each time? What happens to the worlds when no one can get to them?"

The spinning was slowing. Yuri sucked in a long breath and tried to calm his still rolling stomach. Could the effects of the Master's blood be amplifying the feeling or was the movement that powerful?

"It's unknown," Theo said. "Perhaps destroyed?"

"Have any that have been closed, reopened in another Fracture?"

"No," Theo whispered, and Yuri heard the pain in his voice, the fear. His people were gone. Perhaps lost forever. Did Theo have a family he had lost? Friends? Lovers? Perhaps children?

"I'm sorry," Yuri whispered. "I lost my mother two years ago. She was all the family I really had. I understand the feelings of losing everyone and everything that is important to you." They sat longer, taking comfort in the idea of sharing the emotions of losing everything. It made Yuri wonder about the Fracture, as it seemed to have let other worlds into the human world. Did that mean that closing it, or stopping the Fracture, would close other worlds? Wouldn't that make it a bad thing? "Does closing the Fracture always seal off other worlds?"

"Sometimes? During the Fractures, many simply seem to collapse in on themselves. Ours vanished when the Fracture closed, the way to travel between worlds, gone."

Yuri looked up, finding Theo radiantly beautiful and terribly sad. "When there is no Fracture, you can travel between worlds?"

"Some can," Theo agreed. "Few worlds are safe. Filled with the monsters, as you call them. Without the archangels, the seraphim are prey to many other species. More so in worlds filled with darkness when we are the only remaining light."

"And the vampires can control monsters? You said they aren't actually demons, but they look terrifying, and sometimes eat people," Yuri wondered. "And the angels live with the Master. There were others in the bath before you arrived. They were seraphim, right?"

"Yes. Other creatures are drawn to the Onari, as they have always been beings to traverse worlds and times. Legend states the First Fallen created them as his warriors to span the worlds and protect the mortals. When they weren't bound as Lucifer was, the archangels cursed the Onari to hunger for mortals, so it is a war of conscience for them. Protect those who are prey."

"Own-R-eye?" Yuri copied Theo's pronunciation.

"Vampires, as you call them. Their magic remains powerful in all worlds. Though the Master claims it is lessening. He can no longer control the movement of the castle. It shifts around under the influence of the Fracture."

That sounded really troublesome. "The Master used to move the entire castle?" No wonder his power had felt like fire beneath Yuri's veins.

"Not all the Onari are that powerful. Many have vanished into other worlds that closed. Lost or trapped? It is unknown,"

"The Master said there were many gods... The monsters were created by other gods?" Yuri asked.

"The creator of mortals was one of many creators, or gods as the mortals sometimes call them. The First Fallen created the Onari, which would make them a god of sorts, if that were the case. Most worlds have creators. It's a level of power. Many no longer exist having given all they are to create an entire world. Some worlds have many creators, the mortal realm does. Species mirror others because creators often find intrigue in one thing or another and replicate with minor changes. Archangels created the seraphim, but they are not our gods. Think of it as the way mortals have children. They create a child, but that child is a being of its own with only pieces of its creator embedded within. How much control does the parent or creator really have?"

Yuri thought about that for a while. It made sense. His years in the cult taught him that children were supposed to be obedient and worship or obey their Leader like a god. It was against his free will, though Yuri had tried to behave. Was he never meant to exist under the rule of some supreme being? He would have to spend some time thinking about it. Would life lose meaning without some higher being calling it to purpose? Or was life's purpose only to exist?

The movement came to a jerking stop. Yuri squeezed his eyes shut. Had they landed somewhere? Shifted to another world, perhaps? Yuri was both intrigued and terrified. What if it was a place where more monsters existed? Or worse, a demon realm that even the seraphim feared?

"The castle will settle in a few more minutes," Theo said. "It's slow to lock into place sometimes. Everyone inside is on alert until it's done."

Yuri nodded, taking deep breaths as he could feel the magic

releasing like small ties of tension slipping away. "Did the Onari have their own world that was lost?"

"Not lost. Badly damaged by the Fractures, but it's still accessible. We were there for a brief time before landing near the camp where the Master found you. The Master's brother is there." Theo shivered. "The Master says he is not an evil man, but no longer kind. Broken, perhaps?"

Vlad Dracula, Yuri recalled. "He really has a garden of corpses?" Yuri asked, remembering what the Master had said.

"Yes. They warned everyone to keep away from his lands as he was one of the last original Masters. Most of those staked outside his home are beings from other worlds. Not all are dead. Some creatures are harder to kill."

He had living creatures staked and suffering, unable to die? That sounded horrific. Yuri felt like he could open his eyes and not upchuck. He was rewarded with the intense beauty of Theo's face, which was much better than the idea of a garden of writhing and tortured beings. "You're so beautiful. Like I dreamt an angel might look. I see you and wonder if it's all real? And I feel insane for being giddy about all of this. Worlds. Magic. A puzzle to solve. It sounds wonderfully enticing, even if there are terrifying things everywhere."

Theo's smile was warm and genuine. "The Master's castle is one of the few safe places for the seraphim who remain. Some of the other creatures attack us on sight. You will find many of us here, all happy to chatter with the few who see us and don't want to eat us."

That was sad and strange. "But the Master can control the ones who try to attack you?"

"Some. He has fae who can wield enough magic to control pockets of the monsters. Others they war with and beat them back. If demons actually open a portal between the worlds, we'd be quickly overrun. There aren't enough of us, even with the handful of fae mages, and even fewer Noble Onari, to keep them back for long."

Yuri thought about the fae who'd brought him here. "There was a woman who found me. The Master called her Sono. She is fae?"

"Yes, Sono is one of Master's generals. She was high court Sidhe."

"And all the vampires that he leads? They are Onari?" Yuri wondered. "They differ greatly from the Master. Giants in armor?"

"Onari, yes. Not the Noble Onari like the Master. Nobles have magic."

"Those giant soldiers don't?"

"Not like the Nobles. The general population of Onari is much like the legends of vampires recorded in mortal books. They feed on blood and can't walk in the sun. The Nobles don't have those restrictions. Next time we land some place with sunlight, you'll see."

There were places that still saw the sun? Yuri could barely remember what it looked like anymore. Would it hurt his eyes? Burn his skin? Was it too much to hope he'd ever experience it again? "What about the things that eat people? They don't wear armor. They look like demons." Sort of bug-like sometimes. Cockroaches on steroids, with giant eyes and lots of legs that ended in spear-sharp tips.

"Species from another world. Some of the fae, like Sono, can call them and control them for a while. You won't find the unruly hordes in the castle. We've never even been besieged. The Master's magic protects it." Theo paused, though his fingers kept dancing lightly over Yuri's skin. It was a gentle distraction. "Most of the house is warded. Don't wander. Especially not beyond the large double doors. We could lose you forever in parts of the castle we don't even know exist. Pieces of other worlds stuck within these walls. Portals perhaps? Those who wander in search of other ways home become lost themselves. Never to be seen again."

Yuri recalled the giant door the Master had led him through. Was that the one Theo meant? Everything beyond that door had been almost normal, before it had been chaos.

The door to Yuri's room burst open. The blond man from the siege at Yuri's camp stood there, looking angry and ready to fight. Yuri shoved Theo behind him, readying for an attack, but the man lingered in the doorway. He was physically smaller than the Master, but his presence preceded him, an edge of doom clinging around him like an aura of dark despair. It wasn't the too much power of the Master, but a sizzling taste of something similar. A bite of chocolate so dark it was bitter. That glow of energy surrounded him, much as Yuri had seen with Star and the Master.

Was this man another Noble Onari? Yuri's gut clenched in hunger, as though something about this man made him desire to devour him. What a crazy thought that was?

The man was beautiful, and breathlessly handsome with hair a pale golden brown, brushing his shoulders and cascading down his back several inches, face clean-shaven, oval, and defined. He had an icy blue gaze that snapped with anger, and yet swirled with confusion, reminding him of Star's rainbow encircled, sky-blue eyes. Not ethereal like Theo, nor the imposing dark beauty of Radu, this man looked like he could be the mortal adaption of an angel. Perhaps part angel? Was it possible to blend beings from other worlds? The Onari and the seraphim? If an archangel created the Onari, did that make them angels too?

Hope and Indifference

The auras Yuri saw meant something not human. No one in the camp had ever had an aura. But in the past day, since the course of his life had again been interrupted, he'd noticed a dozen different waves of rippling color.

Radu, the Master, had been reds and oranges, not unlike fire. This blond man wasn't a vampire, or at least Yuri didn't think he was, as his aura wriggled with only the barest flicker of the Master's, and not at all the same as the warriors or the fae mage, Sono. But Yuri didn't know how to decipher the dark wash of blues, greens, and purples swirling around him like a film on the fritz. It almost looked like a bruise. Soul damaged? Sadness? Or some type of magic he had yet to discover?

Yuri's stomach growled. He flushed, embarrassed by the sound. "I'm sorry," Yuri apologized again. "I've not been this hungry in a while."

"You're healing. Onari blood is filled with magic. It's necessary for the bond, extending mortal life and offering resilience." Theo kissed the back of Yuri's neck and stroked his hair.

"Did you need something, Lucian?" Theo asked.

"I came to escort the *touched* to get food." The man, Lucian, said.

"He should rest," Theo protested.

"He needs food to continue his healing. Have you forgotten how delicate humans are?"

"Have you?" Theo threw back.

"I am half human. I think I understand their intricacies better than you. How many centuries since you had a ward to guard?" Lucian demanded, his expression turning neutral. "Can you walk, human?"

Yuri was torn. He wanted to stay with Theo, but as the last sensations of the castle settling faded, so had his nausea, leaving him starving. "Real food? I won't have to eat blood or anything?"

"Actual food," Lucian agreed. "I partake regularly, though I don't need it as much as you do. The Onari feed in other ways, and I am more Onari than human."

Did he mean blood? Yuri tried not to think about what the vampires ate as he examined Theo's face. Was Lucian safe? Theo had his arms wrapped tightly around Yuri but didn't look afraid. "Theo?"

Theo sighed and turned to plant a gentle kiss on Yuri's cheek. "You need food. We don't have any here and the servants don't respond to us."

Lucian leaned against the doorframe. "The servants don't see the seraphim. Most are mortals, though not human, and not lucky enough to be *touched*. You'd have to find your way to the dining hall and hope you don't get lost on your own."

"I have to go beyond the double doors?" Yuri asked.

"We can leave here," Theo said.

"And chance drawing the shadows into the main part of the house," Lucian agreed. "They love devouring the souls of angels. Perhaps if your brethren hadn't abandoned you millennia ago, you'd have more than a tiny pocket of my uncle's house in which to hide."

There were shadows in the house that devoured angels? Yuri frowned. What could that be if not demons? The excitement over this new world faded with the more terrors he heard.

"I will bring him to the others. Regis will feed him there," Theo defended.

"Not outside of regular mealtime," Lucian corrected. "Regis does not make special accommodations for the humans. Even the *touched* ones."

Yuri struggled to his feet, drawn by the allure of food, but also afraid. "Shadows that devour angels are in the house?" He thought the Master controlled them, or at least the fae magic that was supposed to protect the house.

"It's rare," Theo said.

"Happens sometimes after a move," Lucian offered, looking bored. "New pieces added to the estate sometimes come with pests attached. Do you wish to eat or not? The blood of the Onari can only heal so much."

A shadow that could devour angels was only a pest to the Onari? How powerful were these creatures? Yuri took a deep breath and glanced at Theo. "I would like to eat."

"The seraphim never really go as far as the dining hall," Lucian stared at Theo. "You're welcome to come if you'd like," he shrugged.

Theo vibrated with tension. Fear?

"You don't have to come with," Yuri said, releasing his hold on Theo. He felt stronger, like he'd had some rest, but the ache in his gut, carved out from years of not having proper nutrition, echoed with pain he couldn't ever recall feeling.

Lucian smelled divine, which was still strange. Was it

because he was half human? Yuri couldn't recall smelling anyone before and thinking about food. But Lucian's scent danced of cake, sweet icing and a delicate lemon and strawberry sponge. Yuri's mouth watered as the memory of the flavors returned with a visceral clamping of his stomach. Was it because he'd had the Master's blood?

"I will deliver him to the library once he's eaten. The others can show him where to begin. Since he's here to be useful and all that." Lucian waved a dismissive hand like he didn't think Yuri would be useful.

"Lucian could bring you food," Theo whispered.

"Lucian is not a servant," Lucian said of himself. "I merely offer to show the mortal to the dining hall since I'm headed that way myself."

"Keep him safe," Theo demanded.

Lucian shrugged and turned away, like he couldn't be bothered. Yuri cast one last longing glance at Theo, then hurried after Lucian and the promise of food.

A MOVING CASTLE'S CHAOS

"The Master is your uncle?" Yuri asked as he followed Lucian out of the room and down the hall to the flight of stairs.

"Your Master is my uncle, yes. You'd do best to learn to speak only when spoken to. Unless you have some vision of impending doom?" Lucian paused as if waiting for an answer. "I thought not."

"I don't know how this *touched* thing works," Yuri said. "Does everyone have visions? I dream sometimes, and sense things before they happen, but I can't say that it's ever been a vision as I would picture it written in a book might be."

"Some of the more useful ones have visions."

Yuri trailed close through the long, maze-like halls until they reached the giant double doors. His stomach flipped over with worry. Would he be able to find his way back if something went wrong? Beyond this door, knowing shadows ate angel souls sounded terrifying. He had walked through it before, unaware danger lurked, or even noticing anything unusual. If a soul eating shadow wasn't a demon, what was it? Would a human like Yuri interest it at all, or was his soul too weak?

The doors opened as they approached without touch or command, but they groaned as the heavy weight of them parted. "The doors remain sealed most of the time. After a move, this area of the castle turns wild," Lucian said, "unpredictable and dangerous."

Yuri followed him through the doors to find the wide entry area a living thing of writhing staircases, doorways, and halls, undulating as though it was a snake. "Holy fuck..." Yuri muttered.

The hall they stood in pulsed like a heartbeat, making him dizzy as he could feel the life in it. Or something. Maybe it wasn't the same life force as a human, but the castle seemed to be some sort of sentient being. He didn't realize he'd frozen in place until Lucian noisily cleared his throat, sounding more than a little annoyed.

"This is not a place to linger."

"Sorry," Yuri said as he hurried to follow Lucian's impatient steps down the hall. "Does anyone know where all the paths go?"

"No, and many shift after a move. There is always someone who goes missing, never to be seen again." Lucian shrugged. "Explore, if you wish. Don't expect anyone to go searching for you."

Yuri sucked in a deep breath and focused on following Lucian closely. It was clear the man didn't like him. Personal, or simply because Yuri was human?

Another dozen halls passed, all looking impossibly similar, and yet Lucian's step didn't slow or falter. Finally, they entered a giant kitchen, the space cavernous with a mass of various types of stoves and fireplaces, counters and cabinets, and the scent of food. Yuri's stomach flipped over with nausea, the mere smell of baking bread making him want to vomit. Was there something wrong with it, or was it because it had been too long since he'd eaten anything more than water weeds?

The room bustled with activity from creatures cooking and cleaning. They didn't look human at all, more like gnomes of legend, smaller with bark-like skin, giant noses and bulbous heads. Yuri tried not to stare. He had often felt like he'd stepped out of reality and into some novel, and the more creatures he experienced, he wondered if the novels he had read were filled with kernels of the truth, embedded in fiction to hide their peculiarity.

Everything stopped. All the creatures turned to stare at Lucian and Yuri. Yuri swallowed hard and took an unconscious step behind Lucian. He hugged himself hard, a chill reaching into his bones despite the raging fire only several feet away. Was any of this real? Or was he perhaps locked in some strange coma-induced dream while he waited for the end to come?

It felt real. The floor at his feet, the scent of baking bread, the bubbling of some sort of soup and the prickling touch of ice giving rise to goosebumps on his skin.

"Food," Lucian said. He made his way to a large counter area with chairs. "For myself and the mortal. Stew and bread are fine."

The group startled back to movement like a game coming back to life. They raced around each other, retrieving bowls and utensils, and filled them with food. Yuri sat down beside Lucian, watching the creatures warily. They didn't speak or even more than glance his way.

He watched them drag a fresh loaf of bread from a large stone oven and winced at the smell. The yeasty scent of it making his stomach turn and cramp. It smelled as he remembered, unmistakable even after years of its absence, and it appeared fresh, steam rising from the warm loaf. A creature set a bowl and a plate down in front of him. The sizable chunk of bread, soft and fluffy, a thick pat of butter added to the top, which quickly melted into the sponge.

Yuri lifted the spoon and stirred the contents of the bowl, examining the soupy chunks and worrying at his lower lip. Was it only the bread that made his stomach churn, or the idea of food? The stew smelled meaty, but it had been years since he'd had anything close to this. "What is in it?" Yuri asked hesitantly. Would they snipe and berate him for daring to ask? A starving man shouldn't care, right? And he was starving, but also badly nauseous and dreaded taking a bite.

"Root vegetables in broth," Lucian answered. "Nothing nefarious."

"Is there meat?" Like people? He didn't ask the last part, but the idea stuck in his mind, having spent the last decade watching monsters devour humans outside the walls of the compound.

"They make the broth from animal tallow," Lucian said. He dug his spoon in the bowl and lifted it to eat. He shrugged. "No meat. It's broth and vegetables."

Still Yuri hesitated. Was Lucian trustworthy? The man ate with gusto but didn't seem to care what the soup's taste or texture was. Did he need the food at all, or was this some sort of elaborate game to torment Yuri?

Yuri lifted the spoon and took a small taste of the broth. It was salty, but mostly flavorless, not unlike the watery weeds Yuri had survived on for the past decade. He tried a cream-colored chunk that looked like a potato. Nothing. Bland mush for texture, with a bit of salt, but nothing else. Was it purposefully bland?

"The Master is your uncle. Does that mean Vlad Tepes is your father?" Yuri asked, trying to find something else to focus on as he picked at the stew.

"He is. As unfortunate as that may be."

"You don't get along?"

"My father has let himself drown in grief. His pain saturates the landscape of everything surrounding him."

Yuri frowned. "That sounds terrible. And sad. He grieves your mother?"

Lucian's look was scalding. "Yes." The short tone told Yuri not to press that topic further.

"Your father has a garden of corpses?" Yuri asked. His mind going back to that as he stared at the soup and wondered at the disconnect between what he saw and the complete lack of flavor. "Some not truly dead?"

"My father has many quirks."

"It's not near here, right?" He stared at the soup again, wondering if they grew the food supply in a field of decaying corpses. "Attached to the castle?"

"No. He is across the veil in the world of the Onari. The brownies cultivate the food supply in lands attached to Radu's power." Lucian's gaze narrowed on Yuri. "Do not waste their efforts. It is difficult to grow any food when we cross into your world. Mortals spent so much time destroying the environment, the conditions are less than optimal. Were it not for my uncle's magic creating a barrier, you would likely starve. As long as the gardens don't get replaced with some useless mortal dwelling, like a museum—we have three attached now—our supply will last for years. Mortals collect strange things. Bowls, weapons, clothing, corpses, and lock them in glass cages. Do you fear the dead returning for them, or something else?"

Yuri choked at the idea of ghosts coming back for their artifacts. Was that possible in this crazy, broken existence of theirs?

"Not all that unlike my father's garden of corpses, many a mortal waged war on its own kind and slaughtered any who approached. My father simply warns anyone away from his space as to not taint them with the weight of his grief. Think of it as a kindness." Lucian finished his stew, sopping up the last dregs with the bread.

Yuri ate slower, each bite sinking into his stomach like a rock. "This food can sustain mortals?" He asked. Was food grown by brownies normal food? Weren't brownies a type of fae? Did that mean the food was magic? "Is it magic?"

"Magic food?" Lucian asked. He handed his empty plates off to a brownie. "Is that a thing in your world?"

"In stories," Yuri agreed. "The fae would trap people by tempting them with delicious treats, then enslave them to their will for eternity. Once a mortal ate the food, they could never leave the fae mound."

"Fascinating," Lucian said. "The mortals fear a lot of unusual things. The world of the fae was closed before I was born. I will have to ask Sono if the stories hold any truth. I wonder what tales she'll tell. The fae are tight-lipped, but I can't imagine that mortals have much use to fae, weak creatures that humans are. Fae magic rivals only the Onari, and our peoples were allies long before the Fractures began. Onari love the flavor of fae, and the fae adore anything that is pretty. The noble class of Onari is renowned for its beauty."

"Onari eat fae?" Yuri tried to make sense of that. Did fae bleed the same? "Blood?"

"Rarely," Lucian said, annoyed. He waved his hand at Yuri's food. "Eat. There is no magic other than it grew in a magic moving castle. Take that for what you will. Plenty of mortals in the palace eat it, and you are already a slave to my uncle, bound to him until he releases you from your contract or you die."

Yuri swallowed hard, understanding in that moment how right Lucian was. The blood bond decorated his skin in lines, and Yuri didn't think for one minute he could step outside the castle and run free. He'd accepted it willingly. A lamb to the slaughter? His malnourished brain trying to give him hope even when his only choices were slavery or death?

He stared down at the bowl, hoping the bland food would at least fill his stomach. It would be a terrible burden to survive, but never fill the aching hunger that had plagued him for years. Yuri dug into the stew and bread, swallowing down the flavorless textures and trying not to think too hard about them. He didn't feel less hungry, and it sat like a weight in his gut. He frowned at the bowl. Maybe it was the bond that made everything flavorless? Had the Master's blood changed him somehow? The Master denied it would make Yuri a vampire, but was Yuri human anymore, or something else?

A brownie held out a hand to take away the empty dishes and Yuri passed them over, flushing as the creature gazed at him. In fact, they were all staring at him as though he were an anomaly.

Lucian rose from his seat and motioned for Yuri to follow. "I will escort you to the other mortals. They are usually in the library at this time of day."

"That's what I'm here for, right?" Yuri asked as he got up. "To help study books?"

Lucian shrugged. "My uncle has many uses for mortals."

They made their way back to the hall. Anxiety rose in Yuri's gut alongside the heavy weight of the food he'd eaten, which didn't move and sat uncomfortably weighty. The edge of fear, a rippling vibration that began at the base of his spine, was familiar, common almost in the world since the Fracture had landed. Usually, it meant something dangerous was nearby, demons, monsters, whatever they were, coming close enough for Yuri to sense them. Was there something in the castle? He paused outside the kitchen, waiting and sensing like he knew how to decipher the wriggling unease.

"What are you waiting for?" Lucian snapped from the end of the first hall. "I don't have all day to play host."

Yuri clenched his fists and rushed to follow, fighting through the pain of anxiety that narrowed his vision. The sensation was like static pinching his skin and intensified as they walked. A few hallways of turns and twists, Yuri feeling helplessly lost after the first three, as they all looked the same. He tried to keep close to Lucian, but the ache in his gut turned sharp. Maybe he shouldn't have eaten actual food. Years with nothing more than watery weeds probably left his body unable to process the actual food. He'd been desperately hungry and forgotten that.

He wrapped his arms around himself in a tight hug and slunk after Lucian. Twice, movement caught his eye, making him pause and look. Each time he found nothing, and his vision swam a little from the tide of anxiety and the rolling pain, but he didn't think it was all in his head.

Lucian vanished around the corner ahead, and a prickle of icy terror ran down Yuri's spine. He raced around the corner, swallowing back bile as he fought the urge to throw up, looking for Lucian.

The hall was empty.

Yuri's stomach flipped over in fear, forcing him to double up and fight to keep conscious. Where had Lucian gone? There was only one hall?

He stumbled forward, smashing into the wall a few times on the way and turning to find another empty hall, then a room beyond with a half dozen doors. Yuri stared in horror at the options, his heart pounding in terror at having to decide. What if the doors led to some closed off world? Or a monster waiting to eat him? Which way could Lucian have gone? Yuri didn't recall coming through a room with these many doors. Was it part of the castle's shifting construction?

A shadow slid across the edge of Yuri's vision. He whipped to the right, trying to track it, hoping it was Lucian, but found a well of pooling darkness forming in the doorway behind him. The inky blackness oozed from the floors, walls and ceiling, eating up all color and light, like a void of oil devouring the castle drip by thick drip.

Yuri sucked in a stuttering breath, half choking on the air as he stumbled backwards. "Lucian?" He called, praying the man would hear him and return.

Yuri's gut cramped hard. A growl of something inhuman rippled from it as though he had an alien inside him. He blinked, gripping his stomach, vision spinning, and feet unsteady. His back hit the wall between doorways, and he didn't know which way to go. How did anyone navigate a magic castle?

The mass of black pooling shadows continued to grow, reaching across the distance like an ooze of liquid, spreading across the floor, reaching for Yuri. What was it Lucian had said about the shadows? They loved devouring the souls of angels.

Shadows *devoured* souls of angels. What would they do to Yuri? He turned and ran, not debating doorways, but taking the opening closest to him. He could still feel the darkness surging behind him, reaching for him as he raced down corridor after corridor, forced to follow sharp turns and entry-less halls. A dozen or more and his heart raced, his stomach cramping with brutal pain. He turned another corner, praying for freedom or at least something familiar, only to be met with a dead end.

He slammed into the wall, and turned, breath coming in pants, his entire body aching as the pain in his gut expanded. Maybe he shouldn't have eaten. He probably should have stayed with Theo. His heart hammered in his chest as he slid to the ground, back to the wall, staring at the oncoming shadows.

The dark mass ate up the distance of the hall, leaving him no way back, and without a way forward. He was dead, right? His soul about to be eaten by this shadow of unknown origins? Maybe it wouldn't want him, since he wasn't one of the seraphim.

He wondered what it meant to have one's soul eaten. A true and permanent death? No afterlife perhaps? Or cast into hell? He shivered at the thought.

He curled his knees up into his chest, wondering where his resolve had gone. When the monsters attacked the compound, he'd been willing to stare into the face of death. Now he didn't want to see. The pulsing pain of hunger beat with the rhythm of a drum in his stomach, echoing through every pore of his body. He hadn't hurt this badly ever. Even a decade of near starvation had never escalated to this level of agony. Was it part of healing? Food that didn't agree with him? Or something else?

Yuri buried his face in his knees, feeling a furious rush of tears on his face as the inky pool of black shadows surged across the empty hall and touched the tip of his sandal. Slowly it slid a cold and greasy grip over Yuri's toe, feeling strange, heavy, and hollow at the same time. He gasped at the icy chill and curled into a tighter ball as if to ward off the attack.

For a few seconds, images flashed through his mind dimming the surrounding room, like memories startled back into place, though they were things Yuri had never experienced in his brief life. A battle over a vast and unfamiliar landscape, bodies and blood strewn everywhere, the stench of burning flesh, guts ripped open, a familiar stink of perforated bowels, old blood, and unwashed people. Shadows arched across the sprawl of bodies, the abyss of darkness devouring the dead, but not the smell. Yuri's heart slowed like the black nightmare was devouring him, too.

A shadow moved, sliding over him, not with a dark ooze, but a subtle blocking of the light. He stared upward, finding a giant of a man, a thick helmet blocking most of his face, massive muscled shoulders expanding for days, blocking out everything else beyond the size and breadth of the man. Although the swirling blue eyes edged in rainbows frequented Yuri's dreams.

"Star?" Yuri said, though no sound came from his lips. He felt himself choking on his own blood, the dimming of the world around him and a rattling echo from his lungs speaking of pain and oncoming death. Had Star hurt him? He tried to reach through the dream, raise a hand or make a sound, but his lungs stopped working, and suddenly he was starving for air, frozen in the final few seconds before death.

Star leaned in close, blood covered fingers caressing Yuri's face. "Rest, Love. I will continue this fight in your place." Darkness swallowed Yuri's sight, leaving him only with the memory of Star's swirling eyes and a ghost-like touch.

"This is no place to linger," an impatient voice snapped.

Yuri jolted, air filling his lungs painfully fast, and he coughed. His vision reformed in pops of color as he blinked the world into focus. Lucian hovered over him.

"What are you doing?" Lucian demanded.

Yuri glanced both ways down the hall that hadn't been there before. The shadow gone, though his heart pumped painfully fast, overworked and aching. His stomach still churned and cramped, threatening to force up what he'd eaten. He met Lucian's gaze with what was probably wide-eyed horror. "There was a shadow..."

Lucian frowned and folded his arms over his chest. "There are no shadows in this part of the castle."

"I was lost," Yuri said.

"You've been behind me the whole time," Lucian said. "Let's go. I have better things to do than play with my uncle's pets." He turned and headed down the hall.

Yuri clutched the wall to get to his feet, stumbling after Lucian, and keeping close enough to touch. Hot tears ran down his face, stomach gurgling in threatening rage, and nerves tingling, Yuri wondered at what he'd seen. Had that been Star? He'd been huge, like a vampire warrior rather than the lithe male Yuri remembered. And had Yuri died? Why didn't anything make sense anymore?

He swayed, sliding along the wall to keep upright, but Lucian didn't slow or look back. The lingering chill of cold Yuri had become used to returned. The benefits of the bath and nap fading beneath a sense of rising unease. He wondered again if all this was a dream, and he was slowly dying, unable to wake from a coma. That made more sense than a moving castle, pretty vampire lords, and the touch of angels.

He sniffled back tears. He was dying. That was okay, right? He'd wanted it for a while, an end to all the pain. Yuri wished it didn't hurt so much, and that the dream would end, leaving him without confusing and anxious memories before plunging him into the void he'd always prayed one day to find.

Yuri followed Lucian with sluggish steps. His gut screaming in agony, and brain a swirling mess of emotions. If it was a dream, it would all end eventually.

Perhaps this was hell. That made him pause.

Not a dream, but death and hell. Pain, hunger, fear, loneliness, those were promises of the damned, weren't they? Was this hell? Yuri wondered what he'd done to deserve hell. He had killed a man, and not been obedient to the Leader, and he'd spent a night in the heaven of Star's embrace. Was that enough to send him into eternal torment?

Was all that a lie? The descriptions of fire, rivers of the dead, and demons to tear him apart? Was it endless cold, hunger, and fear, instead? Yuri didn't know which would be worse. He couldn't help the tears falling down his cheeks as he followed Lucian in a dozen more turns and halls. Every step hurt, each breath adding to the agony in his gut. He fell into the drag of Lucian's shadow, pulled like a magnet, moving only because stopping meant he failed.

Lucian opened a door, and the library stretched beyond it, a massive thing of multiple floors and possibly millions of books. Yuri shuffled forward into an entry to the library, wondering at how many books it could hold, wishing he didn't feel like he was dying and could actually enjoy the beauty of the space.

Heads popped around corners, movement filling the space as people emerged. Gasps from a dozen directions. Humans? They made their way through the stacks as though drawn by Yuri's presence. He heard a half-dozen languages spoken, a mash of brief phrases he could remember from awe to disbelief.

He took a step forward, reaching for the distant railing to steady himself, but his stomach finally had enough. The bowling ball of weight within expanded beyond excruciating pain. He doubled over, losing the fight to vomit. He dropped to his knees and retched, unable to stop his body from convulsing to force everything up. Bursts of color filled his vision. The violent rejection of the food, brutal.

People surrounded him. Touched him and he couldn't help but flinch away as their touch felt like needles on his skin. He couldn't stop throwing up, even as the last of the black sludge stopped flowing, leaving him with nothing but dry heaves.

"Stop touching him," Lucian demanded.

Yuri heard all those voices around him muttering things like *beautiful* and *divine*. How was this pain beautiful? He felt like he was coming apart in a thousand pieces, his vision darkening as the wall of faces closed in around him, making him claustrophobic. But his vision dimmed to darkness, blessed unconsciousness finally ripping away the pain.

INSATIABLE HUNGER AWAKENS

"None of this is normal," an impatient voice snapped. "Keep his face covered."

Yuri woke to voices arguing. A hot rippling of energy contorted around him, and someone pressed fabric over his face. He struggled to breathe for a few seconds, adapting to the weight of it, though it didn't restrict his airflow.

The room pulsed with emotion. His skin prickling with magic of varied flavors. Yuri could almost taste them like long, faded memories of cakes he'd once mastered. How did magic taste like dessert?

He sucked in large gulps of air as a cool compress slid over his face and bare chest.

"Keep him covered," the impatient voice said again.

Yuri's skin burned hot like lava but tingling with cold needles embedded deep. A contrast of pain. He shook with seizure-strength tremors, uncontrolled. His gut was hollow, still clenched with a ghost-like need to expel anything that might linger. He was so hungry, but the thought of food made him swallow back more pain.

"None of the others were ill like this after a bond. I've never had to peel humans off of another mortal before. Was there something in the food?"

"I ate the food and was fine," Lucian said. His voice irritated as it had been the entire time Yuri had suffered through the castle. "Perhaps he was too ill to be saved. They starved him a long time."

"Others have come from worse, and that does not explain the human's drawn to touch him. They were willing to fight each other to get close." Yuri recognized the deep tone of the Master's voice. He and Lucian were across the room, their power sizzling with intensity. Colors flashed across Yuri's closed eyelids, too bright to ignore, and Yuri's body reacted, his cock going hard, and his hips bucking upward, demanding to be touched, while his stomach growled with hunger. The sound of the Master's voice, and the sheer weight of his power, making Yuri crave him like he was the most decadent cake.

He recalled the night he'd spent with Star, and how his desire had been insatiable. This was a thousand times that intensified, perhaps because he had been touch starved? That deep voice demanding he obey, giving him chills and desire all at once.

"The brother mentioned it happened before," the Master said. "He always wore a mask because monsters were drawn to him. I thought he was being fractious."

"He has been unmasked his entire time here," Lucian said.

"And you're drawn to him as well," the Master remarked.

"I'm not."

"Lies," the Master snapped in obvious irritation.

Yuri trembled with the heat in the Master's tone, wanting to reach out and snatch it up like a thick piece of chocolate sponge cake. Vivid images of how he wanted to bathe in the Master's skin ran through his brain.

A soft hand caressed Yuri's back in gentle circles. The touch stirred something in Yuri's stomach. A strange feeling of longing filled him. Like he could take the warmth and comfort to ease the pulsing ache of hunger. The hands paused, touch ripping away. Yuri made a small noise of protest.

"Yuri?" Theo whispered.

"What happened in the hall?" the Master demanded. "Why did you take him through the castle at all? You could have left him with the others and summoned Regis."

"Why hide him away? It's part of his contract to help fix the castle. Shouldn't he see it for what it is?"

"You put him in danger for petty reasons."

"Petty? I'm not the one treating them like coddled pets. They are slaves. Their entire existence spent tearing apart their own world. It's why we no longer let them rule. Use them, fix the rifts before the mortal's greed destroys us all." Lucian's rage rippled hot and biting through the space. The intense heat made Yuri's stomach growl, and he jolted, reaching for the warmth, not a physical action, but something within that yanked on the fire, swallowing down emotion like it was hot chocolate, thick and decadent, to thaw the chill in his gut.

The voices stopped.

Yuri's vision clarified, bringing the surrounding room to life, the bedroom, lights on, space cavernous, his new temporary prison. Theo sat beside him, close enough to touch, but hands clenched against his chest as if he was fighting to keep himself from reaching for Yuri, his expression apprehensive. The Master and Lucian lingered near the doorway, tension between them snapping hot as lava. They were breathtakingly beautiful, a contrast of dark and light, the heavy weight of their emotions giving Yuri a gut clenching desire to eat that he gasped. Did he want to eat them? How was that possible?

The two males stared at him with confused expressions.

"That was..." the Master began.

"It's not possible. He's mortal," Lucian said, hugging himself and taking a step back.

"He needs to feed," Theo said as he scooted toward the edge of the bed. "Like an Onari Noble would." He let out a long breath, his expression sad. "I'm sorry, Yuri."

What did that mean? Theo slid off the bed. He stood at the edge, swaying gently, and clenched his hands into fists.

"You're dismissed, Theodorus," the Master said. "Keep the others away."

"I'm sorry," Theo said again as he bolted for the door.

The Master took a step across the room, slid off his jacket, and dropped it on a chair beside the door. "This should be your responsibility," he said to Lucian.

Yuri salivated as the Master's solid build blocked his view of the other man behind him. Without the coat, the clothing fit like a glove, defining his muscled form, wide shoulders, narrow waist, and long legs. The Master unbuttoned his shirt and kicked off his shoes. It wasn't really a striptease, though Yuri's body reacted as though it were, his cock throbbing, skin screaming with need to be touched, and the writhing hunger in his gut latching onto a wave of desire sent his way. He swallowed the emotion like it was a bowl of sweetened vanilla cream, but it only gave him a few seconds of reprieve.

"Hungry," Yuri whispered, his eyes locked on the Master's defined shoulders as the male shrugged off his shirt.

"He's not Onari," Lucian said from somewhere behind the Master. "He's human."

INSATIABLE HUNGER AWAKENS

"As are you," the Master said. "Leave. Before I make you his first meal. The young are ravenous. Would you survive?"

"I'm not weak," Lucian snapped.

"Out," the Master demanded, blocking everything out of Yuri's vision but him. He was breathtaking, and Yuri struggled to breathe as he desired things he couldn't recall ever wanting before. The scent of the Master shifted, and Yuri closed his eyes to suck in the smell, spreading the comfort of it around him. Indulgent and thick, the faded memory of dark chocolate tickled Yuri's memory. The emotion tied to the flavor felt warm, and it took Yuri a few moments to define it as lust.

When Yuri opened his eyes, the Master leaned over him, bare chested, muscles thick and strong, skin smooth and hot, with a dusting of dark hair. Yuri longed to lick the man, and trace not only the outline of his body, but the flavor of the desire wafting off of him. His erection leaked, body tightening with need, skin begging for touch, he trembled, reaching for the Master.

The Master tugged the fabric away from Yuri's face, gaze hot, and slid his fingertips over Yuri's lips like a kiss, and Yuri wanted that. He gasped at the intensity of that look, and the Master glided his fingers over Yuri's cheek, cupping his face. "You're lovely and will be more so once completely awakened."

Yuri didn't understand what he meant. The Master climbed onto the bed, crawling across the distance to straddle Yuri's body. He unsnapped the button of his pants, and Yuri couldn't rip his gaze from all that flesh.

"I don't understand what's happening to me," Yuri said, unable to look at the Master's face. He wasn't supposed to anyway, right? All that skin and the need to explore it, touch it, taste it, made his brain fall offline. He'd wanted nothing in that moment as bad as the taste of the Master's body beneath his lips. Even his brief adoration of Star hadn't burned this badly. He couldn't stop himself from pressing his mouth to the right pec, only inches from his face. The flesh beneath his lips and tongue burned hot and tasted sweet as salted honey. Each touch blazed with magic. Something within Yuri leeched onto it and sucked it down, begging for more.

The Master gasped. "Ravenous. Where do you come from, sweet Yuri?" The Master shoved off his pants and reached for Yuri's. Yuri swallowed hard at the sight of that giant, thick cock, leaking with precome and begging to be touched. He never wanted to taste something so badly.

"Master?" Yuri begged, uncertain what he really wanted, all the while needing everything he had ever dreamed of happening with Star a thousand times over.

The Master tugged Yuri free of the confines of clothing and traced his large hands over Yuri's hot flesh. The caress was part fire and ice all at once. Yuri shook with the intensity of the need, his cock harder than he could ever remember it being, and his brain locked into focus on nothing more than the rising demands of his body.

"Let me help you," the Master said with that deep and maddening growl. The tone was thick and coated like a wave of honey. It gave Yuri's brain a few seconds of clarity.

He gasped at the intensity of his need and worried at his lower lip, feeling strange for needing so much while unable to process why. "What? How? What is happening to me?"

The Master slid his hands down Yuri's sides, pausing at his hips and lifting him to press him back into the headboard and the mass of pillows. "You're awakening to magic," the Master said.

"I thought you said your blood wouldn't change me?"

The Master crawled forward, sprawling Yuri half over his

INSATIABLE HUNGER AWAKENS

lap, spreading Yuri's thighs and laying him open. Yuri ached with a pulsing need to be filled, both his stomach and his body, while his mind whirled with a thousand questions.

"You must be born with Onari blood to transition," the Master said, his lips finding Yuri's neck. "No amount of blood exchanges would make this happen without a tie to our people." The Master bent Yuri's legs, wrapping them around him, hands on Yuri's ass, sliding his warm fingers up Yuri's crease until the Master found Yuri's hole. A single finger circled the rim, teasing at first, then a slow pressure. "You're wet. We won't even need lube, more proof of what you are."

"What am I?" Yuri asked.

The Master pressed the tip of his cock to Yuri's entrance. "Mine, that is what you are, Yuri Wen. You have given yourself to me in blood." He held Yuri's hips and slid inside, adding fullness and heat to the fire in Yuri's blood. Yuri expected pain after years untouched by others but found only waves of rising pleasure. "Now in body, you'll be mine as well."

Yuri cried out, his hands gripping the Master's shoulders, hips pushing down to meet the first thrust with breathless need. His heart raced, and his skin burned with tingling magic waves of energy. The Master's huge length split Yuri wide, filling him deep and forcing the power inside, as well as the fluttering bolts of it dancing around his skin. He sucked in air as fast as he could, fearing he would pass out and still could not get enough.

"More," Yuri demanded as the Master pressed him into the headboard, grinding their hips together, Yuri's cock trapped beneath the scorching heat of their bodies. He drank down the tides of energy, body aching to drive the male deeper and devour him whole.

The Master thrust, grinding his enormous cock into Yuri's depths, his hands bruising in their grip on Yuri's hips, pressing

Yuri into each plunge. Together their skin glowed, waves of the Master's red-gold magic weaving with Yuri's pale white energy, brightening it until it became blinding. Yuri could only hold on for the ride as the sensations tore apart reason. Every touch left a trail of heat, arousing Yuri again and again. His cock pulsed with an aching near pain need, begging for release, yet not ready for any of this to end.

The Master kissed along Yuri's chest, up his throat, and along his jaw. The ice that had wrapped up the inside of Yuri's soul for the last decade thawed, heat chiseling away at it with power and desire. His heart raced, and he sucked in air, his body riding the Master's with a longing for it to never end.

"Master," Yuri sighed, wanting more and not knowing what he needed. The sensations were too much, endless, and not enough all at once. He drank down the vast waves of heat, body singing as the Master pounded into him in a rolling circle that hit Yuri's prostate with every third or fourth thrust. Enough to keep him on edge and drag him back without being the over stimulation that might deny him a release. "Please." He didn't know what he was asking for, not that it mattered. The Master's sweat-covered abs dragged against Yuri's throbbing dick as he moved and Yuri clung to the male, needing and wanting a last explosion of pleasure.

The power continued to build. Was this an awakening for Yuri? He sensed the edge of something lingering, like a pool of blazing lava continuing to rise. He worried he'd come apart with the final blow and marveled at the sheer intensity, blinding with sensation. The Master pressed Yuri back into the pillows, body grinding hard into Yuri's cavity, deep and filling. Yuri's ass clenched, trying to hold the Master deep, even as his body finally flew off that cliff into the spectacular dance of sparkling pleasure.

He couldn't contain his scream as his cock let loose streams of come he never thought possible, painting the Master in ribbons of white. Deep inside, heat filled Yuri, a physical liquid sensation that was first uncomfortable, and then blindingly hot as it, too, was charged with the magic his soul raced to devour.

He let himself fall boneless in the Master's arms, and the Master's teeth pierced Yuri's neck. It stung for a half second, adding to the rolling waves of pleasure that sent Yuri's body into orgasm over and over, despite his balls being empty with their come coating the Master's stomach and abs, his cock still jerked like it kept coming with ghostly spurts of jiz.

The Master gulped at this throat, sucking down barrels of blood and Yuri's vision wavered for a moment, fearing the Master would drain him dry. But for those few minutes he couldn't have cared, the pleasure overriding all common sense. He closed his eyes, wondering how this act had ripped apart everything he thought he knew of pleasure, even the night he'd had with Star. That had been divine and yet muted. A dream rather than reality? He hated the idea that Star was only a part of his imagination rather than a memory. With the Master's cock still buried deep inside, Yuri compared the now with his memories and feared it had all been a desperate dream to distract him while the world had ended. What if Star wasn't real?

But Yuri's heart ached. He couldn't stifle a sob that rose in his throat as he feared Star would be heartbroken by Yuri's betrayal. Star had instructed him to find safety among the Onari. Yuri didn't think this was what he meant.

The Master pulled away with a snarl. The waves of energy around Yuri rising to snapping pain instead of pleasure, like standing in the middle of an electrical storm, it buzzed on his skin. "Your blood is not Onari," the Master growled.

A wave of fear trembled through Yuri.

"What does that mean?" Yuri whispered, his entire body sizzling with the energy the Master unleashed, as though it were trying to absorb every ounce.

A barrier rose, shoving Yuri's draw of the energy away like a slap. His need fought back, shoving forward into the wall between them, even as Yuri clutched at the Master's arms, trying to use their physical connection to ease the snapping fire of hunger. Ravenous rage filled his gut, still an empty void even after sucking down barrels of magic from the Master. But there was so much more right there in front of him.

"Be calm," the Master whispered, kissing Yuri's hair. "Push back the wave of need, you can control this." He slid his cock out of Yuri's clenching hole, and Yuri cried out, fingers digging into the Master's arm to hold him in place.

"Please," Yuri begged. "Hungry."

"Breathe," the Master commanded, rewarding Yuri with a small wave of energy. Yuri devoured all of it and reached for more, only to find himself smacked away from it again, the wall between them back in place. "That's right," the Master said. "Submit."

The word stung. Yuri hated the idea of submitting to anyone after years of being under everyone's boot. Submission meant endless hunger, pain, and fear. He didn't want to submit. He wanted to fill his stomach with all that decadent flavor of energy, magic, whatever the fuck it was. It didn't matter. Only that he was starving, and right in front of him was the answer to his lifetime hunger.

The invisible shield between them tickled Yuri's senses, and if he looked through the side of his vision, he could see the ripple and catch the flavor of salted caramel. He mentally caressed the barrier, wondering if he could take that, too. His

INSATIABLE HUNGER AWAKENS

gut lurched with need and Yuri didn't realize he had moved a hand to touch the barrier until the thick and sticky sweet and salt flavor of it filled his aching stomach.

"Stop," the Master commanded, and tried to slap Yuri's magic away again. But the tug of energy feeding Yuri leeched onto that, too, sucking it down like a bowl of every food Yuri had missed in the last decade. "Stop," the Master demanded again, and this time the hit was hard, a severing of all that delicious energy.

Yuri snarled as his gut rolled over. His power, whatever it was, gone wild with need. It reached for the Master, demanding more, but met with resistance, and a wave of rage rose inside Yuri. The thing inside him denied and wanting to take. He pressed one hand to the Master's chest, as if to hold him there, but the magic inside him took control and pushed, sending a wallop of energy outward. The Master flew across the room, hit the wall with a thud, and slowly slid to the ground, expression stunned and quickly turning angry.

An explosion of magic swirled around them. Yuri was at a complete loss of control over the beast that rose from his raging hunger. Furniture lifted off the ground, floating for a half second before either smashing into the walls or exploding into a million pieces. Projectiles bombarded the Master with debris, as though Yuri's denied need had turned deadly.

Yuri gasped for air, his vision wavering as everything around pulsed with brutally bright colors and pops of heat to blind him. The Master blocked flying daggers of wood with magic, which Yuri's power would then grab onto to feed. But the Master kept severing that tie of magic, shoving Yuri back, and fighting the onslaught.

A dozen stake-like pieces of wood landed, driving deep and drawing both blood and a grunt of pain from the Master. He narrowed his eyes, the burgundy of them turning blazing red, like fire snapped within. He glared at Yuri and slowly rose to his feet, an untouchable barrier now between them, expanding to fill the room with a balloon of righteous anger. The floating furniture and debris tumbled, stripped of Yuri's power, and the Master shoved through the madness.

Yuri backed away in fear, grabbing a blanket as though he could wrap himself in a barrier of his own, but unable to control the writhing power and drawing hunger. "I'm sorry. I'm sorry," Yuri whimpered. "I don't know what's happening. I can't stop it..."

The Master pulled the daggers of wood from his flesh as he and his immense well of power moved through the room. The insane level of energy stole Yuri's breath, like the Master's massive abilities shoved all that raging hunger back inside Yuri, using Yuri as a bottle to be corked. That feeling of too much returned as the strength of Yuri's need floundered beneath the battle. The red/gold fire of the Master's magic drowned the white light of Yuri's power, and Yuri's vision darkened. He wondered if he was a flame to be snuffed out by this insane power. He recalled briefly that Theo told him the Master could move a castle. Powerful was an understatement. And Yuri prayed silently for a few seconds Star would come and rescue him from this nightmare.

A giant sword appeared in the Master's hand. Fire swirled around him, batting away the last pieces of debris and healing the Master's injuries instantly. The male's size increased, muscles massive, height towering over Yuri like an avenging angel in art might. The Master's skin glowed, a dark burgundy staining his flesh.

Yuri trembled with fear, his lungs aching with smoke and heat, the furnace of power shattering the last of the ice inside, and flooding his fading vision with rainbows. Was his power still trying to devour the Master? It was too much, the Master too strong, and Yuri too weak.

"*Foni captue*," the Master uttered in that achingly deep voice that made Yuri's cock jerk to life again.

The bonds etched into Yuri's skin burst to life, turning into chains, constricting and biting into flesh, binding him until blood flowed from a dozen wounds. He gasped and struggled, the heat of his blood pooling over his skin. The spell slammed him into the floor, bound up in chains that kept tightening until Yuri feared every bone would break. The Master reached out, hand larger and clawed more like a beast than a human, closed his fist and jerked it forward toward his chest.

The chains dragged Yuri to the Master's feet, leaving Yuri breathless, bleeding, and on the edge of blacking out. The Master towered over him, rage snapping, and face changed to give life to all the frightening stories of vampires. A beautiful monster, sword ready to slice Yuri to pieces and devour the waves of power circling through Yuri like a universe of chaos lived in his gut. The Master lifted his sword, and Yuri closed his eyes as it came down, darkness ripping him from consciousness as the blade pierced his chest.

INCUBUS DREAMS

Yuri awakens to dreams of Star and nightmares of rising magic power.

Bonded to the Master, Yuri discovers the magic inside him has grown a taste for power and lust.

The Master's attempts to satiate Yuri's rising hunger evolves into a whirlwind of need, a decade of starvation giving the magic a life of its own, making Yuri dangerous and unpredictable to all who surround him, including an angel who only wishes to protect Yuri.

To save the last remaining seraphim, Yuri is sent to Dracula to learn control.

Will he find salvation or madness with the Monster of Legends?

SOUL HUNGER

Darkness lasted a short time, but Yuri opened his eyes to the gentle touch of someone sliding a careful hand over his chest. He tensed, fearing it was the Master and that pain would follow, but when he opened his eyes, it was to find Star leaning over him. Yuri gasped, his heart leaping with joy and fear. Would Star know the Master had claimed him? Would it matter?

"Star..." Yuri whispered, unable to voice the millions of dreams and fears running through his brain.

Star leaned in and kissed Yuri's forehead. He was cold to the touch, more like ice than the raging heat of the Master. Yuri couldn't help his flinch.

"I didn't know," Star said. "Or I did. My soul recognizing yours. Seeking you without realizing it was you I had found." He let out a long breath, body draped over Yuri's, blocking out the rest of the world. "It's been so long. I thought you were gone forever. Lost to all worlds." He traced his fingertips over Yuri's face. "The light is buried, but not extinguished. Mine was only ever but a shadow of yours."

"What does that mean?" Yuri asked.

The rolling hunger rose again. Insatiable, but it didn't recognize Star as food at all. He frowned, staring at the beautiful man holding him. Was it a dream? Yuri made a pained sound, realizing it had to be. He couldn't feel more than a ghost of a sensation from Star's caress. He reached up, trying to run his fingers through Star's hair, but his hand went through the man. "Star," Yuri said, his heart flipping over with loss and sadness. Was this because Yuri had let the Master claim him?

Star bowed to press their foreheads together, and Yuri stared into those swirling rainbow-circled blue eyes. Like a day of blue skies after a vanishing rainstorm, they reminded Yuri of a long-ago time when he had hope.

"Please," Yuri begged.

"Soon," Star promised. "The veil is weakening."

What did that even mean? "Don't leave me," Yuri pleaded as Star faded and the world darkened again, threatening to take him back into the void. "I didn't mean to betray you..."

"Free your light, my love. I'm coming for you," Star said as unconsciousness stole Yuri from his arms once again.

Yuri drifted for a while, wishing for dreams, mind searching for Star, but rolling in a tide of an unruly ocean of darkness. The hunger took over for a time. Sometimes Yuri would taste chocolate, or vanilla cake, or the sour bite of lemon meringue, or a dozen other desserts he had once tried to master. Emotions, he realized, energy and life, as they all slid through him, filling his stomach or aura or soul, or whatever it was, seemed endlessly insatiable.

Occasionally a lull in the raging need of his hunger would settle him to calm of rest, and he'd dream for a short while, usually of baking, or of his mother, or even one of the many memories of books he'd read with sword fights and dragons would take shape. He knew they were dreams as they drifted by, faded movies of times long gone, unchangeable. He glimpsed memories of Star, some in ways he couldn't recall actually happening. Times when they came together in the flesh, or when Star looked at him in adoration. Those memories far removed, felt like snapshots, nearly emotionless, and each time Yuri reached for them, they vanished into the ether. Stripped of emotion and life, had they ever really happened? Yuri ached to feel everything attached to the rare glimpse into their past. Another existence, perhaps? There were other faces, most blurred and too vague to imprint inside his head.

Then another wave of emotions would rise to give his magic something to reach for, knocking him away from the memories and into a game of flavors, emotions and life force. He wasn't certain he understood any of it. Fear, he recognized, the thick flavor of butterscotch coating his tongue. He sucked on that for a time, letting it ease another round of devouring hunger. He savored it slowly, feeding the flavor into memories, searching for more snippets of Star, or another way to reach him. His heart ached at the thought of being alone again, like it had long been severed from the arteries feeding it the blood of life. Cold. Star had been cold. Cut off.

Yuri trembled.

A hint of peppermint startled him out of the dark for a time, then a smooth well of dark chocolate. The salted caramel of the Master trickled between the flavors, careful and limited, as if Yuri was being fed through a straw. He chased the taste several times but hit a wall and dropped back into the dark.

He'd awake again hungry, needing, body aching to be filled in a dozen ways, fed snippets, and plunged into the dark a dozen times, maybe even a hundred times. He lost count. For a time there seemed to be others who touched him, his body taking everything they offered, but those memories quickly faded into the dark beneath the rolling tide of magic dragged within. The well inside him filled, though endlessly ached for more.

The last trickle of butterscotch faded. Peppermint chocolate vanished beneath the fear that had seemed to ease the starving rage of his hunger. He opened his eyes, the weight of them finally lifting until he could blink into darkness. The surrounding light, a faint glow, made it look like he was in a stone cage? How was that possible?

He lay on his back, staring up at the rock, and focused on his breathing. For a few seconds, he thought he might fall back into the dark, but the cool air around him filled his lungs with clarity and the ease of his raging hunger to let him think. He could hear a heartbeat. Many actually. But they were distant, varied, like his brain could classify types. He could tell if some were human and many were *other*.

He was still alive. Had the sword piercing his heart been a dream? That felt real, not like the faded ghost caress of Star. Yuri recalled how the Master had changed. The pretty gentleman of Yuri's wet dreams turning into some sort of monster. Not really unexpected, Yuri realized, as he'd seen vampires before. The *Onari*, as Theo had said, perhaps the Master's original visage had been some sort of glamour? Yet Yuri had seen through Sono, the fae's glamour, easily enough. Wouldn't he have seen through the Master's?

The Master's form had been massive, claws, fangs, skin red and glowing like cooling lava. A demon? Was Yuri bound to a demon? How much of what any of them told him could he believe? Was the blood of the Master what changed him? Or had Star's touch changed him?

Yuri pushed himself up, moving slowly because his body

felt stiff, chilled, even while fire raced through his veins. He blinked to clear his vision to the space around, realizing he had to be in some sort of prison cell. Walls of impenetrable stone surrounded him on three sides, the last side, a wall of narrow bars flowing with magic.

He recalled feeling sick until he vomited food, and his skin turned to fire. Fever? No. He had changed, demanded sex from the Master. Writhed beneath the man's touch, and in that moment his body ached to be filled again. It was a strange, empty sensation of need, like he could never get enough. Yuri dropped to his knees and lowered his head to the floor, trying to breathe through the sudden rise in desire.

Yuri put his hand to his chest, pressing it over his heart as though he could will it to slow. He expected a wound as he vividly remembered the sword piercing his chest, but his skin was unblemished.

Yuri was nude, the stone floor chill against his skin, even while his flesh heated with need, his cock heavy between his thighs again. He reached down to touch himself, remembering the Master's touch, and the pleasure of being draped over the male's lap, the length of the male buried deep. Yuri gasped as his body reacted, coming that fast, the memory all he needed to erupt. Come painted his thighs and the floor, and he gasped for air like he'd run a marathon.

He pressed his forehead into the cold floor and sought clarity, any sort of focus beyond the amplified needs of his body. The hunger had eased a little, but the void demanding more magic seemed endless, like he could drop an entire world of power within that abyss and still not touch the volume required to quiet the gaping wound. It was almost as though someone had cut his soul out and released it to the bottom of the well.

Only filling the emptiness would reunite him with himself and quiet the anxiety of separation.

Yuri trembled, holding himself to the floor a while longer. The sexual heat of his body calmed the longer he stayed prone, his focus on breathing instead of the pulsing need between his thighs. He had been touch starved for over a decade, but the desire felt unquenchable. The magic in his bones fed him an overwhelming network of information. He could feel the area around him as if he had some sort of invisible hand to crawl the distance. Yuri could picture the walls, solid rock several feet thick, other cells with metal bars, not all enchanted with magic, spread around him for an enormous distance. The cell across from him was empty, void of life, but within something lay cold and not stone.

A body. Dead. Drained of all energy, life, being. Possibly even its soul. Had Yuri done that? He hissed in fear and withdrew his senses, crawling backward until his body found the farthest wall, and he had to stop, crouched, curled in on himself, afraid. What was wrong with him? His skin burned with heat, and the ice-cold stone did little to cool him. A trickle of life flickered from far away, alerting Yuri's magic to the flavor and he wanted to reach for it, devour the flavor, and savor it, even if it meant more sex with his body demanding to be taken over and over.

His heart flipped with worry. Thoughts of the Master's claim, and Star's adoration, a confusing mesh of emotion. Yuri could define emotions by the flavors of others around him, but his own mangled mind could barely clarify a single set feeling from the jumbled web of his thoughts. Fear? Need? Desire? Thinking of either male made him hard again. The worst game of whack-a-mole Yuri had ever thought to experience. He would shove down a memory of the Master's lips on his skin to find a vivid one of Star gripping his hair and feeding Yuri his cock.

He bowed over his knees, keeping his back to the wall and closed his eyes, tired, hungry, depressed, and body screaming with desire for things he'd never imagined before that moment, like the Master and Star taking him at the same time. One buried in his ass, the other between his lips. He shook with the ferocity of the need and forced himself to suck in large gulps of cool air.

Silence etched through the space, the heartbeats too far away to reach, and faint. No other sound or flavor reached him. Imprisoned and left to suffer, Yuri wondered how he got there. The lines of the bond were still etched into his skin, and he could recall them tightening into tearing thorns in his flesh, but his skin was unblemished and whole. In fact, gone were the emaciated limbs with outlines of bones stretched between underfed muscles. His hands and arms, even his thighs, had filled with healthy muscle to surround and support the bones beneath.

Yuri sat up and ran his hands over his body, confused by how it had changed, and still felt oddly familiar. Was it a trick of the light? He traced his ribs with his fingertips, searching for the bony protrusion he'd grown used to over the years, but lean muscle coated his frame. His stomach was flat and undefined, and he could trace the barest outline of his hipbones, but every part of him had somehow spurted lean muscle like the end of the world had never happened. Had the Master's bond done that? Or the strange feedings Yuri had fallen victim to?

A clack of footsteps from hard-soled shoes on stone made Yuri gasp. The sound familiar and made Yuri hard again as the memory of the Master and the bonding circle replayed in his head. He could imagine kneeling in that circle and begging the Master to take him.

An invisible hand of magic wrapped around him, careful, but strong. Yuri shuddered as he thought to rip that shield away and blast through the cage to fill the endless need. But the approaching footsteps reminded him of a growling command to "Calm."

His heartbeat echoed the steps, easing from a racing sprint to a slowed and sleepy pace as they grew closer. Yuri knew the flavor of salted caramel, even as the bits of it fed to him were little more than nibbles. He stared through the cell doors, no other movement around. Everyone was dead, he realized. Not only the one across from him, but all around. The void he felt when he touched them was a need to push them back into the earth to be renewed. Fodder. The dead were fuel for rebirth, even soulless death.

Yuri frowned at the thought. Where had that come from?

The Master approached the cell wall, easing free from the dark hall like he'd stepped through a magic veil. He appeared human-looking again, beautiful and regal, like a king. Yuri's body reacted to his nearness, and he folded his hands over his raging cock to hide the desire. The Master's expression an etch of neutrality, and he was alone. Yuri imagined the male entering his cell and how Yuri would reach up to free that fine cock and suck it down. He shivered.

"What's wrong with me?" Yuri whispered.

"Four dozen prisoners and still you hunger," the Master said, his deep voice bringing Yuri to the edge of orgasm again. Yuri curled himself into a ball as though he could stop his body's response. "You need to control this."

"I don't even know what's happening," Yuri said.

"Awakening to magic," the Master reminded him.

"Do all Onari desire like this?" Yuri asked. His ass clenched with a demand to be filled.

"You are not Onari."

"What am I?"

"I don't know," the Master admitted. He kept his distance from the bars and continued to give Yuri only sips of his salted caramel flavor. The teasing made Yuri crawl forward. The Master took a step back and the caramel flow stopped.

Yuri groaned with need.

"How many more will you kill?"

"What?" Yuri whispered. He pressed his hips into the cold stone, trying to ease the aching heat of his cock.

The Master pointed to the cell across the bars from Yuri's. "You've drained four dozen creatures of life. We had to evacuate most of the prison, but were too slow to save them all." He shrugged and folded his arms over his chest. "Most sentenced to die, traitors and monsters. But you are what you eat, and I would not have preferred to feed you that sort of filth. Are you too far gone? Lost to the madness of lust for fear and pain?"

"I killed them..." Yuri said, tasting the truth of the words and understanding the roll of flavors he'd experienced while he dreamed.

"You are feeding like an Onari Noble, but you are not Onari. None have ever been this ravenous upon awakening, and your blood tastes like light, wind, and sunshine, rather than wine."

"Light?" Yuri wondered. How did blood taste like light? "What am I?"

"Not human as we thought, still *touched*, perhaps. Not Onari, though you feed on emotion like one. Perhaps the bond awoke something dormant in your line? I've already sent a message to search for your brother in case he has the same strange blood," the Master said.

"You changed me into a demon?"

"Whatever this is, was already inside you."

Anger snapped within Yuri. He'd been in the camp for a decade, starving and mostly normal, until the Onari had taken him, changed him. It was their fault he was coming apart, morphing into whatever the hell sort of monster they wanted him to be. Making his body scream to be touched, and mind go mad with desire. The rise of the rage made anger pool inside him, the well of magic rising until it lashed out, whipping forward toward the Master.

The power hit the bars with a sizzle and a snap like electricity hitting water. It stung and backlashed, smashing into him with twice the force. The bonds etched into his skin tightened and blood flowed. Yuri blacked out for a half second, the pain stripping away the desire as he struggled to breathe.

The anger faded beneath the pain.

Tears filled his vision, and he sobbed, cheek pressed to the floor. "Can you kill me, please?" Yuri begged. He wanted to be done with the pain, endless hunger, and exhaustion.

"We tried," the Master said. "You healed."

Yuri blinked as that thought made sense in his head. They had tried to kill him and he survived.

"We have tripled the wards to keep your power from leeching into the castle, but you keep breaking through them," the Master stated. "It seemed expedient to dispatch you rather than worry about you breaking through."

"I can't die?" Yuri asked, horrified because his suffering would never end.

"We have other ways we could attempt to end you, none of them pleasant. It was Theodorus who thought we could teach you control before we resort to removing all your limbs and setting you on fire."

Yuri's stomach flipped over at the thought of experiencing that. He'd always wanted a fast and painless death. Even that was denied him, now? "I'm not doing anything. Not on purpose. How do I control this?"

"Pull it back. If you were a young Onari, you'd have enough of the hunger satiated to create a barrier to hold it back. Can you find that control?"

Yuri sucked in a deep breath and searched for something he could use to hold back the hunger. It felt like a wild thing, some sort of Cthulhu of legend raging from the depths within, tentacles of power lashing out to gather up snippets of energy.

The anger returned, flipped like a switch, spiraling a wave of displeasure toward the bars and the Master. Fueled by the idea of being restrained? Yuri trembled as the bonds restricted further. He feared his bones would break even as blood flowed. His body healed, stitching back together with each drawn breath, but the magic pulsed in static over his skin, a war of the bond and this power taking him over.

"Rage all you wish, Little One. I could leave you here to starve. That would be a slow and lonely death for a creature of abilities like yours."

"You don't even know what I am," Yuri said.

"There used to be many creatures who devoured magic and life. All worlds started that way. Perhaps you're from one of the many forgotten worlds lost long ago. Does that mean the Fractures have reopened them? Or something else?"

Yuri didn't know how to answer that or if he had any answers. "You lied," he said after a while. This was not a comfortable life researching books.

"As did you," the Master stated. "You did not disclose your otherness."

"I didn't *know*," Yuri snarled, anger smashing the bars again, showering him with sparks. He passed out another few moments while the bonds nearly ripped him in half. When he startled back awake, it was to the Master squatting outside the cell bars, studying him. "I don't know how to fix this," Yuri said.

"Instinct is often the best instructor," the Master said. "Let me show you the monster you've become."

Yuri didn't want to know. Footsteps echoed in the distance, heading their way. A heartbeat nearing that made Yuri's power hunger.

The Master glared into the darkness beyond the cell door. "Come," he commanded.

A shiver of magic tickled Yuri's flesh at the sound of that word on the Master's lips, like he wanted to respond, obey, and drop himself at the Master's feet even while the command wasn't directed at him. A vampire warrior appeared from the hall. Not the breathlessly beautiful type like the Master or Lucian, but without the armor, he was massive with muscles and an alien sort of chiseled fineness that made Yuri's body ache. He could imagine riding the male's cock and vividly taste the salty meat of it even if he had yet to see it.

Yuri gasped, his heart racing as he didn't know this creature at all. The flavor of butterscotch filled his senses, thick and decadent.

"He killed your kind, though we had ordered him not to. Two women and a child, fed on them," the Master stated. "There are so few mortals left, it's the height of stupidity to destroy the feeding stock." The Master waved his hand, and the bars parted, vanishing in the middle, shield opening, and Yuri's magic sensed it lurching forward. But the Master grabbed the vampire by his neck and tossed him into Yuri's cell, slamming the bars back in place behind him. The vampire landed hard on his knees, inches from Yuri's bound form.

Butterscotch. Yuri shuddered, kept only from crawling forward by the bonds hog-tying him to the floor. He'd have let the male mount him while he fed, could feel the need of it deep inside, even as Yuri's hunger rose to reach for the vampire. The warrior scrambled backward, trying to get away. The wards of the cell door stopped him as they crackled and hissed.

Yuri's stomach growled, his mind filled with images of lust and gore, as if letting the beast fuck him and then devouring the vampire whole was normal. The indulgent flavor of butterscotch with a hint of salt coated his senses, not distant like it had been, but right there, close, and all his. Yuri's magic lassoed the creature, a whipping rope of energy that dragged it away from the bars and toward Yuri's bound form. The vampire shrank in on itself, flailing to no avail, unable to escape.

It shrieked a sound of a wounded animal as Yuri's magic gulped down that thick flavor of terror. His stomach filled with a warm rush of heat, his cock hard and pulsing despite not being able to touch himself. He stared at the horrified face of the vampire as the male shriveled. Life yanked from it with each swallow. Yuri was doing this, killing the vampire by *eating* his emotions. Perhaps devouring his soul, if he had one. And Yuri couldn't stop. He was so desperately hungry, and this was a feast. The rise of magic within snapped at the bonds, forcing them to loosen until Yuri could crawl forward, inching toward the dying vampire.

The idea of taking him, even on the verge of death, made Yuri come again, untouched. He growled, ripped himself away, rolling toward the distant wall and forcing the hunger down. What sort of monster had he become? His magic felt like tentacles or pulsing limbs demanding to be fed. He pulled them back one by one, coiling them around himself, and lost count at two dozen, but once they wrapped him up in an invisible cocoon, he could finally breathe again. They warmed him, almost purring with heat and comfort. His body calmed, the ache between his thighs eased and he could suck in air that didn't feel filled with icy needles.

"I'm sorry," Yuri whispered, tears dripping down his cheeks. The power wrapped around him, comforting, but also a wild thing he feared could rise again at any moment. He stared at the ceiling, not wanting to look at the vampire or the Master, for fear of triggering it again.

"You stopped before death," the Master said, "Interesting. Perhaps you can be saved. Though sparing him now is not a mercy."

Yuri turned his head to see the shriveled thing of the vampire lying near the bars, wrinkled up like a raisin, its body little more than paper-covered sticks and face contorted in shrieking terror, only no sound came from it. Beyond the bars the Master changed, going from immaculate Onari prince to the demon with a sword of glowing light.

Salted caramel. Yuri's senses crawled forward. Hunger rising at the temptation of the Master's power. He could feed a long time on the Master. Perhaps even quiet the ever-raging hunger.

"Pull it back or I will separate your head from your body," the Master warned.

Yuri turned his head to stare at the ceiling and count silent breaths as he coaxed the heat to return to him. It was like convincing a stubborn cat to come sit in his lap. He even thought, *oh I'm so cold, how shall I get warm?*, and that seemed to give the magic something to focus on, as it wrapped him in a glowing wave of heat.

The cell door opened. Yuri sucked in a hard breath, keeping his focus on the warmth rather than the approach of the delicious flavor of the Master. The bonds yanked Yuri back toward the wall, and he didn't fight them at all as the Master stepped into the cell looking like a dying warrior. He stood over the vampire, staring down without pity.

"It doesn't always pay to be kind, Yuri," the Master said as he brought the sword down on the vampire's neck, lopping off the creature's head.

Yuri gagged. The vampire dissolved. His senses told him there was nothing left to return to the earth but ash, nothing to rebuild. Not like the ones in the distance he could sense. Maybe being close had allowed him to feed too deeply?

"Can you control it?" The Master asked, standing over Yuri with that giant sword that had to be as large as Yuri. "You can choose pleasure over fear and pain. But you may not take pleasure without consent."

Yuri blinked. Had he forced the Master? "What?"

"You call others to you. To feed you with their bodies, their desires, their souls."

"I didn't..." Yuri shook his head in denial. "I would never."

"You did. But you will not again."

Yuri turned his face away from the horror of everything around him. "Please kill me."

"Prove you can control it and we will train you."

"I don't even know what I'm doing."

"Look at me," the Master demanded. Yuri turned his gaze to the Master, still huge in his demon form, but he had unbuttoned his shirt and shoved it aside to show his bare chest and the spread of defined muscles. Yuri gasped as his cock hardened again, the power uncoiling with need. The bonds cinched tight, digging into him again.

"Fuck," Yuri cursed. His magic wanted all of that. He could imagine a thousand ways to break free of the bonds and crawl to the Master, freeing the beast's thick cock from the man's pants and sucking it down, or rolling over to present himself to be taken. "Help me," Yuri begged as he felt the hunger take over.

"Pull it back and I will give you what you want."

Yuri licked his lips as the Master's free hand went to unsnap the button of his pants, letting the fabric gape to give Yuri a peek at what lay beneath. The arch of a hard cock outlined under the cloth with the tip leaking to wet the material. "Please," Yuri pleaded.

His magic kept crawling forward, even while Yuri tugged it back, trying to wrap it back around himself, or tie it in a knot. And the bonds dug in, making him bleed while his own power healed the cuts. A cycle of chaos and need.

"Must I force your hand? Or do you really wish to die?" The Master asked.

TASTE OF THE MASTER

Yuri closed his eyes, though the image of the Master's cock threaded deep into his mind. He worked to breathe and tug the need back. It was another internal battle to convince the magic to return. It raged at him like a petulant child, demanding a cookie right in front of him. But Yuri held onto it with everything he had. The bonds loosened. He slowly opened his eyes, fearing seeing the Master would trigger the magic again.

That stunning sight, a demon if that was what he was, of a divinely carved male, his pants fully open, cock splayed out in temptation, gave Yuri the strength to get to his knees. He waited for the bonds to stop him, but they didn't. As long as he kept his magic coiled and settled around him, shoving it down into a well deep inside, he could breathe and focus on what he wanted, which was to taste that flesh.

"Please," Yuri begged, licking his lips, chasing a ghost of flavor. The salted caramel of the Master's power tickled his senses, tempting, but not as much as that thick length weeping for his touch.

"Submit," the Master said, his voice filled with command.

Yuri sank instantly into the position from the binding circle, on his knees, back straight, core solid, head bowed. He dug his fingers into his thighs even as his cock jutted between his legs in obscene need, his ass clenching, empty and wanting.

Internally Yuri's power wanted to whip back with anger, telling him he was stronger and could take what he wanted, but he took a deep breath, thinking instead of making bread as a distraction. He closed his eyes and mentally rolled through the process, his body aching, but the rage fading beneath a familiar comfort. He sensed the Master approach, looming massively over him in a size that should have made fear rise, but the scent of his spend was close as well. Yuri longed to reach out and taste it.

A hand caressed his cheek, gentle fingertips tracing the lines of Yuri's face. He fought to keep his eyes closed and his body still as the Master touched him. He longed to fling himself at the man, but knew if he did so, the power would unleash again. The Master curled his fingers in Yuri's hair, grip slowly tightening, and Yuri felt the nudge of something at his lips.

He sucked in a deep breath, tongue flicking outward for a taste of what he knew was there for the taking, but fearing if he looked, he'd lose control. The salted caramel flavor coated Yuri's tongue. He lapped at the tip, careful, calculated, savoring the taste burst to life from the ghost of a memory to reality.

The Master's grip kept him in place, not close enough to do more than lick the head of the Master's cock. Yuri counted a handful of breaths and slowly opened his eyes, needing to see, wanting to admire and study the divine shape of the man. Through half-lidded eyes beneath his lashes, he stared at the enormous cock in front of him, needing to feel it between his lips. His ass twitching with the desire to be filled. The Master had taken him once already, but not in this form. Would it even fit?

A sound of pure animal need fell from Yuri's lips at the distance. He could only taste the drops of precome and barely touch the enormous head of the Master's cock with his tongue.

"Please," Yuri whispered. The magic coiled within purred as though waiting. Could he hold it back?

The Master's grip on his hair tightened to the edge of pain. Yuri gasped, but the Master pressed the head of himself to Yuri's lips, sliding along the seam of his mouth until Yuri let him in. Yuri opened his mouth wide to receive the engorged heft of the man, lapping at the decadent flavor of candy and letting the Master slide deeper.

The Master's hold on him was unbreakable, and he was in complete control, slipping himself into Yuri's mouth until Yuri's jaw stretched around the girth of him, and the Master butted against Yuri's throat, causing him to gag for a half second before the Master retreated. Yuri breathed through his nose and swallowed hard, his throat spasming from the pressure, though the Master didn't retreat fully and all Yuri could do was stare at that huge cock as it slid between his lips, slow and deliberate at first, as though the Master practiced caution, waiting for Yuri's power to lash out. But the pool of desire in his gut purred at the touch, demanded it keep going.

Yuri had little experience, his night with Star, which he wasn't sure was real, and now this. But he let the Master guide him, couldn't stop his tongue from searching for more drops of come to add explosions of flavor to his rising need. Yuri's cock ached, jutting between his thighs, and his ass clenched over and over. He felt hot and wet there, as though his body knew what it needed, and the tease of having the Master slowly fucking his tonsils wasn't enough.

The Master slid deep, another bump to the back of his throat, which made Yuri impulsively swallow, throat contracting, rewarded with more salted caramel, and the Master's murmurs of approval. It wasn't what Yuri wanted, his body needed to be filled, and this was only half of the fantasy in his head, but he sank into the submission of letting the Master use him as if he were some sort of sex doll. The power of the Master trickled over him, not only from the cock stretching his lips wide, but the grip on his hair, and the Master's fingertips tracing Yuri's cheek, modifying the tilt of his head to get a deeper angle.

Yuri kept his gaze half-lidded, fearing that if he looked at the Master, saw all that burgundy flesh and rippling muscle, he'd jump the male to drive the length of him deep into Yuri's begging ass. The teasing feed of magic soothed the rolling hunger inside, like a table full of delights in which he could only sample a little of each, fed nibbles, until he thought he might burst with the weight of it.

The Master slid his hips back, freeing his cock from Yuri's mouth. Yuri gasped, sucking in air, realizing he'd been barely breathing but chasing the taste and stretch.

"Please," Yuri begged, licking his lips and staring at that fine male flesh.

"You are insatiable," the Master muttered, his grip on Yuri's hair hurt, and fed into the pleasure Yuri's body demanded.

"Please," Yuri begged again.

"Can you control it if I take you again?" The Master inquired. "Give you what you need?"

Yuri trembled and almost came at the thought of the Master splitting his ass wide with that enormous cock. "Please."

The Master released Yuri's hair, and Yuri cried at the loss. "Turn around, chest to the floor, ass in the air."

Yuri rushed to obey, his body moving fast to fill the rising desire and demand of being filled. The stone was cold on his chest and he felt exposed with his ass in the air, hole clenching as though it needed to be filled for him to breathe. The Master slid his hands over Yuri's ass, the sharp edges of nails feeling dangerous, but careful. He lifted Yuri's thighs, one in each firm hand, and adjusted Yuri's body to spread him open wider. It was a strangely vulnerable feeling, but one that made Yuri shiver with anticipation.

The purring content of the magic in his gut intensified, as if it were waiting to pounce. He prayed it didn't attack the Master again, as he didn't want this to end.

"You're delightfully wet, sweet Yuri," the Master said, a large finger tracing Yuri's clenching hole, teasing, but not pressing inside.

It reminded Yuri of Star again, and how he would whisper endearments to Yuri while they made love.

"You still look human, small, breakable," the Master muttered, sounding somewhat disappointed.

Yuri let out a sound, sadness perhaps, or anxiety that he wouldn't get what he needed. "Please, Master."

"I should return to my human form," the Master said absently. He knelt behind Yuri, and his enormous hands spread Yuri's ass cheeks wide as if to study the most intimate part of him.

"No, please," Yuri said. He turned his head to watch the Master, needing to see the male's cock fill him. "Please."

The Master hesitated, fingers caressing Yuri's rim, gaze hot enough that Yuri could feel another wave of energy sliding over him like he was bread to be buttered. Finally, the Master eased forward, pressing his enormous cock to Yuri's needing hole.

"Yes, yes, yes," Yuri said in a chant, as the pressure of the male shoved against the raging heat of him. He hadn't realized until that moment that the chill had grown in his body again, rising as if ice reformed if he went too long without touch, and the Master's body was an inferno to melt the wall encasing his heart or maybe his soul.

His body provided only half a second of resistance, giving in to the pressure and allowing the Master inside with only a hint of hesitation. But the size stretched Yuri to the limit. His arms crossed beneath him, he ground his fingertips into his forearms and pressed back into the rising pain of *too much*. The Master's power, the Master's body, the Master's cock, all of it *too much*, and not enough at once. Yuri wanted more, needed more, even as his body worked to accommodate the enormous girth and length of the male taking him.

The Master rubbed a soothing palm over the base of Yuri's spine, as though encouraging his body to relax more. His other hand had a firm grip on Yuri's hip, tips of his nails digging in to draw blood, but only added the barest bite of pain. The stretch didn't hurt, not like Yuri expected it to. It was uncomfortable. A large force barreling forward, agonizingly slow, pushing him to the limits. Yuri's body adjusted over and over, accommodating with each movement until the man's hips pressed flush to Yuri's ass cheeks.

The Master let out a sigh that sounded dirty and decadent all at once, and Yuri echoed the sound with his own. The Master's cock nestled deep within, pulsing hot and delivering tiny waves of magic. It took Yuri a few seconds to realize it was a heartbeat. The thick veins of the Master's cock with blood pumping through it also feeding Yuri's internal beast.

"Not human," the Master said as he put his hands to Yuri's hips and shifted him in a tiny circle, which embedded the Master a hair deeper. "No human could take this," the Master said. "Even most Onari couldn't." He reached around Yuri to find Yuri's cock, fingers gripping the length and tracing from tip to balls, before letting Yuri go to run his hand up Yuri's chest to his throat. The Master's hand closed over Yuri's throat, lifting him until his back was pressed to the Master's chest. The hand tightened, restricting his air, but not cutting him off completely.

Yuri gasped.

"Not even afraid," the Master said as he kissed Yuri's shoulder. The grip on Yuri's neck tightened, stars popping up with the lack of air as the Master's other hand draped Yuri's legs over the Master's thighs and pressed his body into the wall. The grip on his throat loosened before Yuri could black out. His body clenched around the Master's cock, and the chill of the stones bit into his chest. Yuri's cock ached, but the Master held him to the wall, body nestled deep as the Master trailed kisses over Yuri's neck and shoulders.

Would he bite again? Yuri wanted that. The sting of fangs in his flesh, the Master's mouth on him, sucking him down. His cock jerked as if the image made his body think of his cock being sucked.

"Please," Yuri begged again, needing everything and not understanding what that meant.

"I'm going to feed you," the Master said.

"Yes," Yuri hissed.

"Take only what I give you. If you try to steal more, I will end all of this." The Master's grip on his throat tightened again.

Yuri swallowed hard. "Yes, Master," he barely got out.

The Master's grip loosened and Yuri felt the splitting heft of the male slide out. Yuri made a noise of protest, his body trying to move backward to catch the moment and keep the Master inside. But the Master's grip tightened on his throat again, keeping him in place, shoving his body hard enough into the wall to bruise. Yuri didn't mind. It was a mix of pleasure and pain, divine and yet not enough.

The Master waited again, only the tip inside Yuri. Yuri's body clenching as if it were a fist trying to pull the Master back inside. "Submit," the Master instructed again.

Yuri relaxed, sinking into the command. He turned his head to rest his cheek against the wall, letting the Master's strength hold him, and focusing only on the nibbles of magic dancing over his skin rather than the burning need to be filled. He knew it was coming. The Master shifted his hips and buried himself deep, grinding forward, pressing Yuri into the wall, and drawing a grunt from Yuri. The Master hesitated there, the weight of him against Yuri's back, briefly crushing, but also comforting, like a weighted blanket.

The heat of his touch leeched into Yuri's skin, warming him until sweat dripped down his brow. Still, the Master didn't move. "Please," Yuri begged, painfully still, wanting to take control and feeling like he could, but knowing it would all end if he tried.

The Master slid out again, pausing for a moment. "I worried the slick would be blood, as you're tight, but it's not." He thrust back in, pressing Yuri to the wall hard. Yuri struggled to breathe with that pulsing wedge inside, his body clenching and adapting around it. But the Master didn't pause for more than a few seconds before beginning a rhythm that made Yuri squirm.

The pounding beat, the Master's strength holding him, the chill of the stone against his chest, the building fire in his ass, had Yuri gasping for air. The thick waves of power filled him like a ribbon of warmed caramel rather than nibbles. He could have grabbed a hold of the magic, pulled on it and kept feeding, but a spout opened from the Master to him, a gift that made

Yuri tremble and shiver from overstimulation. He was close to the edge, teetering on an orgasm as his stomach filled, calming that raging need and soothing that inner desire to purr in contentment.

Each time he thought he'd tumble over the side, the Master's grip on his throat tightened, slowing his air, or nails would pierce his hips, drawing blood, or adding a touch of pain to pull him back, but the feeding continued. The Master's supply seeming endless as he poured the thick waves of magic into Yuri with every thrust of his enormous cock.

Only when Yuri stopped struggling, the magic pool inside feeling overfull, did the caramel flow ease to a dribble. Yuri sucked in a deep breath, his body screaming for release, the magic filling him deeply, inside and out, rippling on his skin. Stars of colors danced around his vision, his lungs gasping for air, the tiny bits fed to him by the Master's careful grip keeping him on edge, but unable to speak.

The Master released Yuri's hip, his body pressing Yuri into the wall to drive his cock deep and traced his fingers around to grip Yuri's cock. The Master licked up Yuri's neck and Yuri shivered, wanting badly to be bitten again. "Come," the Master's deep voice rumbled in Yuri's ear as the grip on Yuri's throat loosened.

Yuri screamed. His body unleashed in a clash of popping lights, rainbows and rippling magic, ass clenching around the Master's cock, which felt a thousand times bigger and every inch making Yuri's body come over and over. His cock spurted in the Master's grip, coating the wall and Yuri's chest, hot and laced with magic. If this was an awakening to magic, he never wanted it to end.

He didn't know if he blacked out or the stars of colors in his orgasming mind blinded him, but he found himself cradled in the Master's arms, their bodies still linked, but Yuri feeling boneless. He sucked in cool air, his skin still pulsing with heat and waves of energy, his flesh oversensitive, feeling everything, and sending him into more trembles that made his body grip at the enormous heft of the male buried deep inside. It felt too large to be real, and so insanely good, Yuri shuddered at the barest movement, driving him over the edge of pleasure again.

"I've never had a mortal take my knot," the Master said. His fingers traced Yuri's jaw, down his throat, and his other hand caressing Yuri's quivering thighs. "What are you?"

"Yours," Yuri whispered, feeling that as deeply as the bonds. Could he have chosen in that moment between the Master and Star? He didn't know which he would pick. Could he have them both? Star's tender caress and slow worship, or the Master's brutal assault grinding deep, spreading him to the limit and making him scream for more?

The Master rested one of his giant hands over Yuri's stomach. The tip of his claws rested close to Yuri's cock, but not touching, rather searching for something. Yuri struggled to keep his eyes open. The Master's magic tiptoed through the edge of Yuri's mind, the bond tickling his skin in recognition. Whatever had been raging inside Yuri quieted with satisfaction. He didn't know how long it would last because his skin ached to be touched. He knew he could reach out and call others to him, fulfill the endless desire for hands all over him.

"You still hunger?" The Master inquired.

"Yes... and no," Yuri whispered, unable to describe his need. With the Master nestled deep inside, he could breathe, reason with the longing to be touched, even if his body thought they should be worshiped.

The Master's knot released. Yuri whimpered as his body tried to grip the Master's retreating length. Hot liquid gushed around the Master's cock as he pulled out, coating Yuri's ass and thighs with spend. It was unfathomable, the way his body ached and suddenly felt empty.

"Can you control the magic?" The Master asked, sliding his cock between Yuri's cheeks as though teasing. Yuri thought there was no way he could have taken something that large in his body, but wanted it again and again.

"Yes," Yuri said, feeling the coils of his energy wrapped up inside keeping him warm and slowly lapping at the pool of salted caramel magic filled by the Master.

"Yet your body demands to be filled again," the Master said. He reached around to trace a careful claw over Yuri's still engorged cock.

"I don't know what's wrong with me," Yuri whispered, but couldn't stop his hips from moving, grinding into the Master's cock and thrusting into the Master's fist.

"There are many extinct species like the Onari. Those who feed on emotion and sex."

"Demons?" Yuri wondered. "Incubi?" He tried to recall the reading from decades ago when he'd lost access to libraries and anything other than religious texts.

"The Onari are incubi, and succubi, if the terms are familiar to you," the Master advised. "Not demons. Only beings who feed on emotions. Lust and desire are easy. Given freely, they can keep us satiated for long periods of time. There are some of our kind who feed on fear, pain, and anger."

They were what they ate. Isn't that what the Master said before? He'd prefer Yuri not to feed on fear and pain? "But I'm not Onari."

"No."

"And you don't know what I am."

"No," the Master said. "An Onari starved for a decade

would not feed as you do, not even a newly awakened one. You devoured more than emotion, taking prisoner's souls, and leaving nothing but a shell to decompose. Onari can feed that deeply, but it's rare, and only the purebreds of old were that powerful."

The Master changed, shifting into his smaller human form. Yuri made a noise of protest, wanting to be filled again, and not lose the pulsing heat of the man behind him. The power coiled up inside of Yuri reached out, trying to bind the Master to him, like a rolling chain of electric energy, wrapping the Master to draw him back.

"Fuck," Yuri cursed, trying to pull it back before he got himself killed. He bowed forward, pressing himself to the icy wall, and begging the power to return. His stomach made a noise, like all the energy the Master had given him was already draining away, leaving room for more.

"Can you control this?" the Master asked.

Yuri heard the rustle of clothing as the Master righted himself and moved away, to keep from touching Yuri. The few feet wouldn't have made a difference. Yuri knew he could reach out and latch onto the power, seduce the Master back to his side and fill him again, but he kept both hands on the wall, pressing his cock into the icy stone, and giving himself clarity.

"I would hate to sacrifice more of my people only to find you can't control this," the Master said. "I've been advised to kill you, whatever it takes, to save us all the trouble, but the Convergence wants you for something. It brought us to find you. What if you are the key to fixing the worlds? What if I destroy you and lose the chance we all have of survival?" He sighed heavily, standing up behind Yuri, and stepping away. The sound of his boots helped Yuri breathe.

His steps retreated to the door and Yuri sank to the floor,

feeling vulnerable, but well used as his ass still clenched with need. The Master's shoes echoed a soothing rhythm that Yuri used to focus on as he felt the barrier go up between the Master and himself. The bars of the cage zapped back in place, and the hunger rose again. Maybe in protest to the Master leaving? Yuri trembled. Would this never end? It might be kinder to kill him at this point. Were a few moments of relief all he would ever find?

A CHOICE OF DEATH OR DEVILS

Footsteps echoed down the far hall. Not the Master's retreating, but someone approaching. Yuri trembled, refusing to look, fearing it would be another vampire or incubus for him to murder. He hugged himself hard, digging his nails into his arms until they bled, trying to keep from sensing whomever approached. But his magic, whatever this internal monster of his was, knew power headed their way. Not the level of the Master's, but nothing delicate or as weak as the vampire warrior had been.

He hadn't realized he was moving, kneeling, crawling toward the door until the Master snarled, "Submit."

Yuri shrank back, taking the submissive pose on his knees, head bowed, breathing hard, hands clenched into fists, and fought to keep himself from moving again. Wards rippled over the bars of the cell, a rainbow of color that Yuri examined through his lashes. He licked his lips, knowing he could rip through the wards, perhaps even suck down that energy too, and his skin buzzed with need. More food was coming. Power. Life. Lust.

"Control it, Yuri," the Master commanded. The bonds tightened again but didn't shove him onto the floor. He bled, and held the submissive pose, fighting for breath and coaxing that endless need to stay with him and not reach out.

The fae woman, Sono, stood beside the Master. A glow around her telling Yuri she would be delicious, like a cool custard topped with real heavy cream. He couldn't feed on her as long as he could the Master, but Yuri knew it would be a divine meal. His gut cramped as he reprimanded himself. People weren't food. The magic coiled within protested, and Yuri could sense that it wasn't seeing people as food, but as energy. The fuel to create things. What did that even mean?

A wave of magic slammed into the bars separating the Master and Sono from Yuri, making them sizzle with renewed fervor. Yuri gasped, each hit delivering an electrical backlash that dug needles of currents into his skin. He lost his focus for a few moments, bowing over his thighs, forehead pressed to the floor. Sweat dripped from his brow as he sizzled with the heat of electricity raging over his flesh.

Behind Sono, someone hid. Yuri caught the edge of chocolate and a tart pop of cherries, the flavor desperately rich and alluring. His gut flipped over with need and he crawled toward the door, his body completely out of control as the magic demanded to dine on that flavor. That it was his, belonged to him, or was meant for him, circled in his head while Yuri gasped and clenched his hands into fists, digging them into his eyes to stop his body from moving. He ground his hips into the stone; the pain biting into his sensitive flesh but stopping his progression forward.

He could recall a candy class the year before the Fracture, and how he'd learned to make chocolate-covered cherries from scratch, a touch of bourbon adding to the divine temptation.

And it was all right there, a few yards away, hiding behind Sono.

"He's mad with hunger. I'd rather not sacrifice a seraph for this," the Master said.

"Yuri?" a soft voice called.

Yuri sucked in large gulps of air, trying to focus on the hints of cream or even the salted caramel he'd gorged on, as both powers assaulted him, as if trying to distract him. He turned his head to stare through the bars, catching wide eyes and the ethereal beauty of Theo hidden behind Sono.

Mine. Yuri's magic thought. The resounding wave of need made him wrap his arms around his chest and curl up into a ball to control it. He couldn't move away, didn't have the strength to crawl back to the far wall and create distance. His entire body writhed with need, not to be taken, but to take and let himself drown in the decadence.

"Can you pull back the hunger?" Theo asked. His glow surpassed Sono's, not in power, but like light itself lived in his skin. Yuri wanted to blind himself with that luminescence, soak his skin until he glowed as brightly.

"Mine," Yuri grumbled, gaze focused on Theo. He licked his lips and wished Sono would move so he could see the pretty angel behind her. He imagined stripping Theo bare and sinking into him as the Master had done to him, bringing him over and over until he could drown in the roaring pleasures.

"Not yours," the Master stated.

Yuri snarled and had to bury his face in his knees to keep from rushing the bars. He waited for the bonds to re-tighten and make him bleed again, but they only ached. What were they waiting for? Didn't they know Yuri was dangerous? The Master said he'd killed people, ate their souls. Was he some sort of monster? Maybe the shadow from the hallway had infected him.

"Hungry," Yuri whispered.

"It seems like a transition of sort. Incomplete, but I'm unsure what he needs to finish it, or what he'll become," Sono said.

"An Onari would never hunger this deeply. The well of need within him seems endless. I've filled it twice, only for the hunger to rage again in a matter of moments," the Master said.

"Nothing in the records accounts for this," Sono said. "Not even the dragons. Though they have been gone a long time."

"We have lost many records over the years. Entire libraries vanishing into worlds cut off in the Fractures," the Master mused. "Why is he drawn to the seraph? What did the dragons eat?"

"Power," Sono answered. "They've been gone for over a millennium. The records misinterpret the rest."

"I can try to help," Theo said.

"He wants to devour you," the Master reminded him. "You are no archangel to vanquish a demon, only a guardian long cut off from his world."

Theo flinched. Yuri wanted to reach for him and comfort him.

"Maybe he's a dragon?" Theo whispered.

"My time was after the dragons had already been lost," the Master said. "But he's not a dragon. He's too delicate, and mostly human."

"You didn't break him," Sono said. "Perhaps he is transitioning to something dragon-like? If the worlds reopen, would the creatures pour from them, or be reborn from the few walking between worlds?"

"I don't like the uncertainty," the Master said, sounding annoyed.

"Mine," Yuri murmured again, his gaze finding Theo's beautiful face. He licked his lips, wanting to taste an unobstructed mouthful of that sweet liquor center.

"Let me try," Theo said.

The Master sighed. "Damn seraph. What good will sacrificing yourself for an unknown do?"

"What if he can fix the worlds?" Theo asked.

"Will it matter if you're not here to experience it?" The Master countered.

"The universe is larger than my existence," Theo answered. "Let me try to help."

The Master waved a hand, opening the bars to allow Theo through. "So be it."

Theo stepped around Sono, and Yuri's gut clenched with need. He trembled and kept a vice grip on the power, wanting to snap forward and ensnare Theo. The seraph drew closer as the bars behind him closed, encasing them both in the stone cage.

"Yuri?"

"I don't want to hurt you," Yuri said. He dug his fingernails into his arms, drawing blood and keeping himself curled into a ball, even while his cock still ached and skin burned with the constant electrical beat of the surrounding wards.

"Then don't hurt me," Theo said as he tiptoed forward. The flavor of chocolate-covered cherries intensified and Yuri swallowed hard. Theo paused.

"He'll devour you," the Master warned.

Yuri shoved back the magic, letting the thick flavor fade as he trembled with the strength needed to control it. He didn't know if he'd be strong enough, especially when

Theo touched his hair. A delicate hand running through the messy curls and over Yuri's face. Yuri hadn't realized he was crying until that moment, when Theo brushed away his tears, coating a warm spread of light over his skin.

"Help me," Yuri whispered, gazing up into Theo's face. "You're so beautiful. Light and sunshine, and chocolate-covered cherries." He couldn't help the tiny sips he took, like the magic licked at Theo's power, life, soul, whatever it was it wanted, teasing, nibbling, but careful.

Theo's expression pained, but his touch didn't stop. "It's okay. Take what you need, Yuri."

"Don't want to hurt you," Yuri said through clenched teeth. The bonds tightened as the power trickled forward, reaching for Theo. Blood dripped as the bond became barbed wire tearing into his flesh.

"If my sacrifice helps, even a little, it would be a fine reward. I've been alone a long time." Theo traced Yuri's cheek with his fingertips, tucking his hair behind his ears and crouching close. Theo leaned down and pressed his lips to Yuri's. Yuri gasped, unable to stop his magic from grabbing hold of all that light.

It blazed between them, strong enough that Yuri gasped and lost all sense of the room in the blinding spread of sunlight. Warmth coated him at the very core, rising to pool on his skin, healing him, even as the bonds continued to bite and bleed him. The thick flavor of chocolate, tart cherry, and bitter liquor slid down his throat.

"Stop, Yuri," the Master commanded. "Submit, before you destroy him."

Yuri sank into Theo's touch, savoring his kiss, and drinking deep of his light. Theo made a pained noise, not one of pleasure, and Yuri ripped himself away, rolling over to break free of the light.

He shuddered at the strength it took to stuff the need and magic back inside. "No."

"Yuri..." Theo said, reaching for him again.

"You're just food," Yuri said, feeling the truth in his gut. He could devour Theo and still be hungry. Theo couldn't hide the fear on his face, though he didn't run away. He was willing to die, for what, a few seconds' reprieve for Yuri? It was all a lie, anyway. There was no candy, only Theo's terrified face, and divine light. Yuri felt like a monster for making him afraid and even worse for desiring to drink down that brightness. What sort of demon devoured angels?

"Kill me," he begged the Master. Yuri shoved the magic inside while it snarled and snapped at him in rage. It tore him up like it had barbs, ripping at his soul and making him feel like he was seeping energy. His physical healing slowed, the blood and wounds digging deep where the bonds wrapped him up like chains. He bled and cried, sniffling into the floor, hungry and exhausted, defeated, but keeping a tight grip on the magic.

A soft hand touched his cheek, brushing away the tears and blood again, and delivering the barest hint of brightness. Yuri didn't chase the light, though the magic inside screamed at him, *mine!* He shivered and closed his eyes, sinking into the touch, and letting the gentleness of it give him strength.

"There you are," Theo said. "You're stronger than this. You can control it."

"Hungry," Yuri said. "Won't hurt you." He was determined not to. He turned his head to glare at the Master, a wave of rage at the idea that the Master would sacrifice Theo, making him unsettled. Yuri counted deep breaths, steadying himself

"He's controlling it," Theo said, looking up at the Master.

"It's a start," the Master agreed.

"He's too strong. We don't know what it will take to truly feed him or finish his transition." Sono frowned at Theo. "Only the demons desired the light of the seraph because they were cast into the dark for so long."

"He's not a demon," Theo said. "I'd feel it."

"You've met a lot of demons in your time?" The Master inquired.

"None," Theo admitted. "You know those worlds were closed before I was created." Theo petted Yuri's hair, then crawled in close to cradle Yuri's body. Yuri trembled with need, but the light saturated his skin, delivering warmth and soothing the cycle of ice that continued to rebuild within him each time the feeding faded.

He blinked into Theo's beautiful face. "I almost ate you." The bonds loosened, and Theo ran delicate caresses around the wounds, spreading warmth that healed Yuri. Yuri sank into his touch, keeping the beast inside him coiled. More than magic, he thought, a demon. That made sense. Everyone had always told him he was evil. Maybe the shadow he'd seen in the hall really had found its way inside him, filling the void where his soul was supposed to be.

"The shadows in the house?" Yuri asked. "They devour angels?"

Theo stiffened. "Seraphim vanish into the shadows."

"A shadow touched me in the hall," Yuri whispered. "When I was with Lucian."

"Lucian said no such thing," the Master said.

"I'll send for him," Sono said. "Though I've never heard of the shadows showing interest in a mortal."

"Maybe it's using me?" Yuri wondered. "Because I'm *touched*?"

Theo traced soothing circles on Yuri's face. It was distracting and clarifying all at once. The tiny bites of brightness warming him, a teasing, but not uncomfortable. "It will be okay, Yuri. We will figure it out."

"He's not safe," the Master said. "I have a castle full of seraphim. I can't chance him losing control again."

"I can put him into a stasis, but with his strength what it is, I don't know how long it will last," Sono said.

"I won't let you kill him," Theo said, sounding defiant.

"It won't matter if he devours you first," the Master said. "Odd that a seraph is so attached to a mortal creature. Another conundrum."

"We could send him to where there are no seraphim," Sono said thoughtfully.

"No," Theo said, his tone suddenly sounding worried. "Please. I can help."

"You are nothing but food," the Master reminded him. "Until he finishes his transformation, whatever that is, he's a liability. The way the mortals were drawn to him, I wonder if he planned to devour all of them too. Like a siren call from mortal legends, he even draws me near; I do not appreciate being controlled."

"He can't help it," Theo said. "None of us knew. Only that he shines with a brightness like a crystal buried in the depths."

"And will you sacrifice the others for the unknown?" Sono asked. "Your fellow seraphim or the *touched* mortals in the house? Perhaps he will call more shadows to him. It's not safe for him to stay."

"The convergence needs him for something," Theo said.

"And we don't know if that means the ultimate destruction or an actual fix," the Master replied. He turned his gaze to

Sono. "We will put him in stasis. Send him to my brother. There is none to hurt there."

"Please, my lord," Theo begged. "The darkness will destroy him. He needs light." Theo cradled Yuri's head in his lap, stroking Yuri's hair, and filling his mind with warmth even while Yuri kept his magic bound up tight inside.

"I almost ate you," Yuri whispered. He lost consciousness for a few moments, fearing he'd attack Theo, but awoke to the sensation of sun warming his skin. A decade without light and he could have sprawled beneath the rays, soaking in the warmth until it fried him to a crisp.

"You're doing so well," Theo praised him, his touch sweet and the light coming from him.

"Not hurting you?" Yuri asked, wondering if he wasn't pulling the light from Theo, why it felt so amazing.

"No. I'm warming you like I would have the children I guarded. Sometimes, when they were afraid, they would sink into the darkness. But I have always been good at drawing them back to the light."

Mine. The magic in Yuri muttered, but it sounded more docile now, like it recognized the heat, and was soaking it up slowly.

"He has gotten better at controlling it," Sono said. "It could take years for him to finish the transition, if that is happening. We don't know if he would need to devour the entire household to change. I've never met a beast more ravenous."

"I've fed him twice," the Master stated. "Not small amounts, either. Feeding him in my other form should have been enough to quiet any Onari in heat."

"I'd rather not risk you again," Sono said, folding her arms over her chest. "The wilds would be safer, cast him out, and let him find his own way."

"No," Theo said. "Please."

"He might be strong enough to devour your brother," Sono said. "My compulsion no longer works on him. Will any of your brother's tricks?"

"Hmm," the Master hummed, seeming thoughtful. "I can't say whether that is a good thing or a bad thing. I wouldn't normally subject a young Onari to that darkness, but none of this is natural. Vlad is strong. His fist is iron compared to mine."

"He'll kill Yuri," Theo protested.

"If Yuri can't learn control, it would be a kindness."

"Please kill me," Yuri begged. "I don't want to hurt anyone." Maybe he'd sleep and dream of Star again. Maybe he would drop into a void of nothing. Either way, he'd no longer be a danger. Everything had turned into a nightmare the day the Fracture had fallen. The years starving in the camp seemed like nothing compared to this. Yuri sensed the magic inside him like it was a beast needing to be freed. He trembled at the strength it took to hold it back and keep it from latching onto Theo.

"Please let the Master train you," Theo said, leaning over to kiss Yuri's forehead.

Theo's beauty made Yuri's heart race. He knew he could release the smallest amount of magic and absorb all that light. He couldn't help that he reached up to wrap a hand around the back of Theo's neck and draw him down until their lips met. Magic pulsed between them, and the coil within Yuri snapped into action like a snake waiting to strike. Chocolate-covered cherries with a thick bite of bourbon filled his senses, wrapping around Theo, drinking him down.

The Master was suddenly there, ripping Theo away, and casting the seraph out of the cell. Sono's wards surrounded herself and the seraph like a brick wall. Yuri's power latched onto the Master for a half second before he was smashed back into the floor, bleeding as the bonds tightened again, forcing him down as he sobbed.

"I don't want to hurt anyone," Yuri whispered.

"I will give you a choice. Death or train elsewhere."

"Would the seraphim be safe?" Yuri wondered how many remained in this world and how his magic purred at the idea of devouring them. He really was evil, wasn't he? What sort of nightmare devoured angels?

"My brother has no seraphim. In fact, he has few in his household at all," the Master stated. "He is more powerful than I. But also, less patient."

His brother. Dracula. Vlad Tepes. Yuri shuddered in fear. What sort of nightmare was he if the Master, who could be an enormous demon with powers that moved a castle, was weaker than him?

"Choose," the Master said, his deep voice growling in irritation.

"Elsewhere," Yuri whispered. They had already tried to kill him and failed. What sort of torture would he survive if they tried a dozen ways, and he still didn't die? Would it not be easier for him to be cast away from all this? Hidden away with access only to a monster much like himself. An iron fist, Yuri thought. Did that mean he wouldn't be able to kill anyone else? He hoped so.

"My brother is no longer the man he once was. He has spent years devouring pain, anger, and fear. And we all become what we eat," the Master warned. He tightened his fist in Yuri's hair, turning Yuri's face to look at him. "I wouldn't wish him on my worst enemy."

"But I can't control this," Yuri said. "And I'm afraid I won't die."

The Master sighed and let Yuri go. He stepped away,

making his way to the bars and stepping beyond as the wards slammed down to cut Yuri off of everything, even the trickle of salted caramel. Yuri shook as the ice spread inside again. His magic writhed, refusing to remain bound as its source of food vanished.

"Ready the transport," the Master said. "I trust you can put him in stasis for the trip?" He asked Sono.

"Yes, Sir," Sono said.

"I could go with him," Theo offered.

"Absolutely not," the Master said.

Mine, mine, mine! Yuri's power screamed as it lashed forward, showering them all in sparks as it tried to dismantle the wards and reach Theo. "No," Yuri said, clenching his jaw tight as the magic delivered him pain and wouldn't sink back inside, no matter how he tried to coax it.

"Sono?" the Master asked, and suddenly darkness walloped Yuri, dragging him out of the pain and into a void, which was fine because he bled and couldn't breathe. Death would have been kinder, but rest would have to do until he met his next jailor, a monster to hold a monster. Yuri thought it might be justified, and even felt evil in those few seconds as his mind dreamt of devouring Theo while he plunged his cock into that delicate body and watched it shrivel around him, suctioned of light, life, and everything that made him good.

THE SON OF DRACULA

"I noticed nothing peculiar," Lucian defended. He glared at a magic wrapped box, not unlike a coffin, as they loaded it into a carriage. The seraph's anger was righteous, but they had never liked him much, anyway. Too human or not human enough, Lucian did his best to ignore the angels who flitted around his uncle's home like they were fairies rather than incarnations of light.

"You're dismissed, Theodorus," Radu said. The seraph hesitated, but Radu raised a brow. "Yuri is bound."

"I wish you'd let me go with him," Theo protested.

"If Yuri didn't eat you, my brother would. Foolish to waste you on that. The *touched* adore you, and you keep them calm, working for a cure to all this madness. Would you give that up for a single being?"

Theo stared at him, his resistance saying everything he didn't voice. *He would.* Strange. Lucian frowned and studied the box of wriggling magic that it took to contain Yuri. What was he?

The seraph stalked toward the doors of the castle. They

rarely came outside. The trip into the shattered mortal world often drew dark species to cling to the spires, trying to find a way past the many wards. Seraphim were food for a lot of creatures. That Yuri desired to devour them too, wasn't all that unusual.

"You'll accompany Sono," Radu stated, clearly annoyed, looking at Lucian.

Lucian gasped. "What? He's not my pet."

"And you shouldn't have removed him from his room without permission," Radu said.

"We don't know that this wasn't always going to happen," Lucian said. "He smelled like a normal human to me. *Touched* or otherwise. Why do I have to guard your pet?"

"You are not guarding my pet; you are accompanying Sono. You know your father hates the fae."

Lucian's father hated everyone, even Lucian. "If you want the boy dead, why not kill him?"

"I tried," Radu admitted.

Lucian blinked in horror. "What?"

"I drove the *Lightbearer* through his heart and he repelled the blade. Then I tried to drink down his power to weaken him, but he latched onto mine instead, forcing me to cut off our connection, which led to him devouring half the prisoners in the dungeon. He's more volatile now than when this mess began. I'm uncertain how to kill him."

That was impossible. No one was stronger than Radu. Well, perhaps Lucian's father was, but not some half-dead mortal. And the *Lightbearer* was a sword of legends, said to have been given to them by the creator of their entire species. The weapon could cut through steel like butter, slice armies into ribbons with an arc of magic, and only Radu had ever wielded it, at least since Lucian's father had given up the

THE SON OF DRACULA

sword. Lucian didn't think Vlad Tepes could touch the sword anymore. The light glowing through the magical artifact made it blinding to look at and burning to touch for the darkest of things.

"And you think it's safe for Sono and I to travel across the veil with this time bomb?"

"Sono has him bound. Yuri is resting in stasis. You should check in on your father, anyway. He has been alone far too long."

"Do not meddle in our affairs," Lucian snapped, wishing, not for the first time, that he was a power to match his uncle's. But Lucian's father was right. Lucian was weak, too human to really be any good to the Onari nobles, even if he had an extended life and the ability to feed on emotions rather than blood or mortal food.

"You are family, both you and your grumpy father, even if you hate to admit it. We are all the last of our fading species in worlds ripping apart around us. Shall we all sit back and wait for it to come like Vlad does?"

"No, you would rather poke a hornet's nest by wrapping up some sort of supernatural unknown to send to the most volatile of our kind," Lucian said.

"You're drawn to Yuri," Radu said, with an edge of teasing in his tone.

"Like I want your sloppy seconds."

"That is the human in you showing through. The Onari aren't limited in our affection, and you wouldn't torment him if you weren't enamored. Sono told me it was you who made the army stop at their camp. The scanners reported everyone was dead, but you saw past it. Sensed him, perhaps? Intriguing, as your abilities have never superseded Sono's. But your teasing is childish. I raised you better." Radu waved a hand at the box, which fizzled and snapped with magic. Was Yuri still trying to get out? Even while unconscious? "You're not strong enough to be the iron fist he needs, and I am unwilling to sacrifice more of our already dying stock, hoping he can learn control."

"And if my father kills him?" Lucian asked.

Sono put her hand on the lid of the box and rewrapped a dozen more wards, unfazed by the lashing monster of power, seeking freedom. The sizzling faded, but the box buzzed with energy Lucian could sense even a dozen feet away. The fae had balls standing that close, and Lucian dreaded the idea of being stuck in a small carriage with that nightmare at his feet. Even a young Onari's first transition didn't leave a dried-up husk after they fed. Lucian's hunger had never been more substantial than a taste, likely because he was part human. It was the number one reason his father found him worthless and weak. He'd been sent to Radu for training with the command to make a warrior out of him or dispose of him. Lucian would never be the power most Onari Nobles were, and his father's disappointment burned in his gut. Radu wasn't unkind, but he wasn't a doting parent either.

"Perhaps you share some similarities with the mortal," Radu said.

"Human perhaps, but not Onari." Lucian frowned at the carriage and the horses with glowing eyes. He really despised the fae beasts that could help them travel through the veils.

"He is something," Radu said. "I have everyone combing the library for ideas. You can spend some time exploring him yourself while you check in with your father."

"My father will not agree to train him," Lucian pointed out. Vlad Tepes had even refused to train Lucian, his own son. Why would he agree with some random mortal?

"What better time to test your negotiation skills?" Radu said.

Lucian bit back a curse. "You're setting me up for failure."

"You are stronger than you realize, Lucian. Can you resist the mortal's pull? Convince your father he has value? Perhaps you can help teach him control yourself? You have yet to pull your eyes from the box in which he's bound."

Lucian gasped and yanked his gaze away, realizing Radu wasn't wrong. "I don't want him." He did. Since that first moment Lucian had glimpsed those pale blue eyes, a smoky gray blue clouded when sad. They should have felt cold and chilled his soul to peer into them, but Lucian found warmth there, like the first warming sun after a terrible blizzard. He couldn't explain the jealousy that rose in his gut after finding Yuri in Theo's arms, without a mask for the first time, the face beneath revealed and breathtaking.

The mortal made him do stupid things. Centuries of care and caution, unraveled by such a small thing. And no longer starved, his body filled with muscle, and hints of light dancing beneath his skin, adding color to the art he'd drawn on his flesh, made Lucian ache to explore and claim. Claim. That had never happened before. Lucian wanted to rip Yuri from Theo's touch. The seraph's beauty was divine, and Lucian possessed only a shadow of what an Onari's attraction should be. He had been driven to feed the mortal, try to heal his body and nurse him back to health despite his uncle's claim.

But Lucian hadn't expected to lose sight of him in the hall. That the house moved around them, changing passageways that had long been untouched, had made him fear the house had taken Yuri. When he found the man curled up in a ball, terror wafting off of him like a bitter wine, magic filling his skin, Lucian had thought the mortal overwhelmed. Was the food healing him that quickly? Perhaps it was more than that. Had the castle attacked? Perhaps the shadows had found a home within Yuri, as though he could act as host to feed them and finally free them from lurking in the morphing monster that was Radu's home. What was Yuri?

Lucian had only glimpsed the man before they had stuffed him, unconscious, in the box. Yuri's skin was golden bronze, as if he'd spent weeks in the sun. His limp and damaged hair cascaded over his shoulders in gentle waves, a fine mix of rich dark brown laced with strands of platinum blond. From its distance it almost appeared touched with gray, mixed with a dozen shades of color, even a hint of copper red. Lucian suspected if he stared long enough, he'd find a rainbow of color to match the art painted into Yuri's skin.

He didn't realize he was swaying and staring at the box, inching closer, until Sono blocked his vision, arms folded across her chest. Lucian blinked and glanced back to find Radu a dozen feet away, unmoved other than the smirk on his lips.

"I don't want him..." Lucian protested.

"Hmm," Radu mused.

"Will it be wise to take him from the castle?" Lucian asked. "It seems to want him."

"Until he can control this, yes. And should the castle follow..." Radu shrugged. "Then I suppose we know he has more value. Only time will tell. Will it be so terrible to see your father?"

"He hates me," Lucian said, feeling like a lost child and hating that emotion. He barely remembered his mother, but distinctly recalled how his father's rage had grown over the years since she vanished. His icy anger tainted everything, saturating even Lucian's minimal light in the pain of darkness.

The castle had landed in Europe somewhere, a region of

barren snow and ash. A nearby rift would take them across to Dahna, the world of the Onari, though it would take a few days' travel after passing through the veil to reach his father's estate. At least Dahna still had sunshine. The mortal world ached with a bitter death, the landscape frozen, people vanishing, and the world itself in ruins, dying as the planet ripped itself apart. Lucian didn't see the point in saving it. He tried to muster up some joy at the idea of being back in Dahna. Sun, good food, more of his kind, fewer beasts and bitter cold, but facing his father sucked the joy out of it.

"He doesn't," Radu said gently. "He fears for you. Worries that if he loves you, you'll be stolen from him as well."

"He's achieved that admirably, not loving me *to keep me safe*." He glared at the box, which rippled with magic again. "What if *it* breaks free from the box?"

"Sono will see he doesn't."

Lucian sighed with irritation. His uncle might have endless faith in the mage, but Lucian didn't have faith in anyone. "If he eats me..."

"You'll simply have to make it pleasant for both of you, won't you?" Radu teased. "I assure you; his body is divine. I've never met a mortal more accommodating, even in my other form."

Lucian looked back at his uncle warily. He had taken Yuri in his Onari form? And Yuri lived? Lucian didn't have another form, not like his father or uncle, another weakness, but that Yuri, who was an average size human male at most, could survive an encounter with the power and mass that was one of the original Nephilim, human giant hybrids full of magic and now called Onari? Lucian gaped at his uncle. "That's not possible."

"I assure you, it is," Radu stated. "He even took my knot."

No one said no to Radu. He was the master of desire and lust, feeding never difficult, but to have changed while taking a mortal that seemed unlike him. "Did you lose control?" Lucian wondered.

Radu flinched and glanced away. He had. Unbelievable.

"And you think I have a chance against whatever this thing is?" Lucian asked and waved a hand at the box.

"I'm sending him to your father."

"Who feeds on death, pain, and anger."

"Your father has always been stronger than I," Radu admitted.

Did that mean anger was stronger than lust? "Promise you won't let him keep me," Lucian begged.

"You're far too old to heel to your father's will."

"That doesn't mean you'll rescue me if he locks me away."

Radu sighed. "You are only accompanying Sono. I have no plans for you to stay in Dahna. Drop off the human and return."

As if it were ever that easy.

"Stand up to your father, Lucian. You are not a child anymore, you are a warrior," Radu said. "I have trained you as I have trained my most powerful generals."

"I know how to stand up to him," Lucian said. He avoided his father like a plague. It was better than arguing with the beast inside the monster.

"You ran away," Sono said. She finished securing the box to the carriage, a dozen wards scrawled on every surface, though it still sizzled with power.

"I didn't." The last time he had *visited* had been a nightmare, locked in his room until he'd escaped when another Noble had arrived. His father had killed the Noble. Lucian had used the distraction to break free.

"You did," Radu said. "I understand. Vlad didn't want you on this side of the veil. It was why he locked you away. But you came anyway, finding me in a chaos of broken worlds."

"To help," Lucian said.

"To escape his madness," Radu corrected.

"And you're sending me back..." Lucian shivered at the idea of stepping back into his father's control. "The human is a mess and Father has little patience for mortals on the best of days." Radu's castle exuded the desire, lust, and joy of his power, but Vlad's home was saturated with darkness, despair, and depression. "This is a terrible idea. If Yuri isn't already insane, he will be soon."

"He fed on pain and fear in the dungeon. I think your father is a better tutor for that than I."

"What if he can only feed on the dark things?" Lucian wondered.

"He wouldn't have been tempted by the seraph. He tried to *claim* Theodorus. The seraph will sacrifice himself for Yuri. That tells me there is something we aren't seeing."

"Theo didn't fear him?" Lucian wondered if that was why Theo had drawn Yuri's power, as the mortal had been feeding on fear. Would a seraph's fear be more alluring than their light?

"He did not," Radu said.

Theo was hardly the most powerful of their seraphim, as a guardian for children. The seraph's small and androgynous beauty comforted the *touched* Radu collected. They had messenger class seraphim who appeared more warrior like with muscles, height, and weapons made from light. The handful of guardian seraphim in the household kept buried within the wards of Radu's safety, away from other species and the worst areas of the house, fearing the shadows. And yet Theo hadn't been afraid of Yuri becoming as dangerous as a shadow.

"This is madness," Lucian said.

"The seraphim love to bask in the glow of mortal energy, which he still has," Radu said. "It reminds them of home, though their world has long been lost. It is not unusual for them to be self-sacrificing, only uncommon for them to meet anyone worth the expense these days. Whatever the seraphim sense from Yuri is important, only none of us know what it is yet."

"The end of the world," Lucian growled, annoyed at being cast into the center of this. Fucking angels. Why did they like humans, anyway? They were weak, smelled, often got sick and died easily. They were too breakable. Lucian hated his human half for that fact, one of which his father had proven to him repeatedly. Weak. Not the incredible strength of the Onari, with little to no magic. It had surprised him when they'd been journeying back to the castle past the camp the scouts had already said was dead, and he'd felt something. His heart had sped up, and his gaze sought the still walls built up around the space. Something was in there. Now he knew it was Yuri. Whatever the fuck Yuri was.

"Perhaps," Radu acknowledged. "The seraphim claim he is filled with light. That rarely means an end in the mortal languages."

The seraphim told Lucian nothing. "They don't like me much. I have little light."

"You've always buried your light. I thought your father taught you to do that." Radu frowned, staring at Lucian now, his gaze assessing. "Do you not do that intentionally?"

"I don't shine like humans."

Radu stared at him a while longer until Lucian felt ready to squirm under his scrutinizing gaze. Finally, Radu sighed. "Go. See Sono across Dahna. You have plenty of time to think of ways to convince your father to train Yuri. Perhaps it will wake him from his dark stupor. He helped close the last rift."

"At the cost of my mother," Lucian said.

"Yes. Though I wonder if he could have kept her affection. He was always a brutal man with little patience. I had hoped your mother, and her gift of you to him, would teach him otherwise."

"Well, that was an epic failure," Lucian remarked.

"You have your own strengths, Lucian. I don't see you as weak. Perhaps one day you'll find them yourself and use them." Radu walked away, heading back to the castle, likely to plan raids to search for survivors. Sentimental bastard. Lucian would have let them all die.

"Do you fear riding with him or me?" Sono asked in a smug tone as she climbed into the carriage. He choked back his biting reply and followed her inside, curling up on the bench as far from the magic-wrapped coffin as he could. A small box sat on the bench beside her, and the coffin itself was bound to the floor at their feet, separating their seats.

"He better not fucking eat me," Lucian said, though his body reacted to the idea of Yuri's lips on his. He'd never felt drawn to a mortal like this before, and hated it. The doors closed, and the carriage moved. Not the smooth ride of one of the many rails Radu had installed over the years, but it wouldn't be a terribly uncomfortable ride, except for traveling with a fae lord and a volatile mortal. "What's in the box?"

"Books. What he took with him from the camp. The titles were already in Radu's library, and Theodorus suggested they might comfort him in the darkest hours of your father's stronghold."

"This is really the worst idea. What if he can only feed on negative energy?"

"Then we train him for battle, put him in an army and let him feed," Sono said. "We were led to him for a reason. *You* were drawn to him. Can you voice the reasons?"

He couldn't and said nothing.

"Our numbers are dwindling. Perhaps he's another weapon to use in the war."

"Your faith in my uncle's mission is maddening. The mortals aren't worth this."

"Better to have faith in something than wait for the inevitable end like some docile pet. I prefer to keep fighting until there is nothing left to fight for. You should rest. The trip is long. I won't let him eat you while you sleep."

Lucian sighed and wrapped his cloak around himself, as if he could use it as a shield. "Wake me when we reach the garden of corpses. Wait... never mind, the stench will rouse me first."

A FIELD OF CORPSES

Yuri drifted in the dark, feeling the ghost of someone pressed against him. He absently wove his fingers through familiar hair, imagining it was that teal tinted thick waves he'd sought since the night the world ended.

"Star?" He whispered, feeling disconnected, tired, as though his consciousness was in chains, making his brain processes slow as a molasses spill.

Lips pressed against Yuri's, but he couldn't open his eyes. Each time he tried, the wards ripped him back down into dreamless darkness, only sliding back to semi-consciousness when he stopped fighting. Soft kisses danced around his face, and Yuri held carefully to the hair in his fist, though they were in a narrow space which made it hard for them to move.

What is happening to me? Star? Are you there? Please don't leave me. Yuri wished he could voice those words but forced himself to not fight the bonds holding him in the dark. He had already lost chunks of time and felt the shift of the world around him. The aching power of the castle vanished. Distance perhaps?

You're awakening, my love. A soft whisper danced through Yuri's sleep-bound brain. It tickled his senses like the touch that ghosted over his body, as if someone was there, but he could only partially feel them because they were across the veil, or in another world. The memory of the Master attacking him with a sword flashed through Yuri's thoughts, ripping him back into the dark again as his magic lashed out instinctively.

He returned to more kisses and a swaying chill he now recognized as Star's presence from wherever he was bound. Whatever separated them was too strong to break through, leaving them only a phantom of longing.

"Star?" Yuri muttered, his lips drawing out the name. *I don't want to hurt anyone.*

"Rest, love." It felt like that dream again, the one of Yuri dying, and the warrior version of Star standing over him, reaching down to close his eyes to end the pain. Was Yuri dying again?

Never again. Star's voice echoed through his thoughts, filled with conviction. *I will let no one take you away again.*

Yuri clung to those words, floating in the dark and bathing in the breeze of Star's touch, hoping it wasn't all a dream, though tears still stung his eyes. He wondered what he was becoming, briefly remembering the dead vampire, the horror of Yuri's rising power, and the Master showing him pleasure. Would Star be angry? Yuri's body reacted to the memory of the Master's touch, and pain sizzled through him, dropping him back into the dark again.

He sighed as he floated back upward, on the edge of consciousness. Magic wrapped him in layers of spells like chains. He knew they were moving, felt the glide of something tugging them through sparsely populated lands. Magic radiated from every crevasse of the land they wove through. A temptation to drink from that well of power rippled with need through Yuri's soul. The surrounding bonds tightened again.

Yuri could sense the fae nearby, and the edge of his consciousness warred over the idea of devouring her power or begging her to teach him control. The ghost of Star's touch came and went, sometimes encasing him in a chill that soothed the raging heat demanding release inside. Yuri would dream for a time. Then the power would rise again. The surrounding box crackled and sizzled as his magic sought a path to freedom. It was a dance like a puppet on the end of elaborate strings pulled in multiple directions.

Buried beneath the many wards of the fae's power, Yuri caught the hint of something decadent, but unfinished. At first, he couldn't taste anything from them, rather a void of their presence. Was it the wards? Yuri's magic reached a careful caress toward the other. Male, which made Yuri's body react, sending him back into the darkness again. When he rose from the depths, his consciousness sought that unusual hint of something indefinable again.

It became a game of control, caution, and curiosity, seeking the other beneath the incredible magic of the fae. Yuri thought the male's flavor should have been more intense. He caught a rare glimpse of fear when the box sizzled, but it tasted of rock candy, only slightly sweet and missing any definition to add interest. Beneath, something lingered and Yuri wondered if he could coax it free, drink down the deep well of hidden energy, and pull it forward into something as divine and drawing as the Master had been.

Occasionally the sound of voices flitted through the edge of his awareness, starting as gibberish, then slowly forming words his brain translated. Some sounded lyrical, like poetry or spells from a sonnet than the languages he was accustomed to. It happened a handful of times, startling him out of the darkness to listen, and twice forcing him to reach out with his magic, which plummeted him back into the dark. It was a frustrating game he didn't think he was winning. But he learned to listen, soothing the inferno inside, even while it rippled with growing ice again.

So hungry.

By the fifth round, he understood they weren't speaking in a dozen languages. His brain was translating what they said. How was that possible? He didn't even know what the languages were. Was it because he was *touched*?

It was an excellent distraction, giving him focus to help keep the magic wrapped around him as he translated their conversations, tones, and emotions. The hunger didn't ease, and he found himself thrown back into the abyss a half dozen times by the fae's power, but would rise again quickly enough.

Yuri ran his fingers through Star's hair. The beautiful man wasn't really there, and Yuri couldn't move at all, but he let himself craft the dream. Star's touch added to the expanding ice, but Yuri refused to push him away.

I'm sorry, my love, Star apologized. The chill kept Yuri calm and slowed the hunger, even as he shivered from the intensity of the cold. The slow torture of icy needles spreading through his skin, his breath forming fog, and his body becoming feverish to cast off the chill forced Star to pull away. Yuri grabbed for him, but even the ghost of a touch vanished, and the heat lashed outward, trying to warm him, which meant the wards shoved Yuri back into the dark.

He let out a long sigh as he rose back up from the pit again. His consciousness only barely touching the surface of the world around him. They were still moving, the fae and the other nearby. They passed something that Yuri could sense danced with flavor. Was it emotions? Life? Magic? He didn't reach for it as he knew he'd be cast back down into sizzling pain and then nothing.

"You could stay here," Sono said. "Your kind adores the city. Far enough away from your father to give distance."

"And overcrowded, filled with pompous royals who live lives as twisted and corrupt as my sire, while pretending they don't drag mortals to their bedrooms to drain them of blood and emotion until there is nothing left but a shell. At least my father is an honest monster."

"I never thought you cared for mortals," Sono said.

"I don't. It's a waste that my uncle rescues creatures of other worlds only for the nobles to eat them."

"Only the disobedient," Sono affirmed.

"I was never disobedient," Lucian growled.

A stretch of silence rippled through the carriage, adding a wave of chaotic emotions, too fast to define the flavor, and quickly stuffed away, unreachable.

"Your father would never..." Sono whispered.

"Wouldn't he?" Lucian snapped. "Do you think I mean anything to him?"

It was Lucian who tasted of bland rock candy. Slightly sweet. Emotions constantly shifting but buried too deep to have real flavor. The pain that flickered through the whirl of emotions had a momentary hint of bitter coffee. Yuri had long missed that vice. Was Lucian's lack of flavor because he was only half Onari? Maybe his power only wanted the Onari or the seraphim. If that was true, perhaps he could convince them to let him stay with humans instead.

"You could find a high court suitor," Sono said.

"Not when they are used to having me at their feet," Lucian replied, sounding tired.

Another long silence permeated the air of their small space, and Yuri relaxed into the lack of aggression. Lucian's minimal flavor calmed something he didn't understand. Not that Lucian felt like nothing, only that Yuri sensed power or will tied to it buried so deeply it might as well have been absent. Yuri found himself awed by that control.

"Your father never..." Sono began but stopped as though she didn't want to know.

"Raped me? No, that was saved for the nobles he sold me to," Lucian snapped.

Rape. The word stirred something in Yuri. His power snapped and fizzled again, the box and wards clenching down on him as though trying to crush him. He fought the darkness, wanted to hear more, and yet didn't want to know. Unconsciousness ripped him back down even as he heard the startled yelp of Lucian and Sono from the box jumping as though he'd smashed it with his power. The world vanished again.

When next he opened his eyes, it was because the cold encased him, raging fire inside barely flickering with life, and his stomach ached with a hunger deep enough to devour the universe. He trembled at the need, the gut-wrenching ache flipping and rolling with the sense of *food* nearby. Yuri wondered if it was Sono and Lucian again but couldn't feel them at all as a buffet of flavors filled his senses. The wards on the box snapped and wriggled, trying to hold his power inside. He could picture a table full of delights, and couldn't help but sample each, from cakes, to bourbon candies, to salty meat, and delicate sweet breads.

The fire in his gut erupted outward, demanding to feed, cracking the ice covering his soul. Yuri jolted wide awake. The box around him seething with the magic of rainbow-colored wards as his power instinctively ripped apart the delicate bonds, absorbing the broken pieces. He curled his hands into fists as he fought to regain some control of the hunger. This was a thousand times worse than the dungeon had been. His desire for Theo and the Master magnified by a million as his body responded too, power seeping free from the box and reaching for the coming buffet.

"This isn't good," Sono sounded strained. "He's going to break out."

"He couldn't wait until we arrived at Father's doorstep?" Lucian cursed. "Strengthen the wards, Mage."

"I'm trying," Sono said.

Flavors rolled over Yuri as they got closer, teasing at first. A touch here or there. His power crept over a few already gone, left to rot for fuel, only to find others with a thick coating of delights that Yuri sucked down greedily. The box and the wards might as well have not been there. They held his physical body, chaining him in place, but his magic, energy, power, whatever this hunger was, surged free, devouring everything it touched, drinking down the masses. And it was endless, branching around him, a handful gone, his mind shattering the withering remains to nothing as he flowed to the next squirming chaos of zest.

The carriage jerked to a halt, but Yuri was beyond caring. The ice chiseled away inside his gut as he drank down everything he could touch. He sensed Sono escaping the carriage, covering Lucian with her shields, and didn't care at all. The feast surrounding him, his only focus. It was a swirl of colors, his memories attaching to the emotions and life with images of things he had once eaten. Cakes, candies, roasted turkey and mashed potatoes with thick gravy, fresh buttered bread, and delightfully sweet dessert wines filled his aching soul. The box rocked and sizzled, wards fighting to hold him and failing miserably.

Yuri sat in the eye of a hurricane, the magic growing in strength and swirling around him to gather every tidbit it could find. He hit a barrier. Something shielded a thousand times stronger than the fae, but it didn't matter as his hunger flowed around it, finding more to devour despite the roadblock in the center. The bonds burned, the etched chains breaking his skin to make him bleed again, acid burning in his blood and tightening his lungs as though trying to force him to stop.

But the fire was free. The ice melted away and unleashed a healing energy, the last of the resistance faded, too tired to keep fighting, and the hunger overwhelming, Yuri released the power to do whatever the fuck it wanted. Something inside him rose from the depths of his soul, filling the abyss of need inside, and his body filled as he fed until his skin felt too small to contain him.

He slammed a fist upward, expecting to meet the top of the hard box, but went right through it. The wards shattered; a cascade of rippling power erupted outward like shards of glass. Yuri's whirlwind of hunger caught them, dragging every ounce of magic into the funnel the coil of need had created, sucking it into the depths of his soul.

It fed. The leviathan of desire within him, expanding Yuri's consciousness, making him long for Star or the Master, or even Lucian to take him, split him wide, and bring all that insane power to a final climax. The box exploded, the eruption blasting the top off the carriage as Yuri felt too large to be contained, even while he bled, and continued to feed. He gasped and wobbled on the edge of darkness for a moment while heat like lava poured down his spine.

Yuri's muscles contracted and cramped, bones aching with

a charge of electricity that made it impossible to breathe. Was he dying? It all felt like too much, and he prayed he'd turn to ash instantly, as he was certain he was burning up from the inside out.

Star! His mind screamed as he felt like his brain was melting, body throbbing with need even while he hurt more than he thought was possible before death. In the distance Lucian stood with Sono, the two swirling with powerful shields, dark horses tucked behind him. A fizzling blue haze kept Yuri out, but that was okay because he was still feeding, even while he stared in horror at the graveyard surrounding them. Bodies by the thousands dangling from giant stakes, some little more than bones, others still thrashing, many shattered into ash as Yuri's power slid over them, taking the last bits until nothing remained.

The bodies stretched as far as he could see, a looming monstrosity of a giant castle in the center of it all, like some maddened mausoleum. A tornado of color danced above the area, expanding whipping winds to gather all the power in rainbows of lightning bolts. The magic rolled through the cemetery, sliding over the mostly dead and ripping them from this world, ending their pain, filling his gut as the bodies dissolved, feeding the remains of life and power into the demon within Yuri's soul. The bonds bled, but he healed and they bit deep again, a wave of pain and pleasure, Yuri's body aching as his gut filled, truly filled, for the first time since his change had begun in the Master's castle.

A furnace of heat poured down Yuri's spine and something burst free, tearing his back open wide. Blood rained over him like fire and he rose from the ground. Yuri screamed in pain, blacked out for a half second as his muscles and bones reformed, the energy of his feeding racing to heal whatever he'd done. A wallop of energy jolted him awake, floating far above a field of prisms, light sucking down every bit of darkness, death, and pain. The power filled him to the brim, spilling over in dancing waves of magic that curled through the landscape, absorbing the ash, and turning the abandoned stakes into mulch, mushrooms, and growing vines.

Yuri sucked in large gulps of air, his vision limited by the blinding light and pain arching up his spine. He blinked back stars of colors, finding himself high in the sky, wondering if he'd fall suddenly like a bird who questioned their ability to fly. The garden of corpses vanished as Yuri's power slid over them, extinguishing their pain and suffering and scattering the overfilled well back onto the land to grow real flowers.

A garden of life and beauty rather than death and agony.

The garden stretched in a wide ring around the castle, and Yuri's magic drank it all down, unable to break through the shield on the castle, and not really bothered, as he was full for the first time in decades. Trees erupted in fresh growth, adding to the forest, which had been cut to allow space for the gruesome cemetery of only partially dead creatures.

Yuri hovered up high, several dozen yards over the broken carriage. Sono and Lucian stared up at him in horror. What had he become? He still bled and healed, and bled and healed, the energy of the dead filling him like a disturbing candy bowl of long-lost flavors. The muscles in his back shrieked with pain, warning he was growing tired even with his stomach full. As he turned his head, he realized he had something wing-like, moving in a flurry that kept him in the air, but the motion faltered from exhaustion.

He dropped like a stone, smashed into the ground seconds later, startled, bones breaking, and instantly healing with a brutal pop back into place. Yuri sucked in gulps of air, not pushing himself up as he trembled and twitched. His wings flapped and twitched, adding to his pain as he couldn't stop from flopping around on the ground like he'd been a bird thrown into a window or hit by a car.

The last of the energy stored in the graveyard of corpses slammed into him in a wave of fire, the vortex of whipping energy snuffed, and he lay exhausted, face in the dirt, blinking at the convulsing of his muscles. The bodies vanished beneath a wall of trees and growth, sprouting up to towering lengths that nearly hid the castle from view. Like a bomb of green exploded, rippling with enormous stalks, flowers the size of cars, and glowing mushrooms, life expanding all around from the finality of death and suffering.

Yuri gasped at the beauty of it for a moment, awed by the transformation into some fantasy world he could only have dreamt of reading about in a book.

A roar of rage slammed into Yuri's senses, shoving his power back and away from the field, cutting off the growth, and making Yuri moan in pain as his healing slowed. A well of magic approached him with an intense heavy sense of *too much*, not unlike the Master, but this wasn't desire or beauty. It was pure rage.

The chains around Yuri tightened, yanking his limbs back until his hands and ankles were all bound behind his back, wings aching at the angle. A shadow towered over him, anger pooled over Yuri's body, wrapping him in chains of fire that sizzled through his skin, and he cried out.

"Death eater, that was *mine*," a bitter voice growled at Yuri. Strong hands gripped Yuri's right wing and yanked. Overwhelming pain flared brightly in Yuri's mind, but thankfully dropped him back into blissful unconsciousness.

Monster of Legends

Imprisoned in Dracula's dungeon with an incubus prince, will either of them survive?

A gift from Star, bestowed in a dream, helps Yuri control his power while locked behind magic wards. As time passes and he starves with the only possible meal nearby, Lucian, the son of Dracula, Yuri is certain feeding his magic would be suicide.

Lucian has returned to the nightmare of his youth, locked away and treated like the useless half-human his father claims he is. Only Yuri's presence in the opposite cell keeps him sane and drives him mad with desire.

Can Yuri find comfort and strength with a man everyone fears?

DREAMS OF LOVE

Pain came and went with a strange floating sensation that wouldn't untether him from the last of reality. He opened his eyes to a soft caress running over his face and hair and found himself curled beside Star. Yuri's heart leapt with joy, but exhaustion kept him from reaching for the man. He sucked in a contented sigh and sank into Star's embrace.

"I won't let you stay," Star said. "This is not the place for you." He leaned over Yuri, a soft smile on his lips, his touch and appearance more solid than Yuri could recall since the first night they'd met.

"I don't want to leave you," Yuri pleaded. Star's skin ached cold against him, and more a tickling sensation than reality. Tears filled Yuri's eyes with the stinging realization it had to be a dream again. "No more dreams..."

Star kissed a trail over Yuri's face, chasing away the tears and filling everything Yuri saw with him. He was so beautiful. "As soon as I'm free, we will be inseparable."

"I had wings," Yuri whispered. Had that been a dream, too? His back ached from the movement or the horror that had dropped him back into the dark of someone ripping one of them off. Maybe that was okay since they hadn't been beautiful like he was certain Theo's must be, rather, made of darkness and shadow. "Am I evil?" Yuri asked, basking in Star's touch. "Is that why I have to suffer?"

"Not evil at all, my love," Star said. He rested his palms on Yuri's cheeks, tilting Yuri's head a bit to capture his lips in a devouring kiss. Yuri sank into the exploration, faint as it was, wanting to feel Star again in all ways. When Star broke the kiss, his eyes glittered with tears. "I would give you everything."

"Please," Yuri begged. He reached up with his arm feeling like a lead weight but slid his hand through Star's hair. The chill of his touch biting, but if that was all Yuri could get, he'd take it. His dreams had never been this defined before, memories of the barest hint of his face rather than the fine detail of those beautiful blue-sky eyes. Only they weren't as bright as Yuri recalled. The sun no longer shone behind them. His teal-streaked dark hair, peppered in gray, like ice grew from his scalp, and there was a thick chain around his throat.

Yuri released Star's hair and traced his fingers over Star's face, down to the collar, a blackened thing almost four inches thick. How could he even breathe? Before Yuri could touch the bond, Star captured his hand and kissed his palm. Similar links wrapped around each of his wrists and all the way up his arms. Yuri gasped. "Star?"

"It's all right, my love."

But it wasn't. "Is this why I can barely feel you?"

Star rest his forehead to Yuri's, holding his hand in a tight grip. "Time."

"I'm tired of waiting," Yuri said.

"You and me both…"

Yuri sucked in a huge breath, trembling at the idea that he

was alone, always alone. Star was bound, unable to reach him. That was why he suffered. "Please," Yuri pleaded with tears in his eyes. "I don't want to hurt anymore. Can't I stay with you?"

Star painted Yuri's face in kisses again, a feathered touch that calmed his racing heart. "My gifts have only brought you pain so far. If I could go back and undo all I did..."

Gifts? What did that mean? Was the hunger Star's? Yuri thought about his time with the Master and the pleasure. That hadn't been pain. Did Star even know? He remembered back to their first meeting and how Star told him no one wanted his touch. Was that what *touched* meant?

"This thing inside..." Yuri began. "Did you put it there?"

Star gave him a sad smile. "If I had, I'd take it back. I was never one who agreed with *required* suffering. It was the whole reason the war began and why they cast me out." He gripped Yuri's fingers with one hand and ran his other through Yuri's hair. "You and I never fought about this. They betrayed your love for them. I won't let that happen again. It matters not how many chains they bind me with, or realms they close to keep me leashed. You are mine, and I will return to you."

Yuri relaxed into Star's touch, even if it was cold, and made him sleepy. He didn't feel out of control with hunger or rage, and the magic inside, fighting to break free, was absent. "The power is mine?"

"Yes," Star agreed.

"It's terrifying. Too much for one person," Yuri said. He shivered at the desire. Was that okay? "What if I touch others?" He feared Star would turn him away if he knew.

"It is our nature," Star said.

Yuri blinked. "Desire?"

"And lust, and love. You always gave your heart too easily."

Star breathed deeply, as if he were savoring Yuri's scent. "The more you gave, the more they raged, until..."

"Until?"

Star shook his head. "If you never remember, it might be better. Love has its own pains."

Love. Lust. Desire. These were the things the Master said he fed on, and Yuri had dined heavily on the Master's power, even when the Master tried to keep him out. Was Yuri some sort of Onari? "What am I?"

"Life, beauty, and love, Yuri. What else do you need to be?"

"Yours," Yuri hoped, wishing he could rip Star free from those chains. "For this to not be a dream, and to know when I wake that you really will be there someday."

"Love, I am yours first. Always have been. I will burn down all of existence for you."

"But this doesn't feel real."

"Transformations are never easy. Creation is sometimes painful. You taught me that." Star sighed deeply, curling himself against Yuri. "And how to love. I thought I'd lost the ability until I found you again. Cold darkness ate away at my sanity. I longed for the day to break free and rip it all to shreds. Destroy them all for taking you from me. And there you were, shining your brightness over me. My heart beat again. Love warming my soul, even if it's only a buried flicker of life left."

Yuri's heart warmed at Star's confession. If it was only a dream, it was a nice one. He wanted badly to be loved, always had. His mother had given him glimpses between all the beatings and pain from the camp leader's demands. Then the end of the world had ripped away the last bits of affection with his mother's death, and the shattering of reality around them. Monsters ate people. Humans slaughtered and raped other humans to steal food or control. And Yuri had slid into the darkness, trying to hide from the endless pain.

He thought of their night together and the heat of Star's skin on his, the passion of his kisses, and how his touch delivered love with every caress. Desire was part of it, but the warmth of that bright emotion had been his first taste. An awakening to what he desperately had been missing his whole life. "I need love," Yuri whispered.

Star nodded. "Yes. You'll need a lot of love to grow strong again. Can you embrace the desire and cast away the hate? Let me take all that rage. It was never meant to be yours."

"I love you," Yuri confessed, feeling that with every part of him, even if he wasn't certain Star was anything more than a figment of his imagination. "Are you even real? Or have I gone mad?"

Star tugged Yuri's hand up between them. The familiar-colored snakes tattooed over his hands shifted and moved as if they were living things. Yuri blinked at them as one slid up Star's hand and encircled Yuri's. It was a cool touch of textured skin, though Yuri couldn't recall ever touching a snake in real life. The creature didn't snap or hiss at him, rather it curled around Yuri's arm and sank into his flesh like an elaborate and detailed tattoo. The snake even slid under the edge of the bonds on Yuri's arm, as if to ease the biting cuffs that could control him.

"How?"

"My vow to you," Star said.

Yuri stared at the ink painted over his skin. Would it be there when he woke? What did any of this mean? The sensation of the textured skin wriggled over Yuri's body, engraving itself beneath the bonds that tore into him each time they were used. A cushion, perhaps? Yuri's vision blurred as he realized Star was fading again.

"I told you I wouldn't let you stay. You don't belong in the dark," Star reminded him.

Yuri choked back a cry and tried to tighten his grip on Star, but the man vanished as Yuri was yanked backward, plummeting him through the dark at lightning speed and finally dropping him into the pain of his body, too small and riddled with agony. He lay gasping for air. The snake tattoo slithered up his arm, easing the pain. Healing him?

Yuri trembled as the soothing edge of magic trickled over his skin, careful, gentle, with a hint of cold. He knew in that moment Star was real. The textured chill of it slithered over his flesh, new and yet familiar. The sensation of the snake soothing magic over his flesh, repairing damage, was unsettling as he feared for a half second something worse touched him. But a calm whisper eased through his mind, affection, no real thought, only adoration and peace. Star was with him.

DUNGEON OF SORROW

He caught the scent of food. Not the sweet delights his power craved, but a salty hint of roasted chicken. How long since he'd had chicken? Almost a decade, he thought as he sucked in gulps of the flavored air. Not magic, but actual food. Was he in some fever-induced dream?

He blinked open gritty eyes and found himself on his back on a stone floor, the bars of a cage around him on two sides, and stone walls on the other two. Not a dream, or the camp, but another cage. Was he back in the Master's dungeon? It didn't look the same, and his body no longer ached. The serpent slid back into place around his arm. His skin tingled where it became art, and he examined the tattoo in awe. Star had given him a permanent reminder, and something to help him heal, perhaps?

Yuri sucked in deep breaths, resolving that he would find Star and free him. He had more questions than answers, but that was okay. Star loved him. Star was real. They would be together again.

Yuri stank, dried blood and dirt covering him. His back no

longer hurt like someone had tried to cut out his spine, but a dull ache throbbed in reminder. He didn't have wings anymore. Had they even been real?

The scent of chicken remained, tickling his awareness with rising hunger.

He curled onto his side, rolling over to search for the source of the smell, and enjoying the cool stretch of stone on his oversensitive skin. The magic coil of need in his gut lay silent, wrapped around him, sated and warm like a blanket. He let out a grateful sigh as his mind felt clear and calm rather than maddened by feverish desire. Was the worst over? Had he completed some transition? And into what?

Yuri closed his eyes and savored the scent again, imagining old Thanksgiving dinners as a child, before food had gotten scarce. The smell of roasted meat and the salty memory of gravy filling his mind.

A heartbeat echoed nearby. Not his, as he could feel his heart in his chest, a steady rhythm that the beat he heard didn't match. Was someone else there?

It was too dark to see much beyond the bars, but Yuri thought there might be the outline of another. "Is that chicken?" Yuri whispered, worried it was his magic again.

"I'm shocked you can smell anything over your own stench," Lucian's voice snapped back, angry and cold as ever. "The water will turn on soon. I recommend you use it. You reek."

Yuri rolled onto his side and peered through the narrow spread of bars. They crackled with energy and a wash of rainbow colors. Magic? He waited for his hunger to leech onto the rippling electricity of power, but it stayed quiet, sated, the non-physical part of his hunger at least. His gut growled with hunger, the distant and visceral memory of chicken making him want to crawl through the bars and reach it.

He and Lucian shared a wall of bars. Why was Lucian imprisoned? "Didn't we arrive at your father's castle?" Yuri asked.

"He's not thrilled by your arrival. Which means I suffer as well. Not unexpected, though irritating. I warned Radu. It's what I get for daring to stop him from grinding you into dirt."

Yuri recalled the garden of corpses and how his power had suctioned every ounce of life remaining in it, scattering it back to dust and reforming something out of a fairytale. A forest of mushrooms and massive trees? Had that been a dream? The flavors still drifted across his memory like the buffet they'd been, vivid on the back of his tongue, as though he could still taste them. He had eaten the dead? Not dead, he thought, not completely. "They weren't dead," Yuri said out loud. "He had a garden of suffering, *living* creatures."

"Which you devoured. Father is enraged. He's been cultivating that nightmare for centuries," Lucian said, his voice monotone, as if he didn't care.

"It tasted like a buffet of food. Things from a hundred memories," Yuri admitted. *Death eater.* That was what he'd been called. What did that mean?

"I'm shocked he killed neither of us. Perhaps it's a matter of time. He's never liked me much. It would be a fine opportunity to get rid of me. At least Sono got away. I hope she will report my sacrifice to Radu." Lucian sounded tired. Yuri wished he could make out more than the vague outline of the man. "I don't know why they bother to feed me."

Yuri swallowed, catching the scent of chicken again, and the sound of a sliding plate. He realized his hunger wasn't the soul devouring kind, but a normal *I could eat* type. Could he eat? He recalled the stew and how it sat like a stone in his gut. Had that been part of his transformation? A trigger or a symptom?

"Can I have that?" Yuri whispered, waiting for Lucian's biting retort.

A gush of water turned on a few feet away in a corner with a drain making Yuri jump. There was no privacy, but the area had a toilet and a shower spout.

"Clean up first. I'd rather not smell you anymore. The stench of unwashed mortals is vile."

Yuri flinched and slowly climbed to his feet, worried the bonds would tighten again, but he could move. He stepped beneath the spray. It hurt at first. The lukewarm needles were an unfamiliar sensation on his skin, like it had been too long since water assaulted his skin. He had no soap or anything to wash himself with, but scrubbed at his body and hair anyway, letting the water wash away the worst of the remaining blood and grime. Yuri drank several mouthfuls, then swished and swirled, trying to clean his teeth and ease the dry paper coating in his throat.

The water stopped before he was ready, and he stood there dripping, sad that it was over, but feeling a little cleaner. Yuri finger-combed his hair into a thick braid, the wet strands helping it stay together. He had nothing to wear and ward off the chill.

"Here," Lucian said, sounding a little closer. He shoved a pile of fabric through the bars into Yuri's cell. If the glowing energy of magic separating them affected him at all, he gave no sign of it. He watched the shadow of Lucian's presence back away from the bars before approaching.

Yuri picked up the fabric, finding a shirt.

"Might be a tad snug, but I have little else to share."

Yuri tugged on the shirt, surprised his arms and shoulders stretched the cloth, but it buttoned and the length allowed him to hide the worst of his nudity as it ended mid-thigh. He squinted through the bars to find Lucian sitting a distance away, dressed in only a pair of pants, his long coat spread beneath him like a bed.

"The coat is more fitted than the shirt, and doesn't button," Lucian said.

"Thank you for the shirt."

Lucian huffed.

Yuri's gaze lingered on the man, surprised by the stretch of pale skin and defined lean muscle tone. Lucian traveled with the warriors, and it made sense that he would be one. Fully dressed and standing beside his uncle, Yuri had barely noticed Lucian's build. Now he couldn't help but notice the musculature of the man. Not a pampered prince, and likely no less strong than the Master had been in his human form. Smaller overall, but not weak. He and Yuri were similar in height, with Lucian only a few inches taller.

Yuri's body had changed, muscles where they hadn't been after years of starvation. The shirt pulled tight over his hips, his thighs touching as he tried to keep his groin covered. Had devouring the garden of almost-corpses changed him? He stared at the snake tattoo that began at his knuckle and wove around his arm to his shoulder, and rippling waves over his entire body. It carefully avoided Yuri's other tattoos, but knit itself beneath the black markings of the Master's bond, a touch of purple and teal rippling through the scales with an iridescent shine.

Yuri ran his fingertips over the head of the snake, wondering if Star could feel his touch. It was hope, he realized.

Star had given him hope, and Yuri planned to cling to it with everything he had left.

Lucian shoved the plate close to the bars. It wouldn't fit through, and Yuri hesitated to get any closer. Actual food, a large chicken breast and a handful of veggies, made Yuri's mouth water. He eyed the rippling magic of the cell. He sat a half dozen feet away and could still sense the waves of it, as if him getting too close would instantly cause pain.

"The magic doesn't bother you?"

"Magic?" Lucian asked.

"The bars are coated in magic," Yuri said. "You don't see or feel it? I'm not even close and it aches. A burning edge of electricity that my mind tells me will hurt if I get closer."

Lucian blinked and reached a hand out to touch the bars, wrapping his fingers around one. Nothing happened. "Hmm," Lucian hummed.

Yuri slowly put his hand up, not touching the bars, but hovering inches away. The magic snapped and crackled, zipping to life and slamming him with a hard jolt of electricity. He pulled his hand away; the muscles convulsing as if he couldn't control them yet, and he swallowed a curse. The plate and food were out of reach, and his hand ached, numbness replacing the pain as he held it against his chest.

"That was unexpected," Lucian said. He picked up the piece of chicken, threaded his hand through the bars, and dropped it on Yuri's side.

Yuri scooped up the chicken with his uninjured hand and took a bite. It wasn't warm anymore, but that was okay. It was salty and still soft. He chewed slowly, worried it would cause more pain as everything seemed out to hurt him. He waited, letting it sit, analyzing how he felt before he took another bite. No pain or discomfort rose. His stomach rumbled. A call for more and Yuri ate slowly.

"Is this chicken?" Yuri hoped so.

"The Dahna version, yes," Lucian said. "They are larger here. Is it hurting you?"

"No. Tastes like regular food," Yuri said.

"The stew didn't taste like regular food?"

"It didn't have a taste."

Lucian seemed to think on that for a few minutes. Yuri finished the chicken and eyed the veggies. He was still hungry, but he also didn't want to be greedy.

"Sono thought the castle might have done something," Lucian said after a while. "That it needed whatever you are to awaken. I thought she implied I wasn't to blame, which is odd, as she's not kind. Though I am glad my father didn't leave me here for you to eat."

"What?" Yuri gasped. But that had been exactly what had happened when Radu had put him in a cell. He had devoured the prisoners. Was Lucian the only one close? Yuri couldn't sense anyone, and he could only vaguely hear Lucian's heartbeat. Something had changed in him. He'd never heard other heartbeats before.

"My father doesn't keep prisoners anymore. He adds them to the garden. I supposed it should thrill me not to be writhing outside with a stake up my ass. A sick display, as it would take a long time for me to die that way."

"I ate his garden," Yuri said, remembering the vortex of power. "Not corpses..." Which was worse? Feeding on death or the last dregs of life?

"Father has fed on pain and fear for centuries, but I have known none who feed on the dead and dying the way you did. Not their emotions, but their life," Lucian cyed Yuri warily.

"And things grew. My entire life outside of this castle has been corpses. Now it is some sort of fae forest."

"I don't know what happened," Yuri admitted. He tried to tug the shirt down further to keep his bare ass and thighs from touching the cold floor, but it only barely covered his rump if he wanted his groin hidden. There were no blankets, or anything of comfort, only stone walls, magic bars, and the wet room area with a toilet.

"I wonder what you are," Lucian said absently. "Devouring an entire legion of nearly dead monsters, and now able to eat actual mortal food. You are a quandary. And you had wings. There are very few humanoid species that have wings. The seraphim, of course, but everyone sees you fine, in fact, are drawn to you like flies to honey. Your wings weren't seraph-like either, made of shadow and leather rather than glowing white feathers."

"The Onari don't have wings? I thought Onari are like vampires? There are stories of vampires turning into bats," Yuri said, thinking back to his years of reading.

"Strange mortal myths. The Onari never had wings. They also are not shapeshifters."

"Your uncle changed forms."

"He can mask his true form with magic, making himself less intimidating. It's not all glamour like the fae can do, but not a true shape change. More a contracting of his mass. There are actual shapeshifting species, some animals to humanoid, but I've never heard of one who could actually fly. The size of wings required defies science and magic."

"But the seraphim can fly?"

"Yes, they are also creatures created almost completely of light. Do their wings work as a bird's might? I don't know. Don't care. They are dreadfully dull creatures."

Yuri got the impression that Lucian didn't like anyone very much. He thought through all the man had told him so far and frowned at one thought. "I slept a week?"

"Father was quite angry. I thought he killed you. Sono was wise to take the horses and escape, but the fac are excellent at self-preservation." Lucian's gaze turned back to Yuri. "You were very broken. The fall and my father's rage, shattered bones, blood splattered everywhere. Organs on the outside. It was quite gruesome. You were already unconscious." Lucian flinched and said, "He ripped off a wing. Like a belligerent child dismembering a dead moth. I stepped in to protest. My mistake, thinking maturity gave me immunity." He shrugged. "I earned my beating, I suppose."

Yuri peered through the bars, the flickering lights of magic making it hard for him to see much. Was Lucian injured? He could only make out the barest play of skin, and what he'd thought was shadow, but realized it had to be healing bruises.

"He hit you? His own son?" A bit of angry fire erupted in Yuri's gut, hot and whipping at the idea that Lucian's father beat him for something Lucian had no control over. The bars crackled and flared. Yuri sucked in a breath and slid back a few more feet to give himself distance from the wards.

"Pummeled me into the ground," Lucian waved a dismissive hand, as if it were so common it didn't matter. "Mostly healed now, and he did not damage me as terribly as he did you. You slept and were still a long while. I didn't know if I was rooming with a corpse."

"I feel fine," Yuri said. Even the ache in his back had faded. He glanced down at the serpent wrapped around his arm. "I'm not *touched*, am I?"

"Perhaps?" Lucian sighed. "Mortals weren't the only ones *touched*, though other species rarely share their insight. The worlds are in constant war. Do we know every creature from all worlds? No. Even though my uncle may claim otherwise. His pets spend their days researching, but sometimes the veil splits and something new steps out."

Yuri thought of Star and wondered if he could find a way to where Star was bound. "I have wings, eat life, and can see seraphim. It sounds terrifying." Yuri frowned, realizing that Lucian implied he'd been left there for Yuri to eat. "Your father locked you up with me thinking I would devour you?"

"I had thought as much until you stated your side was warded."

"Fuck," Yuri grumbled.

"Would you like the vegetables?"

Yuri thought it was strange that Lucian was being kind. Maybe he wasn't? "Aren't you hungry?"

"No," Lucian said.

Yuri stared at the outline of the plate, hungry but not *hungry*. "Maybe?" What if he could only eat meat? The stew had been all vegetables, hadn't it?

Lucian got up, retrieved the plate, and began feeding the vegetables through the bars. "Take them. I need very little, and I'd rather you not turn ravenous again. My father may have confidence in his wards, but you blew through Sono's as if they were paper dolls, and she is one of the last of the Sidhe court mages left. They were the only species who could rival Onari power, but you snapped her wards like a twig."

Yuri gathered up the veggies and took a tiny sample, waiting to see how his stomach would react. It tasted fine, like food. Cold, cooked broccoli wasn't anything to write home about, but it had flavor. He knew a divine recipe for baked broccoli with parmesan cheese and fresh garlic sprinkled with olive oil that he could eat buckets of. Maybe human food wasn't exciting here because the Onari didn't really need it. Yuri slowly made his way through the veggies. They didn't hurt, and his stomach settled, hunger easing a little.

"No discomfort?" Lucian asked. "I should have noticed in the hall the way you clenched your stomach. Feared we had given you something too heavy. My uncle blamed me for your illness."

"I feel okay," Yuri said. "Maybe the castle did something?"

"Indeed."

They sat in silence for a while. Yuri closed his eyes and focused on the strong, rapid beat of Lucian's heart. Did that mean Onari had internal organs like humans? Or was it only Lucian since he was part human? The sound was comforting. Another life nearby. Yuri huddled in the shirt, hating the chill, and trying to not let the silence get to him.

"Being imprisoned is boring," Lucian remarked.

"You've been here before?"

"I was five when my father dumped me down here the first time. My presence had always annoyed him. I suspect it surprised him to find me alive when he returned several weeks later. But the staff brought me small things of comfort back then. I don't think any of them are still living."

"Five?" Yuri asked. "That's not... what the hell? You're his son."

"Whom he never wanted. Radu has several dozen children, all warriors. My father has none but me. Deficiency or design?"

Yuri growled at the idea of Lucian as a child stuck down here. There was nothing but a bathroom space. No bed or blankets, and the chill bit into Yuri's skin. He couldn't sense any life other than Lucian's nearby. The space was a void of sensation, only lights provided by distant candles outside the bars which neither of them could reach. How could a child subjected to this not go insane? It made sense that Lucian trusted no one and hated everyone. His own father had been his jailor and tormentor.

The bars crackled and popped, warning, though Yuri hadn't moved. His anger made his power wild.

Lucian chuckled. "There's a touch of excitement, wondering if you'll rip through my father's wards and eat me. At least wake me if you decide you need to? I'd rather die with my eyes open than devoured in the middle of a nightmare. Masochistic as that may be. I am my father's son, after all. Pain doesn't frighten me anymore." He curled up on his jacket, nestling his knees to his chest, and back to the bars that faced outward into the darkness.

Yuri sucked in a deep breath and ran his fingers over the serpent tattoo, seeking comfort and control of the rising anger. He barely knew Lucian. The abuse made him want to tear through the wards and find Lucian's father, devour him, or at least make him suffer. Why? He was a monster, right? Yuri had met a lot of those. And Yuri had suffered similarly under the Leader's abuse. As a youth his mother had been tortured to force Yuri to behave. As he got older and she died, the pain passed to him. Locked up a half dozen times in a shed outside the camp. No one ever spent more time there than Yuri had.

After the Fracture, it had been because he burned some food. An accident, but he was beaten and locked in the shed for three days to starve and freeze, listening to the terrors of the world outside the walls. His other trips were because sometimes a man would notice him, stare, or even follow him. Which led to Yuri being punished, though he never understood why that was his fault. He learned quickly to never be caught without the mask or clothing by anyone.

When the world fell apart and Yuri was struggling to

survive, a gang of men had jumped him. He didn't know why, as he had nothing then but the clothes on his back, stained and dirty as they had been. Long run out of food, he'd been traveling by foot south, hoping to find a safe place, but aiming for *home,* which was his mother, even if it meant going back to the cult and abuse.

He remembered little of the attack. Only that he'd blacked out and woken alone, hurt, but alive, a stack of clothes piled up next to him; Warm clothes, real boots, and even the gas mask he took to wearing permanently. He vaguely recalled one of his attackers had been wearing it but didn't know how they had vanished and left him things.

"Star," Yuri muttered, realizing that it had to be his lover's intervention.

"What was that?" Lucian asked.

"Nothing," Yuri said. "Will your father let you out soon?"

"Who knows?" There was a biting sadness in Lucian's tone as though he tried to pretend he didn't care, but the hurt bled deep. They weren't all that different, he and Lucian, were they? Both raised by monsters, abused and abandoned, mixed breeds thought to be powerless.

Yuri's rage built like a furnace of energy. At least it warmed him, even if the magic was a rippling thread of irritation as the bars snapped and sizzled in reply. Lucian fell asleep, Yuri listening to his breath and heartbeat, using the sound to focus the rolling intensity of his anger. Injustice, he realized, made him teeter on the edge of losing control.

They had abused Lucian until he buried every part of himself possible from the entire world, not unlike Yuri. Yuri watched his magic coil expand, braiding itself in colored ribbons and picking away at the ward. He should have been alarmed, but it was food, energy, and he wondered if he could give Lucian warmth and free them both. It probably wasn't a good idea. He was as likely to eat Lucian as free him, and Yuri's body reacted to that thought. Not food, as his cock hardened, and he thought about having Lucian the way the Master had taken Yuri. Pleasure, an emotional sort of meal, or sucking the life from the man?

Yuri crawled as far away from the bars as he could. He tugged off the shirt and cringed as he put his back to the ice wall, using the thin cloth as a barrier between them. Lucian didn't need more abuse. Yuri refused to be that monster. He curled himself up in a ball and shivered, hoping to sleep and dream of Star. A gentle squeeze from the snake around his arm told Yuri he wasn't alone, and that was all he needed.

Legends in Magic Books

Three days passed. Lucian was right about imprisonment being boring. Yuri slept a lot, often seeking dreams of Star, but finding nothing but memories of his faded youth scattered with dreams of other worlds and lives he thought might have been memories of the past. He got up and showered when the water ran, and tried to wash the shirt Lucian gave him, since it was all he had.

Food came only every other day, and only to Lucian. Yuri worked hard to control the magic that craved energy, even pulling it back from its slow nibbling at the bars that separated them. The wards responded to his assault by increasing the electricity of the wards and pushing him further away. He didn't want to devour Lucian, anyway. The man rarely spoke to him but shared his meals as meager as they were.

Yuri's magic came alive a handful of times, usually snapping him out of sleep to battle with a rage of magic that would shower sparks from the wards over him in stinging needles of pain. He would roll over, cradle the arm with the serpent tattoo, and focus on his breathing, reminding himself he'd free

Star soon and everything would be okay. His power had a will of its own, and his control waned the hungrier he got. He could identify the differences between body hunger and soul hunger now, or at least that was how he thought of them. One was very physical, his stomach rumbling from time to time as it cramped with hunger, and the other was deeper, louder, sometimes burning him up, until he was dripping with sweat, trying to hold back the magic.

Lucian often huddled in his coat, shivering. The cells were icy. Even the water had grown chilled over the last few days. Yuri caught a scent from Lucian recently, not an unwashed smell, as they both had a little of that despite trying to maintain some sense of cleanliness, but of illness. Was he sick? He ate very little. Yuri tried to encourage Lucian to take more of their small food deliveries, but the man ignored him, instead dropping the food through the bars to quiet Yuri's noisy stomach, all while complaining the sound kept him awake.

Yuri suspected the biting words were armor. Lucian kept others at bay and hid his weakness with verbal barbs and distance. But Yuri had also memorized the fading bruises covering Lucian's thinning body. He knew he shouldn't stare; it was rude and an invasion of privacy, but he watched the man sleep, finding comfort in his breathing, the subtle beat of his heart, and even an occasional pained sound he made while he dreamed.

The bruises infuriated Yuri. Beaten by his own father, the knowledge brought back a lifetime of childhood trauma. He could feed the coil of hunger inside him for a long time on that buried rage. It didn't matter if he dripped with sweat and trembled; he refused to be another monster, hunger be damned. And those bruises, fading to yellow as time passed, didn't ease

LEGENDS IN MAGIC BOOKS

Yuri's anger. How long before they vanished, hiding the damage, and leaving an internal scar?

No one came. Yuri never even saw the food delivered. He would awake and find the plate there, Lucian dumping food through the bars. Yuri tried to draw the man into conversation, anything to pass the time, but Lucian said little. A bitter edge of lemon tainted his usual rock candy flavor. Depression? Yuri knew it was sour and growing by the day which added anxiety, as he worried he'd not be able to resist shoving his magic through the bars.

Yuri kept himself as far from their shared wall as possible, but the wards crackled and zapped as if he sat right next to them. His power grew erratic. Was this meant to be some slow torture for both of them? The past few hours, Yuri found definition in Lucian's flavor, not unlike the crisp bite of a Granny Smith apple. More than a decade without it and he could imagine the snap, his teeth breaking the flesh and sinking into the sour flesh of the apple, juice running down his jaw.

He didn't know why Lucian tempted him more each day. Was it the touch of illness he was scenting? Yuri had devoured the last life dregs from a field of long tortured and near-death creatures. Was Lucian dying?

Yuri hesitated to ask. The man was prickly on his best of days, rarely said more than a single stinging reply, and didn't respond to questions. He slept a lot, sometimes his breathing labored, heartbeat slow. Hunger?

Yuri vowed the next meal would stay with Lucian, though he didn't know how to combat the growing sadness. His or Lucian's. He felt like he was watching Lucian as a child, trying to survive again, lost in loneliness, afraid to trust, losing himself in silence to quiet the urge to scream. Yuri's fury grew. He would free Lucian before his magic destroyed them both, if he could. He didn't care what it was and who it hurt.

He took to humming, part comfort for himself, soft, but sustained, hoping it reminded Lucian he wasn't alone. The man never complained about the melodies Yuri ran through, even if all he remembered were rock songs from popular radio in his college years. Yuri fell asleep humming most days, finding it helped him maintain control.

A week passed, three days now with no food, and Yuri's physical hunger battled his soul hunger. He roused from a broken sleep to the feeling of something delicious passing by, honey on a fresh biscuit, piping hot. He didn't know if it was actual food or magic until the coil of his power reached out to snatch the taste of it and the wards slammed into him with an electrocuting force. His body writhed and convulsed; the ward a thousand times stronger than he'd grown used to. He even lost control of his bowels, which made his face burn hot with embarrassment. Yuri couldn't speak or move for over an hour before the pain finally faded. He lay panting, heart racing, breathing hard, but dragged himself to the shower to clean up, the water icy over him.

The shirt Lucian had given him would not last much longer. It smelled, the sweat impossible to remove without soap, and Yuri wondered if it mattered if he remained nude. Lucian didn't seem to care.

He crawled out of the shower, finding a spot clear of his accident, and caught the metallic scent of blood. Was he bleeding? The jolt hadn't tightened his bond, rather acted more like a taser than the thorns he was used to. Yuri ached from his muscle contractions but didn't think he actually had bled and could find no sign of it in his cell.

Was Lucian hurt?

"Are you okay?" Yuri asked, the wards rippling and raging still, preventing Yuri from seeing into Lucian's cell. Yuri sucked in a deep breath and quietly counted to calm the magic.

Lucian's sigh was long and annoyed. "I'm fine." He didn't sound fine. "They feed me like I'm common get. Disgusting. Like I should appreciate that they feed me at all?" The angry whipping of the wards faded as Yuri wrapped the coil of hunger back around him, soothing it mentally as though he were petting the snake Star had given him.

A goblet sat near the opposite bars.

Yuri remembered the goblet he'd drank from to bond himself to Radu, the Master. His body reacted at the thought of the man, cock going hard, ass clenching to be filled, magic purring with need. Fuck, that was going to be a normal thing, wasn't it? Was it because of the bond? Yuri curled up into a ball, trying to hide the way his body reacted.

"You don't drink blood?" Yuri asked, trying to distract himself from his body's desire. It sounded like the Master drank blood from time to time.

"Not by choice," Lucian said.

"The Nobles feed on emotions, right?" Yuri recalled how it worked. Lust and desire were the Master's choice. Yuri understood how much of a draw they had, his magic using emotions to sink into the soul and magic of another. Maybe he was part Onari? He couldn't help but think of the Master's hands on him, his enormous cock filling Yuri, growing at the base to lock them together in a dance of pleasure.

"We can eat blood, though we prefer the blood of powerful creatures like the fae or the seraphim," Lucian said after a while. "This is... less than quality," he sighed heavily, "it's like giving a human watered down porridge. A bare minimum of nutrients. Hardly enough to keep any Onari living, even the most ordinary of our kind."

There was nothing appealing about the smell. Yuri couldn't sense any magic or life from it. It might as well have been foul water to him. Did that mean he didn't need blood? "I'm sorry," Yuri said. "I would offer you my blood if it would help, but I can't get close to the bars."

Lucian said nothing for a while but didn't touch the cup. "It doesn't appeal to you like the food?" he asked after a while.

"No," Yuri said.

"I wonder what you are." Lucian stretched out a hand and retrieved a book from a stack near the far bars.

"They brought you books?" Yuri asked hopefully. He could use some type of distraction.

"They are not in your language," Lucian said.

Yuri frowned, sadness and loneliness rising again. He remembered what Star said about Yuri needing love. This place had none of that at all. No wonder his power was going mad, his mind wouldn't be far behind. He lay down in silence, back to Lucian's cell, and tried to hold back tears. It would be foolish to cry now. Pointless as it accomplished nothing.

"Here," Lucian said gruffly, and shoved a book between the bars, carefully dropping it into Yuri's cell. He withdrew to the other side of his cell and picked up the book he'd abandoned. "It's nothing thrilling."

Yuri crawled across the space and retrieved the book before making his way back to the far wall. It was a worn title, text on the front foreign, and no art like Yuri was used to. The pages were thin, not unlike the Bible the camp had treasured, but the writing inside was a mix of swirls and loops, a bit like Arabic cursive, or at least how he imagined that might look.

He traced his fingertips over the page, following the lines, uncertain if they read it left to right or right to left, only that in front of him were words, perhaps even a story he had never read. Maybe it was about dragons or seraphim or even incubus demons who moved around the world in magic castles.

Yuri stared at the page, trying to decipher if anything looked similar to the little he knew of languages. A few times, out of the corner of his eye, he thought he recognized something, but when he shifted his gaze in that direction, it was still unreadable. He sighed and stared at the open page, letting his eyes go unfocused and wishing he could read it, even if it was a boring dictionary. Anything had to be better than this brooding and lonely silence.

The serpent on Yuri's arm gave him a tiny squeeze. Yuri blinked, glancing down at the tattoo, then back to the page. The words rippled, changing to English before his eyes, or translating for him? He gasped, and gripped the book tight, flipping through the pages, watching it all become readable.

"What?" Lucian asked.

"The book..." Yuri blinked again, watching the swirls return to their unreadable form. His heart flipped over in fear. Had he imagined it? He blinked again, and the pages became readable. Was his mind translating this for him? "Is it magic?"

"Magic? A book? Are there magic books in the mortal world? I heard humans were remarkably good at killing magic. My uncle says the mortals write about magic, but fear it so deeply they destroy anything touched by it. It's why the fae were one of the first worlds to be lost. Humans eradicated half their number."

The page became unreadable again. Yuri growled in frustration. "I thought for a minute I could understand the words. I have read a lot of stories about magic books, but never seen one," Yuri whispered, his hope fading as the words didn't change again. He caressed the letters with his fingertips, wishing to know what secrets hid on the page. "What is this book about?"

"The seraphim. I thought you'd appreciate that, since they adore you so much." Lucian's tone was bitter and biting. Hiding more pain?

"Do you not like the seraphim?" Yuri asked.

"They care little for me."

"Why? Theo seemed nice. I didn't meet any of the others, though saw some in that first bath."

"To humans," Lucian said. "The seraphim protected and guided humans, a little like humans treat dogs and cats. Benevolent caretakers. Though obviously not all seraphim or there wouldn't have been a war."

"But aren't you half human? Wouldn't that mean they'd be drawn to protect and guide you, too?"

"It's not enough, I'm never enough," Lucian sighed.

Yuri thought about that for a while, sad for Lucian, and trying to sort through what little he knew about himself. "I don't think I'm human at all," Yuri said, staring at his hands. He looked human, or human-like. The Master had looked human, as did Star. The Master had turned into some sort of giant. Yuri vividly recalled the feel of the male sliding into him, filling him, making him writhe with pleasure. He had more than one glimpse of memory of Star being larger, warrior like, eyes shining with light and sunshine, and wondered if his touch would be as alluring as the Master's. Yuri couldn't help the way his body reacted to the memories and desire. His soul was hungry. Hadn't that been what the Master had wanted to teach him? To hunger for desire and lust instead of pain and fear?

"Who is it you are thinking of?" Lucian asked. "Me?"

"What?" Yuri wondered, confused.

"I can smell your arousal." Lucian sighed. "My uncle is alluring. He's always had legions of lovers among all species."

Yuri wanted to die of embarrassment. His face flamed hot, and he wished he could vanish into the ether. "I don't know why I react to the memories this way."

"He draws out the deepest desires of pleasure. It's how the nobles feed. Most species exude energy and emotion in waves during sex. Pain as well."

"Is it magic, then? My reaction to him?"

"Not in the way you mean. My uncle never coerces emotions, only stirs what is already there. If you didn't desire him, you'd only react with adoration, as most of the seraphim do. It's why they serve him."

Yuri thought about that for a while, lapsing into silence. "Is it possible to desire more than one person?" He dreamed of Star, lusted after Radu, but desired them both. Only physical? Or something more.

"Certainly," Lucian said.

"Even if I love someone else?"

"Love is a very mortal word."

"Onari don't love?" Yuri asked.

Lucian snorted. "I don't know. Everyone claimed my father loved my mother, though I remember none of that. I've met none who Radu claims to love. He feeds on lust and desire but is careful to keep everyone at a distance. I suspect he fears turning into my father, maddened by loss."

"You've never been in love?"

"I'm hardly Onari, but no. I've bedded plenty of mortals. Lust, desire, sex, they are tools. Love... I'm uncertain it's anything other than a fairytale."

It was the most Lucian had spoken to him in days, but made Yuri sad as his rage stirred again, thinking how much

Lucian had been neglected and abused. "You don't love your uncle? He raised you, right?"

"I hardly like Radu."

"Was he cruel like your father?"

"You are very nosey."

Yuri flinched. "Sorry. He didn't seem cruel."

"He adores his pets. But no, he was not cruel. Reserved, he's one of the last true nobles, a direct descendent from the Nephilim, his power unmatched, and many throw themselves at him only to bask in his power. He taught me to fight, made me the warrior I am, and how to take care of myself, even though I'm barely stronger than the average human."

"He never..." Yuri didn't voice his concern, knowing the Master fed on desire and lust, he wouldn't have forced his nephew, would he? "Fed on you?"

"No. I had control of those powers long before they delivered me to him. Decades as a sex slave in the Onari city of Johi took care of any training I needed."

Yuri sucked in a breath, feeling like that statement had punched him. "You were a sex slave?" He knew Lucian was older than he looked, suspected the Master was centuries old, but had thought the Master took Lucian in as a child.

"My father thought it would help my Onari side override my human one. It didn't."

"Your father forced you to become a sex slave?" Yuri was horrified. His magic exploded as his anger rose. The wards of the cell slammed into him with a ferocity that dropped Yuri to the floor in convulsing pain again.

It took a long time for his muscles to stop spasming after he coaxed his magic back again. Lucian curled up far away, staring warily at the bars that separated them. Yuri could hear his heartbeat and used it to focus the last of his control over the hunger.

"I'm sorry," Yuri said. "The hunger is rising and anger makes it harder to control."

"You're angry at me?" Lucian asked in a small voice.

"No. At your father for being a piece of shit who abused you," Yuri snapped. The rage rose again. He lost consciousness this time, the pain overwhelming, but he was grateful for the reprieve as it also cooled the anger that made him want to rip the entire place apart.

THE KING OF NIGHTMARES

Yuri woke aching, hunger pulsing in waves, both his magic and his stomach. He didn't smell food, but Lucian's crisp apple scent drifted to him from across the space. The man was reading, keeping his distance, but that heartbeat was a familiar comfort.

"Sorry," Yuri whispered again.

Lucian said nothing.

Yuri picked up the book, clinging to it. He dozed a while, in and out of restless sleep, the hunger loud in his head. He heard the water turn on but didn't get up. Long after it shut off, he finally roused to open the book, seeking comfort in the pages even if he couldn't read them.

He stared for a long time as at first he thought he was imagining it again as the words shifted into something he could read, but as his mind devoured the story on the page, he thought there was no way he was making up the entire tale. Angels hated the humans they'd been created to protect. A type of jealousy, it seemed, as they disliked the way the humans were so imperfect, everything from physically, touched by illness, disease, and weakness, to all the stupid mistakes they made. The angels abandoned humanity, turning angry eyes to the creator. There was an underlying sense that the creator had given humans free will but not the angels.

Yuri frowned. If they had given the seraphim the job to protect and guide humanity, but they abandoned it, didn't that mean the seraphim had free will, too?

He wondered if the fall of angels was due to them embracing free will, but the story didn't mention that. Only that they abandoned their duties, and the creator asked one of his beloved archangels, the only one who had not turned his back on humanity, to help the mortals because the other angels slaughtered them on sight. That had been the creation of an angel and human mix, Nephilim, later translated to the Onari. Yuri recalled the Master had said something about being created by Lucifer. Again, there was no mention of names in the book. Were the Onari supposed to guide humans? The angels turned on the Nephilim, but it seemed they were beaten back to their realm?

Eventually, the species separated. The humans wary of the Onari tried to kill them, the seraphim who were angry with the creator taught the humans magic in revenge. Some seraphim created other species to help destroy humanity. It became a battle for control, everyone killing everyone, and so the creator used the last of their strength to separate the worlds, erecting the veil as a barrier and giving only a few the ability to cross it.

"Did the creator force the first Fracture?" Yuri wondered out loud. "To separate the worlds?"

There was a long stretch of silence. Yuri wondered if Lucian was asleep, but had memorized the sound of his heartbeat, and it beat faster than it normally did when he slept.

"That's what the book says. Can you read it?"

"I think so? The words changed..." Yuri didn't know how to explain.

"*Touched...*" Lucian grumbled. "The seraphim, the few old enough to remember, tell a similar story. One of hundreds of creation stories, fairytales for children. It is a theory my uncle clings to, save humanity and save us all."

"One creator? The Master said there are many."

"One creator for the humanoid species, though others copied the design as inefficient as it is. There were rumors that the seraphim created the fae, but no one really knows. None of the original fae are still around."

"The angels didn't fall; they were cut off?"

"I've only heard stories. Tales from the wars, long before my existence. The archangels fought among themselves, seeking the destruction of humanity for all its flaws. Some of the powerful were imprisoned, others had their wings ripped off and cast into the fires of the abyss. Some left as shades to walk the mortal realms unnoticed by all of humanity."

"But the *touched* see angels, right? Even the fallen ones?"

"That is the thought, though not all *touched* are that powerful. Some only sense something. I have long suspected Radu's many pets exaggerate their power to live quiet lives," Lucian said.

Yuri couldn't blame them if they did. He returned to the book, having to give himself a few moments to un-focus and get the words to form again. He didn't know if it was real or his brain messing with him, but he would take whatever distraction he could. Everything in the book was vague, like the choice to fall or embrace free will. Maybe his brain was mistranslating. Was Star one of the Fallen? Was that why he was bound and only Yuri seemed to see him?

He rubbed his wrist, petting the serpent and seeking

comfort, though it felt like his skin and not the creature Star had gifted to him. The more he focused on his body, keeping the magic bound, and his hunger at bay, the smaller things he felt, like the bond from the Master had weight. They might appear as etchings of ink on his skin until they tightened, but they might as well have been real chains, as they coiled around him in a tickling awareness he found a little unsettling. Had his choice to serve the Master been wrong?

Yuri let his thoughts follow the strands of the bond, finding them stretched outward into the distance, toward Radu, king of the moving castle? Yuri couldn't follow it as he hit a wall of magic. The wards of the bars snapped at him in warning again, and Yuri curled up into a ball, breathing until the magic stopped its assault. Time faded in and out again. Sleep? Or forced into unconsciousness. Yuri trembled as his dreams turned to vivid nightmares.

Footsteps echoed from down the long corridor, approaching with a measured step. Yuri's gut clenched, his cock hardening with need, reminded of Radu's calculated gate and how it soothed his anxiety. The hard sole shoes were similar, but not the same. This rhythm was heavier, larger, and with it came an intense wave of thick doom. Far beyond the *too much* sensation of the Master's power. There was no caramel or decadence in the magic waves at all. Rather, it was cold and bitter, like lemon gelato left in the freezer too long.

Lucian's sadness expanded; startling Yuri out of his light doze. Yuri's magic wanted to latch onto the flavor, but the bars crackled and snapped. He heard Lucian recoil, backing as far away as he could in the small cell, and Yuri put the book aside, hoping it wouldn't get damaged by whatever was to come.

Pain headed their way. The bite of it on the back of his tongue was pungent, lingering in his throat like soured wine.

Yuri fought to keep the coil of his magic wrapped around himself, but his hunger warred with his common sense. He recalled those first few months after the world fell apart, and how he'd starved for a long time before giving in to dig through garbage and rotted foods desperate for the barest hint to fill his stomach, even if it would cause cramping later. It was the reason he'd returned to the camp that had been his childhood of torture. Long years of a slow decline of food had eased the worst of the pain until now. The waves of hunger debilitating with their demand that he sink down and let himself be filled so he could finally feed.

Yuri trembled, fear rising as a thousand scenarios played through his overactive imagination. But he knew exactly what headed their way. Who else could have power beyond Radu the Master, who moved an entire castle and seraphim adored? The darkness, pain, and bitter rage wafted from a distance, a call sign for what Yuri could only believe would be Vladmir Tepes, Dracula, the original monster of human legend.

Yuri couldn't stop his heart from racing, and his brain screamed at him to run, fight, anything other than sitting and waiting for the pain. Lucian's heartbeat sped up too, fear rolling off of him in tangible waves. Yuri found that clarifying, and let his rage build to override the pain. Lucian was no longer a child, but his father had hurt him so deeply he still sat in terror, waiting for the nightmare to descend, and Yuri found that infuriating.

Unjustified, he thought, all the beatings, isolation, and humiliation. Yuri had experienced a lot of the same. Beaten over burned food, or not making something last long enough, even if there was little to go around. The many times they had locked him in the shed outside the camp, left to the terror of the frosty nights and sounds of monsters screaming in the dark because someone looked at him in a way he didn't understand.

He'd killed a man and felt less shame than a general looking at him with lust. Yuri understood that expression now, why he'd hidden behind the mask, which had been more than to prevent damage to his lungs from toxic air pollution. He recalled killing the man who tried to force himself on a little girl. He'd met her eyes and found relief shared between them, and then panic as he knew he had to hide the body.

The way others looked at Yuri, their gazes telling him he was an object to be used, that had always burned him up with fury. Not affection, he realized, not even adoration. Yuri thought he lusted after the Master, but it was more than that. The memory of his touch giving a sense of adoration, comfort, and affection. He hadn't been a toy to be used, but a person to be adored. Had it been a dream?

Star treated him with the same reverence. His touch and gaze filled with recognition and love. Yuri remembered Theo's eyes saying much the same. From the first bath in which Theo helped Yuri, and held him like he mattered, to the last moment when Theo had begged to travel with Yuri, even if it meant Theo's destruction.

Yuri tried to cling to the warmth of the memories but felt himself shoved back down into a vivid replay of being beaten for breaking a bowl. A memory from his childhood, held down, ripped from consciousness by pain, and then forced awake to watch them rape his mother, blaming him the entire time.

Yuri shuddered, the memory real enough to touch his mother's screams like daggers in his skull. He knew he whimpered, felt the sound fall from his throat as magic wriggled around him. The bonds tightened, and he smelled blood, but remained locked into the terror of his childhood.

He forced his eyes shut. The sounds as real as that day had been and sucked in big gulps of air. It wasn't real. The past was over. The weight of the power settling over Yuri drowned out his rage, cooling the heat with waves of icy sadness, pain, and hopelessness.

The bars facing outward vanished, and Yuri's magic jolted free, seeking food, desperate for anything to break free of the ice forming in his gut again. He caught the flavor of baked peaches coated in brown sugar, caramelized, glazed in sticky sweetness. He drank it down furiously with need for a few seconds before it was slapped away, and Yuri felt the ice in his gut expand.

Terror slid through him. Something dug into his power, dragging his strength away, drinking from him. He trembled, fear rising from his skin. The bonds made him bleed, even Star's snake wrapped beneath the bond couldn't ease the razor wire blades digging into his flesh, and his air cut off as he levitated off the ground to hover, gasping before a man who looked a lot like Radu. Not the pretty human-appearing king, but the demon with skin the dark burgundy sheen of the Master's, verging on black and wafting darkness. Yuri couldn't raise his head to see the man's face, only the massive body, hips, shoulders and wide chest. He was dressed in black from the floor up, but the breadth of him was impossible to hide beneath clothing. This man wasn't pretending to be mortal or anything nice.

A clawed hand stroked Yuri's cheek, touch dropping Yuri into another nightmare from his past. Yuri fought to find his way back to the surface, wading through the terror, gasping for breath. He briefly recalled the picture Radu kept of his brother, a human rendition, not of the man himself but of the monster he hid within. It failed to give much more than the barest glimpse of that nightmare. No wonder the world found

Dracula terrifying. Madness in living form. A true, living monster.

The clawed hand moved upward, gripping Yuri's hair, and yanking his head back painfully, his scalp burning in agony. He forced him to look up and meet the gaze of terror. The male himself was beautiful, face sculpted with sharp angles, but cold, eyes black, not the warmth of Radu's or even the pretty pale blue of Lucian's.

"You owe me, death eater." Vlad's deep voice twisted something inside his gut.

Yuri choked, unable to respond. He much preferred the Master's seductive growl to the gravel of this black wolf monster. Death coming, or worse, endless nightmares? Yuri thought of himself staked outside, writhing as wood slogged its way through his body, killing him organ by organ. He wasn't human anymore. Did that mean he wouldn't die? He gasped at how real it felt, grasping for reality, knowing what was in his head hadn't happened yet, but he screamed at a sharp point of agony as though they shoved him on the stake.

"Please," Yuri begged, his voice choked, liquid bubbling up from within his gut as if he really was dying, pierced from the inside. Hot tears ran down his cheeks, and all he could see were the glowing black eyes of the nightmare in front of him.

The ice continued to spread, his breath misting as he roughly exhaled, his entire body shuddering in pain and terror. Panic ripped away all logic. He could only dangle there in the monster's grasp, staring up into the horror of nightmares and endless pain.

The grip on his hair tightened, burning Yuri's scalp with agony as the monster lifted him and shoved him into the warded bars. The magic hit him like an electrical current on blast. Yuri screamed until there was no air left in his lungs. His muscles contracting and contorting in chaotic torture. Stars of flashing color and light blotted out his vision as though the magic fried his brain. He blacked out for a half-second, wishing to die, anything to end the pain, but the hand vanished from his hair and now tightened around his throat, choking him, and holding him up to dangle against the wards and add more jolts of insane torment.

The chill ate him up inside, stripping his ability to fight at all, until he lay limp, body reacting only from convulsions of pain and not effort.

"Please kill me," Yuri slurred, unable to suck in enough air to more than mouth the words. Dracula was feeding on him, not blood like all the books and adaptations led him to believe, but his terror and pain. The hand around his neck would loosen a touch to yank him back from the edge into another nightmare.

It wasn't real, Yuri tried to tell himself. But the monster found one of his worst memories and it rose over Yuri's mind, blanketing him in the past horror as if to say, *Not real? Let's revisit real.*

Rescued by the Prince

His mother writhed with fever, burning up. The Leader had forced her to drink the water, though she had said multiple times they had tainted it and they needed to rebuild the system to clean the water. He had slapped her, instructed the generals to hold her down as he forced the water down her throat, before casting her aside to be raped by them, and ordering a rebuild of the system, anyway.

It took only an hour for the sepsis to set in. Her color changed, and nothing Yuri did seemed to help. She lay broken in her bunk, Yuri wrapped around her, trying to comfort her pain, even while she told him she loved him and begged him to let her die. Her death wasn't kind or fast. And he'd been unwilling to end it and see the only person who ever loved him gone forever. The Leader ignored her, refusing to spare a bullet to ease her pain. He threatened to have her dragged outside to be left for the beasts.

Yuri had prayed to a god he never believed in, wishing for an end. For them both to fall asleep and never wake. It had been Eric who'd come in on the evening of the second day of her suffering to put an end to the noise.

"*She's going to bring a horde down on us,*" Eric snarled. He snatched up a pillow and pressed it over her face. Yuri battled his own emotions, guilt, fear, and sadness, his cowardice to not end her suffering or to fight Eric off. The gasping pain and shrieking wails vanished, leaving the room deathly silent, only a rare sniffle from an upset child disturbing the finality.

She stilled, not that she had much fight left in her, the sepsis and accompanying gang rape destroying any will she might have had to fight. But Eric kept the pillow in place for several minutes, and Yuri buried his face in his elbow, hiding his gulping gasps and tears. He prayed then that she'd be free of all the pain and horror, finally escaping the nightmares into whatever finality death could offer. When Eric removed the pillow, what Yuri saw was frozen terror, horror, and brutal death.

He gasped, choking and backing away to fall out of the bed. Memory burned in his brain of his beautiful tiny mother who had always held him and confessed adoration for him, dead. He'd done nothing to stop it. Had selfishly hoped to end both of their pain. And all he could see now was the horror, over and over. Yuri remembered screaming, like something inside had broken. Reality? His sanity, perhaps?

He'd been dragged away, the Leader's generals shoving a rag in his mouth to silence his pained wails, delivering him to the shed outside the walls. Most of the group wandered away, spitting on him, but one remained to press him into the floor, hands on his body, hips pressed into his from behind.

No, no, no! Yuri's mind screamed as the nightmare unfolded, as real as the day it had happened. He clutched for anything to rip him free, but couldn't breathe, a hand gripped his cock through his pants and yanked the fabric off his ass, rank breath filling Yuri's senses adding to the nightmare of icy mud beneath him already covered in excrement from his many trips locked in isolation.

"Stop," a trembling voice demanded, breaking through the darkness. Yuri thought he dreamed the word or even spoke it himself, but couldn't siphon enough air to ease the popping flash of warning lights in his brain.

"Stop," the voice demanded again, stronger this time. Demanding, angry.

A soft caress ghosted over Yuri's cheek. He couldn't help his flinch, locked deeply in pain, but was surprised by the gentleness of the touch. Yuri stared blankly into the colors of the wards snapping around him in blinding array, but the nightmare rape vanished. His first and last, as the mask and hiding in the pigpen, had become his existence.

"You'll kill him. Stop," the voice demanded again.

"And you care why?" A dark voice growled from behind Yuri. The one holding him tightened his grip on Yuri's throat again, and his balls, pressing a too large to be real cock into the crack of Yuri's ass. He'd been turned and faced the bars, chest sizzling in agony, magic burning into him from the wards.

Yuri whimpered, unable to move, breathe, or even be. His heart beat hard in his chest, aching like it tried to burst free and run from the nightmare. Soft fingers traced the tears on his cheeks, carefully wiping them away.

"Grant me a boon," the voice asked, "this one time." Lucian. It was Lucian who touched him, not with gripping terror, but with soft affection. The crisp apple bite muted to nothing, and Yuri realized his power was entombed in ice, buried until he might as well have been an ordinary human.

"He is worthless," the growl told Lucian, then shoved Yuri

into the bars again, setting the crackling to burn into his skin again. He couldn't scream, only cry. "A mixed breed of corrupted worlds."

"As am I," Lucian said.

"And look at the disappointment you are."

Yuri felt Lucian flinch, his touch stiffening, but he didn't pull away.

"And yet you had me anyway," Lucian snapped back.

"Your mother wanted you."

"Was she the only one? Do you dishonor her memory this way?" Lucian caressed Yuri's face. "I don't know why she ever loved you."

The Monster flung Yuri from the bars and he smashed into the far wall. He felt bones break. Darkness wobbled around the edge of his vision as he sank to the floor and watched the giant monster that was Dracula with his hand through the bars around Lucian's throat. Lucian didn't struggle at all, merely looked resigned, sad.

Yuri tried to crawl toward him, even though he hurt and felt as though he were sucking air through a straw. Lucian didn't deserve this, especially not from his own father. "Don't hurt him," Yuri demanded as he dragged his broken body to latch onto one of the monster's feet, a giant boot clad thing Yuri could barely feel. Were his hands broken?

"Enough, parasite. I do what I want with my get," Dracula sneered and stomped his booted foot down on Yuri's back.

Yuri gasped, his ribs breaking, the snap sounding grotesque. He didn't know how he didn't black out. He was desperate for it to end but reached a hand for Lucian. He'd wanted to free him, right? Before the end?

Star? Yuri thought, wishing for the touch of his lover, but even the sensation of the serpent tattoo vanished beneath the throbbing agony of his body.

"Let me have him," Lucian said, his hand around his father's fist on his throat. "If you planned for him to eat me, you wouldn't have warded his cell. Give him to me."

"You've lived too long with my brother. These mortal toys are beneath you."

"He's hardly mortal. You saw what he did outside. A human who could devour souls and rise on wings of shadow and darkness? He lies at your feet, broken in a hundred ways and still he heals. Are you so blind, father?"

"He is a death eater. Like the demons long cast into the hell dimensions. Even now, he wants to devour you. The darkness always eats its own," Dracula snarled, his voice like grinding stone. It hurt Yuri to hear, as though his ears would bleed if he continued, but he couldn't move. The heavy weight of the boot on his back crushing him into the floor. Yuri's head turned at a painful angle, only able to see Lucian's resigned yet sad expression. The touch of fear had vanished, leaving the bitter snap of sour apple and depression.

Yuri thought Lucian was incredibly brave, or had a death wish, as he said, "That makes you the same, doesn't it? The darkness you thrive on? Torture, pain, fear. He at least showed the dying mercy and ended their suffering. And you've wanted me dead from the moment I broke free from Mother's womb. Why not end us both? Save the world the trouble by snuffing out our weakness?"

The grasp on Lucian's throat loosened. He straightened his stance, unwilling to back down even as large, rough fingers cupped his cheek. Yuri focused on Lucian, fearing that if he looked back at the Monster, nightmares would rip him out of reality again.

"You look like your mother," Vlad said quietly.

"And yet hate burns in your gaze. Did you love her? Is that why you hate me so much? This mortal speaks of love. I told him it was a fantasy. Mortal blathering in ancient books written by the delusional."

"Two sides of one coin. To love..." Vlad said, "Is to hate."

Lucian yanked his face out of his Father's touch. "Indeed. I've learned that lesson well."

"You've grown balls, boy."

"Isn't that what you wanted?" Lucian snarled. "I am a warrior. I fought and won many battles, despite my *weakness*."

"And what has it gained you? My brother's affection?"

"Obviously not your respect."

Dracula reached down and yanked Yuri up by the hair, shoving him face first against the bars to stare into Lucian's mask of indifference. "And this is what you want? This dog of darkness?"

"I can't have what I want. You've made that abundantly clear when you sent me to Johi to become food for the nobles."

"You are what you eat."

"Petty and bitter? Indeed. I find the creature beautiful when he's less broken. Do I wish to taste him? Yes."

Yuri felt something inside him defrost at the confession, like Lucian had actually said he liked him.

Dracula dropped Yuri to the floor, stepping back, though his presence didn't retreat at all. "He is your responsibility, then."

"Radu thought you might train him. His hunger is overwhelming." Lucian knelt and ran a hand over Yuri's face. The wards between the bars didn't react, leaving Lucian to caress Yuri's broken body.

"No."

"You warded his cell to keep him from killing me, and now you'll let him devour me?"

"Your wish, not mine. I believed you called yourself petty? As though I am not?"

Anger rose in Lucian. Yuri caught the flavor of salted caramel drizzled over warm baked apples. He trembled as the coil of magic unfurled, cracking the ice. Yuri trembled at the strength needed to hold it back.

"Then let me return him to Radu for training."

"No," Dracula said again.

"You can't keep me here. The council warned you the last time..." Lucian said, his heartbeat speeding up with fear.

"*You* can leave any time you want," Dracula said. "He remains. He destroyed my garden. I shall use him as the first new decoration in its restoration."

"No," Lucian said. "You said he was my responsibility."

But Lucian's biggest fear was being imprisoned here, and Yuri knew it. He could feel the stinging bite of terror rising in the man, amplified by their touch. Did Dracula feed on his son's fear? He hated the idea of Lucian being abused again.

"It's okay," Yuri choked out, blood in his lungs. He was healing, which was unnerving and painful. "You can leave, Lucian. Go back to Radu." Where he was safe from this Monster. "Do what you will with me, Vlad Tepes, but let Lucian go."

"You dare speak to me, vermin?" Dracula snapped at Yuri, reaching out to dig claws into Yuri's gut.

"Stop," Lucian demanded, and Yuri gasped in pain, gaze popping with colors that threatened a black out that refused to come. It had to be the Monster's power, Yuri realized, that kept him from falling unconscious. Hard to feed on fear and pain if the brain shut itself down to prevent it.

"Teach him control," Dracula demanded.

"You've left us both starving for days. This is suicide."

"You're an Onari Warrior, are you not? Was that not your claim? Overcoming your *weakness*? He stays here and dies, or you stay and train him. Those are your only two choices."

"Is this another test?" Lucian asked. "To prove how *weak* I am?"

"That is for you to decide."

"Do you plan to keep us locked in the bowels of the castle while winter breaks?"

"You may bring him to your suites, but not beyond. If I catch him outside your space, I will strap him to my bed and rape his body and mind until there is not an ounce of fear remaining to devour."

"Pleasant," Lucian whispered, "Always so pleasant to be home. Like a never-ending nightmare. I will stay."

The Monster snorted and waved a hand. The bars between them vanished, wards and all. Lucian gathered Yuri in his arms, cradling him, but his heart raced with fear. Yuri nestled his face in Lucian's shoulder, breathing in his crisp apple spritzed with lemon scent, and held tight to his hunger. He prayed to black out, and that his magic wouldn't take control and devour Lucian.

"Your affection is boundless, Father," Lucian said.

"If that were untrue, you'd already be dead," Vlad growled. His power slid away, feeling like slime receding. It left a stain on Yuri's skin that made him shudder. The chill retreated with that suffocating darkness slipping away. "Best hope he doesn't devour you in your sleep."

"It would be a kinder death, I suppose," Lucian said. "Radu

claims his body is divine. I'd rather die with my cock nestled into his warmth, screaming in pleasure than any path of torture and nightmares you've set before me."

"I have never..."

"Thrown me to the wolves? Sent me to a dungeon to be drained by your brethren?"

"Johi was meant to awaken the Onari strength in you."

"And failed miserably," Lucian said. "I am what you see before you. Whatever weakness remains, and still I persist. Despite your best attempts. How *weak* am I to still live?" Lucian glared at his father, the fear fading beneath the weight of rage and... pride. That hint of rock candy returned, and Yuri kept his gaze focused on Lucian's golden hair.

Silence stretched for a time, and finally the last dregs of oppressive magic vanished, fading as footsteps disappeared into the dark. Neither Yuri nor Lucian moved for a long time. Yuri struggled to breathe, his body hurting and the darkness threatening to drag him down. He wanted it, but also feared leaving Lucian alone with himself.

"The devil you know," Lucian cursed. "You better be worth this insanity."

"I'm sorry," Yuri said. "Will you train me? Help me learn to control this thing inside me?"

Lucian frowned, his gaze studying Yuri's face, hand warm on Yuri's cheek. "You understood? We were not speaking your language."

"I understood," Yuri agreed. "In the carriage, too. You and Sono spoke. Sometimes it wouldn't make sense, and then it would change. Like the book..."

"Magic book," Lucian said. "More than *touched*. What are you?"

Yuri didn't know how to answer that. "What if I eat you?"

"I would recommend you don't. My father is a man of his word. And I am a bitter bastard, good at hiding my rage, with no less wrath than my monster of a father. He raised me on pain and terror. I still have a taste for it."

"You taste like apples. Sour when you're sad, warm and spiced when you're angry," Yuri admitted.

"Apples? I feel fine, but you can taste me? Are feeding on me?" Lucian asked. "What was Radu?"

"Salted caramel, thick and decadent."

"And the garden of the dead?"

"Endless. A buffet of foods, but no apples."

"You are strange," Lucian admitted.

"Do emotions not have flavor?" Yuri wondered. He thought he might have a touch of Onari in him, but maybe he was wrong.

"Emotions taste like emotions," Lucian said. "I've never trained another Onari. But you have this strange ability to read texts and translate conversations not in a language you would have any way of knowing. That is not an Onari or a *touched* strength. Maybe Radu is correct that you are necessary for repairing the rift. I may have some untranslated books we can try."

"More magic books?" Yuri found that a pleasant thought.

"Perhaps to you. You like books."

"I do."

"If you promise to try not to eat me, I can try to teach you how to feed on emotions without killing things." He sighed and glared at their surroundings. "As long as they don't continue to starve us both."

"I don't want to hurt anyone. I don't want to be evil. Eating the dead means I'm evil, right?"

"A mercy. Ending their suffering," Lucian corrected. "Had

I been out there, I'd have appreciated the end. Your idea of evil is flawed." He looked toward the far hall. "He left the cells open. It means we can go upstairs. My rooms at least have warmth and some comforts like the daytime sun. I may even open a window now that the garden of corpses is gone. The stench was endless."

"Upstairs has sun?" Yuri asked, hope rising. It had been too long since he'd basked in the sunlight and felt that gentle warmth on his skin.

"You'll only get it through the windows. You heard my father state what he would do if he found you outside my rooms." Lucian sighed. "I've never been good with pets. Father kills things I get attached to."

The words chilled Yuri, but he reached up to touch Lucian's face, realizing the last part hadn't been spoken for Yuri's benefit, as they were in another language. "Why bother trying to train me, then?"

Lucian flinched. "I'm uncertain I like that you understand everything I say. But Radu thinks the castle found you because the rift needs you. What if keeping you alive gives me a chance to get away from all of this forever?" Lucian sighed. "Hope is a dreadful emotion. Useless, but helplessly overpowering." Lucian bent to gather Yuri in his arms, lifting him as if he weighed no more than a child. "I hope you don't eat me. What do you hope for, Yuri?"

"Sunlight," Yuri whispered as he let his body relax into Lucian's grip. "Love," he whispered, knowing that his heart needed it badly. "Star."

"Star?" Lucian asked as he carried Yuri down a long hall and Yuri's vision faded. "You should be able to see stars from my room. The sky is often clear at night here."

Yuri didn't correct him. Seeing a night sky filled with stars would be a dream come true, though not fill the aching need he had for Star's adoration. The darkness rose in gentle waves to tug him down. And silently, Yuri hoped he wouldn't eat Lucian either. He couldn't see how that would be a positive end for either of them.

A Gilded Cage

Lucian paced his rooms, the space feeling smaller than he remembered. Radu had spoiled him: the space, the freedom. He'd forgotten some of the worst parts of his past.

Yuri slept like the dead, the thick energy of his magic curled around him like a snake ready to strike that Lucian could sense, but not see. Yuri healed with each breath. Lucian watched for over an hour in awe as Yuri's body re-knit with some divine influence. Even the cuts through his many tattoos weaving his flesh back together unblemished. If he were mortal, he'd be dead. More proof he was something no one knew how to define.

Lucian continued his pacing. The staff ignored him. Lucian knew his father went through staff quickly. The rare few who remained lived dancing on eggshells to survive. Which meant his father had ordered them to stay away. Lucian had exited the dungeon and found a single servant there to lead him to his rooms. The creature then vanished, hiding from the wrath Lucian could feel radiating through the house. The emotion was thick and technically, Lucian knew he could nibble at it to fill his empty reserves, but that would bring his sire's focus back down on him.

Yuri said emotions had a flavor. Lucian had never thought about it before. Onari didn't eat like mortals, not that they couldn't, only they didn't need to. But rage, now that Lucian could taste it on the back of his tongue, tasted sour, heavy, and he fought not to swallow because he didn't need his father returning to beat the shit out of him for *stealing* the emotion that blanketed the entire house, and he didn't want to linger on the flavor.

Yuri had spoken of a dozen foods; things Lucian had only read about in books. He wondered if he could attach those flavors to emotions if he knew what they tasted like. Mortal foods? The kitchen creatures provided fare that was usually bland and boring, but enough nutrients to get by. That he needed both emotions and mortal food had always been a weakness.

Lucian glared at the new cage. At least he had a proper bed, clothing, and a bathroom with soap. He planned to get Yuri cleaned up and dressed as soon as he could safely touch the man without wanting to eat him. His hunger made him irritable. Pampered by Radu, always a meal close at hand, Lucian had grown soft.

He stopped to stare through the glowing barrier that covered his door. A ward that might as well have been a wall. Lucian could open the door but couldn't leave the room. He hoped it wasn't the sort that would make Yuri writhe and convulse in pain like it had electrocuted him. Lucian had spent too many of the past days watching in sympathy and pained horror, unable to do anything to stop it.

Lucian hammered on the ward, expecting pain, but it did nothing to him. He continued to pace, watching Yuri sleep, pounding on the ward, hunger and irritation rising. Finally, a servant appeared.

Lucian didn't know what the creature had been previous to working for his father. It was a species with pale purple skin, a bald head, and stretched thin, with coarse-looking flesh over somewhat humanoid bones. It had huge glittering black eyes, not unlike an insect, and it glared at Lucian as though he'd interrupted its work.

"Am I to be starved?" Lucian demanded.

"The Master ordered mortal food and blood to be delivered twice a week," the creature answered.

"I am an Onari Noble," Lucian said. "I don't eat blood."

The creature jabbed one of its three digits toward the bed behind Lucian, where Yuri slept. "You have food."

Lucian sucked in a shuddering breath, feeling like he was gut punched. He was meant to feed on Yuri and Yuri on him. Yuri, whose powers were deadly. Training meant to be a trial by fire? Perhaps this was torture, more for his father to feed on, Lucian supposed. Anger burned in his veins. If the ward hadn't separated him from the creature, he would have eviscerated it.

"Can I speak to my father, please?" Lucian tried to be civil.

"The Master does not wish to be disturbed."

Lucian scowled. Of course he didn't. Master. What a joke. "Can you at least bring me books from the library? I will make you a list." He had a sprawl of bookcases filled with some of his favorite reads. But he was curious if Yuri could read the few locked away as ancient, unreadable texts no one could translate.

"I will send your inquiry to the Master," the creature said and turned away, vanishing into the dark beyond.

Lucian growled and slammed the door shut. The space was dark and cold. His last days in residence, he'd used massive curtains to block out the sea of corpses. His father never cared for the light, creating shadows and eternal night by filling the area with a sea of death and torture.

The stories of Vlad Dracula spoke of him existing in the night. Not completely wrong, Lucian knew, but his father never slept. His anger and hate for everyone permeated the entire valley with an oppressive foreboding that drowned out everything.

The nearest city planted a forest to filter the wafting stench of dead and endless spread of his father's discontent. Two different worlds, this nightmare palace hidden with trees and distance, and that elite city with dungeons beneath to enslave the disobedient to Onari whims. They delivered the worst of the offenders to the palace steps, most ending up on a stake when his father got bored with torturing them.

Lucian learned not to get attached and to keep his distance. In a way, it was no less chaotic than Radu's moving castle. Lucian had lived as a ghost there, working with the army, consulting with the generals and mages his uncle put in place. It gave him things to do, and a way to avoid the seraphim simpering after his uncle's adoration in the castle. Occasionally, a human would catch his eye and end up in his bed for a night of mutual pleasure. Radu never used his mortal pets for food. The *touched* were rare and fragile.

Until Yuri.

Dracula's castle was not as aware as Radu's, but something lingered in the dark. A presence of looming danger, like an unforeseen pit into the abyss waited to claim its next victim. Lucian always sensed it the moment he stepped into the space, but knew the ache in the back of his skull, even if his awareness of it faded, remained. What would happen if a nightmare like this place came to life? The end of all worlds? Perhaps demons would pour free of the veil? Lucian tried not to think about it. He tried to think of the house as a sleeping dragon, waiting for the wrong noise to awaken it, startling it into devouring them all, and so he walked softly. Was it his father's power? Or something more? Lucian prayed he was no longer present when it happened.

He should have left. Run back to Radu while he had the chance. Sono was right about his cowardice, but he knew none, not even Radu, who would face the Beast head on.

Yuri had reached for him, begged his father to stop. Broken and beaten, he still faced down Lucian's nightmare. His level of terror coated everything, whatever Lucian's father had shown him with nightmares, yanking away his bravado. Lucian didn't know what moved his tongue and made him claim Yuri. Their time in the cells spent with little conversation. Lucian as he basked in his sadness, used to being alone and still hating it. It had surprised him to wake a few times to the sound of Yuri humming and find it a soothing reminder he hadn't been completely abandoned.

Sometimes Yuri would mutter in his sleep, the words a jumble that made no sense to Lucian, but he listened anyway, desperate for another life to be nearby. Yuri had fallen asleep asking about stars. Would there be any?

With the nightmare graveyard gone, would there be light and beauty rather than pain and horror? Lucian went to the farthest window and slid back the curtain. An unfamiliar glowing world loomed beyond. Trees, flowers, mushrooms, and the grass all bloomed with light, even with the dark sky overhead. Lucian estimated it was late, or early morning, several hours before the sun would rise. How would all that growth look in daylight?

The density of the new garden prevented Lucian from

catching more than a glimpse at the sky, a handful of stars, pocking the navy-blue veil. It would have to do.

Lucian pulled back all the curtains, dust blooming from them. He sighed. They'd cleaned nothing while he was gone. It might as well have been the dungeon for all the filth he'd be living in. He yanked free the fabrics and made a pile. Without the help of the servants, he'd be cleaning much like he had on the battlefield. At least Radu had given him that skill. A roof over his head and a fire were perks he hadn't often had in war. He'd make it work.

He lit a fire in the fireplace. Fueled by magic rather than wood, it didn't have the pleasant scent of woodsmoke, but projected warmth, and Lucian knew Yuri's skin was chilled to the touch. Snow blanketed the stretch of plants. An unusual paradox, the bright luminescence of spring erupting in what Lucian knew was winter. He wondered if the plants would die beneath the cold?

Lucian stared a while longer, until the heat penetrated the room, and Yuri made a small noise, his body rolling over as though he tried to reach the fire. Lucian checked on him, touching his forehead, finding him chilled, but he didn't wake. Was it a fever? Mortals got those, but Lucian thought it was the opposite, and that Yuri would have been hot to the touch rather than cold. He frowned, trying to decide what to do.

After a few minutes of internal debate, he headed to the bathroom and the giant soaking tub, hoping for warm water. It ran hot and clear, making Lucian groan with a desperate need to be clean. His rooms weren't as large as they'd been in Radu's sprawling estate, but the bedroom also had a small study, and the bathroom. He suspected it may not be large enough for himself and whatever Yuri was becoming. Suicide, was that what this was? There were easier ways to die.

Lucian let the tub fill, dug some dusty towels out of the linen closet, shaking them out before setting them beside the tub. He made his way to his closet to find clothing, doubting he had anything that wasn't centuries old. He'd have to clothe Yuri as well but wondered if he had anything that fit the man. Yuri's body had filled out. He'd always been broad of shoulder, but now lean muscle covered his frame, still underfed, as Lucian could see a hint of rib when the male stretched out on the bed. Yuri was shorter through the leg, and maybe wider through the hip? Lucian stared at the contents of his closet in contemplation. He could keep the room warm enough for Yuri to go without clothing, but Lucian knew the temptation would undo him.

He sorted clothing into two piles: one for him and one for Yuri. Everything was dusty, some damaged from years of disuse. He sighed, knowing he'd be hand-washing everything. What had he been thinking? Offering to stay? Asking for Yuri as though his father owed him anything. He should have run.

His gaze fell back on Yuri, sleeping, breathlessly beautiful. A sleek touch of stubble outlining his jaw, the soft curl of his hair softening the sharp angles of his face. Lucian sucked in a hard breath at the memory of those clear blue eyes, bright like gemstones in sunlight. Filled with vulnerability and need, they drew Lucian's attention back repeatedly, despite the physical beauty of his body. Not human, Lucian thought. Mortals could be aesthetically pleasing, but never the divine beauty of the Onari, and Lucian had bedded plenty of Onari in his life. Why did he feel drawn? Like he could drown himself in Yuri's skin forever?

"Unlike you who is self-destructive," Lucian muttered to himself. If there was one thing Lucian had learned over the centuries, it was to survive, and survival meant being selfish.

He found the rising jealousy over the idea Radu had tasted Yuri unsettling. Why did he care?

Lucian stripped off the last of his clothes, casting them aside as trash, too damaged and stained to save. He added his favorite soaps and oils to the bath, and stared at it, thinking he should get in and soak, and that he'd wake Yuri afterward to bathe. Lucian cursed as he stared at the male on his bed, bloody, covered in filth, healing, and fucking insanely beautiful. He made his way over, scooped Yuri up and carried him to the tub. The man didn't stir. He carefully stepped in, sliding into the heat with Yuri in his arms.

The water was divine, and Lucian could pretend for a few moments that his existence wasn't an endless nightmare. He held Yuri up, uncertain if the man could drown, and let the warmth soak through them both. Yuri didn't wake, likely in that necessary healing sleep he'd been in for days after Lucian's father had ripped off his wings.

The memory burned in Lucian's brain with the scream of agony that echoed through the valley. The damage had stopped the growing spread of the glowing forest rising in the valley. Perhaps the power returned to Yuri to heal him?

Sono had told Lucian to run, but rather than mounting one of the horses and following Sono to the nearest gateway, he'd raced to stop his father's destruction of the unusual man. It happened in an instant. One moment Sono was pulling him away, the next he was between his father and Yuri, ready to face down his wrath, and rewarded with the beating he should have expected.

Yuri whimpered in Lucian's arms, as though he remembered too. Lucian ran his fingers over Yuri's face, trying to comfort him, and was surprised at the touch of fear rising from him. Lucian swallowed, the first taste of the emotion heavy and thick on his tongue. He was so hungry, couldn't recall ever being this starved. His fault for going weeks without food before Radu commanded him to accompany Sono, and then caged by his nightmare of a father.

Lucian told himself he'd only take a taste; a touch to ease the worst of the hunger pains. He hated the weight of fear, had used it often enough, a necessary evil. But it felt wrong to take it from Yuri. Radu insisted on consent. He'd have beaten Lucian himself for taking without asking. Lucian stilled, closing his eyes to stop the gulps he suctioned off Yuri. The poor man was probably having a nightmare. Lucian recalled his teaching and how pleasure was better than pain. If he hadn't been starving, it would have been easier. And Yuri cast off waves of emotions, unfettered, even with his healing.

What if he shifted the emotions from fear and pain to pleasure? Would Yuri be interested in him at all? Lucian knew he was not the handsome Onari prince his uncle was. His stomach sang with warmth as he filled it, even though it was the lingering taint of Yuri's fear.

Lucian scrunched his eyes closed and hugged Yuri to him, finally able to stop feeding and feeling guilty for stealing. Yuri would hate him if he knew. Lucian hated the many who had taken from him over the years. He tried to justify the rape of emotions with the idea that Yuri had been tasting him for days. Feeding on him somehow? Lucian didn't feel any weaker, and usually he could sense someone tasting his emotions. Did that mean Yuri wasn't feeding on emotions?

He sighed and opened his eyes to gaze on the sleeping man. Even half broken and covered in filth, he left Lucian wanting. Lucian groaned and propped the man up on the seat and cleaned himself up. He'd wash Yuri from head to toe when he finished, if only to end the smell. It didn't matter that he was lying to himself. Lucian's guilt over stealing would make him do it, anyway. Yuri couldn't consent while asleep, but the coil of his magic didn't move. Lucian could sense it cradled around him and wondered what it was. Not a barrier, more a presence, not unlike Radu's castle with its waves of strange magic each time it moved, or the dark doom of Lucian's sire's castle lying like a sleeping dragon waiting to burn down the world.

"What are you?" Lucian asked as he carefully washed Yuri's hair.

Desires of the Heart

Yuri's body ached with need, warmth radiating from the outside in. He opened his eyes and the light stung, tears filling his vision as he blinked to adapt to the brightness. Heat blanketed his skin with warm lapping water and the body of someone else pressed against him. The coil of his magic unfurled, starving and seeking, as the scent of crisp apple cobbler filled his senses.

"If you take without asking, I will have Father return you to the dungeon."

Yuri sucked in air and found focus on the biting tone, and the man wrapped around him. Lucian. They were no longer in the stone cells but a large room glowing with some strange illuminated stones in a giant bathtub. "What?"

"I can feel your magic moving," Lucian said, his touch falling away.

Yuri coaxed his power back. It was hungry. He was starving, but he wouldn't eat Lucian if he could help it. "Sorry."

Lucian slid back around him, his skin hot to the touch, and Yuri sighed in delight.

"I think my default is warm," Yuri said. "It feels amazing to be warm."

"Not one of the shadows then," Lucian said as he finished doing something with Yuri's hair, braiding it maybe? "The shadows are always ice. I've heard demons are that way, too."

Yuri thought of Radu, and how burning hot he'd been. He couldn't stop his cock from filling and his body aching with need. Fuck, that was hardwired now.

"What are you thinking of?" Lucian asked.

Yuri's face burned with embarrassment.

Lucian sighed. "My uncle?" He slid away, but Yuri wrapped his arm around Lucian's waist, tugging him closer.

"His temperature," Yuri said. "When he changed? I remember thinking at first, he was a demon, and that the demons ran hot. Stories of hellfire and all that?"

"Radu is not a demon. Never met a demon. The shadows are ice. I've heard the hell dimensions are hot, but demons are cold, and that's why the heat doesn't bother them. I don't have an Onari form like Radu."

"You're warm," Yuri said. He let his arm drop; worried Lucian didn't want him touching him. "Sorry. I shouldn't touch you without asking."

"You pulled your magic back easily enough. Are you still hungry?"

"Starving," Yuri admitted, both physically and his soul, whatever that meant.

"I can try to feed you. Onari couples do it all the time," Lucian said, though sounded uncertain. "Feed from each other."

"How does that work?"

"In theory, it's a little give and take. You fed on Radu, and he fed on you." Lucian frowned. "Though you came out of that encounter even hungrier than you went in."

Yuri remembered Radu filling him, not only his body, but the abyss of his soul hunger. The warmth had been part of it, and inside, Yuri ached with ice. The core of him frozen by the nightmare attack. He shuddered with the memory.

"Are you still cold?" Lucian asked. He reached around Yuri and tapped the side of the tub. The water bubbled and heated again, though Yuri couldn't see any buttons.

"Freezing inside," Yuri said. "I don't want to hurt you."

"You've pulled back your magic."

For now, Yuri thought. He balled his hands up to his chest and trembled, his body aching, a desire filling him with a need that bordered on insanity.

Lucian swallowed hard, and Yuri watched the motion of his Adam's apple with fascination. He longed to study Lucian, not with his gaze, but with his fingers, mouth and tongue. The man soaked himself in depression and bitterness. Could Yuri coax joy and pleasure from him? He shivered at the idea of Lucian taking him.

"What are you doing?" Lucian asked.

"Would you believe me if I said I don't know?"

"You don't seem to know much at all," Lucian grumbled. He shifted his hips, giving Yuri distance, which made Yuri groan.

"Please stay," Yuri begged.

Lucian hesitated. "This desire is for my uncle."

But it wasn't. Sure, Yuri would have dropped to his knees before Radu had he been there, but staring at the sharp angles of Lucian's face, his golden hair back in a thick braid, and those luminescent blue eyes that reminded him of a pale shade of Star's, made him hard. Star said desire wasn't bad, or at least that's how Yuri understood it. He needed love, affection, and adoration. Was that why the seraphim drew his attention?

Yuri's gaze roamed over Lucian's defined shoulders and pale skin. He frowned at a legion of scars over the man's torso and reached out to touch a long white line that started at the collarbone. Lucian flinched. Yuri ripped his hand away. "I'm sorry. Did that I hurt? I didn't mean to."

"I scar like a mortal, though heal fast like an Onari," Lucian said tightly. "The entire reason they let me out of the sex pits of Johi was because they didn't find me beautiful anymore."

Yuri blinked. "Are they insane? You're breathtaking." Yuri touched Lucian's face and slid his fingertips down his cheek and to the scar below, enjoying the warmth and soft heat of Lucian's flesh. He paused and yanked his hand away. "I'm sorry."

He shifted his hips because he was achingly hard and his ass begged to be filled, adding discomfort to his hungers. He briefly wondered if he could make himself come and ease himself that way, or if it would add to his frustration. Yuri felt his face heat with embarrassment as he'd rather that Lucian touch him than do it himself.

"Why are you blushing?"

Yuri shook his head.

"You and I are caged together in my space. Might as well be honest," Lucian said.

"I don't even know if you like men," Yuri muttered in a rushed spill of words. "But I can't help how my body responds to you. The images I have of you and I together..."

"You desire *me*?" Lucian whispered, sounding shocked. "You've had my uncle and desire me? I will never be the massive male my uncle or my sire is. What you see is what I am. I am too human for most."

Yuri thought of Star and his slim beauty. Radu had been divine in his own way, massive, muscular, a true Master, and Lucian, thin without defined abs or the giant physique of his uncle, gave rise to Yuri's desire. Yes, Lucian was lovely, desirable, and Yuri's body reacted with need. Because it was hungry and desperate, or because he wanted Lucian?

"You're beautiful," Yuri whispered.

Lucian flinched again, as though the idea of that was a lie or distasteful.

Yuri sighed, remembering all Lucian's biting words. "You hate me."

"I don't," Lucian scoffed. "I would have left you in the dungeon if I did."

"Was that to save yourself, or me?" Yuri asked.

Lucian was silent for a while and Yuri pulled away, though the man's body heat made him tremble with need. Lucian didn't release him. An arm locked around Yuri's waist, holding them close beneath the water.

"Both," Lucian said after a while, his gaze on Yuri intense. "I will let no one take me again."

Yuri thought about those words, picturing Lucian sliding into him, and gasped as his ass clenched with need. "Okay," he said breathlessly. Yuri shivered again, and guided himself closer to Lucian, seeking heat.

"I can't make the water any warmer. Is it not helping?" Lucian asked.

Yuri shook his head. "Cold on the inside." How did he explain that Lucian's father, the monster Vlad Tepes, had done something to him? Frozen his soul? Drained him until he could barely see straight? His hunger warred with his desire. Did that mean they were the same? Or a means to the end. "Do I repulse you?"

"That's ridiculous," Lucian said. "This strange transition of yours is causing this. You don't really want me. Radu began something he couldn't control, or the castle did."

"The cold started long before the castle," Yuri confessed. "I thought it was hunger. That I would finally die from years of starvation. Then you walked in the door, shining like the sun and restoring hope."

"Hope?" Lucian sounded confused. His bitterness sliding away, replaced with a touch of spice. Anger? Yuri sighed at the change, enjoying the added warmth that slid around them. "Me? Shining like the sun? I'm nothing next to Sono. She's one of the high fae."

But Sono didn't spark that visceral need in Yuri that Lucian did. Like that first night when he pressed himself into Star's embrace, aching to find a home, safety, and love. Yuri cupped Lucian's jaw, marveling at that brightness, buried, but beyond the shine of the sun he'd missed for ages. "You remind me of someone."

Lucian scowled and yanked his face free of Yuri's touch. "I am not a replacement."

"No," Yuri agreed. No one could replace Star. Yuri's soul needed Star as though the man were a part of him. Star had told him he loved too easily but needed affection to grow strong. He thought about Lucian's fear and the damage by his father, forcing the man to bury himself in depression and bitterness. "My heart has room for more," Yuri whispered, "Is that wrong?"

Lucian studied Yuri's face. "You seek adoration like Radu?"

Yuri shook his head. "Not adoration. Desire, affection, light." He pressed his hand to Lucian's chest, feeling the beat of Lucian's heart beneath his palm. "Hope. Love."

"Love is a fool's game," Lucian said.

But Yuri sat in his lap, draping himself in Lucian's warmth. He reached down to trace Lucian's stomach, hesitating to go too low. The memories of rape were too vivid in his mind to force another. His touch brought more of that light to the surface, a growing wave of something bright trickling through the waves of depression.

"Did I really force people when I was in Radu's dungeon?" Yuri asked in a small voice.

"The prisoners flocked to you, trying to break out of their cells. You fed on their energy life? I'm uncertain exactly. More than emotion, which is an Onari trait. I've read some of the original fae could drain life from others. Many tried to touch you, but my uncle kept them away."

He recalled drinking down the Master's pleasure, his body soaring with orgasm, hunger filled with salted caramel gooeyness. He didn't need death, right? Or had the Master been too powerful?

Yuri buried his face in the groove of Lucian's neck, tears stinging his eyes at the idea he'd killed others. For what? Some strange awakening of endless desire? He blinked through the tears, sucking in strained breaths, and saw the serpent tattoo around his wrist. Star.

He reached out to touch it, but it only felt like his skin.

"Do they mean something?" Lucian asked.

"Not anymore," Yuri said. Had Star abandoned him? He stared at the snake, willing it to move, even if it was little more than a squeeze, but it was nothing more than art on his flesh. His magic wriggled, almost a protest of need. Yuri took it as a warning. "I think I need to feed or the power will take over?" He flushed and looked away from Lucian. "I could try doing it alone?"

In college, he'd grown familiar with his right hand. Prior to that, he'd feared being caught in camp touching himself.

Lucian slid his hand down Yuri's chest and cupped the head of Yuri's cock. It was a tentative touch, careful, and not at all what Yuri wanted. He shoved his hips up to press himself into Lucian's grip, needing friction and maybe even a little pain. Was that twisted of him? Lucian tightened his hand around Yuri's shaft, squeezing until Yuri gasped, his body screaming for more.

"Would this be enough?" Lucian asked.

Yuri didn't know. "Don't stop," Yuri begged.

"Keep control of your magic and we will continue," Lucian threatened. He worked his hand over Yuri's erection, a rolling motion that squeezed him in a delicious teasing of *too much* before easing to give friction. Yuri ached, unable to find the right thrust to his hips to add to the pleasure and let himself relax into Lucian's obviously skilled hands. Lucian pressed Yuri into the side of the tub, hand working him, while his other hand slipped around Yuri's throat. Yuri remembered the Master half choking him, keeping him from coming, and longed for that, but Lucian didn't cut off his air, merely cupped his throat. "I wonder how your blood tastes."

"I thought you didn't drink blood," Yuri panted.

"We can. Of the more powerful," Lucian reminded him.

"Right," Yuri huffed, trying to get his body to fly over the edge it lingered on. He was so close, Lucian working his cock like Yuri hadn't known possible. "Fae or whatever." He felt Lucian's teeth scrape his shoulder, not enough to break skin but adding a touch of danger, and a tiny sting. Yuri gasped, his vision popping with color, but he still lingered on the edge of orgasm. Did he need to release his magic to come? How frustrating would that be?

The ice inside ached, pulsing with waves of cold that hit each time Yuri thought he'd finally reach flight and come. He shuddered, trembling with need in Lucian's arms. "I don't know what's wrong with me." Yuri clung to Lucian, flying higher and higher with need, his vision lost in waves of desire, but still unable to reach that final explosion he'd found with the Master or Star. "I don't know why," Yuri cried in frustration. "I can't..."

Lucian shoved Yuri hard into the side of the giant tub, his hand tightening around Yuri's throat, making him swallow slowly and gasp for air, which brought his vision back to Lucian's face. Yuri feared he made Lucian angry, but the man leaned in and pressed his lips to Yuri's, tongue seeking entrance at the seal of them, until Yuri let him in. The warmth was divine, and Yuri was desperate for it. Lucian's hand left Yuri's cock, sliding between his legs to cup his balls, spreading more heat and need through him.

Yuri sank into Lucian's touch, spreading his legs as Lucian slid between him, his thumb circling Yuri's hole, teasing. "Please," Yuri begged. The crisp apple flavor surrounded him, soaking into him with every touch. Yuri battled to keep his power wrapped around him. It stilled, waiting like a serpent ready to strike, and Yuri trembled with worry that it would take over again.

Lucian pulled back from the kiss to watch Yuri's face as he pressed the tip of his thumb inside, nothing more than torment when Yuri wanted to be filled. Yuri tried to move his hips, but Lucian tightened his grip on Yuri's throat, cutting off his air. He stopped moving, and the hand loosened. Yuri blinked through the need to find Lucian's beautiful blue eyes, clear like the sky he hadn't seen in over a decade, and a touch icy.

"Please," Yuri begged again, certain now that he needed to be filled.

"I'm not my uncle," Lucian said, sounding bitter.

"Okay," Yuri agreed.

"I don't have another form."

Yuri didn't know why that mattered. "Fuck me, please."

"And if it's not enough?" Lucian whispered.

"What?" Yuri asked, his need the only thing that mattered right then. The heat of Lucian's body warmed him, thawing him slowly, and Yuri needed him inside. "Please." He wasn't above begging. Yuri begged Star a thousand times and had been gifted passion and the adoration he'd always dreamed of.

"Can you control your power?"

"I don't know," Yuri said.

"Let me bind you, and I will continue."

FLESH AND BLOOD

Yuri blinked, processing the words. "Bind me?" He glanced at the bonds painted over his skin.

"I won't use those unless needed, as they cause pain. I mean bind you." Lucian released Yuri's throat and grasped both of his hands in his, squeezing. "Try to break free from my grip."

"What?"

"I am Onari. I may look human, but my strength is far from human. Try to break free. If you're stronger than me, I'll need to use Radu's bond. If you're not, I'll merely chain you to my bed."

Yuri's body reacted with quaking need to the idea of being tied to Lucian's bed. "Okay," he said breathlessly, imagining Lucian's heat warming him.

Lucian tightened his grip around Yuri's wrist, and Yuri tried to pull away. He couldn't move, and frowned, then tugged harder. He might as well have been locked in place with a spell.

"I would have thought the added muscle tone would increase your strength, but perhaps you are some type of hybrid human," Lucian said as he let Yuri go to reach for a stack of towels. "Not stronger physically than the Onari, but more than *touched*. Maybe a drop of fae in your blood? There are dozens of humanoid species, none stronger than the Onari." He released Yuri's hands and stood, his body rising from the water in all its nude glory.

Yuri's mouth watered when presented with Lucian's cock. Erect he wasn't the massive size of the Master, but Yuri knew it would stretch his mouth and longed to feel the heft of it hitting the back of his throat.

Lucian stepped out of the tub, drying himself, and holding up a towel for Yuri. "Do you wish to continue this?" he asked when Yuri didn't move.

Yuri scrambled out of the tub, taking the offered towel to brush off the worst of the dampness, but the chill hit his skin instantly, making him shiver.

"I have the fire lit in the bedroom," Lucian said as he dropped the towel and paraded nude through the door. Yuri followed, his body demanding a million things that short-circuited his thinking, like Lucian's bubble butt and pale peach skin. The heat of the fire pulsed with warmth, though Yuri felt detached from it as it couldn't melt the chill inside. He knew he needed Lucian for that, but the white lines crisscrossing Lucian's back made Yuri's anger rise.

Lucian paused, glancing Yuri's way as he stood beside the bed, with a drawer open in the side table. A wave of emotions rolled through him. Yuri caught nibbles of each, but the one that settled was the familiar wave of depression laced bitterness. "I know my body is distasteful," Lucian said. "Feel free to return to the bath alone..."

Yuri crossed the space to pull Lucian into his arms and kiss him. Lucian stiffened, and Yuri waited until he relaxed into their kiss, his tongue diving between Lucian's lips to taste the man, before running his fingertips over Lucian's skin. He sucked in the scent of apples, a touch of sugar added to the top, which made Yuri think of hope. He broke their kiss to find Lucian's gaze on him, confusion, sadness, and anticipation in his eyes all at once. Yuri wouldn't bring up his rage over someone hurting Lucian. He didn't want the man to retreat into himself again.

"You said something about tying me up?" Yuri asked. "Will it make me bleed like the Master's bond?"

"If you bleed, it will be because I taste you," Lucian growled and shoved Yuri back on the bed. He pulled a heavy set of chains out of the drawer and a container that looked like lube.

"You often chain people to your bed?" Yuri asked.

The edge of Lucian's lips curled upward in a sardonic smile. "I am my father's son..."

"Look like an angel, but fuck like a monster?" Yuri offered.

Lucian bared his teeth. "Indeed. Angel," he snorted. "But the latter, yes." He reached out and snapped one link around Yuri's left wrist, looping it around the metal frame of the bed which was bolted into the wall and having to climb over Yuri to thread it through the bars.

Yuri again was faced with Lucian's cock, still hard, leaking, and close enough for Yuri to lick the tip. Lucian gasped as Yuri laved at the head of Lucian's cock, not close enough to suck it into his mouth, but Yuri craved the flavor of him.

"You play a dangerous game," Lucian muttered, snatched Yuri's other wrist and snapping the cuff on it, leaving Yuri half seated, sprawled against the headboard, hands over his head. He tugged, but the chains didn't give him much leeway.

Yuri spread his legs, his body begging for heat, and Lucian's body against his. Lucian ran his fingertips over Yuri's face.

"Touching you didn't help," he frowned, sitting back on his heels to study Yuri. Yuri felt his ass clenching and opening with need, and heat rising into his cheeks over the knowledge that Lucian could see the most intimate part of him. His cock stood up straight, dripping over his belly, begging to be touched, but Yuri wanted more than that.

"I can't knot you like my uncle."

A vivid memory rose in Yuri's head of the Master's girth, stretching him to the limit, and his body jerked. "Okay," Yuri said breathlessly, needing to be touched. The ice inside ached and his magic curled around him so tightly he struggled to breathe but feared letting it go would end the adventure and possibly Lucian's life.

Lucian shoved Yuri's thighs open wider, and reached for the lube, spreading it on his fingers and then slowly over Yuri's cock and down Yuri's crease to his begging hole. It was torture, and Yuri sucked in gulps of air.

"Please," Yuri begged as Lucian circled Yuri's hole with his fingertips, tickling, teasing, but not entering him.

"I'm trying to understand how you work," Lucian said.

"Less understanding and more fucking," Yuri demanded.

"I think you forget who is in charge," Lucian said, but he slid a fingertip into Yuri, pressure firm until it curved upward to tease Yuri's prostate. He wrapped his other hand around Yuri's cock, applying a firm but slow and torturous rhythm. Yuri nearly came undone, bucking his hips into Lucian's touch, pleading for more. He danced on the edge again, climax close but unreachable as Lucian worked him with skill. "Fascinating."

Yuri blinked through stars of colors popping around his visions and gasped for air, needing so bad to be filled and unable to reach the soaring goodness he'd grown desperate for. "Please."

"You beg prettily," Lucian eased himself forward as he withdrew his fingers and pressed himself to Yuri's entrance. "Demanding though." Yuri's ass clenched with need, begging to be stretched and filled.

"Yes," Yuri said. He pushed out and felt Lucian slip in, a rod of pulsing heat barreling forward. Finally, warmth, life, and desire burrowed into him. Yuri screamed at the raging fire warming him, chiseling away at the ice. He begged incoherently for Lucian to keep going, fill him, fuck him, and unthaw his soul.

Lucian slammed his hips into Yuri, burying himself deep and pressing the two of them against the headboard, grinding their pelvic bones together. Yuri gasped for air, desperate for more warmth trickling through him.

"I expected you to be cold," Lucian said. "But you're raging hot inside, gripping and tight." Lucian's voice sounded strained.

Yuri didn't know if that was good or bad, only that he needed more. "Please," he continued to beg.

Lucian adjusted Yuri's thighs over his, draping Yuri half over his lap, and removing any last distance between them. He put a hand on Yuri's cheek, gaze filled with anger. "Look at me," Lucian demanded.

"I am," Yuri said, unable to pull his gaze away from those divine blue eyes that left him breathless, even while his hips wriggled and squirmed with a need for friction.

"Who do you see?" Lucian demanded, his fingers wrapping around Yuri's throat, squeezing until Yuri's vision popped with color in warning.

"You," Yuri heaved out in a strained breath.

"Me? Who am I? The nephew of your Master? The son of the Monster? Who am I?"

"Lucian," Yuri breathed out desperately.

Lucian loosened his grip. Yuri sucked in air, but Lucian's gaze was no less angry. "What of this other I remind you of?"

Star? Yuri blinked, unable to process beyond his need. "What?"

"You said I remind you of someone?"

"A dream," Yuri whispered. His tattoo didn't move, and his memories of Star faded more every day. The rare dream of them together often happening months apart until recently. Yuri had taken it as a sign he was dying, the end finally giving him some peace. "A wish for joy before I die."

Lucian's grip on Yuri's throat tightened again, cutting off his air until Yuri saw stars and nearly passed out, but his aching body kept him from falling into the abyss. Air returned, and Lucian moved his hips, not a careful glide or even a gentle wave of pressure, but a frenzied pace of bruising intensity. Lucian held Yuri's hips in a painful grip, at an angle that kept his cock sliding over Yuri's prostate with each thrust.

Yuri trembled, hands balling into fists as the chains kept him bound tightly to the bed, his body filling with warmth and Lucian coating Yuri with his apple scent. It was subtle at first, the coil of Yuri's power seeming to absorb the touch, and pulsing with growing heat. He clung to the magic coil, begged it to remain wrapped around him and not attack Lucian, which would have ended all the goodness that was spreading warmth inside of him. Yuri sank into the heat, his power, whatever it was, absorbing the waves of energy Lucian cast off with every thrust and spent emotion. Even the anger had a bite, like cinnamon overpowered the sugar to deliver Yuri a touch of spicy flavor. His body sang with pleasure as the ice wrapping around his soul melted, awakening like a monster stirring from the abyss.

Yuri thought briefly he should be afraid, but the sensation of something enormous lurking deep inside was comforting. The presence ancient and nearly unfathomable, like something locked away for so long that it had grown lethargic and slow, but strong, and willing to rise if coaxed.

Lucian slid his hand up to wrap his fingers around Yuri's braid and tug his head to the side, baring his throat. It felt vulnerable, and Yuri's neck ached at the angle, but his body sang, desperate for more. His eyelids fluttered as he tried to focus beyond the popping waves of color, purple and black, Lucian's bruised soul? His magic slid around the color, examining it carefully, a tentative touch on what seemed to be trauma scarring his existence. The layers of color endless, almost a barrier to keep Yuri from touching him, and Yuri didn't push, rather he skated on the edge of the array, feeling the jagged waves of the color smooth and the dark edges fade into the purple.

Yuri blinked through stars, his body quaking with need, and stared into Lucian's face, the man appearing feral, fangs pronounced and sharp, eyes blazing with rolling purple rings. The mix of need and anger on Lucian's face driving Yuri to the edge of desire.

"Yes?" Lucian asked as he licked up the line of Yuri's neck while his cock pummeled Yuri's hole, grinding him into the headboard. "This is better than my hand on your dick?"

"Yes," Yuri agreed. "Please." He didn't know what he needed, only that he was close. Teetering on the edge of absolute dissolution of self beneath the desire.

Pain pierced Yuri's skin, and he felt Lucian sink his fangs into Yuri's neck, followed by a swallowing suction as Lucian sealed his mouth over the wound and drank while he fucked Yuri into the headboard. Yuri couldn't keep his eyes open, the spinning glory of pleasure dizzying, or maybe it was the loss of blood. Either way, he clung to the threads of his magic, floating on wave after wave of pleasure. Lucian's apple flavor saturating every part of him as though he'd spent months soaked in cider until it became a heady wine, fermented with layers of dancing magic. The line between pleasure and pain wove back and forth, pulling him back and dangling him over the edge until Yuri gasped and shuddered, barely able to keep conscious, until he felt Lucian come. The man ground his hips into Yuri, digging himself deep to spurt all that delicious heat inside, pouring not only come, but waves of unfettered magic, life, and desire into Yuri.

Yuri gaped, spinning off into his own orgasm as his body clenched around Lucian, milking his cock, neck aching from the bite, and a dizzying wave of color exploded in his brain. He had the vaguest sense that Lucian was feeding on him, more than only his blood, but the waves of rocking pleasure. Emotion?

Yuri's magic filled, soaking up all the glowing light and even nibbling away at the purple and black colors that saturated Lucian's magic. Yuri gasped, afraid he was eating Lucian's soul, and blinked until he could see Lucian's face. The man seemed unharmed, licked his lips to dab away the stain of Yuri's blood. Yuri couldn't stop his body from flying up and over the edge into another orgasm as Lucian continued to rock into him, his body draped over Yuri, half boneless, cock filled and still pulsing.

It was a strange dance of give and take. Lucian rode the emotions of Yuri's orgasm, filling Yuri with his come repeatedly. He would pause for a few seconds, gasping and half hard, until he filled again and surged inside again, desperate to continue their rolling tides of give and take.

Yuri soaked up the waves of apple and sugar touched with a spice of cinnamon each time Lucian broke his skin in a dozen places, licking at the blood, and sealing the wound with his lips. Yuri thought they could be locked in the cycle forever, dying beneath the pleasure, and that was okay. The ice inside faded, pulling itself back into a tiny ball, unbroken and aching inside, but the expanding chill paused. The lingering presence inside, aware, but patient, as though waiting.

He blinked a dozen times, surprised by the fading light of the room. Lucian continued to feed and Yuri relaxed, his magic satiated at the very least, even while his body still writhed with wave after wave of orgasm. Yuri wondered if it was possible to die from sex as his vision narrowed. Lucian was part sex demon, wasn't he? And pleasure was a far better way to go than the beating that had almost taken him before. He sank into Lucian's embrace, his body going boneless with submission as the world vanished around him, sending him into pleasant dreams of pleasure, love, and freedom.

Angels and Demons

Lucian paced. Yuri slept like the dead, though Lucian had released his hands and tried to spread him out more comfortably on the bed. He'd had to tug clothing on the man because even knowing Yuri was nude beneath the blanket, his body might as well have been irresistible. It was an act of insane control that kept him from rousing Yuri to indulge in him again. Lucian had never fucked anyone to unconsciousness before, or even had the urge to. Sex, after his years of Johi slavery, had been sex. Pleasure, of course, a necessity to feeding his Onari side, but only divine willpower gave him the strength to pull his cock and his fangs from Yuri's body.

Lucian glared at the fire and continued to pace. Yuri held tight to his magic, though Lucian had sensed it moving a few times. The man's skin glowed with a brightness Lucian couldn't ignore, not unlike the seraphim.

"What are you?" Lucian muttered for the thousandth time. He could hear Yuri's heart beating, the rhythm very human in sleep, and his stomach grumbled. He would need actual food, wouldn't he?

Lucian glared at his reflection in the mirror. He'd showered, fearing leaving Yuri too long, and stepped out from the spray to find his scars fading. Not gone, but no longer pink edged white lines. Had Yuri done that?

Yuri slept curled around Lucian's pillow, blankets tugged up to his chin, mostly to keep Lucian from jumping him again. His uncle had said Yuri's body was divine, which was the understatement of the century. Lucian had his fair share of lovers from all species, genders, and sizes. Yuri's body grew more alluring with every breath he took. Muscles firming, definition clarifying, lean and toned, with a bronze tan painting his skin, the glow beneath making him luminescent. His hair thickened, waves of chocolate brown settling around his face, the braid lengthening as he slept, and touches of color appeared, white, almost silver in some spots, like ice wrapping strands near his brow, and bright purple in others, pops of copper woven here and there.

Lucian couldn't stop staring, gaze drawn to Yuri's sleeping face, and then back to the mirror to examine his scars. Were they fading? What had Yuri done?

He stomped to the closet and tugged on a shirt with a high collar. He had many to hide his body, and he buttoned it without thought, listening to Yuri's breathing and the gentle rumble of his stomach. Yuri needed food. Lucian had given Yuri his meals when they were in the dungeon, and it helped the man's control. The days that passed between feedings had made Yuri's power erratic and the wards had punished him for it. Perhaps Yuri needed to eat more often, both actual food and whatever magic he had gotten from Lucian?

Apples. Yuri said Lucian tasted like apples, but he hadn't sensed Yuri pulling anything from him. He knew all too well the feeling of being drained as someone fed on his emotions. It could be subtle, but if Yuri was some sort of newly awakened Onari, he wouldn't have had that type of control. Restraint, or did Yuri need something else?

The garden of corpses still confused Lucian. Those on the verge of death, so far gone that even his father couldn't feed on their fear or pain anymore, and Yuri had released them all. The waves of power turned all the suffering to ash, which blanketed the ground and grew into some sort of fae forest of giant flowers and mushrooms. How? Lucian had seen nothing like that before. Even Radu didn't have that sort of strength. The number of species left to writhe in endless torture, many immortal and considered impossible to kill, and Yuri had snuffed them out with almost no effort. The heavy weight of oppression blanketing the entire valley evaporated, calming as all the pain vanished.

Lucian knew Yuri warred with himself over the end of all the suffering, but he knew it had been a mercy. How many times had he nearly ended up out there himself? His father had threatened it for his entire existence. In fact, Lucian had chosen Johi to escape the possibility of ending up with a stake shoved up his ass, dangling in the wind for his father's sick display. He didn't regret it, even with all he suffered in Johi. But if he had been staked, he'd have preferred Yuri's tender release than an eternity of torture.

Lucian made his way to the door and pounded on the barrier again. No one came. Why had he stayed? The torture had been too much to watch. Forced to watch Yuri's terror and taste it, his gut clenching with the need to suck it down by the buckets, had made Lucian react.

He paced, listening to Yuri, and kept the fire burning. He even opened the curtains to stare out into a glowing array of wildlife beyond. The sun shone overhead. Lucian could feel the warmth of it despite a thin spread of snow over the tops of the plants but found the resilience of the vegetation fascinating. Yuri created that? How was it possible? Lucian knew some fae could craft illusions of other worlds, but nothing about that spread of plants was an illusion.

"What are you?" Lucian said again, watching Yuri sleep.

Yuri made a small sound of protest in his sleep. Lucian brushed his forehead gently, taking a nightmare from Yuri. His sleep grew more erratic and disturbed the louder his stomach rumbled. He needed food, mortal food.

Lucian paced for several hours. Yuri dreamed, sometimes it turned to nightmares, which Lucian immediately soothed away, absorbing the fear and sadness, and redirecting the man's subconscious to find joy and peace. It was the least he could do as he'd filled his stomach with Yuri's blood and emotions. Lucian had nearly lost control, the sensation of being inside Yuri better than he ever imagined. A touch of jealousy stirred in his gut at the idea that Radu had him first. But Yuri had screamed Lucian's name when he came. That had to mean something.

He pounded on the barrier again, waiting with his arms folded. Nothing.

He cursed in frustration. Yuri was to stay in his room, but Lucian was supposed to be free to move around. He stomped over to the bookshelf, sorting through titles he thought Yuri might want to read, even if they weren't in a language the man should know. The library in the house had a better selection, but it was somewhere to begin. Lucian wondered if Sono had gotten back to Radu. Would Sono care he was stuck here? Lucian thought Radu might worry more about Yuri and how he might help their cause, but Lucian wasn't too much of a coward to admit he hoped to be rescued too.

The oppressive waves of the house made him shudder. He continued to pace, letting himself grow irritated by the silence.

A sliver of something cold ran down his spine.

Lucian froze. He turned his gaze to Yuri, wondering if the man was awake, but he slept on, his body healing in ways that a normal mortal couldn't.

It took Lucian a handful of counted breaths and focused awareness to realize it was the house that changed. The doom and heavy sadness blanketing it, shifting to anticipation and curiosity. He had a few moments of hope that Radu had come himself to face his brother and demand Lucian and Yuri's return, but the servant who appeared at the door looked glum.

"The Master wishes to see you," the creature said. The ward between them vanished and Lucian stepped free from the room, glancing back at Yuri briefly before the ward jolted back into place. He didn't speak to the creature, only followed him through the dark halls of the manor. Every window and door closed as if a touch of light would burn it all away.

Lucian arrived at his father's study, his heart beating a little faster than he'd like, and the sense of dread growing in his gut. The beautiful creature leaning against Vlad's desk made Lucian's heart flip over in terror. It wasn't real. Lucian knew the appearance of the *man* was a façade, like everything else about him them it. Lucian hated him with a passion.

"Your father said you were home," Gabriel said, standing and striding across the distance to reach for Lucian. In this form, he looked like some artistic depiction of the mortal view of the archangel. Massive in height and breadth of shoulders, blond hair and blue eyed with sun kissed skin and an asymmetrical face meant to allure the masses with perfection. If there was one thing Gabriel was good at, it was misleading everyone. His appearance, his words, and his actions, all a lie.

Lucian had spent many years on his knees, bleeding beneath Gabriel's sadistic games. It was the reason he hated the seraphim. They viewed this monster as a protector, and if they even knew he existed, they'd flock to him, and straight to their own demise. Lucian knew better than most that external beauty hid demons. It was the reason he'd hesitated from the first moment he'd laid eyes on Yuri. The draw to touch the man, explore what he was, it made Lucian's fear rise. What hid behind the desire? Another monster like this?

Gabriel slid his hand over Lucian's cheek, the touch feeling like a spread of sludge to Lucian's heightened senses. "I've missed having you beneath me."

Lucian jerked his face away from Gabriel's touch. "I thought I caught a rising stench wafting through the manor," Lucian snipped, unwilling to back down even though his gut clenched in terror.

Gabriel gripped Lucian's hair and shoved him to the floor in half a second of super speed movement. "You forget your place."

"Never," Lucian denied. "I don't belong to you. The council agreed." *Please, please, please* let him not be forced to serve again.

"As though the council decides what I do."

"My brother has spoiled him," Vlad said. "Taught him to fight, and bed humans."

Lucian flinched.

Gabriel dragged Lucian to his feet by his hair, but Lucian refused to utter a sound to acknowledge the pain. "Humans? How the mighty have fallen. Had I known you wished to fight, I'd have put you in the pits when your beauty faded."

"Yet you still touch me," Lucian snapped. "When I repulse you so?"

"I could return you to your uncle," Gabriel offered.

Lucian didn't react. He knew it was a lie and had decades of practice not rising to the bait.

"How many seraphim would trade themselves for you?" Gabriel asked.

None. He made sure they hated him.

"He's got some human creature now. A pet," Vlad said, looking bored. "That *thing* devoured my garden."

Lucian couldn't help his reaction then, his stomach flipping over with anxiety. He couldn't imagine Yuri surviving Gabriel's attention. Vlad was a monster who lived to create fear through nightmares. Gabriel was a nightmare.

"Really? Fascinating. I noticed the change in scenery outside, and thought it unusual. The corpses were much more entertaining."

"He's nothing," Lucian said. "Weak. *Touched*. But little else."

"*Touched?*" Gabriel said. "Does he see the seraphim?"

Lucian didn't reply.

"Interesting."

"Humans are worthless," Lucian said, hoping to remind Gabriel why there were none in Johi. They died too quickly. Humans rarely crossed the veil into Dahna. The only time Lucian could recall any being in the Onari world was on the rare occasion Radu's castle would land there.

Gabriel released Lucian's hair, and Lucian landed hard on his knees, but didn't make a sound. Lucian always suspected the torture Gabriel visited upon him was because of his human half and Gabriel's hate for humanity. "Perhaps I shall go and see?" Gabriel said as he turned toward the door.

Lucian swallowed hard, fear trying to take over as he reached for Gabriel's boot. "Didn't you come to see me?"

Gabriel paused. He reached down with claw tipped fingers, sharp and far from human or pretty now, as he lifted Lucian's face. It didn't fool him, Lucian knew that, but prayed a distraction would be enough to send the monster on his way. Gabriel grew bored quickly. Lucian suspected it was the age. A being as old as time would have little new to spark interest. If he provided a few minutes of distraction, so be it, as long as Gabriel left.

"You throw yourself at me to protect a human?" Gabriel demanded.

Lucian sucked in a breath. "Yes."

"Why?"

"He's mine," Lucian said. "Very little has ever been mine. Why can't I keep it?"

Gabriel's claws tightened on Lucian's face, piercing skin, and fresh blood ran down Lucian's cheeks. "A pet? How unlike you."

"Radu's pets always seemed affectionate. I thought I'd try."

Gabriel's gaze turned to Vlad, who shrugged unbothered. "The human is some unusual hybrid, but weak. I would have devoured him already if not for Lucian's request." Vlad's glare turned to Lucian, and he could feel the weight of the anger resting on his back. "I have instructed Lucian to keep the dog in his rooms. I will need to rebuild my garden."

Gabriel shoved Lucian to the floor and rested his boot on Lucian's chest, holding him in place with no effort. "I have a handful in Johi whom our clientele has lost interest in. I will send a caravan to retrieve them."

Lucian sucked in a breath as though someone had punched him. The cruelty knew no end, but he said nothing. Trying to save others would only end in more dead, tortured, or enslaved, including himself.

"Avail yourself of my son's affection while you're here," Vlad said, turning away, "a reflection of my gratitude. And he seems to have missed you."

Lucian gasped at being offered like a whore. He could only hope that Gabriel's distaste for his scarred body would keep him away, but the beast reached down and sliced open Lucian's shirt, slashing skin and drawing blood in thin rivulets down his chest. Lucian bit his lower lip to keep from responding.

"He does look lovely covered in blood and my come," Gabriel said. His gaze darkened as he stared down at Lucian. "Bleeds like a human but doesn't die." He yanked on Lucian's braid, drawing him upward. "A reflection of the seraphim with that touch of beauty nestled in a human shell. It's an abomination."

Not here, Lucian thought, though didn't fight. He didn't want to be tortured and raped in his father's study, knowing his father would have dined on the waves of fear, pain, and sadness while Gabriel abused him. It was a nightmare. A waking nightmare that faded but never ended.

"The playroom is open," Vlad said, his gaze focused on the wall and the long-faded floral wallpaper. Lucian bit back his joy over the idea of not being raped in front of his father. Small favors, he thought, as Gabriel dragged Lucian away. He could only hope he *entertained* Gabriel long enough to make him forget about Yuri.

ENEMIES AND LOVERS

Locked away with the prince of sorrow, Yuri finds his power adores life, love, and Lucian.

Prince to the King of Nightmares, Lucian has mastered hiding his pain, loneliness, and hunger until Yuri brings him light and bread pudding. With magic erupting with nature to fuel Yuri's magic, the pair find comfort in each other.

But as the Monster's castle begins to wake and the walls narrow, Yuri's flourishing magic wanes as their world is torn apart by shadows. Lucian races to face his sire and free himself and Yuri from the Monster's grasp before they both are devoured by the darkness.

When nightmares and reality merge, will Star let anyone else have Yuri's heart?

BAKING MAGIC

Yuri's dreams were chaotic. He would step into a nightmare, the beginning subtle until the anxiety grew to anticipation of fear and pain, and then strangely vanish, leaving him floating in the dark. He wished for Star's touch, or even to see the man in a memory, but hit some sort of barrier each time he reached for him.

When Yuri finally awoke, he felt like he'd slept for days, his body stiff, but not aching. He stretched, blinking to the brightness of the open curtains and the world beyond which looked like sunlight. He jolted up in bed, casting off the blankets, and frowned down at the loose pants and shirt haphazardly pulled over him. Had he done that? Where was Lucian? He glanced around the room. The fire still crackled and cast pulsing waves of warmth across the room, a stack of books sat on the bedside table, and a tray of covered plates rested on the table near the fire.

Yuri's stomach grumbled in hunger. He slid out of the bed and approached the table, hesitating to touch any of it, though he was desperate to eat, but wouldn't take more from Lucian if he could help it. He swallowed back his hunger and went to the window. The world beyond was something he'd only imagined from a dream. Flowers and mushrooms towering overhead, letting in peeks of sunlight, and a sprinkling of snow that glittered on the greenery like fairy dust. It was fascinating and beautiful.

He heard a startled sound from the bathroom. Pain? Yuri found his way to the open door and large space, worried he would invade Lucian's privacy, but the man sat in the tub, neck deep, head resting on the edge on a towel, eyes closed and face turned away, looking relaxed.

Yuri's magic sensed something off. A sour bite of lemon? Bitter apple? He couldn't quite grasp the flavor, as it was faint.

"It's rude to stare," Lucian snapped.

Yuri jolted, feeling ashamed. "I'm sorry." He didn't explain his concern. Lucian's hot and cold attitude made him dizzy.

"There is food on the table. Eat," Lucian commanded.

"Have you..." Yuri began.

"The food is for you. I took what I could from the kitchen. I do not need any of it."

Yuri flushed, grateful for Lucian's consideration. "Thank you."

Lucian waved his hand, not moving from the tub otherwise, and Yuri turned back to the room to examine the tray of food more thoroughly. It was actually a mix of things, eclectic, like day old bread, a bowl of raw eggs, tea, milk and sugar, and a handful of fruit that was unfamiliar. Yuri looked back at the fireplace, and since he had a decade of experience cooking over an open fire, and a strange desire to taste something that wasn't watery soup, he thought he might use the teapot to cook, and a few of the covering for the plates as mixing bowls. He poured the warm water from the pot into a spare bowl to save it for tea.

Yuri sat down and tore apart the bread. The utensils weren't overly helpful as he tried to cut up the fruit. He tasted a bite of each, taking a moment to savor the unusual flavor and try to define the best way to use it. The texture was a little grainy, not unlike a pear, but had a sour citrus bite, more like a blood orange, or even a grapefruit. Yuri tore the fruit up into smaller pieces, mixing it with the bread before adding a few eggs, the milk and sugar. He dumped it into the teapot and hung it over the fire, then fixed himself and Lucian cups of tea with the remaining hot water and tea.

After letting it steep a few minutes, Yuri brought the tea and the small containers of remaining milk and sugar into the bathroom, setting them beside Lucian in the tub. Lucian didn't open his eyes or move from his long soak, and Yuri left it and the man, to his bath. He returned to the fire and poked at his concoction for a while, the scent of it growing in gentle, sweet waves. Yuri wished he had cinnamon or nutmeg, or even a touch of molasses, as he was certain that would improve the taste, but when he checked again, his little bread pudding mess had come together nicely. He carefully took the pot off the fire and set it to cool, lid off, the smell teasing his stomach with hunger.

Yuri added the remaining eggs to a smaller metal bowl lid with water to boil. He went to the window while he waited and ran his fingers over the latch, worried that if he opened it, he'd bring the wrath of the monster down on them.

A large bush danced in the wind close to the glass, thin stalks reaching toward the light, and a pop of colored orchid-like flowers bloomed. Yuri sat in awe at the beauty, thinking it had been far too long since he'd seen something so delicate and divine, magical in appearance. He wished he could sketch it or snap a picture to save the memory of it.

He pressed his hand to the glass, and the stalks of the bush began to move. He gasped, blinking at the sight, intrigued and terrified all at once. But a flowering stem wriggled and grew, adding more sprouts and blooms until it touched the window where Yuri's hand rested. He held his palm there for a few minutes, heart racing, but joy also filling him at the beauty of the flora in front of him. Was it sentient? How was that possible? What a magical world this was, filled with horrors and terror, and beauty this delicate.

Yuri unlatched the window. It clicked open quietly, sliding a few inches free on its own. The stem slipped around the glass and into the opening, reaching for Yuri's hand. He hesitated a moment, fearing it was some sort of man-eating plant. But a handful of blossoms caressed his palm, not unlike a stray cat newly fed might. Yuri ran his thumb over the nearest petals, breathless at the texture of silk on his skin. He glanced toward the eggs and knew he had to pull them from the fire.

With a heavy sigh, he dragged himself away from the flower and retrieved the bowl before the eggs could overcook. He fished them out of the water with a pair of spoons and dropped them into the room temperature water he had left over, hoping it would cool them enough to stop their cooking. Yuri heard a snap and looked up, thinking he'd find Lucian, but the window was closed, the lock in place, and a small stalk of flowers lay on the sill inside.

Yuri rushed to the window and picked up the stem, fearing the flowers would bleed from being severed from the rest. But the entire bush returned to its unaltered state, and the flowers in his hand attached to a green stem looked like any other bloom he had ever seen. No blood or acid-like fluid to prove it was some sort of sentient life. Had the plant closed the window and left him this gift?

He pressed his hand to the glass again. Sending out a thought of thanks for the gift. The bush twisted and wriggled for a minute, a thousand more blooms appearing along the stalk and it grew instantly, adding several feet to its height as it reached for the sky and the bright sun overhead.

Yuri let out a long breath, the flowers glittering in the light like a rainbow of hope. He took the flower and returned to the table, adding a bit of water to a drinking glass and tucking the bloom in. He hoped treating it like most plant life he recalled from the days before the Fracture would help it thrive. Yuri glanced down at his serpent tattoo and wondered if the flower was a gift from Star. A reminder that hope remained? That life thrived beyond all the pain and torture?

He sighed and sat in the chair, his back to the fire, and peeled the eggs. He made up two plates. Both heaped with his haphazard bread pudding and eggs. Yuri set the second plate across from him, hoping he could coax Lucian to eat, but didn't dare approach the bathroom.

Yuri heard movement in the bathroom. He tried not to tense, as he knew Lucian had left the water. His memory of Lucian's body was vivid and alluring, and also infuriating as he recalled the many scars. Yuri tried to focus on his plate. The eggs were bland without salt and pepper, and a bit of mustard powder, but he ate them anyway. His stomach made a grateful noise as he waited between bites for any poor reactions. He found the bread pudding more successful than he had expected, the flavor of the fruit saturating the custard and bread, adding a bite of sour with a touch of sweet. The texture wasn't perfect, but he had an open fire and the wrong cookware, so that was to be expected. It still turned out better than he anticipated.

Yuri ate slowly, savoring each bite. There was more left, but he knew it would be better as it cooled. He didn't know how often they would get to eat, and wanted to ensure Lucian filled his stomach, too.

Lucian exited the bathroom, fully dressed, from sock-clad feet to a high-collar button up. His hair braided in a tight weave that made his face look more delicate and vulnerable, but the man hesitated as he stared at the table with the setting across from Yuri.

"I made enough for both of us," Yuri said. "Probably for a few days if we're careful," he added.

Lucian frowned as he slowly approached the table. "What is it?"

Had he never seen bread pudding before? "Bread pudding." Yuri said.

Lucian's lips moved without sound, like he was repeating the words 'bread pudding,' but he made no move to sit down.

"It's a custard type of dessert, slightly sweet. I used the fruit, eggs, bread, sugar, and milk."

"Dessert?" Lucian asked as he finally pulled out the chair to sit at the table. He moved slowly, stiff, like he hurt. Had Yuri done that?

"Are you okay?" Yuri asked.

"You'd do best to speak when spoken to," Lucian snapped. He sat at the table with the plate in front of him but didn't touch it.

Yuri swallowed back whatever he wanted to say and took another bite of the custard. He could think of a handful of spices that would improve the flavor, a touch of almond or vanilla extract, or even a bite of cloves or cardamon. Did they have any of that in this magical world?

Lucian picked up his fork and cut off the tiniest corner of the pudding square on his plate, carefully bringing it to his lips.

He ate the piece and Yuri watched with worry. Would Lucian like it? Could the Onari taste food?

A half dozen expressions crossed the man's face as he let it sit on his tongue for a moment before seeming to chew a time or two, then swallowing. He stared at the plate as though it were a mystery but cut off a larger slice.

Yuri hid his smile behind a sip of tea, watching Lucian eat the bread pudding with slow fascination.

"This is bread pudding," Lucian said. He glanced at the hard-boiled eggs on his plate but didn't touch them.

"The eggs would be better with some seasoning, but at least it's some protein," Yuri said. "There is more of the pudding, if you'd rather have that. There are eggs in the pudding, too."

"Eggs in the pudding?" Lucian poked at the remains of his pudding and then the eggs. "It does not taste of eggs."

"It's a custard. Milk, sugar, and eggs baked, make custard."

Lucian picked up the teapot and scooped another chunk of the pudding onto his plate. "Eggs, milk, and sugar. You made this?"

"Yes."

"Out of the little I brought from the kitchen?" Lucian looked shocked.

"I was a baker before the world ended," Yuri said.

Lucian shoved the eggs aside. "You can have those." He blinked and pointed his fork at the flower that sat in a glass between them. "Where did that come from?"

"The bush outside opened the window and dropped it inside," Yuri said. "I didn't know plants of this world could move on their own. It's beautiful. Do you know what kind of flower it is?"

Lucian looked toward the window and back at the flower. "No idea. Never seen it before. Moving plants, you say?"

"Oh," Yuri said, disappointed. He hoped to learn something about all the flora outside. He took the eggs off Lucian's plate and placed them on his own, giving Lucian the remains of his slice of bread pudding.

Lucian ate with a grace Yuri thought befit a prince, even while Yuri devoured the eggs like he was starving. His hunger subsided, but he had to admit he could have eaten everything on the table and still been hungry.

"If I bring you more food items, you can make other things like this?" Lucian asked as he finished the last of his bread pudding.

"Yes," Yuri agreed. "It's nice to cook again. I could do more with some spices."

"What are spices?" Lucian asked.

"Cinnamon? Cloves? Um, they are plants that add flavor to food." Did they not have spices in this world? Maybe since most Onari ate either blood or emotion, they did not cultivate food like it had been in the human world.

"I have read about them in books, but never seen them. Perhaps Radu would know." Lucian let out a long sigh. "Not that I have any way to contact him." He ran his fingertip over a petal. "Even the flora responds to you. Fascinating."

Yuri frowned, not enjoying that he sounded like a science experiment gone wrong. "I'm not doing anything in particular."

"Hmm," Lucian said. He nudged his plate away, and sipped his tea, still stiff in the chair.

LUCIAN'S SECRET

Yuri cleaned up the plates and cooking items as best as he could, taking everything to the bathroom to wash in the sink. Each time he returned Lucian hadn't moved. Something about the way he sat bothered Yuri. Not the sour bite of apples that he recognized as Lucian's depression, as that was something he was growing familiar with, but the faded strength of the flavor. How often did Lucian need to feed his Onari side?

"Did I sleep a long time?" Yuri wondered. Maybe too long?

"Nearly two days," Lucian answered.

"Oh. Wow. That long?" No wonder he had been ravenous. "My magic didn't do anything while I slept, did it?" Like try to devour Lucian? He didn't feel overly soul hungry, if that was what it was.

"No."

That was something, at least. Yuri moved around the room, picking up things, making the bed, busy work, while he monitored Lucian, who sat in the chair, eyes closed, still as a statue. "Do you need to feed again?" Yuri asked. "On my emotions?"

Lucian gave the barest shake of his head and remained at

the table. "The books are for you. I'll try to retrieve more later. Though few are in your language."

Yuri ran his fingertips over the spines of the books, finding a slew of titles that translated before his eyes. Maybe being well fed put his power at high speed? Whatever his power was.

He heard another small sound from Lucian and looked back his way. He sat stiffly in the chair, perching on the edge, as if sitting hurt, and a dark stain colored the shirt near his braid, expanding outward. Yuri blinked, thinking at first it was the dampness of Lucian's hair, but the gray shirt shouldn't be browning from wet hair.

"You're hurt," Yuri cried, making his way across to Lucian's side.

Lucian flinched away from Yuri's touch. "I'm fine."

"You're bleeding."

"Observant, aren't you?"

"Did your father hurt you?"

Lucian said nothing.

Yuri reached for him, turning the chair and noticing stains trickling like veins over Lucian's shirt on both sides. He hissed in horror, unbuttoning the shirt and pushing it off Lucian's shoulders. The man didn't protest, only breathed shallowly, keeping his back stiff. A thousand slices covered his chest, stomach, shoulders, and back. Some little more than scratches, others gaping wounds of spread flesh. It was as though all Lucian's scars had been reopened.

"Fuck," Yuri cursed.

"It is nothing," Lucian said, sitting stiffly, though the wounds wept a steady flow of blood. It was an odd mix of red and gold, almost orange like fire, rather than the dark red blood Yuri was used to seeing. He studied the wounds, muscle torn in

LUCIAN'S SECRET

some places, clean slices in others, a combination of a blade and jagged claws had been used on Lucian.

"I can stitch the worst of them," Yuri said. "If you have a needle and thread?"

"It's unnecessary," Lucian said.

"They need to be closed to stop the bleeding." Yuri crossed the room to search the drawers, not caring if he offended Lucian's need for privacy. For all he knew, gremlins created the clothing here and there was no such thing as a needle and thread.

"In the closet, left side, fourth drawer from the bottom," Lucian whispered.

Yuri raced into the closet and found the drawer. Inside was a small tin with a few needles and thread. He returned to Lucian's side. "I don't suppose you have a stash of liquor in here?"

"Onari don't get drunk on mortal alcohol," Lucian said.

"I'm not trying to get you drunk." Though that would have been a bonus with all the stitching he needed to do. "I'm hoping to clean the wounds."

"I already cleaned them," Lucian said.

Yuri wondered how much it hurt to soak open wounds in warm soapy water, but kept his mouth shut. He brought his fingers to the largest wound on Lucian's chest, a gaping spread of five inches. "I don't want to hurt you," Yuri said as he carefully pressed the edges of the wound together. Lucian didn't make a sound. Yuri brought the needle up. He'd done this a thousand times in the camp, but usually once someone was well and drunk. Yuri had learned to ferment a handful of weeds to create more when they'd run out, even if it tasted terrible.

"I will heal," Lucian said.

"I'm sorry. I hate that this will hurt," Yuri said as he

stitched. Lucian didn't push him away or react at all. He sat stiff in the chair as unmoving as Yuri pictured a vampire might, barely breathing. There were a dozen cuts in need of stitching, and Yuri took his time with each small and careful stitch he knew would leave less of a scar and heal faster. The rest of the scratches seemed to scab over, but Yuri wondered if he could find something from the giant blooms outside to help. Living in survival mode for a decade taught nothing if not resilience.

"Be right back," Yuri said as he patted the last stitched wound dry and got up to make his way to the window. He peered out, staring through the growth for anything he recognized. "Is that yarrow?" He wondered out loud. Yuri unlatched the window.

"You must stay inside. The house will inform Father if you leave."

Yuri cursed, seeing a patch of the familiar weed a half dozen feet from the window. He couldn't crawl out or ask Lucian to do so.

"It's fine. I will heal. I only need rest." Lucian sounded tired.

Yuri held his hand up to the opening of the window, wondering if the vegetation would respond again, and praying for the yarrow. It would help the bleeding stop and ease some of the sting he knew Lucian had to be suffering. The bush didn't respond, but sprouts trickled from the ground in a line toward Yuri's hand. The seedlings grew, spread, and finally a batch of yarrow reached his fingertips, sliding through the open window and spilling a heap of leaves inside.

"Thank you," Yuri said, his heart in his throat, grateful to whatever magic responded to him. He gathered up the leaves, carrying them to the table to make a salve to apply to Lucian's wounds.

"What are you?" Lucian asked, sounding absolutely mystified.

"A friend?" Yuri prompted. He warmed some water and mixed it with the salve before carefully applying it to Lucian's wounds.

"You want to be my friend?" Lucian asked.

"You don't want that?" Yuri asked. He found a spare sheet in the closet and tore it up for bandages.

"Much like love, it's a fairytale," Lucian said.

"Okay," Yuri said, unwilling to argue. He finished bandaging everything and stared at Lucian's pants. Were there more wounds? He sat very stiffly in the chair. How bad off was the rest of his body? "Can you take off the pants?"

"No."

Yuri frowned. Lucian wouldn't meet his gaze and remained still as stone in the chair. "Lucian..."

"I only need rest."

Yuri pushed all the first aid supplies aside and went to bed, shoving back the blankets, and laid down a section of towels to catch anymore bleeding. "Let me help you to the bed to rest."

Lucian didn't move, but Yuri glimpsed moisture beading around the lashes of his closed eyes. Was he crying? Yuri didn't ask. He made his way to Lucian's side and carefully helped him up, letting the man lean on him, and they moved slowly to the bed.

Yuri eased Lucian down, memorizing every small pained sound and area of added stiffness, knowing there were likely a thousand wounds he hadn't been allowed to see. He curled himself close to Lucian's back, putting his own to the door. Not that anyone had come in that he knew of, but he would try to protect Lucian from more damage if he could.

Lucian stiffened from Yuri's touch, the bite of spicy hot

cinnamon trickling through Yuri's senses. Fear and anger mixed. Lucian didn't like anyone seeing him weak. Yuri breathed out a long, measured breath, focusing on calming his heartbeat. He rested a careful hand on Lucian's hip, and thought about his youth, the years his mother taught him about dozens of plants. Everything that could be used for healing or flavoring food. He knew poisons as well and wondered briefly if he could get the monster to eat some, but dismissed the thought. Could creatures as powerful as the Onari be poisoned? He wished he could rip apart whomever hurt Lucian.

"Is it me you hate?" Lucian asked in a small voice.

Yuri blinked. "You sense hate?"

"Hmm. Emotion."

That made sense. "No. Whomever hurt you."

"This world will devour weakness, Yuri. Do not open your heart."

Yuri flinched but didn't pull away. "Love isn't a weakness, Lucian. Kindness isn't a weakness." He ran his fingertips over Lucian's bare shoulder. One of the few places only scratched and not torn to shreds. "Can you only take emotions from me during sex?"

"No."

"Okay. Then I give you permission to take whatever you need to help you heal."

"Permission..." Lucian muttered, as though the thought was ludicrous. "As if I need your permission. You're little more than a pet here."

"Okay," Yuri shrugged. "I had a roommate who had a cat in my first semester at college. That tiny baby used to sit on my chest and purr. She always seemed to know when my heart ached." He recalled how his loneliness and fear would fade with her sweet vibration and warmth. "I'll try to think positive things. Take what you need."

"And if your magic retaliates?" Lucian asked.

"My magic is well fed for the moment." It wasn't a lie. A tiny ball of ice shifted around inside his soul, but the coil of his power pulsed with a gentle warmth, like a heated blanket. His stomach full, and his magic satisfied for the moment, he only hoped he could maintain the control and help Lucian heal.

SWEET TEMPTATION

Two days passed, and Lucian's wounds healed. His movements became less stiff, and Yuri had to cut out the stitches as the flesh held itself together. Lucian wouldn't allow Yuri to see the rest of his body, even banning him from the bathroom for hours while Lucian would soak in the tub.

Yuri's hunger grew, the physical kind stirring up his magic as though to remind him it needed to eat. The hours Lucian spent in the tub, Yuri sat on the windowsill, window open, breathing in the scent of plants, pollen, the icy chill of the wind, and watching the flowers. Gentle waves of peace floated through the flora, and he soaked up the sun, unbothered by the chill. The vegetation continued to grow, leaving a path open to the sky to allow the sun to shine down during the day. The contrast of life and cold fascinated Yuri.

Snow fell often, usually at night. He longed to see the stars, but the cloud-filled sky hid them from him. Were there stars in this world? He glanced at the serpent tattoo wrapped around his wrist and wished to see his Star too. The long stretches between his dreams of the man always left him fearing it was his mind fucking with him, and not an actual memory. But the tattoo didn't fade or change, nor could he recall sitting down in an artist's chair to have it etched into his skin like he could his many others. The body of the serpent spanned his entire torso and beyond, weaving beneath the bonds of the Master's chains like elaborate art. The head of the creature stayed near Yuri's wrist, as though monitoring his heartbeat. Sometimes Yuri thought he saw the head move, the eyes focusing on him, but couldn't tell if his brain was messing with him with wishful thinking or whether it actually happened.

The few pieces of clothing Lucian had large enough to fit Yuri's slightly bigger frame were shapeless, and more like sleepwear. Lucian insisted Yuri keep clothed, even protesting when Yuri removed his shirt. Was the man hungry again? Lucian refused to elicit any more intimate encounters. Yuri suspected it was because he hurt, but as the wounds faded, the spice of fear didn't, the sour bite of depression grew, and he thought Lucian was avoiding touching him on purpose.

Yuri's stomach grumbled, too. The remaining nibbles of bread pudding hadn't lasted long, and his body craved the taste of it again, long starved of delights like sugar and fruit. He stared out the window, glancing back to the cup on the table and the flower stem, which bloomed and thrived as though it hadn't been cut from its host, and Yuri wondered about the flora's response. If he hoped to keep feeding Lucian, he'd have to eat. A balance of his energies, he thought. Keeping his physical side fed seemed to ease the soul hunger, but the longer he stretched between eating, the more both hungers grew.

He sensed Lucian taking small bites of emotions from him from time to time, careful, and almost hurried like a child hiding a cookie. Was Lucian ashamed of his hunger? Yuri didn't dare suggest Lucian leave the room for more food. No one came, and the last time Lucian had ventured out, he returned torn to shreds. The idea of it, and that Yuri had slept through that abuse, made his heart ache. Not that he thought he had any chance of protecting Lucian. The monster who was Lucian's father had beaten Yuri to a pulp without really trying, and Yuri swallowed back a long list of questions that he knew Lucian would not be willing to answer.

Yuri wondered if they would be given food soon, or if Lucian venturing out had cut off any help they might have gotten. He longed for even the bland eggs, or stale bread, but had recently spent hours daydreaming about fruit and the delights of flavors he had once mastered. The bright colors of flowers, some a red that reminded him of strawberries, often had him mentally reciting old recipes for pies, cakes, and even a basic jam. He salivated at the thought, even willing to eat it by the spoonful, knowing the sticky sweetness would likely be too much for him after all these years without it.

A vine curled up and through the window, one long sprout twirling and thickening as it slid by Yuri's feet and outstretched legs. The sprout grew more vines as he watched, tiny buds appearing and opening as he watched in fascination, and bursting into strawberries, white changing to glorious bright red as he stared. Yuri blinked in stunned silence, wondering if he'd fallen asleep, but when he didn't move, the sprout coiled up his leg to reach his hand, which sat open on his thigh, and dropped a handful of ripe berries into it.

Yuri gasped at the weight of it, and how they felt like real strawberries. Was it even a thing in this world? What was this strange magic? He brought a berry to his lips, touching it to the tip of his tongue first, marveling at the texture of the many outer seeds, and then biting into the flesh of the fruit. A juicy burst of sweetness spread over his tongue and he sighed in delight. The vine continued to expand and grow, more fruit arising as it climbed the wall beside the window.

He scrambled down from the sill and found a bowl, taking it to the vine. Yuri didn't have to pick them. The fruit dropped into his bowl, filling it in seconds with a delicious heap of the divine berries. He couldn't recall the last time he'd had them. Probably culinary school before the world fell apart. The climate change that ripped apart Texas after the Fracture hadn't been hospitable for growing much of anything other than root vegetables and hearty weeds.

Yuri ate his fill from the bowl, his stomach bursting with joy and the sweet stickiness of the ripest strawberries he'd ever eaten in his life. The vine refilled the bowl until he feared it would spill over on the floor and he'd lose some of the precious decadent gift. He raced to retrieve more bowls, letting them all fill, and the vine slowed, leaving only a touch of buds sprouting, as if waiting for the bowls to empty. The plant covered the entire wall between Lucian's massive windows. Would the monster find out and get mad? He prayed this wouldn't cause Lucian more pain.

Yuri glanced toward the bathroom, deciding right then to feed Lucian no matter what it took. They were stuck together, and Lucian might try to keep himself aloof, even if that meant starving himself, but Yuri couldn't help but want to touch and comfort him. He marched into the bathroom with a bowl of fruit in his grasp, thinking he'd demand Lucian get out of the tub. As though he could command Lucian.

Lucian soaked in the water unmoving and seeming uninterested. Yuri frowned, staring at him, knowing that they both needed to feed their *other* hungers. Whatever that meant for Yuri, he'd gotten it from Lucian the last time they had sex.

"You are exceedingly rude," Lucian remarked, not moving from his spot in the tub.

Yuri set the bowl of fruit down on the wide ledge of the bath and pulled off his shirt. Lucian opened his eyes and glared at the sound of fabric moving. "You can wait your turn to bathe."

Yuri shoved down his pants, stepping free of them, and feeling Lucian's gaze find his semi-hard cock. Lucian's flavor changed, sweetening a little, but the hot jab of fiery cinnamon remained. Yuri wondered if he could recreate the flavors to share with Lucian how he tasted. Emotions had flavor, and that made Yuri wonder if he wasn't feeding on Lucian's emotions, what was it he tasted, pain, life? He didn't like that thought.

He climbed the steps and made his way into the warm water, stalking toward Lucian with purpose. Lucian's glare didn't fade. "You dare?" Lucian asked.

"I do," Yuri said, sliding his thighs around Lucian's, letting his hard cock rest against Lucian's stomach. He rested his knees on the bench beneath the water beside the man, not wanting to hurt him with his added weight. "You need to eat."

"I have been," Lucian snapped.

"Nibbling?" Yuri ran his fingers gently over Lucian's chest. The scratches had completely vanished. The large wounds he had stitched were pink but fading. Even the old scars Yuri remembered Lucian had been ashamed of, faded, leaving his skin smooth and mostly unflawed. "Is that working for you?" Yuri asked as he pressed his lips to Lucian's cheek, delivering him a soft kiss.

Lucian didn't react. "I think it is you who hunger."

"A little," Yuri agreed. He reached behind Lucian and tugged the bowl of fruit close. "It's less with my stomach full." He held a berry up to Lucian's lips.

"What is that?" Lucian asked.

"A strawberry. Have you ever had one?" Yuri asked.

Lucian said nothing, but parted his lips. Yuri slipped the fruit inside, watching Lucian process the texture and flavor. He chewed and swallowed. "Where did you get these?" He demanded as Yuri pressed another to his lips.

"I was hungry, and a vine grew," Yuri admitted.

Lucian looked at him in shock but accepted a handful of the sweet berries.

Yuri leaned in and licked the seam of Lucian's lips, waiting for the man to let him in, and when he did, finding the flavor of Lucian's mouth sweet with berry juice. Lucian returned the kiss slowly, careful, but Yuri could sense the man's awareness awakening, and his cock lifting to touch the inside of Yuri's thigh.

"Can you taste them?" Yuri wondered as he pulled his lips from Lucian's. "The flavor of the berries? It's a bit like sweet sunshine."

"You are very odd," Lucian said. Yuri fed him a few more berries. He sighed after a few minutes. Yuri's body pulsed with physical need, but he worked hard to not be rude and hump Lucian like he was a dog in heat, no matter how much he wanted the man to fill him.

"I will need blood," Lucian said quietly.

"Okay," Yuri agreed, wanting Lucian's cock nestled inside him, though the idea of having Lucian's cock and his teeth in him made his cock twitch with need. "Do you want to tie me up again?"

"How hungry are you?" Lucian asked. He reached up to grab a handful of Yuri's braid, tightening to the edge of pain, which made Yuri sigh sweetly and sink further into Lucian's lap.

"I ate my fill of berries."

"And the magic?"

"Wouldn't turn away a nibble," Yuri confessed. "Or your cock and your teeth in me."

Lucian sucked in a stunned breath, his gaze narrowing. "Out of the tub," he demanded.

Yuri frowned, but slid away, and climbed out of the tub, dripping water and come from his leaking cock. He waited for Lucian to do anything, needing him badly, and praying that obeying would get him what he wanted.

"Close your eyes," Lucian said. "I don't wish you to look at me."

Yuri blinked but closed his eyes. He wanted to protest because he enjoyed looking at Lucian, from his pretty blue eyes and golden hair, to his slim hips, and divine cock, but Yuri sucked in gulps of air and waited. Yuri heard Lucian get out of the tub, movement of the water, and the sound of a towel, and wished he could lick the water from Lucian's skin. He felt movement from the air stir around them, Lucian close. More fabric rustling covering the mirror? Not that Yuri looked in it often. Next to Lucian's beauty, Yuri was average.

"Keep your eyes closed," Lucian instructed.

Yuri heard him moving around, pausing a minute or two, and tried to focus on breathing. Was Lucian examining him? Did he not like what he saw?

"Is something wrong?" Yuri asked, unable to keep silent as his worry grew. Was his body sprouting roots or something he hadn't noticed?

"Did I tell you to speak?"

Yuri sighed, hating the biting tone. He knew it was a defense mechanism, but had hoped they were past all that, and couldn't help but feel the sting each time Lucian snapped at him.

Lucian's warm fingertips traced down Yuri's back. "This is an elaborate design," Lucian said.

Yuri bit his lower lip to keep from responding, no matter how much he ached to press himself into Lucian's touch. The tattoo was his largest, starting at one shoulder and sweeping all the way around in a mash of some of his favorite fantasy novels, from Middle Earth to moving castles of junk. It had taken him six sessions of at least five hours at a time to complete. Only now that he'd encountered an actual moving castle of magic, did he find his choice of art ironic.

Lucian continued to examine, touch firm and exploring rather than caressing, and gaze hot enough that Yuri didn't need to open his eyes to feel the rise of attraction. His cock ached to be touched, and he licked his lips, imagining the flavor of Lucian shoving himself down Yuri's throat. Yuri's hair had grown, some magic stretching the length until it reached nearly the middle of his back, but he kept it braided, and Lucian slid it out of the way to continue his examination.

Two hands followed, fingertips sliding over Yuri's body, tracing tattoos and muscles, careful, but precise. Yuri sucked in air, fighting to keep his body still when he wanted to fling himself into Lucian's arms. The need to be touched, adored, and fucked senseless grew inside of him to override any lingering hunger.

"Please," Yuri whispered.

"Don't make me bind you," Lucian said.

Yuri bit his lip. Lucian's hands traced down the globes of Yuri's ass, parting his cheeks as though examining him. Yuri prayed for a finger or better yet, Lucian's cock to fill his clenching need, but said nothing, though his breath and heart sped up with desire.

Lucian turned Yuri to face the tub and put a hand to his back to press his chest down on the surface beside the stairs of the raised stone sides of the bath. The rock was cool against Yuri's skin and he felt exposed as Lucian kicked Yuri's legs wider apart, as if to admire the way Yuri's cock hung between his legs and spread ass all at once.

A towel appeared beneath Yuri's chest, Lucian tugging it into place. "I don't wish to scratch your skin on the stone while I fuck you."

Yuri shuddered at the image, wanting it badly. "Please."

"Keep your eyes closed. If your magic stirs, I'll use the bonds."

Yuri nodded, nestling his face into the fabric of the towel, which smelled like Lucian.

"You're naturally wet. How is that possible? Mortal men don't have that function." Lucian said as he tickled the rim of Yuri's opening. "Clenching and gaping like you want to devour me."

Yuri did. He needed it like he needed air. Even if Lucian's touch wasn't the love and adoration he craved, Yuri knew he was desperate to bathe in affection and desire. He sighed, wondering if it was true. Did that make Yuri like the Master? Devouring emotions? Or something else.

Lucian finally slid a teasing finger inside. The long digit sucked in as though Yuri's body was a black hole needing to consume the universe. "You tempt me terribly," Lucian said.

KNOTTY CRAVINGS

Yuri smiled into his folded arms, hiding the expression and spreading his legs wider, hoping for a reward. He'd have preferred languid kisses and teasing caresses, but when Lucian removed his finger and his cock nudged the entrance of Yuri's hole, he hissed with desperate need.

Lucian added pressure, sliding inside, and Yuri fought not to push back and swallow the length of him whole. But Lucian's hands on Yuri's hips gripped him hard enough to bruise. The edge of pain adding excitement. "I could use you like a toy," Lucian said, "fuck you like many of the pets of Johi. They drug many to keep them compliant, but not you. I could take you a thousand times and you'd still beg for more."

Yuri didn't respond because Lucian wasn't wrong. The heat of Lucian driving into him added warmth and movement, life heating something deep inside Yuri's soul that he was desperate to unthaw. That last chunk of ice lingered, like a weight, floating untouched in the lava of Lucian's raging fire. Yuri wondered what it would take to melt that last touch of bound magic.

Lucian moved his hips, testing the thrust, shifting Yuri's hips in his grasp twice before grinding his pelvic bone against Yuri's ass, drilling his cock deep. Yuri groaned, desperate for it, wanting to beg for a pounding and to be filled with Lucian's come. But Lucian took his time, hips pressing Yuri into the stone, fingers still exploring, one hand on Yuri's hip, the other tracing a line down his back, and then changing places.

Yuri whimpered with need, his cock throbbing, ass clenching around Lucian's cock. He wished he could look, even dared a tiny glance toward the big mirror, hoping for a glimpse of Lucian's sleek form shoving into him, but the glass was covered, hiding that view from him. He squeezed his eyes shut as Lucian slowly withdrew, his body clenching, trying to hold the man's cock inside, and he whimpered as Lucian pulled out completely, leaving him feeling empty and desperate.

"Please," Yuri begged.

"I don't like this angle," Lucian said.

Yuri whimpered.

"You wish to be used?"

"Yes," Yuri said.

"Up and to the bedroom. Don't look at me. Press your face into the mattress and put your ass in the air."

Yuri swallowed a thick breath and rose, his body singing with need as he marched into the bedroom, the heat of the fireplace making him sweat immediately, but he forced himself not to look at Lucian as he laid down on the bed, putting a pillow under his head, and his stomach. He adjusted his knees beneath him, to relax into the pose of his ass in the air, cheeks spread. He recalled vaguely that Star had enjoyed this position too, his tongue sliding into Yuri until Yuri screamed his orgasm a dozen times before Star had finally fucked him into the mattress. A dream, or a memory? Yuri counted a long breath to steady himself, waiting and hoping, aching to be touched, and feeling Lucian's gaze on him, even if he couldn't see the pretty man.

He heard Lucian approach, felt the bed dip, and Lucian paused as though studying him. His hesitation made Yuri want to howl in protest. "You taste sweeter when I tease," Lucian said after a quiet moment.

"Like strawberries?" Yuri wondered, barely voicing his question for fear Lucian would stop.

"Sweet sunshine, yes," Lucian said, his hands massaging Yuri's ass, and a second later Lucian bit into one of Yuri's cheeks.

Yuri gasped, the break in skin a touch too much with his blistering need, but Lucian had barely nipped him. A hot tongue lapped at the sting, mouth sealing over the minor wound and suctioning until Yuri saw stars, envisioning the heat around his cock, too. He trembled as Lucian released the skin, licking it a few more times before moving inward. Yuri mentally begged, knowing what he wanted. The teasing play of mastering around his rim had been so long ago he nearly forgot how good it could be.

Lucian slid his tongue down Yuri's taint, teasing the back of Yuri's balls and back up to the rim, and Yuri's hips trembled. He shook with desperate need.

"Now we are getting there," Lucian said, his warm breath teasing Yuri's crease. "The flavor of your emotions is sweetening. How high can I make you fly?"

"More," Yuri begged.

Lucian licked Yuri's undamaged cheek, teasing it with his tongue before filling his mouth with the meaty flesh. It was too much for him to bite, Yuri knew that in the back of his mind, but couldn't stop himself from wanting it, anyway. Lucian released the flesh, lapped at it again, and nipped, breaking skin and drawing another desperate gasp from Yuri. His cock ached with desperate need, ass gaping as if demanding to be filled. But Lucian continued to tease, sucking at the tiny draw of blood and returning to his play between Yuri's taint and rim, purposely avoiding Lucian's begging cock and heavy balls.

"Please, please, please," Yuri couldn't help but beg. He gripped the pillow beneath him but couldn't stop his hips from shoving back into Lucian, as the man's tongue teased his entrance.

Lucian slid not one, but two fingers inside, and lapped at the sensitive flesh of his opening. "Can you not come unless I do?" Lucian wondered; his breath hot on Yuri's hole. He dug his fingers in, finding Yuri's prostate, which drew another moan from Yuri. "You are an unusual creature."

"Yours," Yuri agreed, not caring about anything else in that moment, but the need to have Lucian in him. It didn't matter that Lucian teased him to the edge of orgasm, then would deliver another bite to drag him back from the edge a half dozen times. It felt like heaven, and Yuri wished he could tumble over that cliff of desperate need. Lucian fed on more than blood. The tiny nibbles on Yuri's desire grew to thick swallows as Yuri shivered uncontrollably.

He gasped when Lucian moved, mouth and teeth leaving his ass but fingers remaining as he shoved his cock in beside them, stretching Yuri to the limit, pressing on his prostate, and filling him when raging heat.

Yuri screamed, thrusting his hips back into Lucian's grind, but floundering to find his rhythm as his body swirled in a blaze of orgasmic pleasure, rippling heat, and coating magic. Lucian ground Yuri into the mattress, cock sliding home over and over, pressing Lucian's fingers into all the right places. Yuri seeking something he didn't understand until Lucian gasped and withdrew his fingers.

Yuri wanted to protest, but as Lucian shoved into him, balls deep, he felt something expanding, pressure widening where they joined until it seemed they were locked together, and Yuri feared he'd tear apart at the sheer breadth of the expansion. Lucian held Yuri's hips in a bruising grip, panting, trembling, and burning hot.

"I've never..." Lucian said. "I don't have a knot..."

But he did, and Yuri groaned at the heft of the man's cock filling him, pressing everything he desperately needed to be touched, and warming him from the inside out. Yuri's body clenched around it, grasping, until the gaping size of it settled against Yuri's prostate, each breath causing a rippling tremor of pleasure.

"This isn't possible," Lucian said, voice strained. But Yuri rocked back, their bodies locked together, the movement causing the barest ripple of added pleasure. Yuri's body clenched again, gripping the rock-hard cock inside him and Lucian cried out, his come flooding Yuri with waves of heat and life, coating him until Yuri echoed his cry, his cock spurting, but hips still moving to rock them together over and over. A dozen orgasms swung between them.

Yuri sensed Lucian drinking down the desire in huge, starving swallows. Yuri's magic latched onto more of the purple edge of Lucian's glow, teasing it away like taffy to wrap around himself. It tasted of saltwater sweetness, and Yuri feared Lucian would push him away as the coil of Yuri's magic absorbed the color and whatever it was tied to.

Lucian ground his hips into Yuri's ass, the knot between them pushing all the right things inside and dragging another gasp of pleasure from Yuri's lips. He was deliciously full, stomach, soul, and ass. If he could stay this way forever, his life would be near perfect.

Finally, Lucian dropped his weight onto Yuri's back, pressing them both into the bed, and spreading Yuri's thighs to keep himself nestled firmly between. "It never ends," Lucian said with awe.

Yuri didn't mind Lucian's weight on him. He imagined the man's touch like a hug he always craved, or the way Star would spoon him between rounds as Yuri napped. He prayed that night lasted forever, and the dream of it never truly vanished, but this was a close second as Lucian's fingertips continued to trace lines over Yuri's flesh. Was it okay to bask in the affection, even if it was temporary? Yuri didn't dare speak. All the words forming on his tongue would send Lucian running away. And Yuri wasn't ready for it to end.

He turned his head, gaze finding the open window and a radiating glow emanating from the plants outside, purple blazing through their range of colors as new life continued to bloom. Yuri sighed sweetly and closed his eyes, ass still clenching greedily on Lucian's cock as if to milk him of every drop of come the man could create. It didn't matter that Yuri lay in a spread of his come coating the bed beneath him, or that his cock twitched and tried to come a dozen more times with each movement. All that mattered was the heat and fullness he revealed in. He thought he could die in that moment and it would be okay. Near perfection was close enough.

Yuri closed his eyes and sighed, a deep contented sound.

IN SEARCH OF ANSWERS

Lucian had to drag himself off Yuri. They'd been locked together for a few hours when his knot finally released, and Yuri had fallen into a deep and seemingly restful sleep. Lucian couldn't help himself from gulping down waves of desire, pleasure, and even joy as Yuri cast the emotions off by the bucket full. Lucian couldn't recall a time he'd been full to near bursting, and a mortal being had never given him more than the barest taste.

"What are you?" Lucian muttered for the thousandth time as he made his way to the bathroom. He cleaned himself up, examining his cock for a change, but the knot was gone, along with any sign it had ever been there. They could have sold him for a fortune in Johi if he'd had a knot. Only a handful of Onari nobles had one, a sign of a male of first-rate magic, rare as they were among their kind.

Radu kept himself distant from the rest of the Onari. A long history of attempts at matchmaking from the elite to create a eugenics type of breeding stairway to power left Radu cold and aloof to most of his people. Lucian heard many a story he thought elaborated over time and knew Radu had a handful of children. None as powerful as he, and all his matches, carefully chosen from families with little to no magic power. Had his uncle been trying to remove power from the Onari? Or keep it to himself?

Lucian wondered if Radu would cast him out now. Would he still be a tolerated nephew, or competition? His heart flipped over with anxiety. He hated that he still cared, as any need for familial affection should have been beaten out of him. Lucian silently cursed Radu for allowing him the freedom to think for himself and the thousands of opportunities to be whatever and whomever he wanted. He didn't know what he wanted, even after hundreds of years traveling between worlds, and still his uncle always accepted his return.

That wasn't completely right. Lucian knew he wanted one thing, and that was sleeping in his bed. Yuri. Lucian sighed, taking his time to wash and braid his hair, thinking and worrying at his lower lip. The taste of Yuri's blood still lingered on his tongue, a little green and slightly sweet. Lucian wasn't certain what flavor Yuri would associate it with. The berries had been unlike anything Lucian ever tried before. Mortal food had been a necessity that frustrated him over his long lifetime, until Yuri had made him bread pudding. Magic in a teapot, and ridiculous that Lucian craved more.

He finished his hair, braiding the front of it back and leaving the rest free. Habit mostly, to hide his neck and shoulders from view. Lucian turned to the covered mirror and pulled the towel off to stare at himself, expecting something different. More like his father or Radu, perhaps? But he was still pale, slim, willowy rather than muscled like Yuri, delicate, was a word often given to him in Johi. He hated it. Had fought to be recognized as a warrior despite his size and the lack of muscle tone. Lucian could be as brutal and bloodthirsty as any Onari warrior.

Lucian glared at his bare chest and turned to look at his back and shoulders, his skin flawless, scars completely gone, as though he hadn't spent nearly a century tortured by an archangel with a sadistic streak. Permanent claw marks should have been etched into his stomach. How many times had Gabriel dug into his gut as though to rip his insides out, marveling that somehow Lucian survived? Enough times that the scars made it hard for him to move unless he worked out often. They were gone, the scarring vanished, leaving smooth and unblemished skin.

He glared at his reflection, hating everything he saw, the weakness and mortality that made his father despise him and his people view him as less. Lucian tugged the towel back over the mirror and went to find clothes. His body reacted to Yuri's nude form on the bed, cock twitching and half filling as though begging Lucian to climb onto the man and fill him again. Staring at Yuri, breathing in his earthy scent, and seeing all that bronze skin made Lucian's cock weep, and his gut sing with joy. It didn't matter that he had sucked down buckets of Yuri's pleasure and blood. Lucian felt like he could lose himself in Yuri's skin forever.

He growled in frustration and had to force himself to move to the closet and dress. Clothing between them was a small help. It muffled Lucian's desire only fractionally. Perhaps that was why Yuri had worn a mask in the camp? Had the humans desired Yuri endlessly as well? Well-fed and healthy, Lucian could understand how anyone would find it difficult to keep their hands off Yuri. When he'd been starved and half dying, he had still hidden. Was it a curse?

Lucian buttoned his shirt and tugged the blankets up over

Yuri's resting form. He studied the wall of vines newly formed between the windows, small buds on the plant forming tiny versions of the berries Yuri had fed him. On the table, several bowls heaped full of the red fruit sat, and both windows were open, letting in the chill.

Yuri often spent hours sitting on the ledge of the windowsill, staring out into the bright swatch of sky unblocked by plants. The strange world of giant mushrooms, bushes, and flowers the size of Lucian's bed twisted themselves in knots to clear that small section near the window, as if they did it for Yuri. Was he some kind of fae mage? He had read stories about fae who could make things grow, but never like this.

The world outside should have been barren and blanketed in snow. The chill normal to this time of year. This valley of Dahna often spent the bulk of its year buried in snow, but the plants seemed unbothered. The way they responded to Yuri made Lucian curious and brazen. He wandered to the door, surprised there was no barrier, at least not to him. He suspected if Yuri tried to leave the room another issue would arise, but perhaps, since it was the early morning hours, Lucian could make his way to the library, retrieve a few things, and get back before he was caught out, or Yuri woke.

Lucian hadn't sensed another shift in the house, meaning Gabriel hadn't returned, nor had the sacrifices arrived. He shuddered, not wanting to think about the death wails that would eventually come. He was also more than a little surprised by his father's silence. Was it because the garden of corpses was gone? Lucian couldn't imagine being given privacy in any normal situation. They locked him in his room for months on end with little contact other than the occasional servant or the shifting restlessness of the house or dragged out to be tortured by watching his father kill some trespasser by shoving a stake through them.

The flora outside his window prevented Lucian from seeing if stakes were already being placed near the front of the castle. Another gift from Yuri, Lucian thought, keeping his view from being a constant nightmare.

Lucian slipped on his shoes and took a single step out of the room, sensing the surrounding castle. Nothing moved. Not even the vague doom sense he always got from the castle itself. He waited a few more minutes, but no one came and nothing moved, so he made his way as quietly as possible to the library. The books Yuri had been working through were part of his private collection, which was limited at best. The library was a world of secrets he'd always thought like a story, pages to be opened and explored.

He'd once heard his mother loved the space. His first nanny had even told him a story he later recognized as the mortal tale of *Beauty and the Beast*, claiming it was his mother and father. That nanny had been murdered in front of him when he was seven. After the third nanny had been slaughtered, he asked to not have any, claiming he was old enough to take care of himself. He'd been eleven. His memories of his mother were vague as he'd been five when she vanished.

Lucian opened the door to the massive library and glared into the dark, enclosed space. It felt like a tomb. With curtains drawn, everything covered in soot and dust, they had not even placed coverings over the furniture to protect it from degrading. He flicked on the lights, a slew of old-world oil lamps run by a magic thread rather than electricity. A paradox of worlds, Dahna had always stolen things it enjoyed from other dimensions, cannibalizing anything useful from their technology to the mortal flesh that Onari found a delicacy. Radu had even used phones and computers until the Fracture had shut them all down.

Lucian glared at the enormous space that stretched out for ages. He'd read every book in this room. He buried decades of loneliness between pages and stories. Would Yuri have found nuances in the many stories to help fix things? Lucian wondered if it mattered. Fix the worlds or not. He should never have returned here. Lingering in his uncle's shadow until the end of his days was better than this oppressive weight of doom. Even well fed and full of energy, Lucian nearly succumbed to the urge to sit down in a chair and cry. He was supposed to teach Yuri control, but the man seemed to have grasped that on his own. Lucian wondered what the point was of him being here at all.

He wanted hope. What a stupid thing. So small and useless.

Yet Yuri gifted him that, didn't he? Healing him in ways Lucian didn't think possible in only a few days together. Did that mean Yuri could do more? Fix the worlds? Seal the Fracture? Would he be lost, like Lucian's mother had been? Lucian's heart flipped over with anxiety.

Yuri was infuriating. Never obeying, and always mothering, hovering over Lucian as if he were a child to be coddled, until he begged to be taken over and over. Lucian's cock hardened at the thought of slipping inside Yuri again. Energizing, revitalizing, Yuri was life. Perhaps that was what Radu had meant. Did he sense Yuri was hope?

Lucian cursed, standing in the dusty room, knowing every book and its place, and still not knowing where to start. How was he to know what Yuri might need? Radu had a library a thousand times this size that grew constantly, both with his *touched* rescues to read, and books recovered from a dozen worlds. His uncle was resourceful having dozens of mortals sort through thoughts, ideas, and philosophies. Wouldn't he have stripped whatever might be useful from this library, or had he not been allowed?

He knew Radu and his brother had waged battles against each other, and that Lucian's sire had attempted to kill Radu more than once but had thought they'd created working peace between themselves. Had that vanished with Lucian's mother as well?

The shelf with books without a translation sat untouched, dusty. Those handful were the only ones in the entire library Lucian had never read. Nothing appeared out of place. Because they were useless, or because Radu hadn't purged his brother's library?

Lucian stacked up the handful of mystery texts, then made his way to a section of books about the fae. He'd been young when he read them. Maybe he'd missed something about Yuri?

He created a stack on the table near the door, pausing briefly to look at the portrait of his mother. Her hair and eyes, even the shape of her face, a mirror of his own. No wonder his father never came in here. She had been beautiful for a mortal, much like Yuri was. That sort of divine, precious touch of something fragile which everyone thought Lucian had but didn't. It mattered little how often they hurt him. He healed. An endless nightmare for him, a game for them.

He sighed, hating the melancholy the house forced him to bathe in. Lucian knew he'd adapted over the years, adding his own waves of depression to the ones forced on him by the supernatural strength of his sire and the monstrous house he lived in.

Lucian picked up the stack and carried it back to his room. They'd work through the entire library if they had to, he decided. His last imprisonment here had lasted nearly three decades. Would Yuri live that long? Would he age and die? Lucian growled at the idea, leaving the books on the table near the fire.

Yuri slept peacefully, a blanket of green ivy looping from the windows to wrap around the headboard and posts of the bed. Even while he dreamed, the vegetation reached for him.

The box of battered books Yuri had brought with him caught Lucian's gaze. It sat on the floor near the closet door, untouched. Lucian made his way to the box, opening it and sorting through the books. He knew they hadn't intrigued Radu since Yuri kept them. And Lucian had read the handful of fiction works in the box. One was a medical guide, which he took out to review. Perhaps it would give him more information on how to keep Yuri healthy.

"Like he's a pet," Lucian grumbled to himself. The last was an enormous book full of food recipes. Lucian flipped through the pages, fascinated by the brightly colored images of foods he'd read about in books but never been able to imagine in real life. Many recipes included the red berries Yuri had fed him. He even found a recipe for the bread pudding.

Lucian ran his finger down the pages of ingredients. Could he find any of these things in the kitchen? He knew many items were delivered from the cities and considered delicacies. Yuri would need food, more than berries, as humans had tricky upkeep. Lucian would eventually need to eat too, his mortal half irritating him with small things like physical hunger. There had been little in the kitchen when he'd limped his way there after Gabriel had finished his torture and loaded up on the few things he could find.

The servant hadn't returned. In fact, Lucian felt no movement in the house at all. Not unusual from his father, or the handful of servants that tiptoed around his father's rage. He tucked the books away and made his way to raid the kitchen and return with as much as he could from cookware to ingredients. Yuri was resourceful, and Lucian allowed his curiosity to rise at the idea of new flavors and experiencing food he had only read about in passing.

The kitchen was empty. Not a soul to be seen, fire unlit. Lucian frowned as he stared at the vacant space. Were there no servants left who ate? That wouldn't bode well for himself and Yuri. Lucian wondered if Yuri could magically grow chickens to give them eggs, or if Lucian would have to hunt them in the forest beyond. Or if he'd even return if he had the chance to run free.

He sighed at the thought, not willing to leave Yuri behind if possible. Sono had been right about Lucian, always running from his father. But Lucian wasn't stupid, nor a slut for pain, and Vlad Tepes was in mortal stories as both a monster and a beast for a thousand reasons.

Lucian grabbed a basket and scoured the kitchen for anything edible, finding the space recently abandoned as there was a handful of eggs, and a pitcher of milk not gone off, a sack of flour, and container of sugar, a few jars of things Lucian couldn't identify, and even a skin of some sort of broth. He contemplated a rack of dried seeds, wondering if they were useful for mortal food, and grabbed the entire rack, heading back to his room. He delivered the array to a spot beside the fireplace and realized he'd forgot cookware. A teapot and the handful of silverware wouldn't be enough, would it? Lucian thought briefly of waking Yuri to ask, but also of climbing into bed with him and sliding into his clenching heat again.

Lucian cursed himself for his lack of focus and stomped back toward the kitchen. The house feeling empty and ghost-like, haunted, perhaps. Had his father left? The lingering edge of doom hadn't faded. He snatched up a handful of tools, shoving them into two pots, and headed back to his room, emboldened by the lack of confrontation.

A high-pitched whine pierced Lucian's sensitive hearing like a sharp knife shoved in his ear. He flinched, pausing, heart rate immediately spiraling upward. Had someone hurt Yuri? He'd only been gone a few minutes, and it didn't sound like Yuri. Lucian memorized many of Yuri's small sounds now, from his dream whimpers to the moans he made while Lucian fucked him. This was something not human at all.

Lucian stood frozen in the hall for a moment, a shudder of familiar terror and pain rippling through the house. He should have gone to his room and closed the door. He knew what that feeling was, but couldn't stop himself from being drawn forward toward the main entry.

The double door gaped wide out to the front lawn, which had been overgrown with magic plants the last time Lucian had seen it. The area appeared sheared. Plants slashed at the base to create a space for stakes, and the writhing death throes of the last few servants of the household lining the walk up to the stairs and doorway.

That dreadful high-pitched noise came from the creature who had answered Lucian's questions days earlier and escorted him to his father's study. The thing looked like little more than a skeleton wriggling on a skewer, and Lucian gagged at the waves of pain and terror rising. Doom blanketed him before he realized it approached and a brutal hand fisted his hair, yanking Lucian back into a powerful chest and the familiar stench of blood, agony, and rage.

"You said I was free to move around the castle," Lucian protested his father's grip. He could feel his energy being drained, unable to control his fear, and nightmares of being the next to be staked filled his mind. His sire never hesitated to feed off of him.

"You're well-fed for having nothing but the pet for several days," Vlad remarked.

"I am doing as you instructed, teaching my pet control," Lucian said.

"As my brother does? Sinking into his heat? Devouring his desire?" Vlad sneered. "You stink of mortal desire."

Lucian swallowed back his honest reply, as it would only get him beaten. "My pet, my choice, is it not?"

"Not if I shove a stake through his hole and leave you bound at his feet to suction the last of his dying pain."

Images of that very horror filled Lucian's mind, blinding him to reality, and he sank into the drowning weight of pain. He had tried hard to keep his distance and not find affection for Yuri. The man was like a puppy, eager to please as long as he got some sort of attention. But the nightmare of watching him die that way made Lucian want to attack.

He had to shove back waves of revulsion and depression to clarify the world again. The cold iron pans having weight in his grip reminded him of Yuri in his bed and the sweet flavor of bread pudding and strawberries. The taste of Yuri's release sat on the back of Lucian's tongue. Not dead, not yet.

The exterior of the house still stretched a horror of death, but Yuri was safe in Lucian's room. Lucian said nothing to protest his father feeding on him. He shouldn't have left his room at all. Or Radu's castle. This nightmare would only end in Yuri's death and Lucian's imprisonment. He sucked in gulps of air and steadied himself. The fear and pain vanishing as he resigned himself to losing everything. It was how he existed for decades, burying his feelings deep. Could he survive losing Yuri?

He didn't want to, but he was nothing if not a survivor. How many had tried to end his existence? His father, Gabriel, thousands of creatures, it didn't matter. Perhaps Lucian would have been better off letting Yuri drink down the last of his soul and free him from this life. To die in the throes of pleasure rather than pain, no wonder Radu bathed in desire. Lucian only wanted to bask in Yuri.

He relaxed into his sire's grasp, waiting for the man to decide if today was his day for torture, but slowly the grip vanished. With no fear to feast on, Vlad would return to haunting his study or staring out at the current victims, waiting for more. Lucian remained until the weight of doom vanished, the chill air stinging his lungs. Finally, he turned, alone in the entry, alone in the house other than his monster of a sire, and Yuri, and made his way back to his room. Without servants, the small amount of food he'd recovered would be all they had to keep Yuri fed. Lucian set the cookware down, listened for Yuri's breathing, which had softened. He was waking.

Lucian closed the bedroom door and put his hand beside it to create a ward. It wouldn't keep his father out but give him warning. It was better than nothing. Lucian had to make a plan. He needed to get himself and Yuri out of this nightmare before his sire turned his hungry gaze to Yuri.

SWEET SACRIFICE

Yuri marveled at the change in Lucian. When he woke to kisses on his face and chest, he had almost expected another dream of Star, but opened his eyes to Lucian's fervent need to fill him again. Yuri didn't mind, basking in the pleasure, warmth, and finally making his way to bathe and find food.

Lucian said little, but Yuri smiled over the items he'd retrieved, everything from spices to books on fae lore that Yuri couldn't wait to dive into. The small space of their room felt a little like an oasis. It was the first time in over a decade that he could remember feeling happy. The garden outside the windows and Lucian's attention made it feel like paradise.

He read through all the books, finding the few Lucian had been unable to translate, little more than genealogy. Lucian had been disappointed, but Yuri found it fascinating as it seemed to link Lucian's family line back to the original Nephilim and their archangel fathers, or at least that was the lore. He even teased Lucian about it. "If the archangels had knots, that explains everything."

Lucian's face heated, as Yuri knew he was still in awe over the change. "I'm not certain that's what happened."

"Some hot angel dude came down from the sky and some girl milking goats was like 'um hi'," Yuri teased. "Angel was like, 'let me show you my pleasure bump'."

Lucian snorted. "Ridiculous. Pleasure bump. Don't ever call it that."

"I love your pleasure bump," Yuri added.

"Hmm," Lucian huffed, but quickly enough had Yuri skewered on his hard knot again, both of them trembling in pleasure.

Yuri used their stash of supplies to make food. It was simple fare, but flavors like soda bread and honey, or an egg salad were things he'd almost forgotten existed. Yuri discovered Lucian enjoyed sweet things, often snacking from the berries as the plant continued to refill their bowls.

Days passed in a routine. Yuri was careful with their supplies, small things substituted by the plants gifting things through the windows, and Lucian's affection. Yuri bathed in Lucian's touch, but a strange hunger rose. He should have been endlessly full, his stomach satisfied and his body always aching from rounds of pleasure, but Yuri's coil of magic vibrated with something he couldn't identify. Anxiety?

Yuri worried at his lip as he used up the last of the flour to make their last batch of flat bread. He had fermented the milk to create a sort of yogurt which made the bread hearty, but everything other than the berries was running out. Was his magic anticipating hunger? His sleep had been restless the past few nights, woken by the sound of high-pitched wails on the wind.

Lucian had shut the windows, but said nothing about the sound, or the rising chill. Was it winter causing Yuri issues? He stared out into the forest of plants beyond their small space, and found it comforting, though the colors began to fade. From the cold? Even their wall of berries produced less fruit, struggling to cling to the wall and sprout buds.

Yuri took the last of the bread off the hot plate he'd created in the fire to cool and worked on creating another jar of jam from the berries remaining. The jam would last longer and give them some calories if they completely ran out of food.

No one came. Not a single servant, nor the monster himself, but Yuri felt the house change. Like it half slumbered, and then slowly, as time passed and Yuri grew hungrier and more exhausted, not sleeping more than an hour or two at a time, the house rippled with life. Was it feeding on Yuri?

His stomach grumbled. He set a plate of bread and jam beside Lucian.

Lucian put aside his book but pushed the plate back to Yuri. "You eat. I don't need it."

It was a lie. Yuri watched Lucian's health improve in their short time together. The light beneath his skin glowing with each added day full of sex and food. His hair shone like spun gold, and skin seemed to cast another touch of brightness beneath, an aura of pale blue, not unlike sunshine reflecting from within. Lucian moved around their room, prowling like a cat with too much energy and not enough space.

A warrior, Yuri thought, not used to inaction. Yuri recalled his first few years after the Fracture feeling caged but had learned fast about the dangers beyond the wall. Here it was dangers beyond the doorway. But as their food became scarce and Yuri's unease grew, Lucian touched him less, avoided nibbling on Yuri's emotions, and he'd not taken blood in days. They both knew something was wrong, but neither voiced the concerns for fear of making reality worse.

"Eat," Yuri said. "Perhaps we can open the windows and see if the plants will give us more."

"Best to keep them closed," Lucian said.

He hadn't left the room again, though often stared through the open doorway, arms across his chest, shoulders tense. What happened the last time he left? He hadn't returned beaten or torn to shreds like that first time, but Yuri wasn't fooled by the change, either.

Haunted, Yuri thought as he watched Lucian pace. Something in the house shifted again, a wave of apprehension rising that made Yuri sit on the edge of the bed and clutch his heart.

"What was that?" Yuri asked. The sensation wasn't the same brutal twisting of Radu's moving castle, more a plucking or severing of something from inside Yuri. His heart fumbled for beats, erratically flopping between a stuttering race and stopping.

Lucian caught Yuri as he slid to the floor. Yuri gasped for breath.

"What's wrong?" Lucian demanded as he cradled Yuri in his grasp. Yuri gripped his arm, unable to speak as waves of pain etched a course through his bones. He felt as though someone was ripping his veins out, one by one. He gasped, blinking back stars of overwhelming brightness, his gaze finding the window and the garden beyond, with light growing from outside.

Not new light, Yuri realized, but the fading sunlight from the late day intensified as the plants fell, the shade vanishing from outside their windows. Booming echoes shook the ground nearby as mushrooms the size of giant oaks were slashed and chopped in half like buds to pluck. Flowers and bushes, and a thousand vines ripped free from the ground.

Lucian followed Yuri's gaze and cursed. He lifted Yuri onto

the bed, setting him down and going to the window to close the curtains.

"Don't look," Lucian instructed, but it was too late. Yuri couldn't miss the horrors, both from the death of the vegetation screaming in agony and the distant rise of bodies skewered on stakes, floundering in the wind, some writhing with agony as they either couldn't die or would take ages to wither away.

The vine fell away from the wall, graying and crumbling, as Lucian pulled the drapes firmly shut. Yuri shuddered in pain and revulsion. The ice inside his soul expanding. Lucian slid onto the bed, yanking the blankets up and draping them around them as though they could hide from what was coming.

The monster was restoring his garden of torture, fear, and death.

Yuri shivered and trembled for a long time, the pain flowing in waves, piercing and brutal, bringing him to the edge of passing out, then floating in numb agony for a time, before it would start again.

Lucian held a cup of warm tea to Yuri's lips. "Drink," Lucian commanded.

Yuri sighed, wanting only to sleep, or at least pass out and avoid more pain. The liquid slid down his throat, tasting bland and barely warm. He swallowed and felt as though the world was spinning.

"Rest," Lucian instructed. The distant fireplace intensified in strength, and Yuri wished he were awake enough to ask Lucian how he did it but found himself grateful to be lulled to the deadening edge of sleep. "Rest."

Days passed in a blur. The cold grew, ice reforming inside Yuri like concrete, freezing the coil of his magic as if it were being set in stone. It wasn't a completely unfamiliar feeling, Yuri realized as the days slid by and he couldn't keep down more than a sip of tea. His first few months after the Fracture, he'd burned with fever. He had traveled with a handful of survivors from place to place, trying to find a safe space, but often found himself left behind with his belongings picked through while he burned with illness.

He thought it had been the change in the environment, toxic gases or chemicals in the air. How long had it taken for the worst of it to pass? Yuri couldn't recall as his brain flickered and sparked, sometimes sending him into broken dreams, other times not letting him rest at all as it raced with a thousand worries.

Lucian no longer fed on him. He'd carefully nibbled the remaining food, trying to share with Yuri, but gave that up after a week of Yuri's gut clenching in revulsion. Lucian spent a lot of his time wrapped around Yuri beneath the blanket, or holding him in the bath, trying to comfort him and keep him warm, for which Yuri was grateful, but he also watched the glow and brightness fade from Lucian's flesh and hair. The luminescence buried to hide his growing hunger.

"It's okay," Yuri told him, gazing up at Lucian as dusk fell. The light of the fireplace cast a dancing shadow over Lucian's face. He was expressionless, and silent as always. Yuri could taste the rising sour lemon flavor of Lucian's depression, and fought not to linger on it, fearing he'd hurt Lucian with his growing hunger. "You can feed on me," Yuri said.

Lucian frowned. "You're hardly strong enough to make it to the loo on your own, and you expect me to fuck you?"

"I'm sure I'd enjoy it," Yuri said, though his cock didn't respond. The cold froze him from the inside out.

"It would be better for you to take whatever you can from me and fly free of this place," Lucian said.

But Yuri wouldn't. "You could get away, right? Return to your uncle?"

Lucian said nothing. Something in his gaze looked pained.

"We know a little more about what I am, right? Maybe your uncle will understand? Whatever my connection was to the plants? You could tell him. Come back for me."

"My father wouldn't let you live if I left," Lucian said. "You'd be another corpse on a stake." Was that why Lucian refused to leave the room? He feared for Yuri's safety?

"But my control is okay," Yuri said. "We could go, right? That's what we came here for?" He didn't know if he could hold his magic back if the starvation continued. Whatever he got from Lucian helped, but Yuri could sense his magic becoming wild and unhinged, the need intensifying. He wondered how he'd kept it buried for a decade or if bonding with the Master had awakened it. He licked his lips at the idea of the Master sliding into him. His body didn't respond at all, but the coil of magic wrapped around him stirred, hungry.

Lucian flinched.

"Sorry," Yuri whispered, holding onto the magic with an iron will.

Lucian squared his shoulders and pulled away, leaving Yuri cold and with fear rising in his gut. "I need to face him. It's cowardly to sit here while we both suffer."

Cowardly? Or self-preservation? Yuri wondered. "I'd rather you stay," he said, hoping it would keep Lucian from being hurt again.

"I'm not strong enough to resist you," Lucian admitted.

"Then stay," Yuri said, feeling a wave of joy slide through him. As sick as he was, the warmth of having Lucian wrapped around him made his heart soar. It was probably reckless as he grew weaker and less able to control his magic, but he adored Lucian's touch.

"You taste like strawberry custard," Lucian said. "I want to drink down all that happiness."

Yuri had made him the delight one of their first days after he'd raided the kitchen for supplies, and Lucian had murmured over the flavors, which meant Yuri made it over and over until the ingredients ran out.

"Okay," Yuri agreed. It would be a pleasant way to go.

"I fear it would be suicide," Lucian said.

"For me, or you?" Yuri wondered.

"Both?" Lucian turned away to pace, and Yuri missed his warmth. "If I feed on you and trigger your magic, you devour me, and my sire will come and devour you in the most horrific way possible."

"Is that why you won't leave the room?" Yuri asked.

Lucian sighed. "He's already gifted me with nightmares of what he wants to do with you. I assure you, it's nothing as delightful as what my uncle did. Radu is a connoisseur of pleasure. My sire prefers the nuances of a thousand types of pain and terror."

"But Onari aren't limited to one emotion, or even one set of emotion, right?" Yuri asked.

"No," Lucian said. "And my sire has promised to chain me to your feet as you die in agony. I'd rather not. But I will have to face him soon. Demand for food or release... something."

Yuri rolled over and opened his arms, throwing back the blanket. "You're a soldier, right?" he asked.

"Of course."

"Then come fill yourself and prepare for war," he offered.

Lucian sucked in a pained breath; eyes filled with lust as his gaze roamed Yuri's bare body. "You're some sort of demon."

"I thought Onari were supposed to be the sex demons?" Yuri teased.

"You're too tired to respond," Lucian said, though he couldn't tear his gaze from Yuri's flesh.

"But I'll still enjoy it," Yuri promised. He spread his legs and shifted his hips, begging to be filled. Lucian's physical heat warmed him a thousand times more than the fire could, anyway. "Please."

Lucian groaned but unbuttoned his shirt. "You'll be the death of me."

"Sweet way to go," Yuri said, feeling bold despite his exhaustion. He watched Lucian undress and marveled at the man's slim beauty, not unlike Star's, and it gave Yuri hope for dreams of peace in the end, like his decades of dreaming about Star had. He missed his first lover and hoped that whatever existence found him after this, they would finally be together. Perhaps Lucian would find him again, and the Master, and Yuri could bask in all of their affection, let it warm his soul, his heart, and his body. He sighed sweetly as Lucian slid into him, and felt the man's fangs pierce his neck, the knot expanding to lock them together.

If Yuri weren't half frozen with numbness, he'd have moved with Lucian's furious need, but he relaxed into the man's touch, closed his eyes and let Lucian devour every bit of joy, hope, and love Yuri could give him. Not suicide, Yuri thought, as the world darkened around him, sacrifice. "Free yourself," Yuri whispered to Lucian. "Take it all." He sank willingly into the darkness, gifting everything he had to Lucian and praying the man could escape the nightmare waiting for him.

DRACULA'S CASTLE AWAKENS

Lucian fed deeply, drinking down the deep well of Yuri's emotions. Yuri's body was pliant and warm, but still. When Lucian finally pulled himself away, Yuri barely breathed. He had survived a decade of near starvation, being torn apart and beaten by Lucian's sire, and skewered by Radu's magic blade. Yuri would certainly survive Lucian drinking deeply of his blood and emotions, right?

Lucian trembled with an edge of anxiety and rage, mixed like he couldn't recall ever experiencing before. He'd spent the past few weeks gorging himself on Yuri's divine roll of emotions until the man became too weak to get out of bed. Guilt plagued him, anxiety that he'd drained Yuri like this, leaving him little more than a shell of a creature.

Onari didn't kill to feed like vampires of legend, or even like Yuri who absorbed whatever remainders of dying souls leaving nothing but dust, but they could drink deeply enough to leave most beings in a coma on the verge of death with a void of emotions or the strength to create them, mortal creatures died. Lucian saw it happen all the time in the Johi sex pits.

Many started out there joyous, welcoming the sex and the feedings. The Onari were revered for their beauty until they left the creatures as nothing more than a slightly warm hole absent of emotion.

Lucian stood over the bed, his cock still half hard after coming a nearly dozen times wrapped in Yuri's heat, and worried at his lip. Lucian watched the colors and life fade from Yuri's flesh. His gut rolled with anxiety that he did this, though he could never feed as deeply as the nobles. His human half made him weak in a lot of ways, and Yuri had been fine when they had food and a wild jungle outside their windows.

The plucking of the garden caused a ripple effect within Yuri. As though the life of the plants gave him strength and ripping them out caused his bronze skin to sour and the waves of purple to fade to white in his hair. Without proper food, he starved, but his emotions hadn't faded until the plants were cut, windows shut, and death lingered beyond the window. Would he have to devour the dredges of nightmares again? Could he? Or had that been some consequence of a decade without food and his uncle's touch awakening something within?

Lucian couldn't recall any story about a mage with that sort of intense tie to the earth, not in any fae lore, though there were vague references in older translated works about Earth, the mortal world, created from a living being, Gaia in some cultures, Mother Earth in others, a goddess with a thousand names. Did that mean Yuri was somehow related to a goddess? It would explain some of his draw and his divine flavor. It took a huge amount of willpower for Lucian to drag himself away from Yuri's decadent body, even unconscious as he was right then.

Lucian's heart ached, but he slid the blankets over Yuri and made his way to his closet to find clothes. With his body thrumming with the divine pleasure of tasting Yuri over and over, Lucian planned to use that strength to face his sire and demand both he and Yuri's freedom.

They had met their bargain. Yuri controlled his power. Lucian sensed the stir of it a dozen times, yet Yuri kept it leashed, wrapped around him like a shield. He suspected if Yuri released that energy, he could have devoured Lucian as easily as he'd suctioned all remaining life from the gruesome garden of corpses.

Lucian's sire had already rebuilt a large part of his garden, likely with anyone who displeased Gabriel in Johi, and Lucian prayed he could convince the monster to release them. It was reckless, but Yuri needed food, mortal fare, and some sort of connection to the plant life. That much Lucian understood. Would Radu know more? He trusted his uncle, and the staff of a thousand *touched* pets to find an answer to Yuri's peculiarity. He had to free them both from this nightmare.

Lucian stepped outside the room and shuddered as the house rippled around him with awareness. Parts of Radu's castle bore the same oily chill that radiated from the walls of Lucian's sire's manor, but Lucian couldn't recall it ever feeling this awake, ready, as though it were waiting for something. He paused, sucking in air and smelling only mold and death, then made his way to his father's study, the dark halls feeling oppressive, nightmares and piercing wails of the dying or tortured things trickling through the walls. In a way, the noise reminded him of his youth, an odd comfort of the familiar while knowing how ghastly the reality was.

Lucian paused in the hall, frowning as he knew he'd gone the right way, only he turned and found another doorless run. Had his sire's manor turned into something like Radu's shifting mess of a home?

He stood in the hall, looking both ways, his heart racing with added fear over the change. What if he couldn't find his way back to Yuri?

His heart suddenly in his throat, he pivoted and followed the path he'd come, praying to return to his room. He would gather Yuri up and spirit him out the window if need be. They could lose themselves in the forests beyond, and somehow find a way back to Radu.

Lucian cursed his uncle for sending them here. How many times had Lucian said his father was a lost cause? Did Radu care so much for his brother that all his sins were forgivable?

He rounded the corner that should have led to the hallway to his room but found another empty stretch of hall. Lucian snarled and slammed his fist into the wall, anger rising, and red staining his vision with a wash of blood rage. Yuri was his. He had claimed the man, kept him alive, dined on his body, marked him with his come and his fangs. *Mine,* Lucian thought fiercely. He wasn't about to let the house and its arcane magic steal Yuri from him.

He raced down the hall as though speed could prevent the manor from changing and keeping him from Yuri, but he met empty room or barren hall after barren hall. Lucian struggled to breathe, rage and need burning hot in his gut, the threat of it igniting under his skin like he would burn himself from the inside out. His blood boiled like lava and it hurt. The idea of not having Yuri seared worse than any other pain Lucian could recall experiencing in his long life. Lucian had to find him, and they had to escape.

A Ray of Light

Yuri sank into Star's touch. It was a dream come true. He sighed sweetly, exhausted, but welcoming the familiar chill and soft caress.

"You should not be here," Star whispered, peppering Yuri's face with kisses.

"Can I stay with you?" Yuri pleaded. Lucian's face flashed through his mind for a moment, making him flinch with worry. Would the monster let Lucian go if Yuri were gone? He was so tired, it would be okay if he rested a while, right?

"You should not be this weak," Star said, sounding angry.

"I told him to take it all," Yuri said. "And free himself." He recalled Lucian's kisses, and the pleasure of the man's heat sliding into him, warming the eternal chill and worshiping him in ways Yuri had only dreamed of. It was a pleasant way to die, much better than the many dreams he had of battles gone wrong and pain turning to numb bitterness before the darkness took him.

Star growled. "You always give your heart too easily. Does he deserve your love?"

Yuri blinked, finding it hard to focus on Star's face. "Yes. But I still love you. Is that okay? Please don't stop loving me."

"I would never stop loving you," Star said. "You're mine until the end of existence." He sighed. "I thought you went to the Onari. It's rare for them to have only one lover. You should have a legion to rebuild your strength."

Yuri didn't delve into an explanation. He only wanted to rest in Star's embrace. He didn't care if it was a dream; it was a pleasant one.

"Open your eyes, Yuri," Star demanded.

Yuri struggled with the weight of his eyelids. Exhaustion making him cold, and barely able to feel Star at all, or a tether to his mortal body. He blinked a half dozen times before finally focusing on Star's face. "You're so beautiful," Yuri said breathlessly.

"You need another. Someone full of light," Star said.

His gaze intensified as he cupped Yuri's face. Yuri felt as though Star slid into his mind, searched his memories, riffling through them looking for something. He touched the memories of Yuri and Lucian together, and Yuri worried Star would be angry, but he wasn't, only continued seeking. The waves of power and lust from the memory of Radu tried to rouse Yuri's flaccid cock, but it did little more than twitch, as he was out of strength.

"Not enough light," Star said. "You've taken a lot of darkness and need a balance."

A dozen more faces passed through Yuri's memory, many long gone, some making Star pause with a jolt of anger.

"Dead," Yuri muttered, letting Star know those who hurt him had met gruesome ends, many in that last battle with Radu's army.

A RAY OF LIGHT

Theo's face appeared in his memory, a smiling ray of warmth as he helped Yuri bathe, then comforted his pain. Yuri's reaction to the memory was visceral. He wanted the angel badly, recalling how he wanted to eat him, and drink down that divine light. Now he thought it would be easier to bask in pleasure and drown in the beauty of Theo's flesh. He knew it would feel like sunlight, heat, and joy.

"That one will do," Star said.

"I don't want to hurt him," Yuri begged, but he wanted Theo badly. Was that fair at all?

"Shouldn't it be his choice?"

To sacrifice himself for Yuri? Yuri didn't think he was worth that.

"Let us ask his thoughts, shall we? You were adamant the seraphim have the ability to think for themselves, even if many refused to do so." Yuri's world shifted as Star dragged him along some strange super highway of flashing lights. It was magical, like something out of a movie, and Yuri basked in Star's grip, feeling weightless and precious all at once.

They stopped with a jolt and a door opened, an entire world before them leading to a brick-lined hallway filled with light. Theo stood there, frozen, expression filled with apprehension and confusion all at once. His breathless beauty made Yuri sigh in contentment. Being near him was like sitting in the sunshine.

Theo blinked at them, standing in the doorway between worlds, and Yuri wondered if he could really see them in this dream. Was it a dream? Theo struggled to drag his gaze from Yuri to focus on Star. He gasped, mouth falling open with shock.

"He needs light," Star said. "Will you be his light?"

Theo blinked and gaped, mouth opening and closing for a few seconds, but his gaze fell on Yuri again. "Yes," he said.

"I don't want to hurt him," Yuri said, feeling like little more than a ghost with Star holding him together.

"Then don't hurt me," Theo said. He took a step forward toward the doorway and reached for Yuri.

"You'll have to become one of mine," Star said.

Theo didn't hesitate. His fingers slid over Yuri's cheek as he stepped through the doorway and Star embraced him, circling them back down. Theo squeezed his eyes shut but didn't let go as they landed back in that dark space that was becoming too familiar for Yuri. He sighed as they cradled him between Star's precious touch and Theo's blazing heat.

"What do I have to do?" Theo asked, his gaze directed at Star. "I will give him all of me if necessary."

Star sighed. "Seraphim are so self-sacrificing."

"In their image," Theo whispered as he focused on Yuri and stroked his cheek. "Did you not do the same? Isn't that why you are here?" He pointed to the chain locked around Star's wrist.

"Indeed," Star said. "We never learn." He held out a hand, sitting up as though to draw Theo in for a kiss as they leaned over Yuri. "You'll become one of mine. A vessel to guide him back to strength, even if that means the destruction of all you are."

Yuri gasped. "No. I don't want to hurt him."

"Yes," Theo agreed. He took Star's hand and Star pulled him forward until their lips met, a kiss filled with deep passion and a pool of glowing energy, blinding in its intensity, Yuri blinked back tears. He gasped at the beauty of the men together, his body stirring with need even while he was too weak to respond with more than a twitch of desire.

He thought about watching Star slide into Theo, and the seraphim's sweet cries of pleasure. Yuri would happily join in, showering them both with kisses, basking in the delight between light and dark until the very end of everything.

Theo gasped, the kiss breaking, and turned with a blazing blue gaze toward Yuri, Star's magic filling him. Yuri sucked in a deep breath, wishing he had the energy to delight in Theo's beauty, but the seraph leaned over him and pressed his lips to Yuri's.

It was a few seconds of fire, *too hot*, burning with strength, but Yuri's magic stirred, the magic coil of power wrapped around him, thawing and lifting with interest. He tried to grab hold of it, fearing it would devour Theo, but it slid over the seraph like a caress, nibbling at the energy, spreading warmth and healing over Yuri, awakening his body to sensation again, and easing the numbness.

Theo's kiss delved deep, but unskilled, which was okay as Yuri reached out, capturing the back of his head with a gentle hand and pressing them together to taste and explore the seraph, as he'd only dreamed he could. The chocolate cherry flavor trickled over his tongue, magic fueling their touch, and Yuri couldn't stop his hips from moving, seeking friction, even if he wasn't strong enough to roll Theo over and slide into his raging warmth.

Yuri feared he'd hurt Theo, but Star spooned himself around them, offering sweet words and soft caresses, his touch leaving neither of them, adding balance to Yuri's need. He wanted more than friction and kisses but delighted in the slow melting of the ice encasing his soul. The drip hurt less than Radu's molten heat, turning ice to water instantly, a shift of desperate need, to sweet desire.

"He'll need life and love to continue to heal," Star told

Theo when Yuri released Theo's lips, breathing in the scent of his arousal and joy.

Theo rested his forehead on Yuri's, gaze focused on Yuri's face, fingers tracing a line over his cheek and lips, their bodies pressed close together.

"He's not strong enough for more. I will lend what I can."

"What do I need to do?" Theo asked.

"Keep him safe, Guardian. Fill him with adoration, love, desire, and life. Know that there will always be those seeking to destroy him before he can become."

Become what, Yuri wondered, but couldn't pull his gaze from Theo's to ask. It reminded him of his days sitting on the windowsill, basking in the sunlight and scent of pollen from the plants outside Lucian's window, warmth and happiness filling him. He sighed as he realized it had to be a dream, as everything felt real, and yet faded. "Am I asleep?"

"Yes, and no," Star said. He looked at Theo. "You'll have to help him get free of the wards. I couldn't touch him there, even in dreams, until he sank near death."

Theo put his hand over his heart. "I will do my best."

"And I give you any strength I have to spare," Star agreed. He reached for Theo again, fingers catching beneath his jaw to lift him for another kiss. Yuri watched in divine fascination but felt himself being dropped back into the weight of his physical body, warmth fading. He flinched but opened his eyes to stare into the darkness of Lucian's bedroom. The fire was out, which was strange. It had burned the entire time they'd been in the room. Yuri thought it was Lucian's power that fueled it. Did that mean something had happened to Lucian?

"We have to go," Theo said, tugging Yuri up. His body ached, ass giving him a reminder that he'd been well stretched on Lucian's knot. Theo found Yuri's pile of discarded clothing and frowned at them. "It will have to do. We need to go. I can feel the house moving."

Moving? "Like the Master's?" Yuri wondered, his movements sluggish, body slow to respond to his command like he'd slept too deeply, but he let Theo guide him.

"Yes, and yet no. It seems tethered but shifting. Radu said something happened. Rumors abound, spreading through all of Dahna about Vlad's castle going wild, and awakening. He was gathering his army to descend on his brother's estate to ensure your return." Theo guided Yuri to the door. Yuri paused, glaring warily at it, knowing there was usually a ward there, and that if he stepped outside the room, the house would know. Where was Lucian? Was he already free?

"The door is usually warded," Yuri said. "I have to free Lucian. We can't leave him here. His father is a monster."

"It's not safe," Theo said. "I think if I can get you outside the wards, we can find Radu's army and be safe. Sono is with them." Theo put his hand up and the ward over the door rippled. It shattered under his touch.

"I'm not leaving without Lucian," Yuri said.

"What if we send Radu back for him?" Theo asked. The taste of his chocolate-covered cherry flavor soured with fear.

"You don't have to go with me," Yuri said. He captured Theo's face between his hands and kissed him lightly. "Wait for me outside the wards. I'll find Lucian and get out."

"You're not strong enough..." Theo clung to him.

"I ate the last garden of death the monster created. I can do it again, right?" Yuri knew what was outside the windows, the horrors that Lucian tried to hide from him.

"You don't have enough light to balance it."

"What does that mean?" Yuri wondered. He had a thousand questions, but they needed to escape. He could feel a slithering sense of doom stirring, like some dark demon rising from the depths. It was cold and suffocating. "Help me find Lucian. Please," Yuri begged. He knew Lucian worked to make himself unlikable to ward off rejection, but Yuri refused to leave him behind to suffer more. "Please, Theo."

Theo sighed but nodded. "Let's hurry."

Rage of the Morningstar

Lucian stepped through the only doorway in another similar hall and found himself in the library. He glared at the space, anger raging from deep within. The books, dust, display of weapons, and dated furniture all reflecting a life he'd never known beyond stories. His father's creation for his mother, abandoned when she vanished. Was his love for her that deep or truly shallow?

Love. What a worthless emotion. It wouldn't save Lucian from his father. The monster hadn't been able to save himself. The castle should have been a sanctuary of memories filled with light and love. But the walls heaved with shadows and pain. How did wallowing in nightmares honor his mother?

Lucian slammed his fist into a small table and sent it ricocheting through the window, shattering the glass in a thousand shards.

Moonlight pierced the space, casting shadows of the dead through the room and his mother's portrait. The stench of loosened bowels and rotting flesh trickled through the window and

Lucian approached the broken window, enraged by the sight beyond.

Had Gabriel sent half the population of Johi? Lucian expected a dozen corpses, but found hundreds, and more still struggling, trying to survive despite their actions skewering them further with the horrific effects of spilling organs and splitting flesh.

Lucian yanked a sword free from the wall, determined to end his sire's feeding and force the monster to face him, free him and Yuri. He wasn't a child to be cowed and locked away anymore. Lucian was a warrior and an Onari Noble. He might not have legions of seraphim bowing down to him in adoration, but he had commanded armies, and traveled a hundred worlds.

He gripped the window and leapt through it, not caring about the glass that bit into his skin and drew blood, only at the overwhelming anger at being kept from Yuri. His gaze found a half dozen seraphim wriggling like worms on a hook. It would take them a long time to die that way. Maybe centuries before the waves of their light completely faded. Where had Gabriel found the seraphim? Radu fought to keep the angels nestled safely within the walls of his traveling castle.

Lucian didn't recognize them, though he avoided those who gathered around his uncle. He'd have given a lot at that moment to see Theodorus on a stake. The memory of the way the seraph had clung to Yuri, as if to claim him all for himself, grated at Lucian's nerves. He stalked toward the writhing seraphim, their pain flavored with a salty cream Lucian couldn't quite identify. Yuri taught him flavors, awakened him to delights like caramel custard and strawberries. The pain, fear, and sadness rolled off the bodies in waves, a meshing of a thousand flavors Lucian wished he could share with Yuri. The pain and fear added bitterness and salt to the tastes he tried to identify, the sweet delights like cream and berries buried beneath all the rising sour.

Lucian raised the sword, slashing through the nearest seraphim, cutting it in two with the stake. It stopped moving; the light fading completely, all pain and fear vanishing from the quickly fading body. He watched the corpse dissolve into dust, not unlike what Yuri had done when he'd released all the dying to final rest.

A kindness, Lucian thought, and at the same time it filled him with satisfaction that he would cut away at his father's power. Dracula did not feed on the dead; he fed on fear and pain from the living. Keeping them near death and suffering added to his power. Lucian glared at the array of wriggling bodies. Yuri would want them to be free, even if that meant true death. They would all die anyway. Few could survive the brutal torture of being pierced with the stake digging itself deeper with every movement.

Lucian stalked forward and cut them down, one by one, not watching them pass, but leaving a wake of shriveling corpses, severed stakes, and a stretch of silence. His rage grew with each death, a rippling of the landscape shaking the ground. Soot covered him, ash of the dead, clinging to his face, and clogging his nose, but he was determined to clear them all.

The rising sense of doom approached, his sire's presence suffocating, but Lucian refused to back down. The monster would either let them go, or finally kill him. He'd embrace the end.

Lucian turned his gaze back toward the manor, watching it shift with magic like it was a living thing waking and stretching. Radu's castle never felt as monstrous, even the darkest moving stairways.

He spied the window he knew to be to his bedroom. If he

could break Yuri out, he would take him and run free before the nightmare completely woke like a dimension to hell opening up. Before he could reach the window, movement caught his gaze from the front edge of the house.

His father stalking forward, the massive beast of legends, with glowing red eyes, fangs and claws like a monster, and holding Yuri around the waist. Lucian gasped. How had his father gotten to Yuri? Had that all been part of his plan? The beast paused, his face full of challenge, and Lucian could recall a thousand insults, beatings, and nightmares granted by the monster. His rage took control. Yuri was his, and his father couldn't take that from him, too.

Lucian raced forward, sword outstretched, ready to run that nightmare through once and for all. Seconds before he reached his sire, Yuri moved, throwing himself forward and shoving the beast away, skewering himself on Lucian's blade.

Lucian gasped in horror, his body suddenly frozen and Yuri slid forward on the blade, hot blood coating Lucian's hands and splattering over him in a gruesome burst of essential things broken inside. Yuri blinked at him, expression stunned, and blood burbled up from his lungs, spurting out his mouth as he sagged.

"No!" a voice screamed, bringing Lucian's gaze up behind Yuri to his sire. Only the monster no longer stood there. It was Theo, the seraph, eyes glowing icy blue. His wings appeared behind him, an enormous glowing span of soft, white feathers. Theo caught Yuri, the seraph dragging him away, gathering the bleeding man in his arms and kicking off into the sky.

Lucian trembled with pain and horror; his heart ready to explode. Was this all a nightmare? He prayed he was still asleep beside Yuri and not standing amidst the corpse cemetery of his sire's creation, having slaughtered the man he loved.

"Yuri..." Lucian whispered, dropping the sword and falling to his knees as Theo flew upwards in a spiral, with Yuri cradled against him. Hot blood blanketed the ground, vegetation cropping up instantly wherever it landed.

The world of stakes and wriggling corpses vanished, leaving only a handful of the dead and a dozen slashed and empty stakes. Had it all been a nightmare? Lucian trembled in dismay, realizing his father had crafted this to feed from him, weaken him, and keep him locked inside the manor.

The monster emerged from the house, hand raised as though to strike Theo out of the sky with a blazing lightning bolt, and Lucian helpless to stop it. But light flared and something snapped, like a chain popping as the sky turned molten. Pain ripped Lucian from consciousness. The world spiraled into darkness, and Yuri vanished beneath the wave of supernova power.

THE SERAPH FALLS

Yuri blinked open tired eyes. His pain had eased, allowing him to rise from the floating haze of darkness that had tried to drag him deeper a thousand times. A canopy of flowers blanketed the ceiling of their space with color and blooms. It was breathtakingly beautiful, the scent of pollen, and floral waves of honey sweetness made him breathe deep to take it all in.

A warm body stirred next to him, and Yuri turned to find Theo stretching and waking. The area of light and life made Yuri want to stay forever, but he caught the memory of horror on Lucian's face and jolted upright, instantly worried.

"Where is Lucian?" Yuri asked.

Theo wrapped his arms around Yuri. "You need more rest. You're still healing."

Yuri studied the seraph, surprised to find a streak of teal color in his hair and other strands black, as though the original white was vanishing beneath the spread of colors. In the light's brightness, Theo's hair was a pale blue, like the sky on a clear day, not white at all. Had the color changed or was it merely a difference between natural light versus firelight?

Yuri reached for him, wrapping the seraph's thick braid around his hand and studying the mix of colors. Several expressions crossed Theo's face, none happy.

"What's wrong?" Yuri asked.

"Do you hate it?" Theo asked in a small voice.

"Hate what?"

"The darkness."

Yuri blinked. "You mean the colors in your hair?"

"Yes."

"No. Not at all." Yuri studied the strands mixing color through Theo's pale blue.

"Even the dark bits?" Theo bit his lip. "It's very different."

Was color bad? Yuri lifted Theo's chin to study his face. One eye was Star's familiar sky blue, a vibrant cyan, the other a honey gold. It was startlingly beautiful, life in action, and Yuri could imagine Theo wrapped in a thousand colors, light dancing over his skin. He tried to pull the seraph close, but a wave of pain gripped his side. He flinched.

"Don't tear it open," Theo said, pressing his fingers gently to Yuri's chest. "We are helping you heal."

"We?"

Theo's lips moved as if to say something a thousand times, but a shadow rippled across his eyes, like something lived in skin beneath the surface. "You call him Star."

Yuri sighed sweetly at the reminder, his heart filling with emotion and affection. Was he still there? "You can use his power?"

"I accepted his bond," Theo said, looking down. Was it a bad thing?

"I'm sorry?" Yuri said, wondering if it was his fault Theo

was unhappy. He recalled Star carrying him through magic waves to face Theo and give him a choice. Something about becoming one of Star's. Star's what? Yuri wondered. The sunshine and life of Theo's strength amplified by Star's touch, which Yuri basked in, feeling warm and calm.

"I would do it a thousand times for you," Theo replied. He pressed Yuri down onto his back, and slid down, like a living blanket, and Yuri sighed in relief, the warmth of Theo's touch easing the last of the pain in his abdomen.

Lucian had stabbed him.

Yuri flinched at the memory. Lucian's eyes blazed red, but unfocused. Yuri had glimpsed his golden hair outside a window they passed, and begged Theo to take him out to call Lucian back. Yuri hadn't expected him to lunge at Theo, and his reaction had been instant, reckless, he realized, as the sword slid through him like a hot knife through butter. He had only a few seconds to see the horror on Lucian's face before darkness took over, his blood spurting, heart stuttering, and struggling to beat. With Yuri's magic drained, he was too weak to heal it and unable to stop the darkness from closing in.

For a few moments, he'd felt weightless and cradled in Star's embrace instead of Theo's. The chill sinking into his bones, even as they took flight. Yuri wished he could recall the rest but had passed out.

"I healed?" Yuri said. Hadn't the Master tried to kill him with a sword, too? Yuri had eaten the lives of the Master's dungeons to heal that injury. "Are you okay? Did I hurt you?" Was that why Theo's hair changed colors and he was upset? Yuri studied the strands of Theo's braid, wanting to unravel it and sink his fingers into the silky length as he pressed himself inside the seraph's sunny warmth. "Did I do this?"

"No," Theo said. "My choice, not yours, but I don't want you to find me ugly."

"Never. Why would having colors make you ugly?" Yuri wondered. He waved his hand at the flowers surrounding them. "Look at all the beauty."

A few minutes of silence stretched between them as Yuri took in the weave of colors, a thousand flowers, and endless green.

"You created this," Theo said. "As you healed."

"Me?" Yuri asked. The coil of his magic wrapped tightly around him, warm and filled with a rolling awareness, not unlike having a cat in your lap, purring and happy, but also ready to pounce if startled.

Theo took Yuri's arm, still stained with blood, but the skin now painted in multiple serpents, the bond, and a mess of Yuri's tattoos. Star had given him more gifts? Wouldn't the power to grow pretty things be Star's then? "Star's power?"

"Star's energy," Theo corrected. "He funneled a lot through me to heal you." Theo shuddered. "That's why my hair and eyes have changed."

"Did it hurt?" Yuri asked, suddenly concerned. He didn't want Theo to suffer.

"No. It's only that seraphim are light," Theo said.

"Are you less light because you have shades of teal and brown in your hair?"

"No?"

Was that a question or an answer? Yuri wondered. "Are all seraphim shades of white?" He thought of the sun. "Maybe yellow like light?"

"Yes," Theo agreed.

"But scientifically, light comprises a rainbow of colors, a prism, and spectrum all at once. Shouldn't seraphim be a rainbow?" He studied the pale blue of Theo's hair. Could the seraph not see the blue?

Scientifically, Theo mouthed without releasing a sound, as though he didn't understand the word.

"Nature," Yuri continued. "Do other worlds not have science? A way of studying nature, evolution, and physical structure through observation and experimentation? Isn't that what the Master was doing? Or do magic worlds throw out the idea of science?"

"I don't know," Theo admitted. "The seraphim watch over the mortals in the Master's care. He doesn't share with us what he does and we don't ask. He gave us purpose and guidance."

"Seraphim never come in other colors? Like red hair or brown hair, like humans?" Weren't they supposed to reflect each other? Humans and angels? Did that mean Star wasn't a seraph?

"Only the Fallen," Theo said. His eyes changed, blazing gold before turning blue in both, and Yuri felt the warmth fade to Star's familiar chill.

Yuri sucked in a deep breath, grateful for the touch. "There's a lot I don't understand," he admitted.

"Or remember," Star agreed, "and that's okay." Star felt more real this way, not the faded dream touch that had become so familiar. Was that because he was using Theo?

"Don't make Theo do anything he doesn't want to," Yuri said as Star pressed his lips to Yuri's.

"Until I'm free, he's all we have," Star said, brushing his lips over Yuri's, then decorating his face in kisses. "I can't have you nearly dying every time you wish to see me. My heart can't take it, and you need to heal and return to your full strength. The millennia have stripped you of much."

"But if he doesn't want to touch me the way you do, I don't

want to force him." Yuri hoped Star understood. He needed Star desperately. Would give anything to be back in his arms, and bed permanently, but he would never use another for that purpose.

Star sighed heavily, but the blue faded from one eye, leaving it honey gold, and Theo looking back at Yuri. "It's okay," Theo said. "I have little experience in worldly things but would never turn you away if you need my touch."

Yuri shook his head. He would enjoy rolling Theo over and teaching the seraph songs of pleasure. He knew that blaze of power would feel divine on his skin but could sense Theo's hesitation.

Unease.

Were seraphim expected to be chaste, or had it been because Theo was a guardian who hid among the dying covens of his own kind to escape the Fracture?

That Yuri was healing meant his body grumbled with hunger, both his stomach and his cock, as though food and affection were two sides of the same coin and necessary for existence. But he would force no one. Theo's adoration warmed Yuri, and though it was a slow trickle of energy, he felt like he could suck on that flavor, like old-fashioned root beer candy, and keep his hunger from overwhelming him. Whatever had been awakened in him needed energy, warmth, affection, and love.

If Lucian were close, Yuri could slake his desire with him and help him understand Yuri knew it wasn't his fault. The sword, the madness in his gaze, the raging array of red fire in his eyes. He'd looked demonic, but not all that different from the Master's true form. Had he been changing into a true Onari like his uncle? Lucian had mentioned he'd never had a knot before it expanded in Yuri's ass like a gift Yuri hadn't known he'd needed. If he was hundreds of years old, perhaps thousands, and didn't have an alternate form, but suddenly changed, would that drive him mad? Would it have been Yuri's fault? Did Lucian hate him now?

"Is Lucian close?" Yuri asked.

"No," Theo said, looking away.

"Don't be angry with him," Yuri said.

"He nearly killed you. Twice." A touch of Star's power slid through Theo's eyes again, the dark shadow beneath rising with no warning, though his tone deepened.

"Not his fault. I think the monster was messing with his mind," Yuri said.

"He *hurt* you," Star said, grinding out the words through Theo's lips.

Yuri sighed and pressed a kiss to Theo's forehead, hoping he wasn't pushing the seraph's boundaries.

"You are too forgiving," Star muttered, but the blazing blue faded from Theo's eyes again, leaving Yuri with the seraph.

"He's not here," Theo said. "Star got angry and broke one of his chains... he is still bound, but I wonder if all the chains are weakening, or if he lets himself remain bound." Star didn't reappear to answer, and if he shared the answer with Theo, Theo didn't share it with Yuri. "Star cast the manor into the Fracture," Theo blurted and flinched.

"What?" Yuri said in horror. "What about Lucian?"

"I don't know. Please don't be angry with me," Theo begged. "We had to get you away. I found a spot deep in the forest for you to heal. Star did the rest. I'm not strong enough even as his scion. I'm only a simple seraph."

Yuri's heart raced with anxiety. Had they left Lucian behind, or had he been cast into the Fracture too? He felt a stir of anger at Star for being careless, not only with Theo's safety, but Lucian as well.

"I didn't plan it," Star said from Theo's lips. "Anger overcame me. Betrayal burns deep. That any dared harm you again..."

Yuri grabbed Theo's hair, turning his face toward Yuri so he could see into those blazing blue eyes. "Do not sacrifice others for me."

"You are all that matters," Star said.

But Yuri knew that was a lie. There was so much more to life and love than one tired pastry chef. If the end of the world had taught him anything, it was that people didn't exist as islands, and living things needed each other. He studied the pain on Star's face, not a physical thing from Yuri's grip on Theo's hair, but the type of pain that burned the soul, loss, fear, and the scars of trauma embedded deep.

"If I lose you again, there will be nothing left of me but madness," Star confessed.

"Do you know where Lucian is?" Yuri asked.

Star sighed. "No. The Fracture is like a broken mirror, rippling in a thousand directions. I was aiming for the monster's manor more than anything else, and it seems I left a mess."

"How?" Yuri wondered.

"Rest longer, and we will show you," Star promised as he settled in beside Yuri, letting Theo's warmth return. "You're not fully healed."

They stayed a few more days in the garden beneath the canopy of the forest, basking in clean, clear water, and endless blooms providing fresh berries which made Yuri sad, as they reminded him of Lucian. When Theo examined Yuri's chest, fingers careful, but finding everything healed, he agreed it was okay to look, though fear turned his flavor sour again.

"Do we have to get close?" Yuri asked. He wondered what sort of power Star had when he was mostly bound in another realm somewhere. Enough to hurl a castle into the Fracture, which sounded impossible, but the magic of the worlds opened since the shattering of the veil in a lot of places defied things Yuri thought had been logic.

"No. We are up high in the mountains," Theo said. Was that why they were climbing? Theo meant for them to view from above? Couldn't he fly them up? Yuri wondered, as he still had yet to see Theo's wings, and his own had not returned. Had that been a dream? He couldn't imagine having them ripped off had been something pleasant. Maybe that had been another nightmare from the monster.

They found a cliff edge with massive pines that stopped right before a drop off, and Theo pointed down. Far below in the valley, probably miles away, a hole gaped in the ground as though something had taken a giant spoon, carved out the castle and the surrounding death field, and flung it away.

Yuri stared at the space in shock. Star, mostly bound, had used Theo to funnel power to carve an entire chunk of the landscape out? He gazed at Theo. The seraph had to be a lot stronger than he pretended to be.

A spread of tiny figures moved in the distance on the opposite side of the giant hole. An army? "You said the Master had gathered his army because the castle was awakening," Yuri recalled from their escape, hope filling him. Would the Master help? Would he know how to find Lucian?

"We can't go to him," Theo said.

"What? Why not?"

"I'm no longer seraphim. Radu has welcomed none of my kind among his people. And he adores his brother. For all the faults of Vladmir Tepes, Radu cares for him. He will blame us for this and do everything he can to seek your destruction. He already tried to kill you when he couldn't control your power. The strong never like having to cage things they can't control."

No longer a seraph? Theo looked like a seraph to him. Was it the hair thing again? Yuri frowned, realizing this too was his fault, his and Star's. Theo couldn't go home. Yuri was bound to the Master. Could he use that bond to find him? He had seen the Master's rage when Yuri attacked him in self-defense, and that hadn't been intentional. How much worse would it be if the Master focused his rage on destroying Yuri in revenge for losing his brother? He shivered, saddened by the idea the man would hate him. It was a dagger to his heart, making it hard to breathe for a minute.

Theo wrapped his arms around Yuri, holding him up. "We have to go before they see us."

"Go where?" Yuri wondered. Was there anywhere safe?

"To the Fallen."

Fallen angels? Yuri turned his gaze to Theo again. Was that what was happening to Theo? Why he was changing colors? Is that what it meant to become one of Star's? They were Fallen angels? "Theo?"

Theo pressed his lips to Yuri's, tears sliding down his cheeks, but he didn't look sad. "It will be okay."

"But..."

"My choice," Theo reminded him. "You always wanted us to have a choice."

"Will we be safe? Among the Fallen? Aren't they evil?" Yuri asked.

"Am I evil?" Theo asked.

"No," Yuri said.

"Then trust me to keep you safe. I am a guardian, even if I'm out of practice." And he had the power of Star coursing through him. Yuri had a million questions, but he took Theo's hand in his and let the seraph guide him. He would get Lucian back, break the last of Star's chains, and the time it took to get down the mountain gave Yuri plenty of time to think and plan.

Want to read Scion of the Morningstar before everyone else? Join Patreon at: https://www.patreon.com/LissaKasey

SCION OF THE MORNINGSTAR
A WORLD OF BUBBLEGUM MONSTERS

Lucian's vision erupted in a flare of light and heat, shoving him into a rolling wave of darkness until he landed with a bone breaking jolt. The entire landscape shook, but Lucian blinked into a blind array of brightness, unable to see from the massive flare. His gut heaved and hurled like his stomach wanted to be on the outside, and he rolled over to retch. He hadn't eaten food in days, but sludge spewed from him for several minutes while the ground still shook.

His vision slowly returned, spotted with stars, gut settling with a wobbling rock. A spill of black ichor puddled where he'd retched, and Lucian crawled away from it, disgusted by the mess that seemed to writhe and undulate like a living thing. Where had that come from?

Lucian blinked through the brightness, a sun shining overhead with a strange pink and purple glow illuminating everything. The manor appeared to half landed on the edge of a hill, the walls splitting in the middle with giant cracks as one side tipped downward. The attached field of corpses, only a dozen, wriggled in ghastly detail, the gore clarified by the blazing light of the sun. Beyond the chunk of mansion and rock island, a world of cotton candy trees, painted in pastel pinks, purples, greens, oranges, and yellows, peppered the landscape like some creepy board game. Lucian's retrieval team had recovered dozens of mortals in the past decade, the children sometimes bringing with them games, toys, and strange artifacts from the past. This world reminded him of a game filled with candy, and a story he'd once listened to about a witch luring children to a cookie house to eat them. The stuff of nightmares.

Something had shoveled Vladimir Tepes' castle out of the world of Dahna in some sort of god-like hand and hurled into a bubblegum world of brutal pastel bright flora.

Where was Lucian's sire? He blinked back more stars, his eyes aching as if the world were too bright, and found his father prone near the front stairs, but slowly rising. Vlad kept his hand up over his face, flinching from the brightness as Lucian worked his way to his feet. He glared at the sword on the ground, still tainted with Yuri's blood, refusing to touch it. His sire's fault, Lucian thought, but also Lucian's weakness. His sire played his fears like a fiddle.

A high-pitched squeal pierced Lucian's hearing, forcing him to cover his ears and search for the source of the sound. Small fluffs of brightly colored fur leapt onto the shelf of the castle's spread. Only a handful at first, then a dozen, and quickly multiplying. They weren't large, less than a meter by human standards, but didn't seem to have faces at first, as they moved like giant hairballs, hopping and rolling. But the sound came from their direction, and one turned Lucian's way, fur sliding back to reveal enormous black eyes.

He stared back at it in a few seconds of wonder, thinking Yuri would want to pet them, but the mass of floofs let out a chilling chitter and launched themselves at the nearest wriggling body on a skewer. The screams horrific, a thousand times a nightmare, as they picked the thing apart with razor sharp fangs and curved talon claws in only a few seconds, feasting on the body and bones of the creature like it was a snack, then racing to the next.

The one with Lucian in its sight bounced forward.

"Fuck me," Lucian muttered, his legs wobbling. He raced for the door, thinking only that he needed a barrier between himself and the murderous fluff kittens. He heard the group feeding and working their way through the bodies behind him, and felt the breeze of the talons slicing through the air as he ran. Too close, he thought, refusing to look back, as that would only slow him down. He dove past his sire, through the open door, expecting his sire to fight the little monsters, but the man was right behind him, slamming the door shut and locking it.

Lucian heaved a heavy breath, his lungs and legs burning from the sprint. He didn't think he'd ever run so fast in his life. "What the fuck are those?" Lucian growled.

"You have not seen them before in your travels with Radu?"

"No. Fluffy murder stuffies are not in the travel guides. This better not be another nightmare of yours." Lucian stalked away from his sire. He needed a plan, and to figure out where the fuck he was and how to get back to Yuri.

"My power isn't working here," Vlad said. "The wards snapped, and I can't recreate them."

Lucian glanced back at his sire; the man looked older than Lucian remembered. A loss of illusion, or something about the change of the world? "Shame. You should go capture some murder fluffies to torture, see if that recharges your power." Lucian stalked away, heading toward his room, eyeing the splitting walls of the manor with caution. At least the hallways seemed back to normal. Whatever blooming awareness had taken over the castle appeared to have vanished.

The door held, but the windows and the roof collapsed in some sections, which meant it was unlikely the manor would remain a safe place. As Lucian neared his room, the hall tilted down, the section of the manor splitting as though it could break off at any moment. Of course, his space had to be the part that landed on the side of the hill, his bad luck.

Lucian opened the door to his room, wishing for a few seconds it was all a dream and he'd find Yuri sleeping in his bed and spirit him away. His heart lurched with sadness at the stillness of the space. The fire out, the entire room askew, furniture tossed in a dozen directions, and no sign of Yuri.

A familiar box sat in the middle of the room; the books Yuri kept. Lucian righted the table and put the box on it. He opened it and pulled out the books. The only one that interested him was the sketchbook. Lucian flipped through it, shocked at some of the intimate acts portrayed, two men together, similar bodies in each picture. Memories? There were a handful of pictures in the back depicting something very different, a large masculine shape with wings black as soot, and horns. Again, no faces. Was it some sort of nightmare for Yuri? Or a fantasy?

The demonic form knelt in one picture, head bowed, posture almost one of reverence, if that was possible for such an enormous creature. Another appeared to be of the beast hugging someone to him, the other form dwarfed by the massive size of the figure, but the embrace was gentle and protective.

Lucian flipped through a dozen more pages. Some sex acts with the creature and the male. Was this Yuri's true form? Some sort of demon of shadows? They didn't look the same, though the smaller male form might have been Yuri. Was this the one Yuri mentioned he dreamed of? Lucian could never compete. He frowned and snapped the book shut. He didn't know where Yuri was, or if this beast existed. And why the jealousy of the beast and not the human-looking male in the first set of erotic drawings? It wasn't as though he and Yuri hadn't done all those things a dozen times. Just thinking of sinking into Yuri made Lucian hard.

He growled and left the book on the table. The room's tilt made the entire space slide a few inches. The house was still shifting. He wouldn't be able to stay here. Lucian made his way to his closet to find a bag to pack supplies. The best thing his uncle had ever given him was survival skills. Training to be a warrior and live on the battlefield meant Lucian knew how to deal with most anything, including a lack of magic. He never had much of that, anyway.

The sound of glass breaking made Lucian race out of the closet to his room, fearing his sire had followed him, but the sound came from the windows on the exterior of the house. A bright purple stalk with suckers the size of Lucian's head wrapped around the outside of the window, crushing the side of the house like it was little more than a sand castle.

"This world is insane," Lucian said. He rushed through his packing, grabbed the cookbook from Yuri's supply, unwilling to leave behind those memories, and the sketchbook. He spied the flower bloom on the floor near the bed, still bright and mostly fresh, and he wondered at the magic of that little thing. It had lost a few petals from the many flowers as Yuri had grown weak, but still had a half dozen blooms.

Lucian eyed the distance from the thing at the window to the bud. It would be suicide to go for that stupid flower, he decided. But his heart ached at losing that piece of Yuri. Would he ever see the man again?

The purple beast crunched another wall, and the bed slid out of the hole, the flower bud with it. Lucian leapt forward, rolling to catch the bloom, his fingers wrapping around the stem as he lost his footing and slid toward the giant suction cups on a limb larger around than the side wall.

Lucian scrambled, gripping at anything he could reach to propel himself upward as the furniture slid past him, his grip on the flower hindering his climb, the pack on his back heavy and pulling him down. He reached the door by sheer will alone, grabbing onto the edge as the room tilted completely downward, leaving his feet dangling.

He snarled, refusing to let go of the bloom, carefully shoving it up over the side of the doorframe, and pulling himself up to rest on what had been the hallway wall. His arms shook from the effort and he heaved for air. He'd never felt so weak before. A lack of his magic, perhaps?

Lucian pulled out the sketchbook, and stuffed the bloom inside, hoping that crushing it wouldn't destroy it, but unwilling to leave it behind. He stuffed everything back in his pack, slung it on his back and carefully made his way toward higher ground and hopefully a way out of the manor. He debated a dozen weapons as he passed, all too old and neglected for to be useful, and decided on a small dagger, which would be easy to sharpen if he found a good stone. The kitchen was barren of food supplies, but he wrapped up the few knives in an oilcloth to have something sharp to use.

When Lucian emerged from a break in the manor's backside, climbing up and out a wall, he stared down in horror at the writhing thing that was the purple beast. Not an animal at all, but some sort of plant. Everything it touched dissolved, like the suckers on it produced acid, and landing in this place had pissed it off, so it was slowly devouring the entire house.

Lucian couldn't see much beyond the trees and the wriggling organic monster, but thought he glimpsed discoloration in the distance, which made him think of the Fracture. Could he find his way back to Yuri by going through the Fracture? Radu didn't need a Fracture to travel; at least until this most recent one, he could move the entire castle from one dimension to the next, or travel that way by will alone. Would Radu know where to search for him? Would he look? Or would his concern be only for his brother?

Lucian glanced back toward the manor and the section he knew to house his father's rooms and office. There was no sign of movement. It wouldn't take long for the plant to devour the entire chunk of land and the manor. Lucian couldn't bring himself to care. It didn't matter that blood related them, and Lucian spent his childhood in that nightmare of a mansion.

"Good riddance," Lucian said, deciding to head toward the coloration in the sky. He had no other plan, couldn't travel worlds like a handful of the original Onari, but wasn't willing to sit down and die, either. Could his sire still travel between worlds? Lucian hadn't seen it in his entire life. Perhaps the last Fracture stole that power from him. Maybe now the monster would know what it felt like to be almost human. Lucian had survived hundreds of years that way, a warrior in spirit more than magical power. He set a goal to return to Yuri, and all the other rules be damned. He lived too long at the whim and will of others.

Several weeks locked in a nightmare mansion should have stripped Lucian of his will to live as it often did, but he'd never felt more alive. First in the dungeons when Yuri hummed to him, and then in his room, where Yuri would bask in the life of the garden outside and give his sweetness to Lucian as though Lucian deserved to be worshiped.

It had been weeks of life and love that Lucian had never experienced in his long life, and he was determined to get Yuri back. If that meant throwing himself in the Fracture repeatedly until he found Yuri, so be it.

Lucian slunk away from the manor, keeping a careful watch on the purple plant and listening for the fluffy murder monsters as he picked his way toward the ripple in the distant sky.

SCION OF THE MORNINGSTAR
AN ARMY ON THE HORIZON

Radu stood at the head of his army, led by Sono, and watched in horror as something scooped out the land and the manor, like a giant hand, and hurled it into the Fracture. The chatter that had rippled through the army as they waited for Radu's orders on the approach to Vladmir's castle fell to a chilling silence.

When the castle hit the Fracture, light flared in a blinding array that burned into Radu's eyes. The Fracture, while easily seen because of its size, was at least five days' travel away. A patch of land several kilometers wide gaped with a giant crater where the manor used to be. Something had ripped the manor out of the ground and hurtled it as though it were little more than a pebble. What had that kind of power?

"Sono?" Radu began, not really knowing where to start as he had so many questions.

"I don't know," she said. "Power. Power beyond anything I've ever seen before."

"Was it Yuri?" They were too far away to see more than a hint of the movement around the manor before the flare. Radu sensed Yuri was hurt through the aching bonds, but something muted them. He knew Yuri had been there because their tie could never be severed, but now he felt nothing. Meaning Yuri was too far away, or had found some way of breaking the bond.

"I don't know."

Radu's vision returned, large chunks of it still bathed with color flares from the burn. The hole was massive, digging deep into the ground, but there was no movement at all around it. He had recalled parts of his army from the cities to congregate near his brother's castle expecting a battle.

It had been a mistake to send Yuri. Radu admitted his affection for his brother, and the memory of their youth clouded his judgment. Vladmir had been a loving man who took care of Radu and loved his wife deeply. Until the Fracture stole her from him and he'd let himself bask in the dark. Radu was a firm believer that their kind, the Onari nobles of original Nephilim bloodlines, were susceptible to sins of their sires. Which meant Vlad devouring the darkness became a nightmare.

For ages, Radu had hoped his brother could find love again and save himself. It was Sono's return and the story of how Vladmir ripped off Yuri's wings, and Lucian had jumped in to save Yuri, that brought Radu to this point. Vlad was too far gone. Radu didn't dare send a messenger. He wasn't willing to sacrifice anyone to his brother's madness. Radu gathered his entire army with the plan to retrieve Lucian and Yuri, knowing his brother would fight simply because pain and chaos were his meals of choice.

"Do you sense anyone alive down there?" Radu asked.

"I think whatever was in that space is now in another world, if it survived going through the barrier of the Fracture," Sono said. "We can send a group of scouts to search, but I sense nothing. Not the manor, which was waking like your castle, or your brother."

Dracula's castle awakening had been one of the most terrifying pieces of news Sono had returned with. Was it the power of the Onari that woke the castles? And why now? Radu suspected it was something to do with Yuri. He could only imagine the terror that his brother would create with the ability to travel worlds. Radu would have to find a way to not only repair the Fracture, but destroy his brother and a castle of living magic.

"Is there a way to sense where the castle has gone?"

"If there is some sentience, possibly," Sono said. "I will have to gather a few other of my kind and search the maps. But you know we haven't seen all worlds."

Radu wasn't in the habit of sending his warriors into unknown worlds anymore. They rarely returned. "Do what you can. We need to see if we can find Vlad and the castle."

The crowd began to move, creating a barrier around Radu, and he turned to see a line of carriages heading their way. The army moved as a unit to block the road, forcing them to stop. Three of Radu's generals standing firm and unflinching as Radu moved forward to the first carriage. He couldn't stop his scowl when the door to the carriage opened.

"Gabriel," Radu said.

"If it isn't the self-proclaimed king of the Onari," Gabriel said as he slid out of the carriage. His size matched Radu's, both in height and body. Radu wondered a time or two who of them was more powerful. Gabriel, as one of the original archangels, should have been the elite of the elite. Though Radu knew plenty of his secrets. He did his best to keep the seraphim away from Gabriel, who would rip them apart like a child pulling the wings off a butterfly, simply because it amused him. Stories spoke of Gabriel as a leader among the angels, delivering messages to mortals about how to live their lives.

Lies.

Gabriel was the king of misinformation. He had briefly fooled Radu until Radu had rescued Lucian from Gabriel's clutches. Lucian never spoke a word about those days.

"What are you doing here?" Radu demanded.

"I was hoping to visit the more pleasant of the Tepes brothers," Gabriel said. "Bringing him a gift of gratitude for letting me spend time with his lovely son again."

Radu's blood chilled in horror. "When were you here last? You saw Lucian?"

"A few weeks ago," Gabriel said. "Had the most enlightening encounter with Vlad. He said Lucian had a new pet that ate his garden and Vlad was quite upset. I offered to take the pet off his hands…"

Radu sucked in a hard breath, clenching his fists at his sides to keep from killing the angel right there. Had Gabriel touched Yuri? Radu would rip Gabriel apart. He wanted to anyway, after learning about what he'd done to Lucian.

"But Vlad was recalcitrant to give me the pet. Said Lucian adored it. I think he wanted to play with them longer." Gabriel waved his hand as if it were an unimportant matter. "Lucian threw himself at me to protect the pet. I'm certain Vlad was feasting on them. There is no greater delight than torturing lovers."

Radu grabbed Gabriel by the throat, squeezing, wanting to rip the bastard's head off.

Gabriel laughed, nonplussed. "I'm immortal. One of the last true immortals, Radu. You are but a fly to me." He kicked, landing a foot in Radu's gut that snapped ribs and shoved Radu several feet backwards, forcing him to let go. Gabriel brushed himself off while the warriors circled closer to Radu. Sono raised a ward as Radu bit back pain and struggled to breathe, channeling energy to healing.

"You're too late anyway," Radu said. "The castle and my brother are gone."

Gabriel frowned, the expression looking exaggerated and clownish on his pretty face. Never human, he struggled when a rare human emotion actually took control of him.

"Let him see," Radu instructed. The crowd moved aside, letting Gabriel pass to look into the valley at the giant gaping crater.

"What is that?"

"Something hurled the entire castle into the Fracture," Radu said. "Didn't you see the flare?"

"I was in the carriage. Perhaps I should have taken the pet..." He sighed. "Now I have all this useless trash to be rid of." He waved a hand at the carriages and the guards opened the doors and began yanking people out, dropping them on the side of the road. Many lay unmoving other than to breathe, none were human as mortals didn't survive Gabriel's touch, but many species, including a handful of fae, lay on the ground like discarded and mostly lifeless trash.

"What is this?" Radu demanded.

"The remains of your people's hunger," Gabriel said. "There is nothing left of these to sustain your kind. Isn't that why you seek to save humanity? For food? We're running short on Johi. I will have to trade for more. Perhaps you'll give me some of the seraphim you hide? I know they are in your castle, have had stories from dignitaries who visit you. The seraphim last so much longer than any other species, and it takes more to squeeze the emotions out of them."

Radu's ribs knit back together, his lungs healing and he let go of his suppression magic to free his true form, calling the Lightbearer to him. The sword blazed with warmth and adoration. It was why Radu could wield it and Vlad could not. He brought the tip of the sword up to Gabriel's throat. "I should end you here."

"Your beloved seraphim would hate you," Gabriel said, not moving. The weapon was the only one in existence that Radu knew could end an archangel for good. The original soul weapon of the most loved of angels severed all life and could craft it anew. Radu could sink the sword into the ground and regrow the earth, or slash it through an archangel and snuff out his existence. "Lose their adoration and you'll no longer hold that sword."

"You'll already be dead," Radu said. "Sounds like a fair trade."

"And your castle will cease to move. Who will save humanity then? And you'll make the Onari powerless. Is my death worth so much?" Gabriel taunted.

Radu growled. The silver tongue of the Messenger was the bane of his existence. It could be complete truth, utter lies, or somewhere in-between, and he would still be believable. Was Radu willing to chance not only humanity, but all worlds, on Gabriel lying? Yes, and no. He cursed silently, vowing to set the *touched* to research if he could kill Gabriel. Radu didn't feast on pain and fear, but he could find the taste for it with Gabriel.

He lowered the sword. "Leave."

Gabriel folded his arms over his chest as if to stand his ground, but Radu pulsed with power, removing the last bits of suppression that held his true blood back. Not only was he direct from the Nephilim, something had changed when he'd tasted Yuri. He'd become more in tune to the castle than he had in centuries, and been able to control most of his section of the castle, minimizing movement. Radu also needed to feed less, his body pulsing with energy and magic like it had before the Fracture in which Vlad lost Celeste, when both he and Vlad were at their peak of power.

It was these changes that made Radu believe Vlad feeding off Yuri awakened the mansion, giving his brother power he hadn't had in nearly a millennium.

Gabriel backed away, giving Radu an exaggerated bow without turning his back to him. "I'll leave the trash for you. Perhaps you'll use them as your brother did." One of his guards opened the carriage door for him. Gabriel got inside and the door closed, the carriage taking off without another word. The rest of the carriages following, leaving ground littered with easily three dozen mostly dead creatures.

"Call for transport and healers," Radu commanded.

"They are likely too far gone," Sono said. "It would be kinder to end their suffering."

"I will let the healers decide that," Radu said. "Send scouts down to search for signs of Yuri and Lucian." He looked at Sono. "Call the fae and see if you can locate Vlad's castle. I need to know he's dead, or the castle is inactive. The last thing we need is the return of the *nightmare eater*."

"Celeste was the only thing that stopped him last time," Sono said. "I don't think he loves Lucian enough to let Lucian hold him back."

"I don't think Vlad loves anything anymore," Radu admitted. "This is my mistake. I thought he'd find the light in Yuri and it might awaken him."

"We all have weaknesses."

"Vlad will no longer be one of mine. Find him so I can put him out of all our misery, once and for all."

DEAR READER,

If you have time, please post a review. :)

Thank you so much for reading *Touched by the Morningstar*, the next wave of serials is coming soon with *Scion of the Morningstar*.

If you would like to read ahead, you can join my Patreon and help support my writing: https://www.patreon.com/LissaKasey

Check out my website at LissaKasey.com for new information, visiting authors, and novel shorts.

If you enjoyed the book, please take a moment to leave a review!

Thank you so much for reading!

About the Author

Lissa Kasey is more than just romance. Lissa specializes in in-depth characters, detailed world building, and twisting plots to keep you clinging to the page. All stories have a side of romance, emotionally messed up protagonists and feature LGBTQA spectrum characters facing real world problems no matter how fictional the story.

Also by Lissa Kasey

Also, if you like Lissa Kasey's writing, check out her other works:

Rise of the Fallen:

Touched by the Morningstar

Scion of the Morningstar (Coming soon)

Simply Crafty Paranormal Mystery Series:

Stalked by Shadows

Marked by Shadows

Conventional Shadows (free short)

Possessed by Shadows

Touched by Shadows (Novella) Boxset only

Sky's Shadow (Novella) Boxset only

Kitsune Chronicles:

Witchblood

WitchMinion (Free Short)

WitchBond

WitchBane

WitchWolf (Novella)

WitchCurse

Pillars of Magic: Dominion Chapter:

Inheritance (Pillars of Magic: Dominion Chapter 1)

Reclamation (Pillars of Magic: Dominion Chapter 2)

Conviction (Pillars of Magic: Dominion Chapter 3)

Ascendance (Pillars of Magic: Dominion Chapter 4)

Absolution (Pillars of Magic: Dominion Chapter 5)

Raising Kaine (Novella)

Pillars of Magic: Dark Awakening

Resurrection (Pillars of Magic: Dark Awakening 1)

Transfiguration (Pillars of Magic: Dark Awakening 2)

Romance a Curse:

Heir to a Curse

Recipe for a Curse

Reflection of a Curse

Hidden Gem Series:

Hidden Gem (Hidden Gem 1)

Cardinal Sins (Hidden Gem 2)

Candy Land (Hidden Gem 3)

Benny's Carnival (Hidden Gem 3.5)

Haven Investigations Series:

Model Citizen (Haven Investigations 1)

Model Bodyguard (Haven Investigations 2)

Model Investigator (Haven Investigations 3)

Model Exposure (Haven Investigations 4)

Survivors Find Love:

Painting with Fire

An Arresting Ride

Range of Emotion

Evolution: Genesis

Boys Next Door Omnibus

Printed in Great Britain
by Amazon

19468048R00253